THE LAST DAY

WILLIAM ODAY

William Oday, December 2015
Copyright © 2015 William Oday
All rights reserved worldwide

All rights reserved. With the exception of excerpts for reviews, no part of this book may be reproduced or transmitted in any form or by any means, electronic or mechanical, including photocopying, recording, or by any information storage and retrieval system.

This is a work of fiction. Names, characters, places, dialogues, and incidents either are the product of the author's imagination or are used fictitiously. Any resemblance to actual events, locations, or persons, living or dead, is purely coincidental.

ISBN-13: 978-1-942472-11-7

Cover by Christian Bentulan

Note that this book was originally titled *The Darwin Protocol* in *The Last Peak* series.

WANT BOOKS FOR FREE?

Join the Readers Group to get a free copy of The Last Day, Sole Prey, and Saint John. One novel, one novella and one short story, all for free. You'll also receive exclusive discounts on new releases, other freebies, and lots more.

Go to WWW.WILLIAMODAY.COM to find out more.

READERS ARE SAYING

"One of the finest stories I've read in a few decades!"

"The best viral apocalypse book."

"Wow, just Wow!"

"Loved it!"

"Truly excellent. A must-read."

"Impeccably paced, it's a tense thriller."

"A friggin' home run."

"One contentious action packed tale."

"My first encounter with the author. I am now a fan."

"Explodes off the pages."

"Will thrill you, move you, and engage you."

EDGE OF SURVIVAL SERIES

THE LAST DAY, Book 1

THE FINAL COLLAPSE, Book 2

THE FRAGILE HOPE, Book 3

THE DESPERATE FIGHT, Book 4

1

One Month Ago
Washington, D.C.

DR. ANTON RESHENKO realized they resembled nothing so much as monkeys, preening and picking at each other to ease tensions and confirm social status.

He stood at the back of the small conference room, quietly waiting to be recognized. The most powerful men and women in the United States government packed the tight space in a conspicuous ordered hierarchy. The senior members each occupied a high-backed, black leather chair at the long rectangular table. The chair at the far end was empty due to the notable absence of the president.

Would that legally cover plausible deniability?

Proximity to that vacant chair reflected the relative power of those seated at the table. The next level removed were the subordinates and staff that stood along the walls behind the chairs of their respective superiors. They stood stiffly at attention, whether obviously military or otherwise, exuding the reflected glory of their seated masters.

And the furthest removed were those, like him, standing at the opposite end of the room, near the door. As if the exit behind served to remind them that they barely warranted inclusion. That their presence might end at any moment with the wave of a hand or a displeased nod.

Unlike him, they were all insiders. Instinctually aware of the invisible web of power and procedure that governed their artificial realities.

The cloying stink of over-used aftershave wrinkled Anton's nose. The latest slide of the lengthy PowerPoint presentation had caused on uproar amongst the room's occupants. The hum of feverish conversation buzzed in his ears. Subordinates scribbled on notepads as they recorded their superior's directives.

The incessant babbling made it hard to think.

Anton's hand slipped into his left pocket and found the familiar disc deposited there. Minted nearly a thousand years ago, the silver Dirham of Genghis Khan was an invaluable reminder of what one man might achieve.

He rubbed it betwcen thumb and pointer finger. The worn edges of the ancient script almost as familiar as the lines of his own palms. One side read "The Just. The Great." Many might argue the former, but none could diminish the latter.

Holding history in his fingertips focused his mind. The small movement was a daily meditation during the development of MT-1.

Anton's shoulders held no stars. The front of his dark, rumpled suit coat displayed no ribbon rack, no medals. Nothing to proclaim a record of service to the world.

That would change.

One day, history would venerate him. Whereas these self-important imbeciles wouldn't merit so much as a footnote. They would be forgotten. In many ways, they were already relegated to oblivion.

Anton looked around the room and caught the eyes of one man seated at the far end of the table, Senator Charles Rawlings, Chairman of the Senate Armed Services Committee. The bespectacled elderly man held Anton's gaze for a moment then turned away.

The senator was the reason for the meeting. The reason for Anton's attendance. Rawlings was twice as smart as the others and yet half as smart as he believed himself to be.

None of them were on Anton's level. He was different, in ways both evident and not. The size of the sideburns that carpeted both sides of his face only hinted at the differences.

The white-haired man giving the seemingly endless presentation leaned on his cane while waiting for the buzz to die down. He'd introduced himself hours ago at the beginning of the presentation. The Director of the Office of Net Assessment, the Department of Defense's internal think tank. The old goat had held the position for over forty years, since the office's inception under the Nixon administration. His title didn't officially hold the weight of many of those seated around the table.

But power often came from unexpected places.

Anton himself was proof of that.

The white-haired man cleared his throat a few times until he had everyone's attention. "Which brings us to the final slide." He flicked a remote and the enormous display on the wall behind him showed a new slide.

It was astonishing how PowerPoint could dull even the most vital of topics. He pointed at the monitor. He shuffled closer and touched the screen, leaving an oily mark. The smudge highlighted large red numbers.

His voice came out brittle but confident, like a bible printed on antique parchment. Like a revelation.

"We've run the sim with every variation we could think of. The result is the same. Under the most optimistic set of conditions, only one thing changes. The timing. And that by no more than a handful of months."

A dead silence descended on the room. Half the people in it turned to Senator Rawlings. He, of course, already understood the predicament as his office had coordinated with the Office of Net Assessment in directing the study.

The other half turned to yet another gray-haired man seated adjacent to the empty seat. The Chairman of the Joint Chiefs of Staff. Four gold stars clung to each shoulder. The general's cold eyes narrowed as he digested the information on the screen. He finally looked back to the ancient presenter. "What exactly are you saying?"

The old man pushed thick bifocals back up the bridge of his nose. His rumpled form straightened for an instant. "*I am not saying anything.*" He pointed to the large, red numbers on the screen. "The data, however, is shouting that we're running out of time."

The general squeezed his eyes shut and took a deep breath. He resembled a child closing his eyes, hoping the bad things would disappear. He finally opened them again and blew out a slow exhale. The colorful assortment of ribbons, medals, pins, and stars on his jacket settled. "How can this be?"

"General, your people have run war games that concluded we're headed for large-scale, persistent conflict over dwindling natural resources."

"Yes, but if what you're showing us is true, you're talking about the end of the United States of America."

The old man nodded. "Our simulation accounted for a

far larger set of initial conditions than anything previously run. Depletion of the fresh water supply. Diminished biodiversity. Climate destabilization. Exploding sovereign debt. The end of cheap oil. We accounted for these and a thousand other pressing issues."

"Are you saying we're doomed?"

"*The data* is saying that we are approaching a peak of many correlated and undesirable trends."

The old man tapped the red numbers.

"And this is the destination."

The general chopped a knife hand at the screen. "This is the land of the free?"

Senator Rawlings stepped into the silence that followed. "Listen, we've dug this hole for ourselves over the span of many decades. The days of perpetually kicking the can have ended."

The nation's highest military officer bristled at the patronizing tone.

Anton vaguely remembered how Senator Rawlings had made the general's confirmation hearing an extended and contentious affair. There was bad blood there, and neither man appeared to have forgotten.

The general glared at Senator Rawlings and then turned back to the old man. "What is the least disruptive solution?"

"My staff have been crunching scenarios for months, and, well, they're all bad."

"Give me options."

"We are about to leave my field of expertise," the white-haired man said. He pointed across the room, and Anton felt the world pivot into place. His time had come. "Let me introduce you to Dr. Anton Reshenko."

Anton stepped forward and smiled as he stroked the mat

of hair on one cheek. Yes, real power wasn't always in the obvious place.

Real power came from one, and only one, place. The unbowed will of an extraordinary man to achieve his destiny.

He walked to the head of the long table and stopped behind the empty chair. He yearned to grip the headrest. Perhaps even to spin it around and take a seat. But these people still mattered. He looked around the room and was pleased to feel the focus of every man and woman present. The deserved weight of their desperate hope. He gave himself a moment to appreciate the spectacle.

To acknowledge destiny.

The day he had worked so long for, so hard for, had finally arrived. It would've been a lie to say it didn't feel inevitable.

The world was his, as he knew it always would be, in the end. Insurmountable problems required men of unparalleled stature to solve them. The world needed him, and he would humbly deliver salvation.

"Ladies and Gentlemen," Anton said, "I'm here today to tell you about the Darwin Protocol."

2

The Last Day
Venice, California

MASON WEST cracked an egg into a sizzling hot pan and stared as it bubbled and turned white. The rich scent of melted butter enveloped the kitchen. He pushed at the gelatinous puddle until a spongy yellow form emerged, something that somewhat resembled scrambled eggs.

Breakfast wasn't his usual gig. He had a long and sordid history of blackened toast and burned eggs.

Arms came from behind and wrapped around his torso. He twisted back and breathed in the morning scent of the love of his life. Elizabeth. She was the woman he didn't deserve. Years could blink by with the right person.

He'd never been happier. Given his record, that wasn't necessarily saying much. But he'd take it.

"Morning, honey," he said. He leaned down and kissed her lips, faintly tasting the earthy sweetness of roasted coffee.

"The same to ya, handsome," she said with a wink.

Mason wondered for a moment if it was an invitation. Maybe she'd changed her mind about leaving early for work? He slid a hand down and cupped it around her curved backside. Her brow lifted in that *what are you up to* way. He planted another small kiss and gave her a squeeze in that *you know what I'm up to* way.

She nibbled his lip and pulled back. "Easy, tiger. You're gonna force me to call in a sick day."

"Okay by me."

Mason's daughter lumbered into the kitchen with headphones on, her head bobbing to a silent beat.

"Gross, guys," she said. "Seriously. Get a room. You have one, right down the hall."

Mason looked at her and the shock of having a fifteen-year-old daughter hit him for the umpteenth time. Any resemblance to the chubby little angel that used to giggle in his arms was more his projection than hers. But Theresa was still his baby girl, no matter what.

"No headphones at the table," Mason and Beth said in unison.

Theresa pulled them off and set them on the counter.

"Morning, uncomfortably expressive parents."

Beth poked her tongue out at their daughter and replied, "Oh, don't be a square."

"Very funny, Mom," she replied as she flopped down at the breakfast table. "Whacha burning for breakfast?"

Breakfast?

The acrid bite of scorched yolk wafted through the air, and he turned to verify the scent. Mason examined what remained in the pan. Black, crispy charcoals changed the breakfast plans. "Cereal. Looks like a milk and cereal morning. How about toast?"

"Can I get it only slightly burned?"

"No promises."

Beth unwound herself from his embrace and grabbed her unfinished coffee from the mottled gray granite counter. "It appears your father has breakfast well in hand. I have to go in early."

"What's up, Mom?"

"Jane's a little off. It's probably nothing, but being so close to term makes me extra cautious."

"What's wrong? Is she okay?"

"I'm sure she'll be fine. Don't worry, honey."

Theresa's face communicated her unspoken worry.

Jane was a fourteen-year-old chimpanzee at the Los Angeles Zoo. She'd been rescued as an infant from the bushmeat trade in the Democratic Republic of the Congo. Beth's heart was as soft as warm butter for the animals in her charge. And it was as hard as carbon steel for those that mistreated them.

She'd been a volunteer back when Jane arrived at the zoo. Nobody expected the sickly, malnourished chimp to survive, but Beth didn't give up. She brought the little chimp home every night for nearly a year to ensure Jane received around-the-clock nurturing. Theresa in one arm and Jane in the other. They were almost sisters in some ways.

Mason had thought she was a cute infant, but that was it. Except that wasn't it because she turned out to be a Bili chimpanzee, the largest subspecies ever discovered. Now, Jane was nearly six-feet tall and weighed a hundred and ninety pounds.

She was a wild animal. Not a pet. She couldn't be trusted. However, the single time he'd reminded his wife of that fact, she'd given him an icy stare that couldn't have been a clearer version of *back away from my baby!*

Choosing to live, he hadn't brought it up again.

The family dog trotted in with a haggard, slobber-matted giraffe stuffie in his mouth. Now here was an animal you could trust. Mason had trusted Max completely with Theresa from the first day he'd joined their family. He exemplified the best of the Bullmastiff breed. Loyalty and intelligence. A gentleness balanced with an eye toward protecting his pack.

Max nuzzled his nose against Beth's waist and looked up with rapt attention. His lower eyelids sagged a little, so he always looked concerned. She smiled and scratched his neck. "She'll be fine, Max." She looked back to Theresa. "Both of you, don't worry."

That was apparently good enough for Max, as he dropped the giraffe on the tile floor and proceeded to hump it without regard for who might be present.

Theresa grabbed the giraffe and tried to tug it away, but Max clung to it while his hips gyrated wildly. "Does no one understand the concept of inappropriate kitchen behavior?"

Max paused in his machinations and straightened up to lick Beth's hand. Did he somehow know Jane wasn't doing well? Mason didn't think it was likely, but his experiences had taught him enough to not reject the possibility.

He'd seen firsthand the power of the primal brain.

"Sorry to change the subject, ladies, but it just so happens that I had a client cancel this weekend. Had to leave town for whatever reason. So, I think we should visit Tito and Mamaw."

The darkness hanging over Theresa melted. The sun shone again in her smile, and just as quickly in Mason's heart.

"Yes! It's been forever," she said.

Beth slung her messenger bag over a shoulder. "Tito said

several chicks hatched last night. They're up to their eyeballs in adorable furriness."

Theresa bounced in her chair. "We have to go!"

"It's settled then," Mason said. "The West family escapes the metropolis tonight." He set a bowl of cereal in front of Theresa. Brightly colored blobs of whatever it was that passed for cereal swam through organic, low-fat milk.

Max left Beth and sat next to Theresa. Mason demanded she not feed him at the table, but she slipped him food anyway. It wasn't simple teenage rebellion because she'd done it since he was a puppy. Beth did it on occasion too, so it was a three-against-one issue.

You had to pick your battles. Some weren't worth the effort or injury.

Beth planted a kiss on Theresa's forehead. "I'll let them know we're coming."

Every weekend at her parent's acreage in Ojai was a good one. It gnawed at her that they'd only been out to visit a couple of times in the last year. But their family had never been busier. Between his clients, the demands on Beth at the zoo, and Theresa's burgeoning social schedule, free weekends were a scarce commodity.

But her parents weren't getting younger. And besides, they were long overdue for a weekend away. As much as he loved the city of angels, sometimes he needed a break from heaven.

Especially living on the west side of Los Angeles. He loved Venice. The bohemian flavor. The easy access to the beach. The taste of life under a sun that warmed the air year round. But it felt like being surrounded at times. With the ocean to their backs, they had ten million people between them and the outside world.

Trapped in paradise.

It only made sense if you lived it.

Beth looked up at him with a shadow of concern in her eyes. "Walk me out?"

Mason wrapped his arm around her and tried to remember she needed to get to work. "Sure."

Theresa gagged loud enough to be certain they heard. "The Crayfords don't want to see your PDA either."

Mason tossed her a smirk. "Quiet. Or we'll continue in here."

3

They stepped out of their gray with white trim, single-story Craftsman, unconsciously hitting the first and third wood steps down off the front porch. The middle step was loose and a lawsuit waiting to happen. It was on Mason's list, but a lot of things were on his list.

The smell of freshly cut grass drifted over from the Crayfords' front yard. Their new electric mower and perfectly clipped, deep green grass evidence Otis had already been hard at work that morning. Even in his mid-eighties, he still insisted on keeping up with things himself.

Yellow Gerbera daisies filled a flower bed below their living room window. Bright petals gave the yard a cheery glow that Mason always appreciated. Especially since he and Beth didn't have a green thumb between them.

Though the bed was looking overgrown and riddle with weeds. Otis took pride in his yard, but his wife's illness had taken a toll on them both.

Mason helped out where Otis would allow it. He'd trimmed the apple tree in their backyard a few months ago.

He made sure their garbage, recycling, and yard waste bins made it to the curb and back every trash day.

The early morning sun warmed his face as he accompanied Beth to her old, rusted black and dulled chrome Kawasaki Vulcan 750. Spock, she called it. Any normal person would've tossed it into the junkyard years ago, but Beth gave the twenty-year-old bike all the care it needed to keep going.

It was a point of love and pride for her.

He didn't like that she rode Spock on the freeways. He'd tried to force her into something with more steel wrapped around it. But then she'd forced him to drive her to work in his Bronco a few mornings. Right into the belly of the morning commute.

What a complete nightmare.

The bike cut her commute time in half. That ended opposition towards her riding. The spoken kind, at least.

Beth was a natural fixer. On a work day, she'd be elbow-deep in elephant dung trying to solve a medical issue. On the weekend, she'd be in the garage keeping Spock alive.

She tossed her bag into the stow compartment, and slung her helmet over a handlebar. She turned to Mason and fell into his arms. Her face burrowed into his chest. "I didn't want to say anything in front of Theresa, but Jane's not doing well." A tear pooled on the inside corner of her eye. "I can't lose her. Not another one. Not again."

He lifted her chin to pull her eyes to his. She loved Jane. But he knew it was more than that. Some pain never really faded. Years could be seconds to the heart.

"You aren't going to lose her," he said. "You're the best veterinarian in the world. And you love her like your own child. She couldn't be in better hands."

Beth moved her hands back and forth in the golden

sunlight, examining them with detached interest. Measuring them. "Depending on how she's doing, I may have to sit out the weekend trip."

"Your dad will be pretty upset. And not just because he won't have his favorite free vet checking out the new chicks."

"I know. But if I can't get her feeling better, I'm not letting her out of my sight."

Her heart was still so raw, always just under the surface.

He wrapped her in a bear hug and squeezed. He leaned down and touched their foreheads. Strands of wavy, black hair framed her sunlit amber eyes. They mesmerized him now as much as they ever did. Maybe more. At thirty-four, she was more beautiful than ever. Small lines had crept into the smooth curves, the ripeness of youth had started to show signs of wear.

The imperfections made her more tangible. More precious. Again, he wished she didn't have to leave for work. He could comfort her with more than just hugs. Before the derailed train of his thoughts totally crashed off the tracks, he gave her a peck on the lips and pulled back.

"Get to work, doctor," he said with an authoritative voice. His work voice. The voice he used when he wanted to get someone's attention and make them comply.

"You're not the boss of me," she said, her eyes mocking and grateful all at once.

"Never pretended to be. If you do have to stay with Jane, I'll take Theresa. Tito can't get too mad if she's there."

"That's a good idea." Beth hugged him again and turned to grab her helmet. She slipped it on and popped the visor up. "I'll call when I know more." Without another word, she dropped the visor and kickstarted the engine to life.

He glanced behind her to verify the driveway and street were clear, checking for anyone that might not notice or care about a motorcycle pulling out. He worried any accident would turn out like a crash test boxing match where her opponent had the advantage of about three thousand pounds.

There were no other moving vehicles.

He watched her pull out and waved at her back.

Max bounded out of the open front door and howled as she rode away. When she didn't respond to his off-key howls, he moped over and begged until Mason offered him a scratch under the neck.

The old bike paused at the stop sign at the end of their block before continuing. Mason was about to head back inside to begin the business of scraping the egg pan when the sky to the north caught his attention.

Far away, the blue sky above turned a murky brown at the horizon. A darker hue than the usual smog that habitually hung over Los Angeles. A forest fire probably. A massive one. The darker brown band stretched from the ocean to the northwest to the mountains to the northeast.

He made a mental note to check the news as it appeared to be directly between them and their possible weekend visit to Tito and Mamaw.

Max sat on his haunches and sniffed the air. Mason glanced at him as if he might answer an unspoken question.

As smart as Max was, he didn't bark any answers. Mason couldn't blame him. He'd never seen anything quite like it either.

Theresa popped out the front door.

"Earth to Dad. I'll incur the wrath of the Los Angeles public school system if I'm late again."

"Got it."

He gave one last look at the unsettling sky in the distance, and then headed back inside.

4

Mason glanced in the rearview mirror of his tan 1978 Bronco to see Max's blocky head obscuring most of the traffic that extended forever behind them. His tongue hung out the side as he panted in the early morning heat. Mason reached back and scratched his neck while trying to avoid the long tendril of drool that dangled from his mouth.

Cars backed up into the intersection as horns blared and people jockeyed to get through. Too many people loved Los Angeles. They loved it to death.

A foul stench assaulted Mason's nose.

"Max," he said as he cracked the window.

The red light governing the intersection of Venice and Lincoln stayed red. Glared red like it enjoyed his growing irritation. This one, in particular, lasted twice as long as any other that he regularly drove through.

He looked over to the passenger seat and watched his daughter's fingers fly over her phone screen. She was a wonder with the thing. He admired the long black hair that looked like a time machine reflection of her mother. They shared the same jaw that could shift from warm laughter to frozen silence so fast he'd be left confused and wondering what happened.

He noticed her shoulders tense and she thumbed out of the texting app.

Busted.

She turned to him with lips twisted up in obvious irritation. Jaws tensed and nostrils flared. "Dad, you're snooping."

"No. Not really. Just daydreaming. Passing the time. Praying this light decides to change."

"It's bad enough you put that tracking app on my phone so you can spy on my every—"

"It's only for an emergency. It doesn't do anything unless you or I activate it."

"Yeah right. Did you also install a text logging app? Something that lets you print the history so you can invade my privacy at your leisure?"

She had her mother's fire.

He looked back to the street light and tried not to let the sarcasm dripping from her words get under his skin. The last year with her had been rougher than any before. At times, it felt about as smooth as a typical street in Los Angeles—one jarring pothole after another.

If only navigating their relationship was that easy. He could see the problems on the road coming. Could utilize skills honed over nearly a decade to navigate and avoid them.

But top-notch tactical driving skills didn't help a lick in avoiding the recurring blowups that were taking a bigger and bigger toll on their relationship.

What had happened to the little girl he remembered?

He didn't feel like a terrible dad. He didn't think he was

unreasonably strict or overly protective. Sure, he preferred to minimize risk. But that was because risk management was priority one. And the biggest part of risk management was having good intel.

So, yeah, he wanted nothing more than to pore through every single text on Theresa's phone, identify possible threats and neutralize them before they could escalate into something serious.

He was a dad. That was his job. Plus, it was his day job as a close protection officer.

Only, it felt impossible in a way no work assignment ever had. Impossible in a way that nothing in his career of protecting Fortune 500 CEOs and diplomats from around the world made easier.

A few clients over the years had made protection an onerous task. Famous people usually. They were the worst. He'd sworn off taking those assignments years ago. The pay wasn't worth the headache.

"Don't be so dramatic," he said. "I looked at you. I'm allowed to look at my smart, beautiful daughter, aren't I?"

"Do I look like an idiot?"

"Not usually."

"Very funny," she said as she looked out her window at the long lines of cars that extended in all four directions at the intersection.

Mason retreated to easier ground. "Mom texted before we left. She told Tito and Mamaw we're coming. Tito said there was one chick, in particular, he wanted to show you."

The clouds parted and Theresa smiled. So easy like that.

"I can't wait to snuggle them. Cute, fluffy little fur balls everywhere. Eeep!" The last part came out in an emotional spike of anticipation.

"And some possible but unconfirmed bad news. Mom may have to skip this visit."

Concern pinched her eyebrows together. "Is it Jane? Is she okay?"

Mason bent the truth, but only a little. For his daughter's sake.

"Everything is fine. Mom just wants to run some additional tests that may take longer than expected."

It was weak, but he wasn't going to break his daughter's heart if he could avoid it.

Theresa huffed and blew out a breathy, agitated exhale. "We already canceled the last two times. We can't cancel again."

"Nobody's saying cancel. Worst case is just us two go."

Mason wanted to go as much as she did. When he married Beth, her parents were a big part of that commitment. They'd welcomed him into their family and given him a sense of rootedness that he'd longed for his entire life. Beth had brought needed stability.

A foundation that kept him from completely sinking, even during the dark years.

He dragged his thoughts back to the present and bristled at the mass of metal crawling by. He longed for the peace and tranquility of Tito and Mamaw's small acreage. Their property was quintessential Ojai. Big. Surrounded by beautiful nature. Chickens and goats underfoot. The braying of a mule somewhere in the distance.

You didn't find that kind of thing in Venice. Not without spending ten million dollars to get it. Maybe not at all.

"We'd better not cancel," Theresa said.

Mason mashed the brake with his left foot and gently tapped the gas with his right. This stoplight felt like a stop-forever-light. He glanced at the cross traffic and saw an open pocket approaching. A dangerously strong urge to punch the gas and roar through the intersection tickled his leg. "Don't worry," he said, as much to himself as to his daughter. "We're going."

Her expression softened. He saw hints of the little girl she once was. Slowly submerging into a woman he often didn't understand.

He prayed Beth would have good news about Jane. At least not bad news.

Theresa's phone beeped and a message popped up. He resisted the urge to take a sideward glance.

"You text more than you breathe."

"Very funny, Dad."

"Kidding. But not," he said as he leveled a look at her.

"Understood," she replied, then nodded toward the road. "Green light."

Mason flicked a look up at the light and verified the change. He glanced at the analog clock on the dash and verified the time. Great. Theresa might be late to class. She'd already gotten a parent report about excessive tardies. He wasn't going to be the reason she got detention.

He dropped the hammer with his right foot while simultaneously releasing the brake with his left.

The throaty V8 roared and lurched forward on oversized BF Goodrich All-Terrain 4x4 tires. Their size put all the surrounding cars on a downward line of sight. He'd seen more than a few surprising things from his high vantage point.

The old beast resembled nothing so much as a proud and aged lion prowling the savannah. Past its prime. Rough around the edges. But strong. Still big and dangerous to the herd of sleek impalas that bounded beside.

Mason smiled as the windows rattled and the round

tuning knob on the old stereo slipped and the station crackling through the single working speaker blended into static.

Through the static, the dull voice of a reporter bled through in sporadic bursts.

"*Fire... threatening the San Fernando... not contained...*"

Theresa punched the volume knob and turned it off.

"Would you mind keeping us alive at least until I get to school?"

Mason flashed a grin and winked. "That's my job."

He turned back and slammed on the brakes, skidding to a stop just beyond the intersection.

Max barked like crazy.

A man dressed in rags stumbled and fell against the front bumper. He raised his head as if suddenly aware of their presence.

Blood streamed from his eyes, down his filth-crusted cheeks. He swiped at the fluid and lurched back, teetering on the edge of staying upright. He covered his face and screamed. "Help me! Please, help me!"

The words gurgled out as red spewed down his unkempt beard.

Horns honked behind them.

A car in the next lane roared by heading in the same direction.

Mason looked in the rearview mirror. A shiny, white Mercedes flew into the intersection, obviously hell-bent on not getting caught at the light.

The man stumbled into the adjacent lane.

He never had a chance.

Sleek, white metal slammed into fragile flesh. The man's head whipped down onto the hood and split apart. The impact flung his body through the air, pinwheeling like a rag doll tossed by an angry child. His broken form landed in a heap. Arms and legs splayed at grotesque angles.

And just like that, whatever dreams or delusions the man harbored ended.

5

ELIZABETH WEST stood alone on the safe side of the thick plexiglass window looking into the Bili Chimpanzee exhibit at the Los Angeles Zoo. It was still before opening hours and she enjoyed the relative peace and quiet before the crowds entered. She stroked her fingertips over the smooth, clear surface as a one-hundred-ninety-pound chimp swished back and forth on the other side. Low, breathy hoots of pleasure made it through the thick glass.

She longed to run her fingers through Jane's fur. To breathe in the musky female scent that only a vet could love, much like a farmer loved the smell of fresh fertilizer. To scratch behind her ears and giggle as the chimp tilted her head to get just the right spot.

Beth would have spent time in the habitat with her, unguarded and unarmed if she could have. She trusted Jane completely. Two things prevented her from doing that.

One was the strict regulation that no one was allowed inside the enclosure while the chimps were out. Only a major emergency could break that rule. Normally, they had to first be lured through the metal door at the back of the enclosure and into the secure holding room. Only then could a staff member enter to do maintenance or whatever was needed inside the enclosure. It was one of a few rules for the larger animals that was inviolate. Bending that one would result in her immediate termination.

Especially considering who would make the call.

Even that knowledge may not have been enough to keep her away. But then there was the second reason.

Jack. A twenty-year-old Bili chimpanzee that made Jane look dainty in comparison. A fearsome beast that stood six and a half feet tall and weighed two-hundred-seventy pounds. Like a jealous boyfriend, he hated anyone that competed for Jane's attention. And his demeanor had gotten worse as more of his troop had been shipped off to other zoos.

Beth tried to convince the new management that the moves were wrong, counter-productive despite the potential good of widening the gene pool through inter-zoo exchanges. Their original troop of six was now down to Jack and Jane.

The transfers were hard on Beth, too. She felt like the exported animals were being abandoned into the world. It didn't help that the zoos were in places like Mongolia and follow-up calls were never returned. The lack of communication made her question the validity of the whole endeavor. Thus far, her appeals to management had fallen on deaf ears.

The loss of so many troop members had turned the dominant male Jack into a neurotically possessive mate. A dangerous one.

Beth couldn't blame him. She'd feel the same way if people took her family members away. The problem was that he'd sometimes take out his frustrations on Jane.

As much as she didn't like him, he was important to Jane. He offered her the chance to live a more normal life. To start a family together. His introduction had been a dangerous gamble but it had paid off. More than she could've hoped.

Beth held her palm to the clear glass. Jane's huge palm mirrored it from her side of the barrier. The dark palm dwarfed Beth's. She rubbed her furry head back and forth and looked like nothing so much as a child needing a hug.

Jane yawned and huge jaws parted wide. Her lips peeled back to show off massive canines. Teeth that could take down a leopard. Packs of Bili chimps in the wild were said to hunt lions. Their size and intelligence made them top-of-the-food-chain hunters in the forests of their home in the Congo.

Her long tongue rolled out like it wasn't meant to fit inside her mouth.

Beth took the opportunity to study the exposed soft tissue. Her gums were an unhealthy pale white. Her pupils were dilated, despite the bright morning light. She wasn't doing well.

Jane's head turned away and froze as a deep barking echoed in the air. Jack. Claiming his territory. Not the ferocious scream of an ongoing fight, but the low rumbling bark warning others not to invade his turf. Promising a battle to any that didn't heed the warning.

Beth couldn't see him. He must've been in another part of the enclosure. She was grateful to have a few undisturbed moments with Jane. The female paced away from the glass and Beth watched her overripe belly sway back and forth with each step. It swung under her like a pendulum.

This was her first pregnancy and added to that was that she was carrying two infants, a very unusual outcome for chimps. The pregnancy was taking a toll on her body. Her left foot dragged awkwardly as the later stages of pregnancy had expanded her uterus and pinched a nerve in her hip.

Beth knew she was in discomfort. At night, Jane whimpered and whined as she shifted back and forth trying to find a comfortable position.

It wasn't a black and white decision, but after analyzing several x-rays and cat scans, Beth had decided not to operate to relieve the pressure. She was near-term and opening her up would put her and the infants at risk. Beth prayed she'd have them before any permanent damage occurred. Anti-inflammatories and close observation were the current best course of action.

Further back in the exhibit, a patch of tall grass parted and an enormous, muscled male chimpanzee emerged. In the prime of his life, his gray fur swished regally as he walked closer. He took his time, knowing the world waited. He was at the peak of his physical strength and vitality. And he knew it.

He sauntered closer and then froze as he recognized Beth at the glass with Jane just feet away. Jane lumbered away from the viewing station, but it was too late.

Jack raised his head and a scream tore loose shattering the morning calm. The surrounding exhibits exploded in hoots and braying as baboons, lemurs, and antelope raised the alert and expressed their fear.

6

The hairs on the back of Beth's neck jumped to attention. There was nothing like that sound. It was a message to every animal within reach and its meaning was clear.

I will kill you. I will eat you.

It didn't get any more primal than that.

Humans weren't so long removed from the web of life that the call didn't instantly get their attention. Genetic memory warned of the multitude of ancestors that heard a similar roar and died soon after.

Jack loped toward the viewing platform and stopped just short of the glass, his large, deep brown eyes never leaving Beth. His lips curled back, revealing teeth that could end her with less effort than she used to swat a fly. She backed away from the glass not wanting to upset him.

Too late.

His teeth gnashed the air as he continued to display. Jane moved further away, not wanting any part of his agitation.

He turned and in one fluid move leapt at her. A giant clubbed fist lashed out at her head.

In her debilitated state, Jane was too slow and it caught her square on the cheek. Her head whipped to the side and she tumbled to the ground. She landed hard and barely had the strength to lift her head and bark in return. Blood welled from a flayed open cut above her eye.

Beth gritted her teeth, seething, wanting to put a boot on Jack's neck. Not that it would have done any good.

The male stood above the mother of his unborn infants, deciding whether or not to deliver another punishing blow.

Beth was already in a sprint toward the door that led to the work rooms, her keys jangling in her hands as she flipped through them for the right one. She snatched the walkie-talkie off her hip and thumbed it on.

"This is Dr. West with an animal emergency at the Bili Chimps exhibit. Is anyone there?"

She'd normally have had an assistant vet to help with situations like this, but the position had yet to be filled after the last one left. More budget nonsense.

"What's going on, Dr. West?" a voice responded.

It was Ralph, the zoo's Security Supervisor. He'd helped out a few times with moving the chimps around. It wasn't ideal, but he'd have to do.

Still sprinting through service corridors toward the equipment room, Beth clicked the transmitter and yelled, "Get some oranges and lure Jack into the holding room. Lock him in and get back to me immediately when it's done. Do not enter the habitat or holding room. And make sure those locks are in place."

"You got it, doc."

"What is going on?" an imperious voice demanded.

Diana Richston. The new Director of Admin and Operations. The boss. The witch. She didn't deserve the position and Beth hadn't been subtle in voicing her opinion. She came aboard when the city of Los Angeles sold the zoo to Milagro Corporation. Yet another public asset sold to the highest bidder because the city was drowning in debt.

"Dr. West, answer me this minute!"

"Not now, Diana!"

Beth shoved through one last door and came to the tall metal safe she was seeking. She fumbled through the keys on her ring and found the right one. She opened the safe and pulled out a packaged, sterilized syringe. She snapped on rubber gloves and prayed as she plunged it into a small bottle of M99. The drug was a thousand times more powerful than morphine.

Sweat dripped from her brow as she measured out sufficient CC's to lightly tranq a chimp of Jane's size. She wanted the minimal dose to ensure Jane and the infants' safety. Just enough for her to sew up the gash above Jane's eye and give her a field checkup.

She transferred the potent opioid into a sterilized dart and carefully set it aside. One drop was enough to kill a human. She pocketed a dose of Naltrexone just in case. An exposed human had only a few minutes to counteract the opioid before a fatal cardiac arrest.

She was in a hurry. But she wasn't stupid.

Beth pulled a rifle out of the safe, inserted the loaded dart, and then slammed the bolt forward. After verifying the safety was engaged, she slung it over her shoulder and locked the big safe. A quick look to verify dangerous gear was stowed and she sprinted for the west entrance to the enclosure. The one closest to the viewing area where she had last seen Jane and Jack.

She finally made it, breathing hard to catch her breath. She found the key but didn't insert it into the lock of the heavy metal door. She waited for what seemed like forever before the walkie-talkie crackled and chirped to life.

"Dr. West, this is Ralph. Jack is secured."

Beth wondered for an instant if Ralph remembered the locking procedure that ensured the holding room couldn't be opened. Chimps were famously clever at figuring out how to get a clasp or bolt released. She couldn't waste time thinking about it.

Jane was out there on the ground. Already weak and now with a likely concussion and bleeding. She was in danger and Beth was the only one that could help.

"Thanks, Ralph. I'm entering the enclosure to deal with Jane."

Diana's voice practically blew the tiny speaker.

"Dr. West, I forbid you to enter that habitat!"

"Diana, there is an injured animal inside that requires immediate medical attention."

"I don't care if it dies in the dirt. What I do care about is you exposing this institution to unlimited legal liability."

"Let me come help," Ralph said.

Diana responded before Beth could even click the transmit button.

"Ralph, if you step one foot inside that exhibit, I will fire you, then sue you to bankrupt your family!"

What a nightmare. The last thing Beth wanted was to get Ralph caught up in the ongoing feud between her and the new director.

"Ralph, I'll take care of it."

"Ralph, get back to your job while you still have one!"

"Yes, Ma'am. Good luck, Dr. West."

Against her better judgment, Beth keyed the talk button. "Diana, it's nice to know you care, but I'm heading inside."

"Don't test me, Elizabeth! Entering the habitat with an

animal present is strictly forbidden. Breaking that regulation will result in an internal review and inquest by the board of directors."

Did she really have to have this conversation now? Right this minute? Unbelievable!

"Jane is in trouble," Beth spat with more venom than half the cobras in the snake house. "This is an emergency."

"The board and I will decide that issue if we must."

"You do your job, and I'll do mine," Beth said through gritted teeth and tight jaws. She cranked the volume dial until the unit turned off and then returned it to her hip. She bit back the taste of bile rising in her throat.

She'd deal with the consequences later.

Beth threw back the heavy steel bolt that held the door tight. She dug her shoulder into the thick metal and shoved. It screeched open until she had enough to slip through.

She wasn't going to lose Jane or her babies. That was the only thing that mattered.

7

THERESA WEST sat in American History class with a sleepy look on her face. She replayed over and over the accident that morning. The blood streaming from the man's eyes. His body in the air. The images circled round and round in her mind.

Despite the buzzing in her brain, her body was tired from staying up late last night. She covered her mouth and stifled a yawn. She seriously needed a Red Bull. Her stomach grumbled in protest at the thought.

It hadn't forgotten two weeks ago when she spent the night with her best friend since third grade, Holly Pearson. Holly snuck some vodka from her dad's liquor stash and replaced the lifted amount with water. They locked themselves in her room and cranked the music, drinking vodka mixed with Red Bull until Theresa ended up in the bathroom puking her guts out. She'd managed to hit the toilet most of the time.

Theresa was going to be super upset if Holly had ruined her favorite drink.

A sickening bubble trickled up her throat and popped in her closed mouth. She breathed out a foul exhale and hoped no one nearby noticed, especially not Elio in the seat diagonally in front of her.

He'd arrived super late to class, even later than she did. He never seemed to care about school. His disinterest should've rung the alarm bells and warned her away, but he was just so awkwardly cute.

Light brown skin matched to mysterious dark brown eyes. A little on the skinny side, but he looked good in the black and gold Los Angeles Football Club jersey he always wore.

Elio was a rabid LAFC fan. Being an equally rabid LA Galaxy fan herself, it was something she had to overlook. Her dad took her to games when his schedule lined up with a game night. She totally loved a night at the StubHub stadium. The crowd. The goals. The players. Definitely the players. Soccer guys were hot. It was like a law or something.

She returned her attention to class as the history teacher strolled through the aisles talking about something she should've been listening to. She stole a glance at him and wondered if her tardiness was going to land her in the principal's office later.

One more tardy mark and she was in trouble. She'd already gotten a big warning after the last one. Probably be after-school detention. She'd done everything she could to get out of the house on time. They would've made it if not for the accident. If not for her dad stopping to help what couldn't be helped. If only he would allow Holly to take her to school, none of this would've happened.

Holly would've run the red light and so they never would've seen that guy.

Most of her tardies were to to Trig class after lunch, and

most of those were definitely Holly's fault. The problem was that Holly saw lunch as a prime socializing time. And once she got started, it was nearly impossible to get her back on schedule.

Theresa turned to look out the window as a raven alighted on a lamp post outside. Glossy black feathers and a prominent black beak. It tilted its head to the side and peered at something held in its claws.

She'd read about how smart they were. That they dropped nuts into traffic and let the cars crack open the ones that were too hard for them to get into by themselves.

Pretty amazing for an animal with a brain the size of a walnut.

Her mind wandered and she recalled how some cultures saw the appearance of a raven as a sign foretelling of dark things to come. She didn't necessarily believe that. Although this time it might be right because detention was likely in her future.

Thoughts of smart ravens and dark futures dissolved as the history teacher rapped a knuckle on her desk.

"Did you not understand the question, Miss West?"

She shook her head, not because she hadn't understood it, but because she hadn't heard it in the first place.

"I presume you read the assignment," he said with a tone that presumed just the opposite.

She'd read it.

Okay, skimmed it.

Okay, skimmed the highlights.

"Sorry, what was that again?"

Holly sniggered, seated at the desk to her left.

"Miss Pearson, do you have something to contribute?"

She shook her head violently and slumped down in the

wooden seat. The kind that made sure you didn't get comfortable enough to doze off.

"No, sir," she replied with her gaze glued to the floor.

Guaranteed *she* didn't read the assignment.

"What a surprise," he replied. He turned back to Theresa. "Why do you think the aftermath of Hurricane Katrina turned out as it did?"

Theresa considered the highlights from the various online articles that she'd read. Glanced through, at least.

From the tragic inexperience of "Heckuvajob" Brownie (all the articles called him that). To the political turf war of local, state, and federal players vying for the spotlight. To the repeatedly ignored warnings from the Army Corps of Engineers about the state of the levees protecting New Orleans. To the just-in-time delivery systems that fed all major cities in the United States and left each with no more than three days of food in grocery stores before another truck needed to show up or the shelves went bare.

From what she'd gathered, it seemed like the abundant, secure reality that seemed so solid the day before landfall was washed away in no time.

As if it never truly existed.

Worse yet, the assumed security of knowing rescue was on the way turned out to be just as false. There was plenty of blame to pass around. But in her mind, it came down to one thing in the end—especially after discussing it with her father.

"There were lots of causes and contributors to the problems. But it boils down to one thing. The people weren't prepared for an emergency of that scale."

The teacher looked at her in quiet contemplation for a moment, as if surprised by her analysis.

"Do you think anyone can be adequately prepare for a category five major hurricane?"

"Not completely, no. But that doesn't mean you shouldn't try. And most people aren't prepared for any kind of emergency. Being somewhat prepared would be ten times better than not prepared at all."

He chewed on that response for another minute.

"And what do you think might happen if a similar event occurred in Los Angeles?"

Theresa's train of thought stumbled and derailed. These were problems that happened to other people, in faraway places. Sure, there might be a freak traffic accident where people died. This was the land of a million speeding cars, after all.

But big disasters?

She'd never considered what it might be like here. If *her* home was destroyed. If *she* was in danger like those people that survived in the days and weeks that followed Katrina.

Thankfully, she realized an obvious fact.

"Um, we don't get hurricanes here."

"No, but we have no shortage of other disasters waiting in the wings. A record drought that has the Los Angeles region buying or stealing water to keep our golf courses and front yards green. Infectious diseases once thought beaten showing up throughout the state. The largest forest fire in a hundred years even now burning out of control up in the San Gabriel Valley. Maintenance problems with the San Onofre power plant requiring an emergency shutdown. The San Andreas fault that is long overdue for a major quake."

Behind him, Holly rolled her eyes, made a pistol with her hand, and set the barrel to her temple. She dropped her thumb and her tongue fell out of her mouth.

Theresa suppressed a giggle and coughed to cover what escaped.

The teacher didn't notice. He looked around the room and paused at the window as he noticed the raven outside. It perched on the lamp post, calmly dipping its head, tugging intestines out of the carcass held in its glistening red claws.

"You never know what the day will bring."

8

MASON pulled to a stop in his driveway and stared out the windshield. What a morning. Witnessing the gruesome accident brought back memories of his time in Iraq. Many that were just as horrible, and a few that were far worse. The vague feeling of danger piqued his protective instincts for his daughter, for his wife.

For Elio.

Elio was the toughest to take because he had so little input in his life. If it were up to him, he'd be more involved, but the boy's mother Maria wouldn't allow it. She'd never forgiven Mason for not bringing her husband David home.

David wouldn't have stood for Elio's flirtation with gang life. Not for a second. But then, maybe Elio wouldn't have felt the draw if his father had been there all these years.

But David was gone and Mason couldn't change what happened. He couldn't magically trade places; a life for a life only worked in storybooks. And thinking about it only threatened to pull him under.

Maria had drifted away after Mason returned from duty. Returned when David hadn't. The widening rift wasn't all her fault. He'd returned carrying new scars. The worst being those not visible to the eye. He hadn't been able to face her for a long time.

He still couldn't face himself.

Mason shook off the shadow. He couldn't go back.

That was history.

His story.

The blackest chapter.

Mason gritted his teeth and stared at nothing in particular. His knuckles turned white from gripping the steering wheel so hard.

There was no getting around it. He had to call her. He'd promised that much, at the least.

A wet tongue lapping at his fingers pulled him up out of the gloom. Max going after the microscopic remains of the failed breakfast that morning. Mason gave him a rough scratch on the neck.

"Thanks, buddy."

He jumped out of the Bronco and Max followed. The dog barked once and bounded for the front door, his thick torso swaying back and forth like a lion. Mason slammed the car door shut and looked to the north.

The sky appeared darker than earlier in the morning.

The fires had to be going strong up there. Depending on the area, the weekend trip to Ojai might be impacted. If they had to cancel, Theresa would be upset. It would be the third time in a row they'd had to cancel plans. He understood that life was sometimes like that. But that didn't make it easier to explain to a fifteen-year-old intent on cuddling and naming newly hatched chicks. And an eighty-six-year-old Tito wasn't any easier to let down.

Disappointment aside, if their safety was at risk, they'd postpone. He'd corral his family on the west side of Los

Angeles for one more weekend. Keep everyone safe on this side of the wildfires. They could hit the beach. For living less than a mile away, it was a cardinal sin how infrequently they got out on the sand.

Mason was about to head inside when Otis Crayford called from the next driveway over.

He didn't look good. Which was saying something for a man already crumpled with age.

"Good morning, Mason," Otis said in a tired voice. He shuffled forward and Mason closed the distance so he wouldn't have to go out of his way. The old man carried a bouquet of freshly cut Gerbera daisies from his flowerbed. Their cheerful glow made the shadow hanging over Otis all the more pronounced.

Max darted at the old man, intent on smelling every millimeter of his pant legs.

"Max! Stop that!" Mason shouted. Max looked back with unfulfilled longing, hoping he'd misunderstood. "I mean it."

Max trotted over and peed on the bushes under the front window.

"Good morning, Otis."

Otis held out the flowers. "These are for Beth. Mabel would want someone to enjoy them while they're in full bloom."

Mason accepted the gift. "Thank you. How's she feeling?"

Otis dropped his gaze and shook his head. "They ended up making her stay the night. I haven't slept in a bed by myself in decades. Fitful, horrible night." His eyes teared up. "Worse for her, I'm sure. Alone in a big hospital."

"Sorry to hear that."

Otis waved Mason off as if he and his wife's suffering were no cause for others' concern. They were old world like that. Otis only let Mason help out when he absolutely had to. That assistance grew bit by bit over the years, as the octogenarian slowed down. Mason was happy to help. He considered it a small payment toward his enormous debt in life.

"I'm heading back to the Reagan Center now," Otis said. "Mabel's most likely tapping her toes wondering why I'm not already back with her over night belongings. Fifty years together and she still has the patience of a child."

The observation might have been harsh, except a smile crept into the corners of his lined face as he said it. They had the kind of love that stuck through thick and thin. Through wars, economic expansions and recessions. Through presidents assassinated or nearly so. Through the rise and fall of grand political theater that tore the world apart, time and again.

Yet, they stuck together.

They were in it to the end.

Mason admired them deeply for their commitment. He liked to think that he and Beth were on the same track, only thirty plus years earlier.

"She'll be happy to see you," he replied.

Otis grinned and a glimmer of youthful optimism showed through the crevices of his craggy skin.

"If I don't make it back by noon, mind checking on Mr. Piddles?"

Mr. Piddles was their ridiculously overweight cat that had a penchant for peeing on the carpets. Hence the name. The rotund feline tolerated Mason because he occasionally fed him when the Crayfords were out. He'd even go so far as to brush against Mason's leg once or twice to indicate he approved of being fed.

"Don't mind at all."

"You've still got the key?"

It hadn't gone anywhere for years.

"Of course."

"You know he gets cranky if he isn't fed precisely at noon."

"Don't worry. I'll take care of it."

Otis paused for a moment, as if assessing whether Mason was a fit guardian. Perhaps deciding he had no better option, he nodded.

"Be back soon as I can."

"See you soon, Otis."

The old man nodded and then shuffled toward his pristine wood-paneled, 1951 Buick Roadmaster. His pride and joy. The thing that he arguably loved as much as Mabel. He patted the flared fender then tugged open a heavy steel door that clearly tested his atrophied muscles.

Mason waved and then strode up the steps to his house, skipping the wobbly second step, and let himself in.

9

After he dropped his keys in the entry table drawer, he poured a tall glass of water from their stainless steel countertop filtration system. The mirror polish made it sit right at home in the contemporary kitchen. It looked good and worked even better. The company claimed you could dump in pond water and it would come out clear as glass and perfectly healthy to drink. Mason had never tried it, but it was definitely the best water he'd ever tasted.

He swigged down the whole glass in one continuous gulp. Partially quenched, he flicked on the TV and flipped to a local news station. A commercial trumpeted in his face. He'd never tested it empirically, but his ears told him that commercials ran at twice the volume of whatever you tuned in to actually watch. He muted it as an adult in a chicken outfit squawked about car dealership deals and closeouts so good they'd be crazy to extend them beyond the coming weekend.

They apparently were crazy as he saw this chicken on TV all the time.

He set the empty glass on the countertop and turned

away from the screen. Even with no sound, watching this garbage was mind pollution. Not facing the screen, he had to face a decision.

He had to call Maria. It had been too long. He dug the phone out of his front pocket and stared at the virtual dialing pad.

He knew the number by heart, even if he rarely dialed it. That wasn't the whole truth. He'd dialed it a thousand times over the years. But then deleted the digits before hitting the green *Call* button. Only a few times had made it to the green button. The few times he'd had something important to say.

Not *the* most important thing. He'd never be able to surrender that story.

Mason's stomach lurched and rolled. He dialed the numbers and punched the green button. It rang a moment and her voice answered.

"What?"

"Hi Maria, how are you this morning?"

"Did you really call to find out how I'm feeling? Because if so, I'm hanging up."

It was never easy. He didn't deserve for it to be any other way. She blamed him for not bringing her husband home. She wasn't wrong.

"Sorry, Maria. I'm calling about Elio."

"I told you to leave him alone. You're not his father. His father is gone."

"Maria," Mason said as he closed his eyes and tried in vain to block out images that appeared more real than the waking world. Images that haunted his dreams. He swallowed hard and continued, "I'm not calling to argue, or bring problems into your life."

"I'm hanging up."

"Wait!" Mason said. "I'm just checking in on Elio. To see how he's doing. It's been too long since I've talked to him."

"I told you to stay away from him, Mason! I don't care what you promised his father."

"Is he still hanging around those Venice 10 gang members?"

"Why do you care?"

"They're bad people, Maria. They aren't kids playing games. They're for real."

"He knows not to mess with them. We've discussed it many times."

"Has he listened?"

"Are you questioning my parenting? How dare you!"

"I'm sorry. That's not what I meant."

"I know what you meant! Mason West to the rescue. My son doesn't need a superhero. He needs a father. Where were you when his father needed you?"

"Please don't make this about David." A spear of hot guilt pierced Mason's belly, doubling him over. He gritted his teeth to the point of shattering. His mouth tasted foul.

"Theresa mentioned the other day that she saw him with those guys. I just wanted you to know."

"Well, thanks for that. I guess. I'll handle it."

"I'd like to help—"

"How many times do I have to tell you? Any help you could've given my family ended in Iraq when my husband died. When my baby boy lost his father. When I lost my husband. Elio wouldn't be in this situation if David was here."

"I did my best, Maria." The words tore out of him like a jagged blade. In war, your best could end up worse than you ever could've imagined.

"Let me be clear, Mason. Stay away from my child."

The line clicked and the call ended.

Mason dropped his head in his hands and fought to control his breath, his heart. Fought to control the acid that scraped his insides.

He would never forget Lance Corporal David Lopez. He'd never had a closer friend.

Mason didn't know then the repercussions of a single signature.

His.

The day he joined the United States Marine Corps.

10

BETH crept through of the metal doorway and tried to secure it behind her. She jiggled and shoved until the stubborn bolt clicked into place. As she turned around to face the interior, the fine hairs on the back of her neck tingled.

A gentle breeze rustled the leaves of the California Black Oaks and Bigleaf Maples that dotted the habitat. The thick foliage drew shifting patterns of light and dark on the grass and dirt below. Thickets of shoulder-high grass waved in a lazy, hypnotic dance.

Her heart hammered in her chest and she took a slow breath to get it under control. There was something different about entering *their* terrain. Even as manufactured as it was here in the heart of the zoo, it was still their turf. A prudent human was wise to remember that.

There was nothing of obvious concern so she headed for the viewing area where she'd last seen Jane. She kept the rifle pointed low but ready. She trusted the female chimp not to hurt her, but then again she'd never entered carrying a rifle. And now she was injured on top of already having a hard time with the pregnancy.

It was better to be ready for anything.

With just a few large boulders between her and Jane, Beth quickened her pace. She had to check on her condition and attend to that wound.

The area opened as she rounded the boulders.

The wall of thick, clear plexiglass held no zoo visitors on the other side because the zoo hadn't opened yet. Not having an audience should Jane to remain calm.

Just over the hump in the ground would be Jane, hopefully not in as bad a shape as it first looked.

Beth crested the small hill, and Jane wasn't there.

She stumbled to a halt, confused. Jane was right there, just moments ago. She must've made it to her feet. Maybe when Ralph was tempting Jack back into the holding pen. She'd been ravenous since the two little infants had made a home inside her. She was eating enough for three.

But Ralph would've told her if Jane followed Jack into the holding area.

She was here somewhere. Various parts of the enclosure were out of sight from this vantage point. It had been designed so that the chimps had different places to get some privacy when they felt the desire for it. It was aimed at making *life in the joint*, as she sometimes joked with Mason, more fulfilling for the animals.

Jane had a favorite spot in the tall grass up on the hill. A few feet inside, she'd flattened a section of grass into a comfortable bed. Beth headed toward it, confident she'd find the giant chimp there.

A low barking rumble spiked the air and vibrated in her chest. Jack's warning call. Must've come from the holding room.

Thank God, he was locked away. Beth didn't want to think about what he would do if he got a hold of her.

She noticed her palms were slippery with sweat and wiped each on a pant leg. Sweat beaded on her neck and pooled in the hollow there. She walked around a shallow pool and made her way up the hill, the rifle heavy and awkward at her side.

The sad whimpering call of an injured chimp sprang from somewhere ahead. Every second that passed tightened the vise around Beth's chest.

She edged forward, her eyes focused and searching.

Fifty feet away, the tall grass shuddered. The stalks swished wildly back and forth. Beth froze and listened.

The stalks settled and rejoined their formerly fluid dance with the breeze.

Beth crept closer.

Now less than twenty feet away.

The towering shoots whipped and shuddered and parted with a flash of motion. A huge head poked through. Its dark eyes focused intently on her. Its mouth hung open, fearsome canines exposed.

A shiver of concern fluttered in Beth's stomach.

Jane.

Blood matted the fur above her right eyebrow. It created a trail down her cheek and neck, tinting the gray-black hair a darker shade. She needed help.

Not for the first time, Beth gave a quick thank you to the universe for giving her this career. She loved caring for all the creatures on the green earth.

Most of them anyway.

Observing Jane for an instant, Beth noticed an unwelcome shallow, quick panting. A slightly unfocused feel to her eyes. An immediate examination was required. No matter what the idiot in the front office thought.

Beth was about to close the distance and start the exam when something odd tickled the edges of her awareness.

The head-high thicket to her left.

What was different about it?

She couldn't resolve it for a moment. And then it zoomed into focus. Clumps of stalks in the middle swished around in sporadic bursts. The movement contrasted with the gentle swaying of the surrounding areas. Beth narrowed her gaze to study it.

What—

An enormous form crashed through, splintering the thicker stalks like toothpicks. The hulk landed on two feet and spread his arms, his posture broad and threatening.

Jack.

Oh no.

11

Cold eyes regarded her with malevolent intent. She shuddered as a chill like an Arctic wind blew over her. Her legs wobbled. Her body a quivering mass of flesh and bone incapable of obeying commands to move, to do something.

Not that any instructions were forthcoming.

Her brain was equally numbed. A thousand thoughts collided at once, threatening to degrade the fight or flight response into a worse option: freeze in fear.

Jack watched her from less than a hundred feet away. A distance he could cover in seconds. His lips snarled and pulled back to reveal gigantic, white daggers for canine teeth.

He rolled his head back and a roar tore from his throat like thunder. The sound touched a primal nerve deep inside her brain. Her heart pounded like a bass drum in her ears. The air seemed to crawl across her skin. Terror tasted like an old penny on her tongue.

She looked toward the locked metal door she'd entered a few moments ago. It was the closest point of escape. It may as well have been miles away. She wouldn't come close to making that distance.

Something slipped in her right hand. Her grip clenched involuntarily to hang on to whatever it was.

She looked down to see what had provoked the automatic response.

The rifle.

Loaded with a dart primed with M99. Enough to make Jane drowsy. Not nearly enough to knock out the much larger Jack.

Still, it was better than nothing.

Jack's roar cut to silence and left behind a cacophony of responses from the surrounding animals nearby. They all screeched one message.

Danger! Danger!

He glanced at Jane to his left for a moment. She held her head low in a display of submission.

With his focus pulled away, conscious thought returned. A ragged breath struggled into her lungs. She thought of Theresa and Mason. Imagined their faces upon hearing of her death. Their pain broke her heart.

And steeled her will.

Consciously moving slowly, she raised the rifle and settled the stock into the crook of her shoulder. She tried to keep the front sight aligned on Jack's broad chest but her shaking hands bounced it around.

One shot. One chance to even have a chance.

He turned his massive head toward her. The vicious intensity of his focus threatened to knock her down. Send her into physical spasms of horror.

She took a deep breath and then blew it out. At the end of the exhale, she paused and let the front sight settle.

Jack leaped forward, his arms extending in front of him and stretching for the ground between them.

She squeezed the trigger.

BOOF.

The dart exploded out of the barrel and spiked Jack in the chest as he rushed forward. He'd already closed more than half the distance.

He was so fast. Too fast.

He bounded closer as another second passed and her life ticked down to a sliver that she couldn't extend.

She stumbled back, buffeted by the tremor of psychic violence that preceded him like a shockwave. Her boot heel caught a rock and she fell. Her arms windmilled in a futile attempt to grab something to regain balance. She landed hard and her head snapped backward and slammed into hard dirt. Bright pain clawed at her eyes. She blinked hard and watched in horror as Jack launched into the air from ten feet away.

His cavernous mouth opened, eager to tear into her flesh.

Beth yanked up the spent rifle, as if it might somehow hold back two-hundred-seventy pounds of primal fury.

Movement streaked across her vision, coming from her right.

Jack stretched for her, his enormous hands extended as he descended.

Beth turned her head. She couldn't watch. She'd done her best.

She never had a chance.

Jack reached for her throat. His jaws stretched wide to finish her. Jane streaked through the air and broadsided him. Though smaller, her speed and fury gave her strength.

Jack's sharp canine caught Beth on the pant leg and gouged a red furrow across her thigh.

Jane's impact slammed both chimps to the ground to Beth's left. They rolled and tumbled in a flying ball of fur and fangs. Their limbs blurred as they tore at each other.

Beth glanced at the open laceration on her thigh and almost vomited. It had just missed the femoral artery. An injury that would have ended her life in minutes. The gash was wide open but didn't look too deep. She got lucky. She struggled to stand, using the rifle like a cane to get upright.

Already, Jane's smaller size and weaker condition began to tell. Jack slashed his exposed teeth and caught her down the side. Red spilled down her ribs and over her swollen belly.

Beth grabbed a plum-sized rock and whipped it at the back of his head. Her aim was true, but it bounced off harmlessly.

This was a fight she couldn't sway. Not without better tools than the one she currently wielded. She needed another dart. A full dose of M99 would do it. She just had to get it before it was too late.

Beth sprinted for the exit and nearly fell as the gash in her leg sent a shock up her left side. She hobbled along as fast as the injury would allow.

The two huge chimps scrambled and rolled in a dust cloud so thick it was hard to see what was happening. Then Jane flew out and tumbled over the ground. She rolled to her feet just as Jack slammed into her.

She couldn't win that fight. It was only a matter of time. And by the looks of it, not much.

Beth limped to the metal door and fumbled at the ring of keys at her hip with numb, unfeeling fingers.

She found the right one, but her shaking hands kept

poking the tip of the key anywhere but the keyhole. She finally managed to shove it home and cranked the bolt free.

The ferocious sounds of the battle subsided. The fight was ending. But not with a truce.

Jane lay sprawled on her back. She offered only token resistance.

Jack stood over her, his enormous hands pinning her down. His powerful jaws around her neck. In minutes, he would starve her brain of oxygen and end not only her life but the life of the two unborn infants as well.

Beth sprinted out and slammed the door shut, in the blind panic of a parent about to lose a child.

In her fevered rush, she neglected to throw the bolt and lock the door shut.

12

Beth fumbled through unlocking the safe in the lab and fumbled further in dosing a dart with enough M99 to incapacitate an adult male Bili chimp in short order. She yanked back the bolt on the rifle and loaded the primed cartridge. She slammed the bolt home and checked that the safety was engaged.

Not wanting to be caught unprepared again, she filled another dart, left the plastic safety tip on, and dropped it into her pocket.

Two shots to take the beast down. It should be one more than she needed.

She locked the safe and started back down the maze of corridors that led toward the metal door on the west side of the chimp exhibit.

She moved as fast as she could, but the wound to her leg slowed her down. And she was keenly aware that precious minutes had ticked by. Jane could already be gone, her body twitching as stray electrical impulses fired muscles that still couldn't accept that life was a rapidly fading memory.

The final turn brought her to the metal door. And to a discovery that sent a violent shudder through her chest.

The door was wide open.

She hadn't left it like that. She'd shut it and locked it!

Hadn't she?

Her lungs sucked at air that felt thinner than at the top of Mount Everest. There was too little oxygen to clear her thoughts, to get her brain functioning normally.

Did she lock it?

Beth stood there, paralyzed by what the open door might mean.

The answer came in the form of a low, deep howl that echoed down the corridor.

Her walkie-talkie chirped.

"Dr. West! Come in, Dr. West! This is Ralph!"

She thumbed the transmitter.

"Ralph, what's going on?"

"Ma'am, I came back to the holding room to grab something and, well, I don't know how it could've happened, but, well..."

"Jack isn't inside. I know."

"Yes. I secured the pen just as you showed me before. I swear I did. I don't know what happened."

"Let's worry about that later. I'm over by the west gate and it's open. And Jack's location is unknown."

Another low growl echoed down the hall. This time, distinctly coming from the direction of the north gate and holding room.

"Ralph, get out of there! Now! Jack is loose in the maintenance corridors!"

There was no response. She waited.

"Ralph! Do you hear me? Get out now!"

The faintest whisper replied.

"He's here now..."

A wild scream tore through the tiny speaker.

Beth sprinted down the corridor. The overhead lights painted patches of light in the surrounding shadows. Her boots slapped the hard concrete floor in a desperate rhythm.

As she arrived at the doorway leading to the holding room, a loud crash accompanied another roar. The sound was deafening in the small space. She made the turn and lifted the rifle stock to her shoulder.

Ralph was trapped under a large stainless steel pushcart. The one they used to transport the daily meals for the chimps. It was now turned upside down with Jack above and Ralph beneath. Ralph's tan shirt had a ragged tear at the shoulder. A dark crimson stain covered the sleeve, all the way down to the cuff.

Beth skidded to a stop and fired.

Jack's head whipped around just as the trigger broke and the dart shot forward.

The small projectile ricocheted off the table and landed harmlessly in the tangle of thick fur at his neck. Jack flinched, pausing to assess what had been done to him.

Which was nothing.

But at least she had his attention now.

Oh no.

She had his attention now.

Beth fumbled for the remaining dart lodged in her pocket. The projectile turned sideways and got stuck in the folds of cloth. With a violent jerk, it finally came free. She ripped the plastic safety tip off just as Jack turned and lunged.

The enraged chimp slammed her backward. The rifle clattered to the floor several feet away.

She crashed to the ground with Jack on top. His

enormous hand crushed down on her chest. He regarded her coolly with mouth open and a rumble emanating more from his chest than his throat.

She reached for the rifle, but a few feet away may as well have been miles. She couldn't breathe, much less move an inch.

She didn't need it.

She gripped the dart tightly, extended her arm above her head, and aimed it at the thick muscles in the arm smashing a hole through her chest. The anesthetic would take more time hitting a muscle group so far from the brain. It might take a few minutes to knock him out.

She wouldn't survive a few more seconds, much less a few minutes.

She jabbed the dart at the meat of his arm.

Faster than seemed possible, a blur of movement, Jack's other hand swatted the dart away just before the needle pricked his skin. The brute force tore it from her grip and sent it skittering across the floor.

That was it.

That was her last chance to stop him.

His attention followed the dart as it came to rest.

Beth lifted her hands above her face, knowing her weak arms were no more an obstacle for him than a silk scarf was to a samurai sword.

"Dr. West!"

Ralph shouted as he pushed the cart off and levered himself up against the wall on visibly shaking legs.

Jack turned his head toward Ralph as the hand on her chest seemed to gain another thousand pounds. She couldn't breathe. Her ribcage creaked, close to cracking like an eggshell.

Between her upraised arms, something caught her attention.

The dart. The first one. Entangled in his matted fur.

She yanked it free. Unfortunately, the movement also got Jack's attention.

He lowered his head and his lips curled back. Enormous teeth that appeared white at a distance looked more yellow up close. Saliva dripped from his lips and down onto her neck. His body was preparing to consume her.

To swallow her in bite-sized chunks.

He opened his mouth and lunged. Huge teeth closed the distance to tender flesh.

Beth turned away as her hand shot up.

The dart found its target and caught Jack in the throat, just below his jaw. It must have spiked a vein because the effect was instantaneous.

His head stopped inches from her face. One long canine pressed into her cheek. His hot breath reeked of blood. His eyes unfocused.

He reared back to his feet in a drunken stupor.

Beth heaved and sucked at air. Searing hot pain tore at her ribs as her lungs inflated.

Jack wobbled back and forth, trying to stay upright. It was no use. Another second passed and his eyes rolled up into his head. His legs collapsed and he fell to the floor.

Beth's heart thundered in her ears, so fast it was hard to distinguish one beat from the next.

The blind terror left her stomach a swirling cauldron. She turned her head and her torso clenched tight. Vomit sprayed out onto the concrete floor. A shaking hand wiped away the tendrils clinging to her chin.

She looked up and a dark form blocked the fluorescent light above.

Her heart skipped a beat.

Ralph stood over her, his skin a waxy, dull hue. "You okay?"

Her ribs ached and a jolt of pain tinged every breath that drew a little too deep. The laceration in her thigh throbbed. "I'll make it. How about you?"

He glanced at his shoulder and smiled. A weak, uneasy thing like the sun in winter.

"Going to need a few stitches, but I'll be all right." He extended his good hand. "Can you get up?"

"I can try," Beth replied as she took his hand. The pain in her ribs flared as she got to her feet. She held her sides and knew some nasty bruises were in store. But it didn't matter. She'd survive. Her years of experience treating wounded animals told her that much.

A more important question bubbled up in her mind. Would Jane survive? She was still out there.

Ralph stared at Jack's inert form. His eyes transfixed by the beast that nearly killed them both.

Beth shook his good shoulder to grab his attention.

"Get a team in here. Drag him into the holding room. Lock it and leave someone to guard it."

"Okay."

"Afterward, bring the rest of the team inside the enclosure. We need to move Jane into the lab immediately."

Beth didn't know if she was still alive or not. And even if she was, there was no guarantee she was going to stay that way.

Beth headed for the door and stumbled a step before catching herself.

"You sure you're okay, Dr. West?"

"Call the team now!" Beth yelled as she disappeared

down the hall. Two thoughts circled in her brain as she went.

How did a locked cage end up open?

And were Jane and her unborn infants already dead?

13

ELIO LOPEZ sat in the school office, slouched over in a hard plastic chair, wishing he could be anywhere else in the world. Harsh fluorescent lights buzzed in the ceiling above. Snippets of conversation floated by in the hallway. The excited hum of students after another day at the education mill.

After the final school bell rang in his last period of the day, he thought he was home free, too. But he didn't have that kind of luck.

The principal had been waiting outside the classroom and ushered him back to the office. He'd been sitting here for a while now. It was all part of the punishment. First, they made you sit out in the front office and wonder. After you stewed in anxiety for a while, only then did you go into the principal's office and receive the punishment.

The first part was working. Elio tried not to imagine what his mom was going to say. She'd be furious. That's all he knew for sure. His head hung so low it looked like his neck had given up.

Suspension was the likely outcome of the coming

conversation. These disciplinary meetings were always called *conversations*. As if two old friends were just sitting down to sort through some misunderstanding. Conversation didn't cover it. It was a lecture of disappointment. His job was to sit there and listen while coming across as regretful for whatever they got him for this time.

Fine. He'd play his part.

It wasn't that he loved his regular visits to the office. He didn't. He just knew there were worse places you could end up. And avoiding those places sometimes required him to do things that landed him here.

It was a stacked deck and he played the hand he was dealt. At this rate, there was no guarantee he'd finish high school.

He was vulnerable and the Venice 10 bangers knew it. They could sense it like you had a neon sign over your head. Once you pinged on their radar, it was almost impossible to disappear.

At least not in a good way.

He'd been late for first period that morning and racked up another tardy. They wouldn't let it slide. They never did.

Elio didn't pay attention to the exact number of his tardies and absences, but he was well within the serious discipline zone.

Suspension might be nice. No school for a week or two. Take it easy at home. His mom would spit fire though. She'd rip him up one side and down the other.

Maybe he could hide it from her. Forge her signature. Pretend to go to school until after she left for her nursing shift. She never made it home before eleven each night anyway.

A figure appeared at the entrance to the office and Elio

groaned thinking that the *conversation* was about to begin. He looked up with a grimace.

And was relieved to see Theresa West standing there. She smelled like flowers. Looked like a goddess. Glossy, long black hair fell around her shoulders in waves. Light brown eyes that even the fluorescents couldn't diminish with their white-blue haze.

She stood there with her hand on her hip and lips pursed tight. "Is seeing me so great a disappointment?"

His mind swirled while his tongue fumbled to say something that wasn't idiotic. "Uhh, what?"

"That look couldn't be less enthused."

"Oh, yeah. Sorry. I thought you were somebody else."

"The principal?"

"Yeah."

"You about to have a *conversation* with him?"

"Yeah. You?"

"Same. Lucky us," she said as she nodded toward the empty seat next to him. "Mind if I join you?"

"Doesn't sound like you have a choice."

"True," she said as she plopped down. Her arm was inches away from his. The empty air between crackled with anticipation. He wondered if she felt it too.

Probably not.

He tried to think of something to say. Something casual. Nothing came.

She filled the empty space. "So, what are you in for?"

He blinked. She made it sound so easy. "Tardies. You?"

"Same."

He nodded, hoping she would say something else so they could avoid another awkward silence.

"Holly said your gangster friends are having a big party tonight."

They were. He knew about it. Cesar told him about it. Invited him—no, that wasn't quite accurate—told him to come.

"They're not my friends."

"Really? I've seen you hanging out with them lately."

It was complicated. She wouldn't understand.

"Yeah, they're having a party. How'd Holly know?"

"She knows about every party happening within ten square miles. She's like the oracle of weekend social activity."

Elio nodded. "Those guys are okay for me. Not for you."

He didn't want her getting anywhere near the Venice 10 members. They were from totally different worlds while he floated in the uncomfortable space between.

"What's that supposed to mean?"

"Nothing. Never mind."

A terrible silence descended.

Thankfully, she broke it.

"Listen, maybe we can hang out sometime."

Did he just hear her right?

His insides twisted up. He panicked. A deer in a headlight. The moon staring at the sun. He didn't respond.

"Or not. If you don't want to."

He wanted to!

He wanted to!

A crease formed between her delicate brows.

No. No. No. He was losing the moment. He blurted out words before they processed through his internal filter.

"I'd love to hang out with you anywhere!"

The words were awkward enough, but the way they spilled out of his mouth in a vomit jumble made it ten times worse.

"Elio Lopez, are you asking me out on a date?"

Crimson fire singed his face. He didn't know what to say. "No!"

She was so gorgeous. So smart. So everything. He didn't have a chance. He was an idiot to think he might.

She looked at him like he was a Martian.

Why did he just say no? He should've said yes. Wasn't she basically telling him to say yes?

Another figure appeared in the doorway.

"Miss West, thank you for taking the time to see me. I'll be a few minutes with Mr. Lopez and then we can discuss the difficulty you have with arriving to class in a timely manner."

She dropped her head in shame. Elio couldn't tell if it was an act or not. In the office, it was always best to look sorry, whether you felt it or not. Elio knew of more than a few girls who turned on the waterworks to get out of deserved punishments.

Unfortunately for him, Elio couldn't bring himself to fake cry to save his hide.

The principal headed toward his open office door.

"Follow me, Mr. Lopez."

Elio stood and followed. A sheep to the slaughter. He looked back just before disappearing through the doorway.

Theresa flashed a smile that left him breathless and no longer caring about what might happen. She mouthed two words to him.

Good luck.

He could face anything with her at his side. If only she'd give him a chance.

14

An impossibly long *conversation* later, Elio escaped the office with a promise to have his mother call the school. Despite the depth of the trouble that he was definitely in, he strolled out casually and winked at Theresa as he left. He exited the school, headed for the bus stop and was intercepted by his friends that weren't friendly.

The V10 gang members.

The afternoon sun beat down as he struggled to hide the tension in his face. The fear. With these guys, showing weakness was the quickest way to become prey. The quickest way to survive was to join them. And for someone like Elio, being on the inside would offer a sense of belonging he'd never felt in life.

The V10 controlled the criminal underground in Venice with a ruthless zeal. No map marked the lines of their territory. But bullets flew and bodies fell when rival gangs probed the boundaries.

He followed them over to one of their favorite spots, a dead-end alley one street over from Venice High School. It had a hill in it half way down so that any cars driving by the entrance couldn't see what was happening at the end. They posted a guy at the top of the alley as a lookout. If the black and whites rolled up, the members had a choice of quick exits through adjacent backyards. The neighbors were smart enough not to interfere.

They also liked it because of its proximity to the high school. A couple members still attended. They liked keeping a few soldiers on the inside. It gave them access and information they wouldn't otherwise easily get.

Elio looked around, wondering if this would ever feel like home, wondering if he wanted it to.

Old couches lined the covered chain-link fences. Gang signs and names covered every nook and cranny. V10 and VX (X being the Roman numeral for ten) were the most predominant tags. Empty forty-ounce bottles littered the ground, mixed with the shards of other bottles. An old import sedan sat up on blocks with the doors gone. It had been stripped down to the point where the make and model were no longer identifiable, the paint worn raw to primer over most of its surface.

Two guys sat in the vehicle, huffing down a huge spliff. The rank stink of old booze mixed with the skunky scent of dank weed. One of them exploded in a coughing fit as the other fell through the nonexistent door and hit the ground with a thunk. He rolled to his back and lifted his arm, noticing countless glass slivers sticking out of his forearm. A mouthful of gold sparkled as he laughed, plucking them out one at a time.

They were insane.

Elio didn't want to have his clothes smelling like a skunk. He hoped they didn't offer any his way. But he knew what refusing would mean—the unmasking of a bleating sheep in a den full of lions.

Six members surrounded him, not counting the one in the wreck and the one on the ground. He was the sole outsider in the midst of a group that considered outsiders one of only two things. A target or a threat. Either case was dealt with the same way.

Elio tiptoed through the no man's land as a potential recruit. It wasn't a safe place to linger.

The members were at ease, as the alley was well inside their turf. Had been since they'd violently ripped it from the Westside Crips in a bloody two-month battle that left twenty Crips dead and half that number of V10 members the same. The biggest blow had been the loss of their previous shot caller.

That's when Cesar took command.

In no time, he'd assumed the status of a street legend. Under his control, the V10 were pushing south, east, and north. Displacing rival gangs in every direction but west, because there was no play in claiming the vast expanse of the Pacific Ocean. Dolphins didn't buy drugs. Sharks didn't rent prostitutes. It was nice to look at, but that was it.

Elio stood in front of Cesar, at attention like a rookie in boot camp. Only in boot camp, the worst that could happen was you'd get yelled at or have to do a ton of push-ups. If you made Cesar mad, you ended up dead. Even if you didn't do anything, you still sometimes ended up dead. He was as unpredictable as he was ruthless.

There were rumors that the previous shot caller didn't end up dead at the end of a black bullet, but a brown one. Nobody said anything, though, because soldiers didn't ask questions. It didn't matter who the shot caller was so long as order remained.

Elio stared at Cesar's huge, muscled chest and not up into his eyes. He didn't want to spark an unintended challenge. The air caught in his lungs as the reek of alcohol-soaked breath rolled over him. He suppressed a grimace. He stilled any reaction whatsoever.

Anything could set Cesar off. At twenty-two, he was only five years older than Elio. But it wasn't his age that gave him authority. It was his size and aggression. He was two hundred fifty pounds of muscled, pitiless ambition. He had exactly one gear.

Domination.

But that same domination could be protection. But that protection came with a cost.

If he joined, any normal future would be lost. And if he didn't join, the same thing might happen anyway. The V10 weren't known for their patience and understanding.

The indecision he clung to was quickly wearing thin. He got the distinct feeling that if he didn't jump in soon, he was going to end up with a bullet in his head.

Probably delivered by the man standing in front of him.

15

"What else you got, vato?" Cesar said, his words spitting down to Elio's level.

"Solo mi madre," he replied. "Nothing else."

"That's right," Cesar said. "Think about it. You get picked off and who's gonna watch after your mama? Nobody. And that's assuming she doesn't take a round herself."

The threat in his voice was inescapable.

Acid climbed up Elio's throat. His jaw clenched and teeth ground together. He wanted to smash this cholo's face in. Leave his nose a pulped mess.

But this wasn't fantasyland where you got even just because you deserved to.

This was LA and the shot caller of the V10. Deserving had nothing to do with it. Good and deserving people ended up dead in a dumpster every day. Cesar put many of them there.

"Entiendo, Cesar."

"Knowin' and doin' is different thangs. You better get to doin'."

Elio nodded and chanced a glance up at all the ink that

laced Cesar's arms and shoulders. More crawled up his neck and covered his jaws and cheeks. The tattoos resembled old photos of Maori warriors. They were a history book if you could read the language. He openly claimed every hit, every murder, every conquest on his body.

It was part of his legend.

Other members, even shot callers of rival gangs, thought he was crazy to give the cops a detailed report of his crimes. Captured in indelible ink right on his skin. If only they could pin one on him and break the code of hieroglyphs. The white wife-beater he wore covered yet more history scrawled across his chest and back.

Cesar had only two unmarked areas of skin left on his upper body, his palms. Elio knew the story. It was gang lore that he was saving those for anyone who double-crossed him. He would kill the traitor and the traitor's family with his bare hands, and then ink the retribution on his palms.

Nobody wanted to end up inked there. Nobody wanted their mother, brothers or sisters to end up there either.

Cesar smacked Elio on the shoulder and his body shook with the blow. Even in jest, the projection of dominance and aggression was obvious. Elio's far lankier form absorbed the impact and he stumbled to maintain balance.

"Come by tonight," Cesar said. "Be good to meet some people." He looked back to the lieutenant behind his left shoulder, Ernesto, Evil E as he was called. Attack dog was more like it. He was short and square, with thick muscles that made him look even shorter. A deeply pitted face that made the surface of the moon look smooth.

"Evil's sister's comin' round. Man you up to tap that."

Elio caught a look from Evil. A look that said he would bleed if he laid a finger on her.

Cesar laughed loudly, enjoying the prospect of his trained personal pit bull disemboweling Elio.

Running with wolves was delicate business. Weakness would get you killed. But a contest of strength could do the same.

"Nah," Elio said, "everybody knows that skank's got the itchies. I wouldn't touch that with E's pole."

It was a risk. Insulting a lieutenant. Even in jest, it could end in an emergency room visit.

Evil practically vaulted over Cesar to get at him, his face a twisted grimace of ugly rage. Cesar's massive arms whipped out and wrapped him in a bear hug. The veins in his biceps bulged as Ernesto struggled to get free.

"I'm gonna kill you, chavala!"

Cesar's other lieutenant, Cuts, stood behind his right shoulder chuckling, his long, lanky limbs shaking with glee. His grin deformed the ragged tapestry of white scars that lined his face. His arms were similarly covered. Cuts was a twisted piece of work. He loved getting sliced up almost as much as doing the slicing. Almost, but not quite. Nothing gave him more satisfaction than watching an enemy fall under his blade.

He raised a wicked looking knife, and his slender fingers caressed the razor edge. "This cholo's got huevos grandes. Maybe we oughtta cut 'em off."

Cesar narrowed his eyes and whispered into Evil's ear, "Tranquilo, carnal. Don't eat the fresh meat 'til it's had a chance to char."

Evil finally relaxed and Cesar released him. Quick as lightning, Evil slashed a right cross and caught Elio across the face.

Elio spun around and fought to keep from hitting the asphalt face first. He slammed down on one knee with a hand extended to stop the fall. Bright pain shot up his arm, the bite of a few slivers of glass in his palm. Blinking hard, he struggled to settle the wobbling world. The sharp bite of copper gushed hot and sticky into his mouth.

Uh oh.

Maybe that was too big a risk.

Cesar roared with malignant approval. "Mis lobos tienen hambre!" He punched Evil in the chest, a message that simultaneously communicated appreciation and also a boundary. A warning not to cross his word again.

Elio swallowed blood and tried to breathe through his nose. Guttering blood washed into the back of his throat and he gagged. He spat it out and was about to stand when he heard a rumble from the other end of the alley, back toward the road.

A cacophony of phones sang with an incoming text.

Elio looked up and saw an old tan and copper Ford Bronco, riding high on enormous tires, charging toward them.

Great.

Like things weren't bad enough already.

16

MASON headed to pick up Theresa. As much as he tried, he couldn't get his earlier conversation with Maria out of his mind. If only she'd let him be a part of Elio's life. He wasn't trying to replace his father. He just wanted to be a friend. Someone who cared.

Max stuck his head forward from the back bench seat and licked Mason's cheek. The wet tongue snagged on his skin highlighting that he hadn't shaved today. One of the pleasures of a day off.

One of too few lately.

The bullmastiff's large head filled the rearview mirror so Mason pushed him to the side and scanned his immediate surroundings. All clear.

He gassed the Bronco and accelerated toward the intersection where the accident had occurred that morning. What a mess that was.

Not wanting to revisit it so soon, he took a right on a side street and elected to take smaller streets. He wound through a number of turns and was about to call Beth when something caught his attention.

Down an alley to his right, a group of kids surrounded a kid on the ground. The one on the ground looked to be bleeding. Mason noticed that the hump halfway down the alley shielded them from any normal height vehicles.

His Bronco, however, had an unobstructed view. He rolled down the window to see if he could hear anything that might offer any intelligence about the situation. It didn't, but the extra moment of observation did show him that the boy on the ground was Elio Lopez.

And he had taken a beating.

The perpetrators were clearly a band of the local thugs that infested Venice like a bad case of termites. Constantly chewing on the sturdy supports of the community. Doing their level best to hollow it out and make it unlivable for regular folks.

He wasn't the type to go looking for trouble. But he wasn't the type to shy away from it either. And right now, Elio was in danger.

Mason noticed another guy positioned at the street corner. The lookout. The guy tapped his phone as Mason hooked a right and turned into the alley. He dropped a few gears and slammed the gas. The engine growled with an ear-splitting roar. Every head at the end of the alley swiveled in his direction.

The Bronco charged down the narrow corridor and skidded to a stop meters away from the biggest thug in front. Before jumping out, Mason unconsciously patted the reassuring lines of the Glock 19 tucked safely into his King Tuk IWB holster. He'd carried for his job every day for over a decade and never found a more reliable, more comfortable combination.

He turned to Max and whispered, "Stay, Max." He didn't

want him involved. There were too many variables already. He jumped out and slammed the door shut.

Before his feet hit the ground, he measured and categorized the threats facing him. Eight V10 gang members. The one in front was clearly a dangerous individual. That must be Cesar, the shot caller. Mason had heard Elio mention the name before.

If he had to use force, that one would go down first. He quickly prioritized the remaining targets and decided on a course of action.

These weren't your typical threats. That was clear. Projecting power and bluffing the use of force wasn't going to impress them into submission. He'd try the path of peace first, as he always did. He just didn't think it was going to get him far with this particular crew.

He didn't want to engage in a close-quarters gunfight with eight opponents. They weren't impossible odds, despite the lopsided arrangement. But Elio would be caught in the crossfire. And getting him killed was the worst possible outcome.

Mason bladed his body to the group to present a smaller target and kept his right hand loose and ready to go for the pistol at his hip. At the same time, he plastered a smile on his face.

One he didn't feel in the least. One he was sure came off exactly as intended.

17

Mason inspected Elio and saw he was bleeding but not seriously injured. He looked back to Cesar and approached to within a few feet. Max barked and growled from inside the truck. That was good. It would give these thugs something to think about. Nobody, no matter how tough they claimed to be, didn't think twice about taking on a hundred and twenty pounds of raging bullmastiff.

Several of the soldiers behind Cesar made a move for weapons they must have had tucked under shirts and jackets. Mason cleared his shirt and was an impulse away from drawing down and tapping a couple rounds of Hornandy Critical Duty ammo into this idiot's chest when the bulked-up monster spread his hands and lowered them with the palms down.

"Tranquilo, carnales," he said. "Let's see what blanco wants first. Maybe he's here to take a pizza order or something."

Mason studied the primary threat without breaking their locked gaze. No weapons in sight, if you didn't count the shredded muscles and malignant look in his eyes.

Doubtless he had a pistol tucked into the small of his very large back.

Judging by how Cesar's dark pants were cinched up high around his waist and the way the outsized bulk of his shoulders and biceps spread his arms, Mason knew Cesar's draw would be slower than his own. A draw down between the two would end only one way. The remaining threats were less certain.

That was a last resort, however.

"So, what you want? Wanna do a beer run for us?"

Mason maintained slow, even breaths, consciously controlling his heart rate and adrenal response. Some fear was good to keep you switched on. Too much was bad as it destroyed your fine motor control. He'd read numerous accounts of close protection officers who had been in gunfights they should've won but didn't. He knew you couldn't miss fast enough to win.

Mason ignored the question and tossed a question at Elio. "You okay?"

Elio staggered to his feet, pinching his nose to staunch the bleeding. "Yeah, I'm fine."

Cesar's eyes held Mason's, unblinking and unwavering. "See hero? Everything's all good here. Why don't you run back to the golf course or—"

"I can't help but notice he needs medical attention. I'll take him to get that looked at." He stepped to the side, toward Elio, with his hand out to help steady him.

Cesar stepped forward on an intercepting course. "Nobody called the cavalry. You best turn around and gallop off while you can."

"I'm not leaving without him."

"You might not be leavin' at all," Cesar said as his arms

flexed and veins slithered under his skin like snakes under silk.

"Dust him," said a squat brick of a human with an acne-scarred face.

"I say we slice him up, eat his heart for breakfast," said a tall, lanky one with thin, white scars all over his body.

The two lieutenants fanned out behind their leader, grabbing space for a fight.

So this was it.

Mason didn't want a gunfight, but he knew that some level of violence was required. And when it was required, it was always better to act first.

The movies always had the good guy drawing fire or getting punched first before responding. In real life, that got you killed. If you had to take action, you didn't wait to be a gentleman about it. You hit first, with everything you had.

Mason pulled his hand away from his side and held both up in front, open with the palms out. He took a step forward and shrugged, doing his best to appear non-threatening.

"I'm not here to make trouble, Cesar."

Using his name had the intended effect. The surprise registered on Cesar's face and left him in an instant of indecision.

That was all the opening Mason needed.

As the last word left his lips, Mason's right hand shot forward on a twenty-inch collision course with Cesar's nose. At the last instant, the target's head dropped. The blow should've glanced harmlessly off his crown, probably breaking a few of Mason's fingers in the process. It didn't though, because Mason had curled his arm back, dropped his torso, and slashed up with an elbow already inside the target's guard.

The hard bone smashed into Cesar's nose. A sickening crunch and a hot spray of blood let Mason know he'd hit his mark. He stepped to the side as a glint of steel shot through the space where his stomach had been an instant before. He snatched the huge hand in mid-air and torqued it upside down with a vicious jerk of his left arm. The force would've snapped the wrist of any normal human being. It got the shot caller's attention.

The knife clattered to the pavement as Cesar grunted in pain.

Mason kicked it away and released the wrist lock. With his right hand, he drew his service pistol and backed up a few steps, his trigger finger lightly along the slide, ready to curl in and empty fifteen rounds at point blank range.

"Nobody move! Kid, get in the truck," Mason said.

"You should leave," Elio replied.

Cesar straightened up, rubbing his injured wrist, glaring at Mason. "You're dead, hero. Dead."

"Get in the truck!" Mason shouted.

Elio walked over, still pinching his nose, opened the passenger door and hopped in. Max immediately stopped barking and jumped on Elio with a barrage of licking and whining.

Cesar's eyes narrowed as he watched. No concern at all about the river of blood pouring down his shirt. He looked around at the soldiers ready to draw down and die if he gave the word. He locked eyes with Mason. "Use that and you won't walk away from this."

"Maybe, but I'm positive you won't."

The barest glimmer of uncertainty flashed in Cesar's eyes before they hardened again.

"Time to leave, blanco," he said. "While you still can."

Mason measured the truth of his words. He saw

something in those eyes. Not fear. But as tough as this guy was, he didn't want to die. And he absolutely would if the bullets let loose.

Mason backed away slowly toward the driver door, his aim never faltering. He rolled the window down and switched the Glock to his left hand. He extended that out the window as he closed the door. The front sight never wavered. He'd trained extensively with offhand drills and was nearly as confident on his left side as his right.

Cesar spat blood on the ground and snarled at Mason through the front glass. "You're dead. Your family is dead."

A threat. One Mason knew wasn't an idle one. But what could he do? He didn't have the legal backing to kill him. The use of justified deadly force was an unforgiving legal doctrine in California. Killing him to prevent some vague future threat would go absolutely nowhere in court.

Mason threw it in reverse and slammed the pedal down. The V8 howled and the Bronco lurched backward, retreating up the alley.

His life had just gotten a lot more complicated.

18

Mason wanted more than anything to call Maria and let her know what happened. But in the end, he'd dropped Elio off at his apartment with a promise to check in later.

He wondered if Elio would tell her, and if she would blame him for the whole incident. Like it was Mason's fault that Elio was there in the first place.

And maybe she wouldn't be wrong about that.

He filled a glass from the kitchen faucet and turned to the muted TV on the counter. He clicked up the volume. What he saw didn't seem real.

The local news had an intrepid, and perhaps insane, reporter broadcasting live on the edge of a massive forest fire. He stood in the middle of a closed I-5 highway. Work crews in blue jackets drove trucks and cranes, moving Jersey barriers into place across the lanes. Drab green military vehicles dotted the road in both the northbound and southbound directions.

Off the road on both sides, and no more than a few hundred feet behind the reporter, Douglas Fir and Coulter Pine crackled in a hell fury. An explosion ignited with a boom and the correspondent ducked like a mortar had just hit. Emergency vehicles in the background went about their business as if nothing happened. Big, white block letters on blue jackets read FEMA.

The Federal Emergency Management Agency.

The federal government never responded to the innumerable fires that California endured every summer. The largest wildfire ever recorded was still handled by state and local agencies. It happened in San Diego in 2003 and burned over 250,000 acres. Before it was contained, three thousand homes and fifteen lives were lost. No federal agency assisted in that operation.

The presence of FEMA didn't necessarily make Mason feel any better. Not after the calamity that followed Katrina. Not after a number of smaller incidents that told similar stories of ineptitude and corruption. It did tell him something though.

This was no ordinary forest fire.

The more he looked at the screen, the more one thing in particular struck him. There was not a single local or state authority mixed in with the menagerie of federal vehicles and personnel. Not one state trooper. Not one engine from a local fire station. It appeared to be entirely composed of federal resources.

Mason clicked the volume louder.

"...Never seen anything like it," the reporter glanced behind him, "Mandatory evacuations have been announced throughout the San Fernando Valley. All northbound traffic on the five, the four-oh-five, and the two-ten have been shut down. Vehicles are being turned around and sent back south toward Los Angeles."

The anchor in the studio cut in, "Tom, has FEMA indicated why they are involved in the containment effort?"

"No official word from anyone yet, Tyrone. All we know so far is that the fire is zero percent contained and has got to be the largest wildfire this state has ever seen." He coughed and spit off-camera.

"Sorry, the air is full of ash." He spat again. "Los Angeles is fortunate the prevailing winds are blowing north right now. Otherwise, the city would be covered in smoke and soot."

"Thanks for keeping us informed, Tom. Stay safe out there. Next we turn to—"

Mason's phone buzzed and skittered across the kitchen counter. He muted the TV and grabbed it.

Miro. Casimiro Pike.

He swiped to answer. "Miro."

"Sarge! Long time no yakkity yak."

"I'm not a sergeant anymore. You know that."

"You'll always be a sergeant to me."

Mason sighed. Miro was always like this. Mason let it slide. He had to. He owed Miro his life. That wasn't a debt that could ever be repaid. Overlooking references to a history he'd rather leave buried was the least he could endure.

"What can I do for you, Corporal Pike?"

"Hey now! That's the Sarge I know and love."

"Cut the Bravo Sierra. What's going on?"

"Got a big ask for you."

The picture on the TV caught Mason's attention.

"Hang on a sec."

He dropped the phone from his ear and turned the TV louder. Another scene of devastation played out. A different reporter stood pointing to an accident in the distance.

Four semi-trailers and their cabs laid out on the highway in a twisted heap. It looked like an IED tore through them.

Their mangled remains extended across four lanes of a large highway. A scrolling banner along the bottom of the screen read "I-10 closed at San Bernardino with no indication when it will be re-opened."

Emergency workers in yellow hazmat suits blasted white goo onto the fires licking through the torn trailers. The backs of the yellow suits had big, white block letters.

FEMA.

What was going on?

Did the end of the world arrive and we were all too busy staring at phone screens to notice?

Every worker wore a black gas mask with round, yellow filters protruding. Thick boots scurried over glistening pavement. Here, too, all of the vehicles surrounding the accident were of federal origin. Similar to the scene playing out north of the city, workers lowered Jersey barriers across the lanes.

The reporter nodded toward the scene behind her. "FEMA officials won't say what chemical is involved or whether or not they believe any has escaped. All we know is that both westbound and eastbound lanes are being shut down. Don't expect to leave the Los Angeles metropolitan area by way of the ten freeway."

The anchor's voice cut in, "Has FEMA said when they expect the road to be clear?"

The woman on the screen shook her head. "Not yet. Thus far, we've been given very little information."

Mason heard a shout echo from the tiny speaker in his phone. He brought the phone to his ear and winced.

"MASON! HELLO!"

"I'm back. Sorry. Have you seen what's going on around LA today?"

"Nope, too busy with a client, which is why I'm calling."

"Oh yeah, a favor. What can I do for you, Corporal Pike?"

"Sarge, it's like this. I'm too popular."

"You always were."

"You see, Sarge, I got a job for you. I know that goes against the usual chain of command."

"We're not soldiers anymore."

"Ain't we though?"

"Close protection is about saving lives, not ending them."

"That's all semantics, Sarge. In any case, I need your help."

Mason didn't hesitate.

"You got it. What do you need?"

"You ain't gonna like it."

19

That didn't sound good. The fact that Miro felt obliged to mention it up front raised big red flags. Miro was an ace on the trigger. A fearless bull on the battlefield. But he wasn't known for being particularly thoughtful in civilian life. The fact that whatever his request was made him think enough to consider Mason's perspective meant something truly terrible was about to land in his lap.

"What?"

"I'm just saying you ain't gonna be happy."

"You ignoring my question makes me unhappy, Corporal Pike. What do you need me to do?"

"I need you to cover a client for me."

"A close protection client?"

Miro was also in close protection. He'd helped Mason get started in the field. Landed him a few cherry jobs that broke the small, specialized community wide open. Mason knew he couldn't say no. But he didn't see a reason why he'd want to in the first place.

"Yes."

"Okay, what's the catch?"

"Two."

"Two what?"

"There are two catches."

"Continue."

"Well, the first is that the job is today."

"Today? As in now?"

You never ran an op with no planning. Intelligence was everything. It was sheer folly to walk into a situation knowing nothing. It was the hours worked in advance that kept a job from going sideways. That minimized that risk, at least.

"Yes. Sorry. I'm in DC now with a client. A bigwig scientist. The world's leading virologist, or so he keeps telling me every time I don't ask. Anyway, he dropped this steaming pile on my boot a few minutes ago. I couldn't think of anyone else to call."

What did a scientist in the nation's capital have to do with him, out on the West Coast?

"Fine. I've got you covered, bro."

It wasn't fine. It was bad news, but what could he do? He'd have to cancel the weekend at Tito and Mamaw's. From the looks of the news reports, it didn't sound like they could escape LA tonight anyway.

"You haven't heard the second catch."

"Hit me."

"This scientist has a daughter. She's the assignment."

Mason had worked with children before. They were no problem. Fun even. They always expected him to bust out kung-fu James Bond moves and start capping everyone in sight. The reality was a big disappointment.

"No problem. She in school somewhere?"

"Nope. Out of school. Twenty-five years old."

A young woman then. He generally preferred working

with women. They didn't come glazed with testosterone and bravado. Egos so big you could hardly get in the same air space. Those sorts of attitudes made protection ten times harder.

"Still no problem."

"There's more."

Of course there was more.

"She's not your average twenty-five-year-old."

Wait for it.

"She's a supermodel with an eye for acting."

There it was.

Mason tried to muffle the groan rumbling in his throat.

Models? Actors? Famous people made protection a hundred times harder.

Mason had several assignments that went sideways because the celebrity clients were imbeciles. In short order, Mason determined that the cash wasn't worth the headache. No amount of money was worth the risk. It was like they thrived on making your job harder.

Never again. He'd sworn off the whole industry after the last job went south. It was a famous actor. Mid-twenties. Impeccably coiffed hair. Teeth spotlight white and cheekbones that looked down on Olympus. The guy was fueled by coke. And not the kind you got from a vending machine. His preferred flavor was the kind you got from Columbia.

Every sensible precaution Mason suggested was stepped on and ignored. The operation ended with them both surrounded by a crazed mob, eager to tear away some bit of enduring fame. It was only Mason's aggressive and overwhelming action that got them out with all their limbs attached.

The mindless moron ended up in the hospital for a few

days. His attorney threatened to sue the agency Mason worked for at the time.

Never again. He swore it, and he'd lived by it until this moment.

Mason let out a slow exhale, doing his best not to sound upset. Favors paid grudgingly were favors half-paid.

"Okay. What's the op?"

"Easy Street. Retrieve her and drop her off at Santa Monica airport for a chartered flight."

That didn't sound too bad. Limited duration. Explicit objective. Maybe it would turn out okay.

"Fine."

"Thank you, Sarge! My client's been flipping out all day. I don't think he knew she was in LA."

"Where is she?"

"We're working on that. Let you know as soon as we find out."

Great.

"Know anything about her?"

Maybe some soft intel could clue him in on how to approach her. Who knew? Maybe he'd get lucky and she'd turn out to be a sane human being.

"You're not going to believe this. Name's Iridia."

The name clicked somewhere in the back of Mason's brain. Where had he heard it before? Victoria's Secret model maybe. The fact that he even had a vague inkling meant she was big time.

The knowledge didn't lend confidence to his assessment of the operation.

"Should I know the name?"

"She's a Sports Illustrated swimsuit issue girl, bro!"

"Lucky me."

"You dumb SOB. What I wouldn't give to get up close and personal with that bit of luscious lady candy."

"What I wouldn't give to let you."

"Sarge, she's smokin' hot."

"I'm married, Corporal."

"I know, I know. I'm just saying. This op is wasted on you."

That was exactly the problem. Usually, these kinds of clients were totally wasted on you. As in drugged up. Drunk as a skunk. Their every whim an instant command to whoever happened to hear it. Their willful ignorance—no, enthusiastic stupidity—made even the simple jobs hard.

Made even the safe jobs dangerous.

20

November 2004
Fallujah, Iraq

MASON stuffed a giant pinch of Copenhagen inside his lower lip. Dark granules of tobacco spilled out onto his vest. Sitting so long had his left leg pincushion numb. The bare metal seat bit into his butt like a bed of nails. What he wouldn't give to get out and stretch his legs. To take a breath of passably fresh air. The air inside the cramped Amphibious Assault Vehicle stank of body odor, farts, and cigarette smoke.

A fleeting gust of thick diesel fumes stung his eyes, but at least it masked the human stench.

He shifted on the hard bench seat, trying to work some relief into his cramped hamstrings and glutes. There wasn't much room to maneuver. Every square inch inside the amtrack was stuffed full with extra ammo, cases of MREs, bottled water, and all the gear deemed necessary for an operation expected to last a couple of days.

All that ammo.

It was hard not to imagine what a rocket propelled grenade piercing the interior would do. While the aluminum walls protected them from small arms fire, a rocket propelled grenade stood a better than average chance of doing serious damage.

Thinking about it didn't help.

This was the mission. An unspoken aspect of the job was that the Marine Corps was expected to do more with less. It was a source of pride for the upper brass. A source of endless frustration for the average trigger puller. There was pride too, but all the rhetoric boiled down to misery for the boots on the ground.

Mason looked around the cramped interior. The red cabin light cast a sullen pall over the men of third squad. He doubted it was just a lighting effect. Spending hours inside a crowded track would be enough to turn the Dalai Lama into an angry old man.

He studied their faces. The men were tense, but ready. A dozen young men from wildly differing worlds came together to do the job America had given them. Mason had worked hard to bring his men closer over the preceding months. They were brothers now, no matter their ethnic or geographic origins.

He looked to each in turn, remembering the shared stories of their lives. Their most embarrassing moments. Their dreams for life back home.

Private Benjamin Hicks. How he ended up in a high school cafeteria with his pants around his ankles. And astonishingly, how that incident ended up with him on a date with the hottest cheerleader in school. The kid had more luck than a leprechaun. It was no surprise everyone called him Lucky.

Corporal Casimiro Pike. The six and a half foot tall

Texan would be an annoying caricature of the Lone Star state if he weren't so funny. And good looking. He swore his record was sleeping with five different girls in one day. And that two of them were sisters. At once. Nobody doubted the claim because they'd all seen how the ladies swooned over him. Miro was aiming to break that record on his first day back stateside.

There were so many crazy stories between them. So much history.

Mason exhaled a breath he hadn't realized he'd been holding in. They wouldn't all make it back. Mason knew it in his gut, but he'd do everything possible to get them all home.

Third Battalion, First Marines had arguably the toughest job in the assault on Fallujah. To clear their sector of the city by going house to house, door to door, capturing or killing every insurgent in their path. Their area of operations included the Jolan district, widely thought to be the center of terrorist activity.

MOUT, or Military Operation on Urban Terrain, was the dirtiest, in-your-face type of warfare there was. They would be taking down the enemy from point blank range. There would be no distance to numb the experience.

The amtrack lurched forward and Mason smacked his Kevlar helmet on a shovel strapped to the wall. He winced as his ear smashed into the inside of the helmet. The sixty-thousand-pound machine didn't do subtle.

Lance Corporal David Lopez sat on the bench opposite him. Everyone called him Lopes because he ran faster than an antelope. He blew the doors off every other man in the platoon, made fast look slow. All gristle and grit, Mason had taken a shine to him on their very first night together in the Marine Corps. The night they both put their own feet on the yellow footsteps at Parris Island Recruit Depot.

Lopes poked his tongue into his lower lip and motioned to pass over the dip. He yelled something to emphasize the request, but Mason couldn't hear a word. The growling five hundred horsepower diesel engine made conversation all but impossible.

Mason tossed the can over. Lopes snatched it out of the air with the easy grace of the naturally coordinated. He grinned and looked around the cabin to see if anyone else witnessed his prowess. Miro sat to Lopes' left. While Lopes waited for applause that wasn't forthcoming, Miro reached over and grabbed at the can.

The whole squad watched as the two scrambled for it. Most laughed and a few shook their heads. Miro and Lopes were a source of daily entertainment. Their Bravo Sierra was an appreciated outlet for the squad. A grunt's life was typified by long stretches of boredom interspersed with brief periods of maximum intensity. Soldiers dealt with it in different ways, but pissing each other off was a favorite.

And Miro and Lopes had it down to a science.

The small, round can popped out of their scuffle and rolled along the metal floor. The track hit something and the whole cabin jumped. Mason pushed off the ceiling to avoid ramming his head down through his spine. The can of Copenhagen bounced up and landed in Lucky's lap.

He grinned and nodded thanks to Miro and Lopes as the rest of the squad broke up laughing. He dug out the remaining dip and tucked it into his lip. After settling it in tight, he tossed the empty can back. It bounced off Miro's desert digital cammies and rolled under the seat.

Miro drew a single finger across his throat.

Mason pulled out another can and passed it over. He

had a few more stashed away. Nicotine was the life blood of a grunt. Whether the delivery medium was dip, chew, or cigarettes, it was the nicotine that counted.

Not that he needed it just then.

Not that any of them did.

They simmered on a low boil. Sick of waiting. Ready for the ramp to drop. Ready to get to work.

21

Yet here they were, stuck in the amtrack while it started and stopped over and over, incrementally bringing them fifty feet closer at a time. Mason ground his teeth and spat a dark glob of juice on the floor. His gums tingled, the promise of an incoming nicotine payload.

At least they were clear of the breach site. That had been a hot mess.

Engineers had blown two lanes through the railroad tracks that ran east-west along the north side of the city. As soon as the lanes opened, hundreds of vehicles attempted to funnel through. In no time, a traffic jam of epic proportions developed. It had taken hours to get through.

Their amtrack charged forward, taking them to the first block of neighborhoods at the northern edge of the city. Somewhere ahead, explosions tore through the predawn air.

That would be the Army's Task Force 2-7 Cavalry beating the path into Fallujah. Their job was to punch a hole in the enemy's defenses, drive deep into the interior, and absorb punishment along the way.

Their Abrams M1A1 tanks and Bradley fighting vehicles were capable of delivering massive amounts of direct fire and also absorbing damage that would destroy the Marines' lighter AAV-7 amtracks. Inside either of the tougher vehicles, the Joes didn't have to worry about small arms fire, RPGs, or even mortar rounds. Most importantly, both were resistant to improvised explosive devices.

IEDs lined every street throughout the city. The mujahideen had transformed the City of Mosques into a death trap. And they'd had a lot of time to get it just right.

As powerful an option as the Army's mechanized armor was, boots with rifles were still required for the dangerous task of rooting out the resistance. One house at a time.

The amtrack's engine spun down as it slowed.

"Prepare to dismount," a crewman's voice said over the intercom.

The men of third squad braced themselves as the vehicle lurched to a stop.

Mason pulled ballistic goggles down over his eyes. The clear lenses kept out dust and shrapnel. He went through last minute checks on his M16A4 service rifle. Magazine seated. Round chambered. Scope uncovered. Good to go.

"Third squad, hydrate," he yelled above the idling engine. You didn't quench your thirst in the Iraqi desert. You hydrated to stay alive. Wearing fifty pounds of full battle-rattle in the searing afternoon sun would knock you down with heat exhaustion in no time. Even in the freezing cold nights, the dry desert air sucked moisture out of your body.

The track's intercom squawked, "Dropping ramp."

Mason stuck the mouthpiece to his hydration pack between his teeth and drained off several gulps.

"Third squad, you know the drill. Push out and establish security. Keep it locked down and we'll be fine."

The rear of the vehicle opened and dim morning light seeped in. The temperature plummeted in seconds. Mason shivered, longing for the scorching afternoon heat and also dreading it. The temperature in the desert never stayed just right for long.

Third squad piled out and set up overlapping fields of fire.

Mason studied the road to the south. It looked like the scene of a Hollywood movie. Twisted metal and concrete rubble filled the street. Huge craters pocked the ground where IEDs had gone off. He'd seen this street through numerous unmanned aerial vehicle feeds as the little UAVs gathered critical intelligence on the enemy's defenses and movements.

Still, a 2-D image on a monitor didn't do justice to this devastation. The first block was almost completely leveled. The destruction was so thorough that Mason didn't immediately see their next defensible position. He needed an intact house for that. He saw first squad ahead, about a block down, working the west side of the street. Third squad was assigned to clear houses on the east side.

The amtrack closed the hatch and turned to head back to the safety of the command post at the train station.

There was no obvious enemy movement. Their immediate surroundings were quiet. Too quiet. Mason knew better than to lower his guard. Somewhere in the city, four thousand jihadis lurked. An international dream team of terrorists that weren't there to liberate Fallujah from the evil, Western oppressor. They were there for two reasons.

To die as martyrs for their faith.

And to take out as many of his men as possible before that happened.

Mason chafed under the rules of engagement they'd

been given. Don't shoot unless the target committed a hostile act or clearly had the intention to commit one. He understood the need to safeguard the remaining civilian population, and also how collateral damage negatively affected the war effort. But his first priority was to keep his men safe and putting that judgement call before every pull of the trigger gave their enemy an advantage.

The task of determining who was a target could be difficult. And yet that split-second decision could mean the difference between going home in your boots or going home in a bag. A haji talking on a cell phone might be nothing. Then again, he might be calling in targets for mortar fire. Or he might be about to detonate an IED in their vicinity. A simple phone call was anything but in a war zone.

Even discerning intent with known hostiles could be difficult. They'd all heard about how an injured muj had begged to surrender and receive medical attention. A corpsman and another soldier approached him to provide medical care and take him into custody. They both ended up dead when he detonated a vest filled with explosives.

One of his guys on point shouted.

"Muj half a click south!"

A man dressed in a white dishdasha sprinted across the street. He held up the hem of the long garment as he ran. He carried no weapons so they couldn't shoot.

"Hold your fire!" Mason shouted.

He prayed the man didn't show up later launching an RPG at them. It was very unlikely that he was an innocent civilian. Army Psy-Ops had plastered Fallujah for weeks with pamphlets announcing the coming assault. Not all the details, just that it was coming and all civilians needed to evacuate. The brass said ninety plus percent of the civilian population had taken the advice and gotten out.

So anyone they ran into was likely to be the enemy. And yet, there was still a required determination before his men could act.

Mason ground his teeth together. It was a tough position to be in. But that was the job.

A distant explosion echoed up the street. Not a single man flinched. Their time at Camp Fallujah had numbed them to the background sounds of war. Mortar and RPG attacks were a daily occurrence at the base due to its close proximity to the city. Pretty quickly they'd keyed into the particular whistling pitch that meant a round was coming in danger close. They'd learned to ignore the rest.

Mason spat out a thick brown stream onto the pavement. He motioned for Miro's fire team to take point.

"Move out!"

He observed as his men moved forward in a bounding overwatch; two men in a covering position while two men advanced and then exchanged positions. They were squared away.

They were ready.

22

The Last Day
Los Angeles Zoo, California

BETH sat on a work table in the lab, her injured leg propped up with a bright lamp illuminating it. Across the room, Jane's inert form lay on the operating table. It had taken several hours to repair the damage Jack inflicted on her. Her body was a mass of lacerations, punctures, and avulsions. He'd torn her right ear off at the base. Her neck got the worst of it.

It had been touch and go for a while after the team had escorted her unconscious body to the operating room. Ralph wanted to help but Beth insisted he not endanger his employment with Diana already on the rampage. She bandaged up his shoulder and sent him on his way. It would be tender for a few weeks, but he'd come out of his brush with death none the worse for wear.

She couldn't say the same for Jane and her unborn infants.

Beth paused and glanced back at the unconscious

chimp. Electrical leads draped across her body and attached to shaved spots on her chest. Her heartbeat beeped across the monitor. She looked like a mangy dog from all the shaved areas around a multitude of bites and cuts.

Jane appeared stable, but she was weak. Very weak.

A tracheal tube was taped to her mouth, securing the pipe that kept oxygen flowing into her lungs and, therefore, brain. Her throat was a bloody mess when they found her in the enclosure. Raspy, gurgling noises bubbled out as she'd struggled to breathe.

She'd nearly died on the table, but Beth refused to let that happen. And she wasn't going to lose her now either.

Beth returned her attention to her leg and tugged the final suture tight. The tear on her thigh closed. She knotted it off and snipped the extra thread.

She took a deep breath and winced as pain stabbed in her chest. Nothing was broken, but the contusions would be bad. She'd get it looked at once Jane and her babies were safe. She applied antibacterial gel to the six-inch sutured wound and wrapped her thigh with gauze to keep it clean. Satisfied that an ER surgeon couldn't have done better, she slipped back into a new pair of khaki work pants.

She'd survive her encounter with Jack. Move a little slow for a month or so, but it could have easily turned out far worse. She got lucky and she knew it. Still, one thing bothered her.

How did Jack get out?

Ralph had practically been in tears assuring her that he'd locked the holding cage. She didn't have an answer when her least favorite person in the universe stormed through the swinging door at the far end of the lab.

Diana Richston.

She marched in like a general delivering the news to

attack. Fire and brimstone burned in her eyes. Her dark business suit pant legs swished as she strode through the door.

"Not now, Diana."

"Not now? Not now? Are you kidding me? You go and nearly get yourself and another one of my staff killed and it's 'Not now.'"

"Yep."

Single word responses seemed the safest bet. If she let out more than that, the dam might break and she didn't know what might pour out.

"Yes, *now*. We'll discuss this *now*. What were you thinking? We have safety protocols in place to prevent this sort of catastrophe."

"Can we do this later?"

Diana set her hands on her hips and her jaw dropped.

"*Later*? *Later*? What makes you think you'll have a later? You'll be fired within the day. You'll be lucky if the board doesn't press criminal charges. And let me assure you, I will very much recommend they do. You're a danger to this organization and I won't stand for it."

"I just saved this zoo's star attraction. A pregnant Bili chimp in captivity is wonder bucks to the public. Don't think I don't know what Jane means to *your bottom line!*"

The last three words spat out like venom from a cobra.

"You, Ms. West, are a danger to Milagro Corporation's bottom line. Every second you remain employed brings the imminent danger of liability and litigation. Consider this your informal notification of termination!"

"Diana?"

"Yes?"

"Get out of my operating room."

Diana's chest puffed as she considered unleashing

another withering outburst. "I'll return later today with your official termination papers."

Without another word, she spun on her shiny black heels and departed. The fading sound of rubbing pantsuit and clacking heels receded down the hall.

Beth sighed and rubbed her aching sternum.

Great.

She'd probably lose her job. The only job she'd ever wanted. Working with animals that daily gave her joy like only they could.

So be it.

If saving Jane meant losing her job, so be it. She'd lose a hundred jobs if it gave the chimp a fighting chance.

She limped over to the operating table and watched as the automated ventilator bladder compressed, pushing oxygen into Jane's lungs. Her chest expanded and slowly collapsed.

Beth slid her palm across the smooth fur on the big chimp's belly. She remembered how much Jane loved getting rubbed there as an infant. She'd grown to nearly double Beth's weight, but she'd always be her second baby.

The one that survived.

23

MASON drove through the parking lot for the fifth time, hoping an empty spot would materialize. It didn't. Whole Foods at five in the evening was always a mob scene. It admittedly had some tasty food, and the deli in particular made a mean brick-oven pizza. But he tried to avoid the peak hours of lunch and the evening post-work rush.

Even considering that, today was different. There was a quiet intensity, almost a desperation, in the people as they jockeyed for parking or hurried through the sea of cars toward the entrance.

He would've loved to bag this trip, but Mr. Piddles hadn't eaten his lunch. He apparently didn't like the Fancy Feast Mason had picked up after he didn't find cat food in the usual spot at the neighbor's house. Otis had a lot on his plate with Mabel sick. He'd likely forgotten.

So here Mason was, trying Whole Foods this time, hoping to get something delicious enough to please the finicky feline.

Mason gave up on parking in the packed lot and pulled out onto Rose and found a spot a block away. He donned his favorite LA Galaxy ball cap and pushed the dark shades a little tighter to his face. The evening sun in the west was a blinding, brilliant orange hue.

He walked the block back and approached the entrance. A uniformed police officer guarded the glass doors. A big hand-drawn sign hung above the entrance read CASH ONLY. NO EXCEPTIONS.

Things were definitely strange. He walked up to the gray-haired officer. A well-earned paunch hung over his black belt, signifying his length of time on the force.

"What's going on?"

"I heard their computer registers went down and the repair guys haven't shown up."

"No, I mean with you being here. One doesn't usually see an LAPD officer posting up at the local Whole Foods."

"Yeah, that. Apparently folks have been getting a little out of hand today. Taking off with groceries and such. It's like nobody carries cash anymore."

Mason did. Emergency cash. He always had at least $500 in small bills on him. Three hundred in his wallet and two hundred in his back pocket. He preferred to be prepared, with backups.

A blast of welcome air conditioning washed across him as he entered. Fresh baked pizza wafted by and made his stomach grumble. He'd grab a slice or two after picking up a few cans of cat food.

He paused at the entrance, looking around. He'd seen it busy before, but this was a whole other thing. The registers all had lines snaking back down the aisles behind. People pushed through each other to make headway.

This was the kind of panic buying you saw before a hurricane swooped into a Florida town. Folks must've been worried about the fires up north. Or else something he hadn't heard about yet.

He twisted and turned his way through the press of flesh and made it to the pet food aisle. The selection was overwhelming.

Non-GMO. Free Range. Organic. Whole Grain. Whole Chicken. There were at least twenty brands that all proudly proclaimed all the same things. One went so far as to guarantee that your cat would eat better than you did. That sounded insane, but Mason decided to go with it.

If Mr. Piddles rejected it, maybe he'd give it a shot. Maybe uber quality cat food was the treat he'd been missing out on his whole life. He grabbed a few cans and headed for the pizza stop. After burning his fingers accepting a steaming hot slice of five-cheese pizza, he burned his tongue taking a bite. He nibbled on the cooling edges as he jostled through the crowd and made it to the end of the shortest line.

It extended only half way down the aisle behind.

After waiting for what seemed like a geological age, and wishing he'd ordered two slices, he made it to the register. As he stepped forward, he noticed a change in the mass of people nearby. A shifting of focus. Their eyes stole glances in a unified direction.

He followed the angle and didn't see anything extraordinary, aside from the sheer number of people.

The barrage of headlines at the magazine stand screamed at his eyeballs. He was about to look up at the infinitely more interesting pipe work in the ceiling when one cover in particular caught his attention.

A headline shouted "Iridia Dumps Ryan!"

Was this the same supermodel Iridia that he was supposed to pick up later today?

The cover had a picture of the dumpee looking the most pathetic he'd probably ever looked. These magazines loved using pics that overplayed whatever story they were peddling. Mason recognized the guy. He was an actor. Had a movie earlier in the summer that was a huge hit. *Death Before Life.* Or something. He played a superhero that saved the world from an alien invasion. Or maybe he played an alien that saved the world from a superhero invasion. Mason hadn't seen it. He just remembered Theresa swooning over this guy and talking about how buff and gorgeous and awesome he was.

Mason picked up the magazine. He wasn't going to buy it, but maybe the story would hold something about Iridia that would be helpful.

The buzz of excitement around him again caught his attention. He realized the focus of the energy was centered on the guy in line ahead of him. He wore a gray hoodie and huge black shades that covered half his face. He was beefy, even under a thick layer of fashionably cut sweatshirt.

Wait a second.

Mason held the magazine up next to the face of the hooded hipster.

"Not your best look," Mason said.

"Do I really look that pathetic?"

Mason glanced back and forth from the picture to the reality. He shook his head.

"Not today."

"They always do that."

"Is it true?"

"The break up?"

"Yeah."

"Since a few nights ago, yes. I got a call from her agent. She broke up with me through her agent. Break up with *me*?

By her *agent*? I just grossed a billion dollars at the box office!"

"What's she like?"

"Gorgeous. Sex like a goddess granted to a mortal. Oh man, the thing she does with her tongue. It's—"

"Yeah, I'm sure it's great."

"*Was* great. It's over now." His head dropped to his chest. "Could my life suck any worse?"

Mason looked away so Mr. Famous MegaBucks wouldn't see him roll his eyes.

And that's when he saw Cesar stroll through the front entrance like he owned the place.

Mason ducked his head and pulled the cap lower. The last thing he wanted right now was to engage that idiot.

"Life can always get worse."

24

The transaction up front finished and the cashier clucked her tongue while waiting for Mr. Famous to notice. The clucking grew louder. You didn't hold up a cashier's line. You didn't mess with their system.

"You're up," Mason said and nodded ahead.

"Oh, thanks."

Ryan dropped an all-natural, vitamin-enhanced, organic spring water energy drink in front of the cashier as her eyes opened wide.

"Are you—"

"Yeah."

"Oh my God! I can't wait to tell Juanita! I loved you in *Death Before Life*!"

She pulled out her phone. "Can I get a pic? She won't believe it without proof. I can't believe it! I knew working here was going to pay off big time!"

Cashiers, however, had no problem holding up the line themselves apparently.

Ryan nodded and smiled. "Sure."

Mason snuck a glance as Cesar turned the corner at the

registers and headed in his direction. His body language was relaxed. He hadn't seen him.

Come on! Come on! Buy the expensive sugar water!

"Hey man, mind taking the picture for us?"

"What?" Mason ducked his head and turned his back to the approaching gang member.

"Take the pic." Ryan stepped behind the register and threw his arm around the cashier like they were old friends. He took the phone and held it out for Mason. "Selfies never get the best angle."

This was not good. This scene within the scene was attracting too much attention. He had to get it over with. Snap the pic and get the line moving.

"Fine." He took the phone and snapped a shot.

"Whoa, now. Let's give her something to remember."

The V10 shot caller drew closer.

Mr. Famous leaned in and kissed the cashier's cheek.

The cashier shrieked.

Mason snapped another pic. "Got it. Good?"

"One more!" she said and planted her lips on Ryan's before he could pull away.

Mason snapped pics as fast as his finger could tap the screen.

"There! Got plenty. Can we move this along now?"

Ryan returned to the customer side of the register.

"Oh my God! Oh my God! Juanita is never gonna believe this!"

Mason picked up the vitamin drink and handed it to her.

"Ring it up please."

Ryan looked at him, through him.

"What?" Mason asked.

"Do you know that guy?" Ryan said while looking behind him.

Mason turned his head, cap still low, and came face to face with Cesar.

He barely managed to duck as a fist the size of a brick flew through the space where his head had just been. Not meeting flesh, the fist continued on and thundered into Ryan's nose. It smashed like a ripe tomato. Blood splattered on the cashier's maroon frock. His legs crumbled and he collapsed to the floor.

Through slurred, wet words, he yelled, "Not my nose! Not my nose!"

Mason didn't have time to worry about the actor's billion dollar nose because Cesar lunged at him. They both went down, fists flying hard and fast. He landed a knee to the shot caller's chin that should've knocked him out. It barely fazed him.

A thunderous punch slammed into Mason's kidney and pain shocked his body, blurred his vision. Another blow struck his temple and his head bounced off the tile floor. He knew he couldn't last. The savage ferocity and brute force would break him.

Mason rolled underneath Cesar and got a foot up under his hip. He pushed with all his strength and managed to get some separation. With the space created, he snapped a kick at Cesar's groin and felt a satisfying impact.

Cesar groaned and his hold weakened. With a gigantic heave, Mason shoved the larger man to the side. He scrambled to his feet as Cesar did the same.

Their eyes locked.

Mason had no intention of getting tangled up with him again. He reached under his shirt and had his Glock 19 up and aimed in less than a second.

The cashier ducked behind the register.

"Don't make me do it, Cesar!"

Ryan curled into a ball on the ground.

"I don't want to die! I don't want to die!"

People surrounding them screamed and pushed back against those leaning in and over to get a better look.

Mr. Famous blubbered and wept, making the situation more dangerous, more charged.

Mason kicked him in the butt. Hard. But not too hard. "Shut up!"

"He's gonna kill me!" Ryan hid his face in his hands.

"Shut your mouth!"

"Someone get my agent! Get my agent!"

Cesar's cold gaze never left his. His hand eased behind his back. Mason knew he'd have a weapon at the small of his back. One thin layer of wife-beater was all that covered whatever he had tucked back there.

"Don't do it!" Mason yelled.

"Drop the weapon!"

Mason turned to see a .38 Special not five feet away and pointed at his chest.

25

The round-bellied LAPD officer stood to the side of Mason with a well-worn revolver clamped in his hands. His hard gaze steady as the muzzle covered him.

"Okay. Easy now," Mason said.

Cesar's hand was still behind his back. Mason couldn't let him draw.

The officer didn't appear rattled. He'd been in gunfights before.

Ryan crawled to the officer and clung to his leg. "This guy threatened to shoot me! I can't die! I have a sequel about to be green lit!"

The officer tried to shake him loose but the actor had a death grip on his ankle.

Cesar grinned and slowly raised his hands, acting the part of the victim.

"This crazy guy pulled a gun on us. He wants to kill us all. He's loco. You gotta shoot him!"

"Drop the gun, now!" The officer thumbed the hammer back and it clicked into position.

"Listen, sir," Mason said. "I'm not the dangerous one here. It's this guy." He nodded at Cesar. "He'll kill us both if I lower my pistol."

"You're the one with a gun in your hand. This is your last chance to drop it."

Mason instinctively felt the Glock's front sight hovering on Cesar's center mass. He glanced back and forth, from Cesar's satisfied smirk to the guard's intense stare.

He was stuck.

If he lowered the Glock, the guard wouldn't shoot him, but he had no doubt Cesar would a second later. The guard would probably die too. If he shot Cesar, the guard would shoot him. If he somehow survived, he'd have a hell of a time convincing a jury the shooting was a justified use of deadly force.

Things were moving too fast. Too out of control.

"Save me!" Ryan screamed as he tried to climb the officer's leg. He grabbed the officer's belt and tried to pull himself up. The officer stumbled forward and his aim fell to the floor as he fought to keep from falling down.

Mason lunged at the older man, his offhand reaching for the hand holding the revolver. If he could get it under control, he could defuse the situation. His hand wrapped around the officer's wrist. The officer yanked back and the revolver fired.

A bullet ripped through the right side of Ryan's face. His previously flawless, high cheekbone spurted blood across the tile floor. The actor collapsed, holding the wound.

"My face! My face! My career!"

Somewhere in a distant part of Mason's brain, he registered the screams of the surrounding store patrons.

The officer was stronger than he looked. He stubbornly

fought to retain his firearm. Mason chopped down on the officer's wrist with the composite Glock frame. Thin bones snapped and the grip gave way. Mason yanked the revolver free and turned to cover Cesar.

BOOM.

Blood exploded from the dark blue cloth covering the officer's chest.

Cesar held a polished chrome .50 caliber Desert Eagle. Smoke wafted from the end of the barrel.

Mason dove behind a health drink mini-fridge as another round fired. Carbonated spray misted the air. He dropped his shoulder and continued the roll, landing in a crouch.

He brought the Glock up and the front sight aligned on an exposed portion of Cesar's shoulder.

He didn't hesitate.

The Glock jumped in his grip and a red hole punctured the beefy shoulder. Cesar dove behind the end of the counter.

"I'm gonna kill you, blanco!"

Mason looked at the actor lying on the ground. He continued screaming about his face, his future in acting. He was lucky to be alive.

The officer's head lolled to the side and their eyes met. He held his heaving chest like he could hold in the air escaping from his punctured lung. His hands covered the wheezing, crimson wound. He choked and gagged as red bubbles frothed out of his mouth. His chances didn't look good.

Mason couldn't continue the fight here. Cesar had no compunctions about killing every bystander unlucky enough to be caught in the crossfire. None of these people deserved to die.

He had to draw Cesar outside. Away from the crowded checkout lines. At least in the parking lot, there would be plenty of steel to stop bullets instead of plenty of flesh.

In a low crouch, Mason ran down the length of the checkout lines and made it to the entrance. He peeked over a counter and saw Cesar lying on the ground holding his shoulder.

Cesar spotted him.

BOOM.

Mason ducked as a round shattered the glass deli display case behind him. He took a quick breath and broke for the automatic doors.

BOOM.

A round zipped behind him as he dove to the sidewalk outside. He scrambled behind a low concrete wall and brought his front sight up on the entrance.

Now he had him. As soon as Cesar showed his face outside, Mason would have him dead to rights. He looked around. Several patrons stood frozen in the parking lot, apparently shut down by being caught in a shootout like they'd seen in the movies.

They were collateral damage waiting to happen.

"Get out of here before you get shot!"

That got a couple of them moving away from the entrance. Incredibly, a few still remained rooted to the pavement. They were going to get themselves killed.

Mason pointed the Glock in the air and fired off two shots.

That did it. The last few statues broke into runs.

Mason looked back to the entrance, to the fatal funnel of fire. Cesar would show up any second now and that second would be his last.

Sirens blared in the distance.

The automatic doors slid apart.

Mason sighted and curled his pointer finger inside the trigger guard.

Terrified customers spilled out of the store and ran for the parking lot. One saw him and screamed.

"There's the killer! There's the shooter!"

Several others screamed and ran away from Mason.

Him? The killer?

The sirens got louder.

A spray of bullets blasted the concrete wall around him. Flecks of masonry bit into his arms and hands. He glanced over and saw one of Cesar's lieutenants from that morning behind a car, an assault rifle held over the hood firing in his direction.

Mason was exposed and outgunned.

Three black and whites screamed down Lincoln and screeched to a halt at the parking lot entrance. He knew they'd have no idea what was going on and that they'd be just as likely to target him as the gang members.

This wasn't a battle he could win. Not without people dying that didn't deserve to die.

Another blast of bullets chewed into the asphalt a few feet away and sprayed fragments in his face. Chunks slammed into the dark lenses of his ballistic sunglasses. The lenses held.

It was an impossible tactical situation. He didn't want to leave such a dangerous opponent on the loose. Not after that opponent had shown such a willingness to use extreme violence. Cesar's freedom put Mason in danger.

Worse, it put his family in danger.

The shot caller needed to be taken down. Sent to jail or sent to the grave. Mason didn't have a preference. But continuing the fight wasn't an option. The likely collateral damage would be catastrophic.

Mason ducked behind a line of shopping carts and took off.

26

The sun dipped toward the western horizon. Mason sat on the porch of his house staring at the orange glow that burned across the sky. How had it gone so wrong so fast? A hollow pit in his stomach seemed to suck him down.

Something nudged his hand.

He looked down and saw Max with a tennis ball in his mouth, wagging his tail and waiting for Mason to take the ball.

Mason patted his head and then took the ball. He flung it to the far corner of the front yard. Far corner in Venice meant about twenty feet away.

He glanced up at the blazing sky and sighed.

The fiasco at Whole Foods was a huge cluster bomb of calamity waiting to explode on his life. He'd tried to do the right thing, but it had ended up making things worse.

Was the officer still alive?

Max brought back the grubby, slobber-soaked ball and dropped it with a wet slap in Mason's hand. He held it, reflecting on the things you did for those you loved, and aimed another throw. This time at the neighbor's wall that ran along the property line.

He didn't know much about them. They were new on the block and weren't big on socializing, and their property reflected it. They'd leveled the tasteful old Craftsman soon after purchasing it and replaced it with a modern glass and concrete structure. To Mason's experienced eye, the result looked more like a bunker than a house.

It stuck out on their street like a sore thumb. The eight foot concrete wall surrounding the front yard was a big part of that.

One of Otis' favorite past times was bagging on the house and the uncharacteristic flavor it added to the neighborhood. Mason would just listen to the rambling indictments and nod.

That said, smearing Max's spit on the gray matte finish of their wall gave him a small satisfaction. He also didn't mind that a spit-soaked ball sometimes ended up in their front yard. It always ended up in his own yard by the next morning.

He winged another throw at the tall wall and the ball hit with a splat. He looked up and caught the last peek of the sun as it descended over the single block of houses that separated his house from the beach and the Pacific Ocean beyond.

A desperate meow made Mason jump.

Mr. Piddles sat on the Crayfords' front porch looking at Mason with expectant disdain. His ample belly covered his paws completely. He looked more like a furry ball than a cat.

"Time for dinner?" Mason said.

Max ambled over to Mr. Piddles and dropped the slobbery tennis ball. Max could tear the fat cat apart if he believed it was possible. When Max was a puppy, Mr.

Piddles had set the pecking order with numerous sharp claws to his wet nose.

So even though now Max outweighed the cat by nearly a hundred pounds, the cat was still king.

Max sniffed at Mr. Piddles and then went in for a lick. Mr. Piddles hissed and slashed a claw at his muzzle. Max jumped back and dropped to the lawn with his rear held high. His tail wagged furiously.

Mr. Piddles hissed and bared little fangs.

"Give him space, Max," Mason said as he walked over between them, worried more for Max than Mr. Piddles.

"Want some dinner?" Mason slowly extended his hand and attempted to pat Mr. Piddles' back. A paw flew at his fingers and he yanked back just in time. He was about to foolishly try again when a thumping bass sound caught his attention.

He turned and froze as a red 1964 Impala turned the corner and headed down the street.

Metallic red paint and polished chrome. The frame floating inches above the street. It approached at a slow speed, slower than any normal person drove.

Mason dropped his hand to the Glock 19 tucked inside his waistband.

Dark tinted windows hid the occupants. The thumping music grew louder as it approached.

Was it Cesar and his soldiers?

Theresa and Holly were inside the house. They'd be out of the field of fire if it came to that.

He didn't recognize the vehicle, but it wasn't unknown to see cars like that cruise down their street.

The Impala crept toward his house and then passed by and kept going.

Mason kept his hand at the ready as the low rider cruised down the street.

They didn't know where he lived. Maybe it was nothing. Then again, Venice wasn't that big. The car took a right at the end of the street and disappeared.

His pocket buzzed with an incoming call. He dug out the phone. Max came back with the sodden ball and dropped it at Mason's feet. He gave it his best soccer kick and swiped the screen to answer Miro's call.

"Miro."

"Sarge!"

"What do you have for me?"

"Got her location. Iridia is staying at The Standard, in downtown LA."

Mason knew the spot. He'd once gone for drinks at the bar on the roof. Typical swanky, hipster watering hole. The place was an operational nightmare. A bunch of drunks jammed into a small space with minimal points of egress and twenty floors of stairs if the elevators went kaput.

"Anything else I should know?"

"Her father is frantic. I mean loony bin crazy to get her on that flight out of Santa Monica."

The loud voice of what was presumably said father boomed in the background. Then the sounds of scuffling and his voice blasted from the little speaker.

"You must get her to the airport! Immediately! Promise me! Promise me you'll save her! My dearest Iridia..."

"Calm down, sir," Mason replied, "I—"

"Save my daughter!"

Great. If her dad was this crazy, his supermodel wannabe actress daughter was sure to be worse. If it was anybody other than Miro asking, he'd tell them where to stick this cursed job.

"You have nothing to worry about, Mr.—"

"Don't fail me!"

Mason was about to respond when he heard the phone change hands again. The volume of the father's hysterics faded.

"Hey, Sarge," Miro said in a quiet voice, "I got a funny feeling about this."

"What do you mean?"

"Not sure. Don't have all the intel. But something big's going down. Been escorting this guy around the last few days. He's way inside the beltway. Been making the rounds all over DC and the Pentagon. Visiting some serious big shots, POTUS included."

The President of the United States? This operation just got better and better. Mason sighed, wishing he could back out. He couldn't.

"Thanks for the heads-up. I'll notify you when we arrive at the airport."

"Thank you, Sarge. And," Miro paused, "can you get an autograph for me?"

Mason bit down on a scathing reply. He didn't have time for this nonsense, but he owed Miro more than could be repaid. "I'll see what I can do."

"Maybe a pic showing some skin too?"

"Don't get greedy."

"Thanks, Sarge. Corporal Pike out!"

The phone went silent and Mason noticed Max in a sit in front of him. Next to him, Mr. Piddles howled.

"You're whining? If only you understood how my day was going."

He stared at the for an instant.

Maybe it was Mr. Piddle's expression, but he got the distinct impression that the cat couldn't care less.

27

The tools of his trade lay spread out on the bedroom dresser. Preparing for close protection work was as much a ritual as gearing up for an op back in Iraq. Only it happened in his bedroom now instead of on the hood of a humvee.

Everything had its place and was addressed in sequence. The sequence was meditative in a way. It also ensured that nothing was forgotten.

In his experience, the thing you forgot was always the single thing you ended up needing most.

He glanced at the digital clock on the bedside table. Half past six. After the call from Miro, he'd fixed a quick dinner for Theresa and Holly, and then rushed through a shower and a shave.

He surveyed the array, satisfied that everything occupied its proper place. He picked up the 9mm Glock 19 and checked the chamber. Empty as expected. He slammed a fifteen round magazine in and racked the slide. He inched the slide back to verify a round was chambered. It was. Next, he slipped it into the Tuk holster and then slipped that inside the waistband of his suit pants.

Downtown Los Angeles wasn't a war zone last he checked. You didn't walk around brandishing weapons. That invited more trouble than it solved.

Next, he clipped an extra magazine to his belt. Then came the 9mm Glock 26. He slipped the subcompact pistol into an ankle holster on his right leg. Next came the Bonowi 26" collapsible baton attached to his hip. In less than a second, he could have it off his hip and snapped into business mode. A big stick was often all the encouragement a situation required.

And a big stick didn't make local law enforcement jumpy like wielding a firearm did. The last thing Mason wanted was another altercation involving deadly force.

Next came the Cold Steel Recon one-handed tactical knife. After clipping it to his belt, he attached four pairs of disposable handcuffs at the small of his back. Close protection officers used them because while you might want to collar a bad guy, you didn't usually want to wait around for the boys in blue to return your cuffs.

His brain clicked off the list as he continued the ritual and ended with slipping on the suit jacket. He straightened the black tie over the sky blue shirt. He inspected himself in the mirror. His belly grumbled, confirming it didn't care what he looked like, only that it had skipped dinner.

"You two about ready to go?" he said loud enough to echo down the hall to Theresa's room.

"Just about," her reply echoed back.

They were leaving when he did to spend the night at Holly's. He would've turned Miro down if it hadn't been an option. There was no he was going to leave his daughter home alone with Cesar and his thugs on the loose.

Especially not after spotting the suspicious Impala rolling down the street.

He made a mental note to call Beth once he got on the road. He didn't want her home without him either. Not until he could figure out how to deal with the situation.

Mason gave himself a final look in the mirror and nodded. His stomach grumbled. He'd grab a couple of Clif bars on the way out.

"Hey Dad, Mom's on the phone," Theresa said as she pranced into the room and handed him her phone.

"Mason?"

"Hey, honey," he said as he immediately sensed the turmoil in her voice. "What's wrong?"

"It's Jane. There's been an accident and she's in critical condition. Sorry I haven't called sooner. We've got her stabilized, but it's touch and go."

"What happened?"

"I can't talk about it right now. I'm just calling to let you know I'll be home late tonight."

"I actually needed to talk to you about that. Make sure and call me before you head home. I want to be here before you arrive."

"Why?"

"I'll explain later. Just do it, okay?"

"Sure," she replied. "Oh yeah, I have to call Mom and Dad about this weekend."

"No need. I already did. Your dad laughed about LA being wrapped up tighter than a Christmas present."

"What?"

"Have you seen the news today? Things are crazy."

"No. I've been busy."

"I'm sure you have. Well, do what you need to do. Theresa is spending the night at Holly's house, and I'll be back before too late. "

"Thanks, honey. I'll call when I know more."

"Love you."

"Love you, too."

Theresa rolled her eyes as Mason returned the phone. She dropped it into her pocket and cast a discerning gaze at his tie. She dug her fingers into the knot, making adjustments only she and her mother could see. She finished the improvements with practiced ease and smiled.

"There. What did Mom say?"

Mason's stomach clenched. Theresa loved Jane like a family member. She'd be devastated if something happened to her. He wasn't going to say anything until he knew something more definitive. It was a cop out. But it was his daughter's heart, and he'd bend a few rules to protect it.

"Mom just said she's staying late tonight. I'm sorry our weekend plans didn't work out."

"It's okay. I'm getting used to disappointment. Maybe next weekend."

She was taking it pretty well. Better than expected.

Holly popped through the open door.

"You two are going to behave tonight, right?" Mason said.

Holly waved him off. "Of course, my parents are looking forward to having over their favorite step-daughter."

Mason's mouth twisted into a smile. "A pair of princesses, huh?"

"You're looking like royalty yourself, Mr. West," she said. "Have big plans tonight with the Mrs.?"

"If only. I'm working tonight."

"Do you have your acceptance speech ready?"

"What?"

"For the Oscars. You look dressed up fine enough to be attending a Hollywood glam fest."

Theresa pushed her shoulder.

"What?"

If Mason didn't know better, he'd think his daughter's best friend was flirting. What would Beth do if she heard the interchange? Would she think it was nothing, or ban Holly from their house forever?

"You two have specific plans for the evening?"

"You know, Dad, we're going to get smashed and go stroll Sunset Boulevard looking for trouble."

"Very funny. Ground rules—"

"Kidding! We're going to veg out to a movie and that's about it. Holly's insisting we watch *Life Before Death*. To honor the wounded. Did you hear what happened at Whole Foods today?"

"Yeah, I heard about it."

Another lie to spare her heart.

"The ground rules are simple. No leaving Holly's house. No doing anything that would make her parents want to call me to complain. And don't blame it on Holly."

He leveled a look at Holly. "Besides, I know Holly wouldn't do anything wrong."

Holly smiled so sweetly you'd think angels sprouted from her eyes. "Don't worry about us, Mr. West. I'll make sure the troublemaker here toes the line."

"Great. I should be finished in a few hours and will be available by phone if you need anything."

Theresa cast him a doubtful look. "You sure it's gonna be that quick? You're heading into prime time rush hour traffic."

"Don't remind me."

Life on the west side of Los Angeles was enjoyable, so long as you steered clear of any freeway travel. Once life forced you onto the clogged veins and arteries of the city's circulatory system, slow and endless torture was guaranteed.

Mason checked his tie in the mirror. His knots really were inferior to both Beth's and Theresa's. He caught Holly's gaze in the mirror.

"Mr. West, did you know you were a real life James Bond?"

"Holly, did you know you were a real life Eddie Haskell?"

His joke met a blank stare.

"Who's that?"

"Never mind."

He turned back to them.

"Girls, stay at Holly's, and stay out of trouble."

Theresa traced her finger in a circle above her head. "You know me."

He did know her. The lifting light of his life. Her heart was generous in ways Mason couldn't fathom. She got it from her mother. She was a good kid. No, a great kid.

Max trotted in with a slobbery tendril jiggling from his lips. He lay down on the floor in the middle of them with his giraffe stuffie clamped in his mouth.

Mason didn't want to see what would likely happen next. "Time to move out," he said. "Are you two ready to go?"

"We're waiting on you," Theresa replied.

The trio gathered their belongings and headed out the front door.

"I'll drop you off." he said as he corralled Max inside and locked the door.

"Dad, it's just a couple of blocks over. I'm fifteen years old."

He didn't need the reminder. He considered forcing the issue, but decided against it. They'd be there in minutes. "Fine. Straight there. No delays or detours."

Holly grabbed Theresa's hand. "I'll keep her on the straight and narrow, Mr. West."

Mason kissed Theresa's forehead. "Love you. Be safe."

Theresa rolled her eyes like he was being melodramatic. Maybe he was.

Holly waved and dragged her away. "Looking good, Mr. West. See you later."

Mason watched them as they strolled arm in arm down the street. The two were almost sisters. And like sisters, they excelled at getting each other into trouble.

28

As predicted, traffic was a snarled mess all the way over. The road closures to the north and east turned the freeways into constricted arteries where the blood didn't flow fast enough to keep the greater organism going. Mason had taken as many side streets as possible to avoid having an aneurism.

There were few things in life more frustrating than navigating rush hour traffic in a city that was densely populated, enormous, and also in love with the automobile. Public transportation never caught on like it did in New York, San Francisco, and other more reasonable cities.

Mason stood at the hotel room door and pounded on it for the fifth time. He closed his eyes in frustration. "Hello! Is anyone in there?"

He'd been standing at the door for the past few minutes working to calm his heart rate as it inevitably spiked higher. His muscles ached to kick the door down. He knew someone was in there, presumably Iridia, because he heard the shower running.

He was determined to deliver Iridia as quickly as possible because it would get him back home faster and because it would mean minimal time with a supermodel client. He lifted his hand to bang on the door again when the lock clicked from the inside.

A muffled voice drifted out. "In the shower. Come in, come in."

Her accent put her in Eastern Europe. Ukraine maybe.

Mason pushed the door open and stuttered mid-stride as a tall, leggy woman glided across plush cream carpet. It wasn't her height that surprised him.

It was her total lack of clothing.

A coiled-up towel perched on top of her head. That was the only stitch of cloth to be found. Her firm backside swayed as she walked back down an entry hall that opened into a large living area.

"Put it on the table," she said with a lazy wave of her hand.

Mason followed her in, doing his best to keep his eyes glued anywhere but her shapely rear. "Excuse me?"

She looked back over her shoulder and a crinkle formed in her perfectly plucked brows.

"Where's the champagne?"

"What?"

"I ordered champagne. Did you forget it?"

She thought he was room service. She was clueless. He should leave now. Before this got truly horrible.

"My name is Mr. West. I'm here to take you to the Santa Monica airport. A chartered jet awaits you there."

"Oh, you're the chauffeur."

His teeth ground together. "No, I'm Mr. West, your close protection officer, ma'am."

She turned and approached him. Also completely naked on the front side.

It took every ounce of willpower to keep his eyes from dropping.

She stopped in front of him, her gaze inviting his to move lower.

There was no way that was going to happen. The first moments with a client established so much about the working relationship. He wasn't going to go there.

Besides, his peripheral vision provided more than enough detail.

"A bodyguard? My father is so paranoid. I mean really." She touched his tie as her chin dipped and head tilted seductively to the side. "But you are handsome."

She ran the tips of her fingers over her small, firm breasts and down her slim torso, resting them on her hips with practiced ease. Her pale skin gleamed with moisture.

Mason steeled his focus, staring into her eyes and nothing else. Long, dark lashes blinked over crystal green eyes. Like splashes of the ocean caught in the mid-day sun. It wasn't difficult to understand why she'd made it big in modeling.

He reflected on the situation. Beth would be angry. Not because he'd ever do anything. Just because she wouldn't like another woman flashing her goods at him. Miro'd be upset too. Because he'd missed out.

"You're too handsome to be a bodyguard."

"Would you mind putting some clothes on? As far as I'm aware, TSA regulations haven't gone so far as to require nudity before boarding a plane."

She bit her lip and batted her lashes.

"Would you like to strip search me?" She pulled the towel on her head free and sandy-blonde hair cascaded down creamy shoulders. She rolled the towel and twined it around her wrists. His handcuffs would have worked better, but he wasn't about to suggest it.

If only Miro could see this. His head would explode.

She licked her lips. "I'm a bad girl."

Of that, he had no doubt.

He pointed to the silver band on the ring finger of his left hand. "I'm here to see that you get to the airport in a safe and timely fashion, ma'am. I'd appreciate it if we could focus on that."

She dropped the towel and retreated into the living room. She picked up an open champagne bottle and emptied the dregs into a tall crystal flute. With a single gulp, she finished it.

The faster this was over, the better.

"Are you packed, ma'am?"

"Packed?"

"For the airport."

"Oh no, we can't go to the airport."

Of course. What else did he expect her to say?

"That's why I'm here, ma'am."

"Yes, well, that's Daddy's plan. It's not my plan."

Mason ground his teeth.

Never actor and never models, much less supermodels. He lived by that rule and business had been far smoother for it.

"What's *your* plan, ma'am?"

"Stop calling me 'Ma'am'. Makes me feel like a dried up mummy. Do I look like a mummy?"

"No, you look nothing like a mummy."

"Then call me Iridia."

"Okay, Iridia."

"What should I call you? Mr. West is so stuffy."

"Mr. West is fine."

"Do you really want to make this difficult? I can be very difficult if I want to be."

That was the last thing he wanted. But it wasn't looking like he'd get his wish.

"Mason."

"Was that so hard, Mason?"

"Great. Now, Iridia, what's your plan?"

"To be famous, of course. Isn't that what everyone wants?"

Mason groaned. He hoped it was mostly on the inside. "I wish you the best, but I'm not sure how that affects you boarding a flight this evening."

"It has everything to do with it! I have a meeting with Bryce Eaton this evening."

She said the name like that explained everything. Any vague interest his primitive male brain had in her female form sunk beneath a thick layer of extreme irritation.

He held her gaze with no problem. He hoped she sensed his frustration.

"He's a director. You'll love him. He's the talk of the town. Had a movie last summer gross a billion worldwide. He's big time. One word and he can make your career."

She clearly sensed nothing. In his experience, the bigger the big time, the bigger the idiot. Iridia herself was adding evidence to that theory.

"I'm sure he's a charming individual, but I have one job and one job only."

"To do what I say."

No. That's what all the famous people thought. It was part of what made working with them such a nightmare.

A close protection officer wasn't a slave. The reverse was

the case. His job was to stay out of the way and only make requests that mattered. Ones that impacted the safety of the protectee.

"Wrong. My job is to keep a mob from ripping your limbs from your torso."

Her mouth dropped at the thought of her million-dollar-body ending up in a million pieces. "I didn't fly out here from New York to miss this meeting. You'll have to tie me up and drag me out kicking and screaming!"

She seductively bit her lower lip and offered her intertwined wrists.

"I'm not going to do that, Iridia."

"Your loss," she said with a shrug. Her breasts heaved with the movement.

Couldn't she just get some clothes on already?

His submerged male curiosity threatened to bubble up to the surface. She was physically gorgeous. Even if he was married and she was an idiot.

Mason decided to surrender a tactical victory to gain the larger strategic victory of getting her clothed and in the general direction of going somewhere.

"Okay. Where and when are you meeting this director?"

She laughed like the world waited on her every word. "We were supposed to meet over an hour ago."

"Wonderful. Where?"

"Mason, you're going to love it! I swear! There's not another spot like it in the city. Give me a minute to slip into something."

He wanted to press for more information, but absolutely wasn't going to derail some measure of forward progress. He followed her through the living room as she headed toward a bathroom that looked like a grenade had gone off in it.

She pulled up to the mirror and admired herself. Still naked and in plain view of where he stood. She applied dark mascara above her eyes with the precision of a heart surgeon. "Be a doll and pack my bags for me. Makeup takes forever and I don't want to miss my flight. My bags are in the closet in the front bedroom."

Mason grimaced. A twenty-five year old supermodel was yanking his chain. He was going to kill Miro.

"Got it," he murmured as he headed toward the nearest bedroom. The room looked worse than the bathroom. Like an F5 tornado blew through. Skimpy panties hung on the lampshade by the bed. Dresses, shoes, skirts, more panties, and other assorted wardrobe covered every inch of horizontal surface. Empty and mostly empty bottles of champagne were mixed in with almost equal frequency.

In some places, the debris looked a foot deep.

Mason trudged through the wreckage and dug five enormous, floral-print suitcases out of the closet. He zipped them open against the wall and flung everything within reach into them.

He'd made it halfway through the mess when he grabbed something wet and squishy. He yanked his hand back and recoiled in horror.

A bright red, thoroughly used condom stuck to his fingertips.

He whipped his hand and the filled piece of thin rubber sailed through the air and stuck to the wall.

Disgusting!

Mason wiped the unidentified goo clinging to his fingers on a discarded towel on the floor.

At least she was being safe.

He laughed. Only a father would think that thought, at that moment.

He scrubbed his fingers in the ensuite bathroom sink until the flesh glowed pink and he felt relatively certain no trace of liquid biological potential remained.

A long sigh escaped his lungs.

He was going to kill Miro until he died twice.

29

BETH gulped down the bitter dregs of some cold coffee and glanced at her watch. She'd normally be home for dinner by now. Not tonight. Jane lay on the operating table next to her, still intubated and in critical condition. An all-night vigil was in store.

She texted Mason with the latest, which wasn't much.

BETH> Still at work. Not sure when I'll be able to leave. Jane doing okay for now.

MASON> Hang in there. Working. Love you.

BETH> Love you.

She pushed the phone onto the counter and rubbed her itchy eyes. She laid a gentle hand on Jane's large chest. It rose and fell in inverse time with the machine's diaphragm expanding and contracting.

She stroked the chimp's face. Soft skin that hardly covered hard teeth. Teeth that she'd never feared because of their shared bond.

"Fight, Jane. Stay strong for your babies. For me."

The lab room door swung open and Diana Richston marched in with an evil grin on her face. What was she still doing here? Seeing her at work one minute after five was unusual. Hours after the closing bell? That was a miracle.

Beth willed her hand to continue stroking Jane. So it wouldn't ball up and sock Diana in the mouth.

"Beth, you were not approved for overtime, but I'm glad you're still here."

"What do you want?"

"I just got off a conference call with the members of the Milagro Corporation board. We had an emergency meeting prompted by your actions today."

Beth recoiled in surprise. She knew Diana would be out for blood, but the speed of her attack was unexpected.

"Your actions put this organization in danger today. Put the lives of my employees in danger. Your lack of judgement is a hazard to yourself and, more importantly, to the zoo. I will not allow you to ruin something so important."

What a sick joke. She hadn't been there long enough to learn everyone's names, and she'd made her concern for the parent company's profits abundantly clear already. It wasn't about the welfare of the zoo. No matter what the words that slithered out of her mouth said.

Beth's temper flared. Her exhaustion bleeding away what little patience she might have normally had.

"Spare me the lecture. I saved Jane today. And there wouldn't have been a problem if Jack had remained locked up. Just how did he get out, Diana? Would you know anything about that?"

Diana ignored her question. "The board has voted and, with one abstention, your contract has been terminated as of today. Dr. West, it is my great pleasure to inform you that you are no longer an employee of the Los Angeles Zoo and its parent company, the Milagro Corporation."

The floor seemed to crack open and a bottomless black

pit pulled at Beth's feet. Taking care of animals was all she'd ever wanted to do. Her time at the zoo, while sometimes a pain because of people like Diana, had been the pinnacle of her life's ambition. The prospect of having it taken away was no different than having her heart torn from her chest.

A confused cauldron of emotions swirled in her mind. Despair. Anger. Lots of anger. But even larger than that was the loss. The desperate sense of loss that she might not get to spend time every day with the animals. And in particular, that she might not be a regular part of Jane's life.

Diana smiled in the most self-satisfied smug way. She crossed her arms, her legs wide. This was the "take charge" Diana that everyone on staff loved to hate. She had no clue how ridiculous she was.

"I'd like you to pack your personal belongings and leave. Now."

Beth jumped to her feet and landed inside Diana's little sphere of authority. The rage dulled the pain in her leg as she landed. "I'm not going anywhere until Jane is doing better."

"That is no longer *your* concern."

She said it in a snarky way that comes naturally to someone who started their career in upper management.

Beth glanced back at the slumbering form of the pregnant chimp. There was no chance she was leaving now.

"I'm not leaving. Call the police. File a lawsuit. Do whatever you feel you have to do. I'm staying until she's stabilized and the babies are safe."

Diana seemed at a loss. Her authority had probably never been challenged so directly. It kicked her world off kilter. Unsure for an awkward pause, she then doubled down.

"You will leave. Now! I don't care if that stupid monkey

dies one second after you're gone. This is my zoo and I decide what happens in it!"

The volume of her voice was in counterpoint to Beth's reply.

"You'll have to drag me out," Beth said in a dangerous whisper. She stepped forward, her eyes dark and foreboding. "Now get out of my lab before I ruin that expensive pantsuit."

The facade of strength and control shattered. Diana stumbled back a step as if struck by a physical blow.

"That's assault! You've bodily threatened me. I'll have you thrown in jail. I'll have your license revoked." She babbled as she continued to shrink away.

The ceiling lights flickered, the ventilator stopped pumping and shrilled in alarm. The room strobed as the lights buzzed and hummed. The lab dropped into darkness a moment and then flickered back into view.

Beth paused, waiting to see if it would continue.

The power flickered again and returned to normal. The ventilator went silent as it resumed its metronomic rhythm. The diaphragm collapsed and Jane's chest expanded.

Beth sighed in relief.

What was that about?

She stared at the ceiling, as if the answer might be found there.

Must have been a hiccup.

Then the room plunged into inky darkness.

30

The lights didn't come back on this time. The ventilator shrilled its battery-powered warning. Beth oriented herself in the dark, remembering the layout of the lab. Her messenger bag should be over by the sink on the far side of the room.

"What's happening?" Diana whispered.

Beth ignored her.

Beth crept forward with her arms outstretched. Her fingertips swished through thick fur. Jane on the table. Her chest didn't move. No air expanded her lungs.

She had to hurry. She had to get Jane on a manual ventilator, but there was no way she could sort through the medical supplies and get it hooked up in the pitch black.

She needed her flashlight.

She edged around the table and left it, stepping into the gulf of open space between it and the sink on the far wall.

"What's happening?" Diana said again, this time louder and tinged with panic.

Beth visualized the room the instant before the lights cut out. Where had the roller chairs been? She crept forward, wondering if she still had five or fifteen feet to go. How foreign the world felt through the lenses of impaired senses.

She took another step and her foot landed on something awkwardly. Her ankle twisted and her foot swept out to the side, throwing her in the other direction. The rolling chair spun around and caught her in the leg, right on the gash in her thigh. A jolt of pain shot through her leg.

The darkness spun and she tipped forward, reaching for the chair to stop the fall. Her searching fingers found empty air as she tumbled forward. The back of the chair jabbed her ribs as she twisted and crashed to the concrete floor.

The chair clattered and tipped over next to her.

"What's happening!" Diana shrieked. Blind terror made her voice raspy and raw. "Help me! I can't see anything!"

From the floor, her thigh sticky with ruptured sutures, Beth groaned with irritation. Pain too. But aggravation overwhelmed the sting.

"Shut up, Diana! Shut your mouth!"

"Beth! Beth!" Diana howled, as if just now remembering the world contained at least one other person. "Was that Jane? Is she awake?"

"Shut up, Diana!"

The woman's hysteria wasn't helping her own struggle to remain focused.

"I fell down. I'm trying to get a flashlight. Don't move. And keep your mouth shut."

A shrill squeak escaped and then gurgled to silence.

Beth picked herself up in the dark, feeling around to get a clue and finding none. The fall turned her around so she had no idea which direction to go now.

Another squeak from Diana told her to move in the opposite direction. She turned and limped forward, praying not to encounter another obstacle that might send her to the floor and completely open her wound.

She touched her pant leg and felt the soaked fabric stuck to her skin.

Her outstretched fingers smacked into something hard. She patted the cool surface of the counter and swept from side to side until she encountered the slick ballistic nylon of her messenger bag. She dug inside and found the cool metal tube.

With a click, a small beam of light shot to the ceiling. She gave silent thanks to her husband for always insisting she carry an emergency flashlight. No matter how many times she said it was ridiculous. She'd never say that again. She'd even remember to change the batteries herself.

She aimed the small, single LED light around the room. Diana stood by the door, her burnt orange, fake-tan skin several shades lighter than usual.

"Give it to me!" She waved Beth over. "We have to get out of here!"

Jane's motionless body jerked. A violent shudder tore through her chest. She settled an instant and then spasmed again.

She needed oxygen. The infants inside her needed oxygen.

And fast.

31

"What are you doing? Give me the light!" Diana shouted. She hadn't budged from her spot by the door as she held her hand out.

Her words barely registered. Beth rifled through the medical supply cabinet and grabbed a sealed plastic, sterile bag containing a manual respirator. She tore it open and hurried back to the operating table.

The chimp continued to convulse as her body reacted to the the lack of oxygen.

"Get over here, Diana!"

Diana blanched, her mouth a twisted grimace of fear and anger.

The final, thin film restraining Beth ruptured. She flew at Diana in a rage. Her boss shrank back as the flashlight came at her.

Beth grabbed her arm and dragged her like a child's doll back to the operating table.

Diana screamed and screeched.

Beth shook her. "Shut up!"

All the fight flooded out of Diana. Her shoulders

slumped and she looked at Beth, her lower lip trembling violently.

"Hold the flashlight, right here!" Beth put the light in her hand and positioned it so the light fell where she needed it.

Fighting the spasming body on the operating table, Beth disconnected the ventilator from the tracheal tube and attached the manual respirator. She squeezed the bladder bag and pushed air down Jane's throat. The large furry chest barely moved. The manual respirator didn't move half the air that the ventilator did.

The light on Jane's face dropped to the floor.

"Hold it up!" Beth screamed. Spit shot from her mouth and peppered Diana's face.

The circle of light came back up to the operating table.

Beth worked the respirator, but it wasn't enough. Jane's thick limbs twitched and then went still. Beth peeled back one closed eye and didn't like what she saw.

Jane was fading.

If she died, her babies would too.

They had to come out. Now.

Beth had never performed a Cesarean on a chimpanzee before. She had on a few other mammals over the years and she knew the anatomy of the chimpanzee as well as she knew her own.

But she'd never done it without assistants. Qualified ones. And she'd never done it in the dark on a dying animal.

None of that mattered, because she didn't have another choice.

"Diana, I'm going to have to get the babies out of her."

"What? Are you insane?"

As much as it would hurt to lose Jane, losing her and the infants would be a blow Beth wasn't sure she could absorb.

"They'll die inside her. It's the only way to save them."

"Save them? Why? They're just animals!"

Beth wanted more than anything to pummel Diana through the concrete floor.

Jane's body jerked and went still again. Beth dug her fingers into the fur on her neck and felt for a pulse. There wasn't one.

The respirator wasn't moving enough air.

"I need you to respirate while I open her up."

Some air was better than none.

Diana's jaw dropped. She stared at the chimp lying on the table.

"Touch that disgusting beast? I won't do it."

Beth leveled a gaze at her that promised murder.

"You *will*."

Diana shrank back in terror.

"Give me the flashlight." Beth took the light and guided Diana's hand through manually filling and emptying the respirator bladder.

They weren't going to give up on Jane or her babies.

"Don't stop."

Diana nodded in silence, her face like a white moon surrounded by night sky.

Beth turned away with the light and sprinted back to the supplies cabinet. A soft whoosh of air, then a sucking sound, then another whoosh confirmed Diana hadn't stopped.

Beth rolled up her sleeves and splashed iodine all over her hands and arms. The dark liquid spilled onto the counter and floor. She tore open plastic packages and dropped scalpels, forceps, and other utensils on a steel platter.

She returned to the operating table and shoved the flashlight into her mouth. Her teeth ached as they bit down on the hard metal tube. She felt Jane's distended belly. She pressed around her abdomen, searching.

No movement.

Please be alive.

Disregarding every precautionary protocol that made sense on a normal day, she picked up a scalpel and was about to press the point to Jane's abdomen when she noticed her hand trembling.

I'm so sorry.

She took a deep breath and then pushed the tip through fur and skin. A pool of red welled up as the blade sliced through skin, fascia, and then encountered the tough uterine muscle. Beth pushed deeper, sinking the thin razor through the fibrous tissue.

The blood flowed in earnest now. Hot, sticky red covered her hands as the blade sank deeper into the abdominal cavity. She felt the resistance lighten as the blade sliced through the interior wall.

Jane didn't respond to the incision. Beth didn't want to accept the implications. She carefully opened the slit to get a better view. She slid a finger down into the punctured uterus and guided the tip of the scalpel lower, making certain no more than a hair's breadth extended beyond the interior wall.

The cut lengthened to a few inches. Blood pooled in the cavity, obscuring everything. She needed an assistant. This was a fool's gamble. What chance did she have not being able to see what she was doing?

Feeling her way along, going so slow she started to wonder if she was moving, the incision lengthened.

Her teeth stung and jaws cramped, but she dared not pull away.

She dragged the tip of the scalpel lower, following her fingertip, drawing it down Jane's belly.

Sweat dripped down her forehead and ran into her eyes, the stinging salt blurring her vision until she blinked it away.

After what seemed like an eternity, she pulled the scalpel away and dropped it on the silver tray. She reached inside the parted uterus and felt a tiny body inside.

She gently cupped her hand around it and drew it out into the world. A blood and mucus covered male chimp emerged. His eyes pinched tight. Delicate little, human-like fingers intertwined with her own. She scrubbed him with small, vigorous motions, mimicking a mother's tongue licking it to life.

A gelatinous cord streaked with blood vessels extended from his belly back inside his mother. Beth severed the umbilical cord and clamped it tight. She continued scrubbing, willing him to breathe.

He didn't.

Her heart pounded. Memories more real than not washing over her.

Drowning her.

She wiped away the fluid from his tiny mouth, set the flashlight on the table, and closed her mouth around the chimp's. She puffed air into his body and drew it back out. Another puff and another inhale.

Come on.

Another puff, and another inhale.

The precious little body kicked and then coughed into her mouth. She drew back and spat the foul-tasting gunk onto the floor.

Soft cooing escaped his perfect little lips.

He was alive!

Beth's heart exploded in her chest.

One more to go.

She gently set the baby boy next to his mother, thinking that if these were to be Jane's final moments, she should spend them with her babies.

Beth noticed the soft whoosh sound missing and swung the light toward Diana.

She stood stone still, staring at the little chimp as it tried to nuzzle into Jane.

"Don't stop pumping!"

Diana snapped to attention and resumed respirating Jane.

Beth put the flashlight back in her mouth and ignored the pain. She slid her hands back inside Jane's cavernous abdomen and located another tiny body. She cupped it and gently pulled it out. Blood spurted from the wound as it emerged.

She rubbed the little body up and down, trying to draw life into a frail and fragile home. She cut and clamped the cord and continued rubbing.

Again no response.

This one was noticeably smaller than his brother.

Beth set the flashlight down and breathed life into him. She knew he would wake up, just as his brother did. He would be fine.

Small puff and exhale. Small puff and exhale.

No response.

She alternated between breaths and scrubbing.

Still no response.

"Come on little guy!"

Fury boiled up inside her. She needed this baby to live. She needed it to survive for all the other babies that didn't. Mostly for the one that didn't.

"Fight!" she screamed as she scrubbed his tiny back and belly. Tears and snot dripped down her face, pooling at her chin.

She kept at it, unable to surrender.

"Dr. West, it's dead," Diana said.

The pronouncement stabbed into Beth's chest like a spear.

She stopped.

The little brother was dead. Died in utero, probably lacking sufficient oxygen.

Beth held him to her chest and tears streamed down her face in a river of anguish. Jane's blood seeped off the edge of the operating table and made a wet sound as it dripped to the floor.

She was gone, too.

Only the soft cry of the remaining baby boy kept Beth from complete collapse.

She gently set the lifeless infant next to his mother. They were together. No longer in this world, but together. She picked up the bigger one and nuzzled him to her neck. His tiny mouth prodded and poked her skin, searching for a nipple that wasn't there.

Beth cried. She'd only saved one. She prayed Jane would forgive her. Would somehow know she did her best.

The sound of softly whooshing air drew her attention. She bounced the light over toward Diana.

Her boss dutifully squeezed the air bladder then expanded it to gather more for another breath of air.

It no longer mattered.

"You can stop."

Diana released the respirator and wiped her face. She squinted into the darkness. "Is that one going to live?"

Grief and joy clashed in Beth's heart. A terrible,

wonderful, sacred concoction that reflected the ending of two lives and the beginning of one more. The miracle of life tinged with the bitter tears of death.

She'd saved one. That had to be worth something.

"Yes."

32

MASON stood in the entry hall of the suite and tapped his toe as if an imaginary pedal might accelerate their departure.

"Coming!" Iridia called from the bathroom.

About time. He'd been standing by the door for the last thirty minutes while she attended to a thousand meaningless things that served to do nothing but delay their departure.

Iridia swept into the hall like a goddess descended from Olympus. A sheer black dress that ended well above her knees. Strappy black heels that made her nearly as tall as him. Sandy blonde hair gathered up in a careless bun that probably took that half hour he'd been fuming.

She was stunning. The involuntary response in Mason's body surprised him. His pulse quickened. He noted the subtle tension that signaled a rise in blood pressure.

Man truly was a beast aspiring to greater things. He succeeded in many. But the animal remained.

"How do I look?"

A girl like this knew full well how she looked. The

question was merely an opportunity for a mortal to affirm her divinity.

He'd never been good at prayer. Besides, his job wasn't to worship her. "Your lipstick is smudged, and I see your panty line."

She narrowed her eyes and gave him a dirty look.

"Liar. I'm not wearing panties."

Mason swallowed hard. "I'm sure the director will think you look fine. Let's go."

She grabbed a minuscule, silver-sequined purse and checked her lipstick in the hall mirror. She had to check. The insecurity of the totally secure. She straightened a thread-like gold necklace and dropped the attached locket between her cleavage. The letters IR were embossed on it.

She turned back to him with a pout puckering her full lips. "I'm asking *you*. How do *you* think I look?"

"I'm not here to placate your ego."

He wasn't going to play that game.

"Fine. Be a sourpuss." She breezed by him. "What are you waiting for?"

He bit his tongue as he reached ahead and opened the door to the exterior hall. "Where are we going?"

"It's a surprise."

"I don't do surprises. It's in the job description."

"Are you trying to ruin my fun?"

Was she trying to ruin his life?

The elevator door opened and they stepped in. He waited for her to press the lobby button so they could pick up her suitcases on the way out. Instead, she hit the button labeled *Bar*. The doors closed and the elevator started up.

Up toward the bar on top of the hotel. The one place he had no personal desire to revisit and every professional reason to avoid. This was getting better and better.

In the silence of the ascent, Mason wondered if she'd heard the news about her previous boyfriend. The news that he had been a part of creating. She hadn't mentioned anything and she clearly didn't seem concerned about anything more than this big meeting with Mr. Hollywood Director.

It wasn't his business to get involved with the personal affairs of a client, especially a brand new one. And double that for one he had no intention of ever working with again. But the afternoon ate at him, whether in a conscious thought or back behind the focus of moving forward. He couldn't stop himself.

"Did you hear what happened to your old boyfriend?"

She turned to him with an angry glare. "Are you trying to ruin my evening? Do you want me to break into tears right before the biggest meeting of my professional life?"

"Sorry, it's none of my business."

"You're right. It's not. But since you asked, he was a lying cheater who deserved worse." She pointedly looked back at the reflective metal elevator doors and checked her lipstick.

Mason had no idea what kind of person the kid was, but he didn't deserve what happened. He also knew that getting what you deserved was a principle that only consistently worked in fairy tales and fables.

The doors opened and Iridia took his arm in hers. "Play along, Mason. I don't want any of these desperate ruffians to think I'm single. Consider my safety. It's in your job description."

Mason shook his head, but understood the logistical advantage. He didn't pull away. Beth was going to kill him.

33

Iridia pulled him along and out into the open night air of the rooftop bar and club. Swanky didn't cover it by half.

A bar lined the wall to the right. A DJ beyond that cranked out beats loud enough to require you to shout to anyone more than a couple of feet away. A sparsely populated dance floor occupied the space directly ahead. A large rectangular pool was surrounded by modern white couches and chairs with low backs and firm cushions. A few swimmers in skimpy suits lounged in one corner of the pool. Sugary looking mixed drinks held up above the water. A rainbow of colored lights from underwater LEDs reflected off their perfectly golden skin.

Beth was going to kill him for not bringing her along. Both to keep an eye on Iridia and to take in this view. She had a posh side that ate up this kind of thing. Besides, she looked great in a bikini.

Surrounding the rooftop on all sides were other skyscrapers. One taller than the rest. What used to be the US Bank Tower was now the Milagro Corporation Tower. A cylinder of glass and white concrete that stretched into the clouds, if Los Angeles ever had any. At one thousand feet tall, it was the highest building west of the Mississippi. A titan among giants.

The crown glowed purple and gold. The Lakers must've had a big game coming up. Circling the crown, glowing white letters read MILAGRO, a reminder to the city of who held the highest perch. A chopper on the helipad at the top blinked red and green lights. Its rotors spun up and it lifted off, banking right and heading east.

Maybe it carried Gabriel Cruz, the charismatic owner and CEO of the company. Mason didn't know much about the richest man in the world, but anyone with a TV had seen his philanthropic pursuits in Africa and other destitute regions of the world.

They had a catchy corporate slogan. Miracles for the masses... or something.

A kaleidoscope of lights adorned the various surrounding buildings. It was Christmas without all the goodwill. The faint smell of smoke scented the air. He looked north and almost stumbled at the apocalyptic scene in the distance. In glimpses between taller buildings, the horizon burned orange. The fires from this distance appeared to be a solid mass of burning brilliance. He followed the glow right and it stretched off to the horizon, eventually lost to the smoggy distance.

A pinpoint of brighter flame flickered closer to the northeast. Several of the white letters of the Hollywood sign roared with yellow licking flames. Only a few still stood.

H L L

How appropriate. The gates of hell were about to admit all of Los Angeles.

Iridia strode forward like she owned the place. For all he knew, she did.

She pulled him right and up a few steps to another level. The chill zone apparently. Enclosed beds like space pods lined the perimeter. Drawn back curtains revealed hipsters reclined and toasting the start of the weekend. A few beds had their curtains drawn and Mason tried not to imagine what sounds might emerge from them if the music didn't drown out everything quieter than a jet engine.

A thick, clear plastic barrier lined the perimeter of the roof. It had likely saved more drunks from death than the seatbelt.

"There he is!" Iridia said with a shout as she tugged Mason toward one of the beds. A man reclined on the mattress, passed out or asleep. He looked twice Iridia's age. Older than Mason by a good span of years. A short glass of amber liquid in his still hand. Whiskey on the rocks if Mason guessed right.

Iridia wiggled his loafered foot. "Bryce, dear! Wake up!"

He shot up like a cattle prod touched his nuts. "What? Who?"

"It's me, Iridia. Hello? We had a meeting tonight. To discuss my part."

His eyes focused, or at least got a little less unfocused, and he glanced at his watch. "Almost two hours ago."

"You can't hurry a girl. You don't think this just happens, do you?" she said as she twirled in a little circle.

Bryce's eyes swept up and down her lanky limbs and whatever anger he harbored melted away. Or was subsumed by a stronger passion.

She finished her turn and extended a hand. Not a hand shake like normal people might do. She extended it like a queen, expecting a kiss of patronage.

Bryce obliged. He knew how to work in royal circles.

"You are a vision." His eyes hungered for her. It was painfully obvious. He turned to Mason. "Is this guy a cop?"

Iridia laughed, a little too loudly. "No. He's my bodyguard."

Bryce narrowed his eyes at Mason and then nodded like that settled the matter. He picked up a small, clear vial from the bed and held it for Iridia. "Care for a bump?"

"Sure—"

Mason dropped his arm between them. "No thanks. She has a flight leaving later." Mason didn't want to get involved in Iridia's personal life and whatever decisions she might make. But there was no way he was going to drop her off coked up out of her mind.

"So?" Bryce shouted with a skeptical look. "I fly to Vegas lit up all the time."

Mason wanted to punch this jerk's face in so bad his fist twitched. He uncurled his fingers and took a slow breath. Caving this guy's head in wasn't going to help.

Seeing that Mason wasn't going to come around, the director shook his head. "Whatever, man." He measured out a crude line on the back of his hand and proceeded to suck it up his nose. His head snapped back and wild light gleamed in his eyes. White powder clung to his nostrils and upper lip.

"You got a little," Iridia said as she motioned to her own nose.

"Oh, yeah," he said and wiped a sleeve across his face. The powder streaked over to his cheek.

Mason almost laughed out loud. Try walking through airport security like that. See how fast you get rewarded with your own personal cubicle and a strip search. He turned Iridia toward him and shouted in her ear to be sure she heard him.

"I'll be at the bar over there." He motioned to the upper deck bar a short distance away. "Fifteen minutes."

She frowned. "That's not enough. An hour."

"Twenty minutes. Should we call your father and see what he thinks about this meeting?"

She pursed her lips, the taste of defeat unfamiliar in her mouth. The green in her eyes iced over. "Fine." She turned back to Bryce and flashed a million dollar smile. Literally.

His eyes glinted with wild, intoxicated abandon. He looked dangerous. Like a feral dog. Mason decided to stay nearby. Far enough to get a good view of the televisions above the bar and close enough to mangle this jerk if he crossed the line.

Maybe it was the frustration talking, but Mason really wanted him to cross the line.

34

Minutes ticked by as Mason caught the odd word here and there of Iridia and Bryce's conversation, only when the music paused before picking up again to continue the hypnotic beat.

He took in a nearby skyscraper. It was all black glass, reflective where the interior lights were out and little dioramas of late night office life where the lights remained on. He could just make out a man seated at a desk in a dim office. His face illuminated by the screen in front of him. He scanned the face of the building, wondering if these people had any idea they were so visible.

His gaze paused on a pane of glass that answered the question. A man and a woman either wore skin-colored, skin-tight business suits or they were in their birthday suits. The details were difficult to make out at this distance, but they were clearly engaged in some very intimate negotiations. She was bent over a conference table, maybe reaching for a pen she'd dropped. He was behind her, urgently pushing her forward to find it.

Only in Los Angeles. They probably wanted people to watch.

Mason shook his head and checked his watch. A few more minutes and he'd drag Iridia to the airport if he had to. The local news station ran on one of the TVs above the bar. It replayed footage of the fires up north and FEMA trucks and personnel scurrying around like a colony of ants under attack.

He glanced back toward the bed and noticed Bryce's hand unmistakably high on Iridia's thigh. His fingertips just under the hem of her dress, which had already ridden up a ways from her sitting down. He said something and laughed. His hand moved higher, disappearing under the black fabric.

Iridia grabbed his arm and tried to push it away. His smile wavered and he pushed to keep his hand in place. She again tried to back him off. He frowned and shouted at her. He jerked his hand back and then laid out another ragged line of white powder. An instant later, it vanished up his nose and his head shot back like a wolf howling at the moon.

He scooted closer to Iridia and slithered an arm around her, whispered something in her ear.

She backed away.

This idiot couldn't take a hint.

Mason edged closer. Not wanting to intrude, but wanting to be close in case he was forced to intervene.

Their words carried over the music.

"I'm not doing that to get the part. I'm a Sports Illustrated swimsuit issue model!"

"Honey, did you really think I wanted you for the lead role? You're gorgeous and stupid. Your lead role is riding my pole." He pointed at his crotch like it was the Holy Grail.

Iridia slapped him with a crack loud enough that people in surrounding beds looked over.

Bryce glanced around, seeing that he was the focus of unwanted attention. "You whore! You'll never get a part in my movie. I'll make sure you never get work in this town!"

"Screw you, Bryce. Go force your little dick on ignorant interns who don't know better."

Mason smiled, happy to see she had some standards, and the strength to keep them.

The director clearly wasn't used to being told no. "You worthless bimbo!" His face contorted as his hand raised above his head.

Iridia flinched, bracing for the impact.

Mason moved in.

Just as Bryce's hand dropped, Mason wrapped him in an arm lock and yanked him up off the bed. The director gave him a furious glare. As if he couldn't believe anyone would interfere.

After regaining his balance, Bryce squared up to Mason and swung a wild roundhouse. It was slow, poorly aimed, and laughable at best. But it crossed the line in no uncertain terms.

Mason almost grinned as he stepped forward and delivered a vicious blow to the solar plexus. It was a hard strike. The bastard would be sucking wind for the next few minutes. Most importantly, it wouldn't leave a mark. Nothing for this clown to show a jury with an accompanied demand of millions of dollars in punitive damages.

Bryce doubled over and collapsed to the ground.

He was human trash, and he deserved a proper beating. As satisfying as delivering that beating would've been, Mason was working and the threat had been neutralized.

Bryce curled up on his side, gagging and coughing for

air. Between ragged breaths, he screamed. "I'll kill you! Kill you!"

Beaten and immobilized, this guy still wanted to attack. Maybe it was empty talk. But maybe it wasn't. People could do crazy things on drugs. He'd seen it before back in Fallujah. He didn't think the guy would come back for more, but additional certainty was a simple matter. Mason spun him around, wrenched his hands behind his back, and slapped a pair of plastic looped cuffs on his wrists. He cranked them tighter than strictly necessary because the idiot deserved it.

Mason reached over to the bed and retrieved the clear vial filled with white powder.

Bryce stopped struggling, even as his chest heaved and rattled, gasping for air.

Mason spun the end off and tossed it at a trashcan twenty feet or so away. It sailed through the air leaving a trail of falling white powder behind.

Bryce screamed like a maniac. Foam sputtered from his lips as words choked out of his mouth.

That business complete, Mason turned to Iridia seated on the edge of the bed. Tears splashed down her cheeks, dragging dark streaks of mascara with them. He gently pulled her to her feet and wrapped his arm around her.

"I can't believe he thought that. I'm not that kind of girl, Mason. I swear I'm not."

"Not my business," he said as he noticed the hurt in her eyes. "But I believe you."

He wasn't positive he believed her, but it didn't matter. He needed to get her out of here before this scene got bigger and more dangerous. Already, they'd attracted a small crowd.

"Let's go," he said in her ear.

She nodded and looked down at the man she'd pinned her Hollywood hopes on.

"I hate you!" She landed a hard kick to his torso before allowing herself to be dragged away.

Mason would've been more than happy to let her kick the stuffing out of him, but his job was to protect her. And that meant keeping her out of court as much as keeping her out of the hospital.

They hadn't taken five steps when the music crashed to silence. The abrupt transition from overwhelming sound to near silence sent the hairs on the back of his neck tingling.

All the TVs above the bar switched to the same local station. Big, white letters scrolled across a red banner on the bottom edge of the screen—BREAKING NEWS. A reporter read from a paper in her hands. Someone clicked the volume higher.

"Details are incomplete at the moment, but we're getting reports that Cedars-Sinai and the Ronald Reagan Medical Center are overrun with patients claiming flu-like symptoms. Neighborhood clinics are experiencing similar problems."

She touched her ear as communication came through the earpiece monitor. "I'm told we have a reporter on the ground at the Reagan Medical Center. Are you there, Kevin?"

An audio feed hissed and then resolved into chaotic shouting.

"Yes, I'm here, Melissa. Just outside the emergency room at the Reagan Center. Sorry, the team is working on patching through a video feed."

"Can you tell us what is happening there?"

"No one knows, to tell you the truth. There are a lot of scared people. We spoke with—"

Horrific screams momentarily drowned out his voice.

"—urging people to remain calm."

"We lost you there for a moment, Kevin. Can you—"

The video feed cut from the studio to a scene of barely controlled pandemonium. A young reporter with stylishly coiffed hair stood in front of the entrance to the ER at the Reagan Center.

The scene resembled nothing you ever expected to see in The United States of America.

35

A mass of humanity swirled around the reporter. A throng of bodies jammed the entrance to the ER in the background. Many people in the crowd wore white dust masks. An ambulance with lights flashing sat abandoned by the door. The crowd flooded around it like a river around a boulder.

Husbands and wives. Mothers and fathers. Sisters and brothers. Grandmothers and grandfathers. Babies. The healthy and sick mixed together in a pack of shoving arms and screaming voices. The mass of bodies lodged in the doorway went nowhere. There was nowhere to go. A line of four police officers stood across the interior door, looking overwhelmed and about to crack. They shoved at the crowd, trying to hold their ground. The inertia from the back pushed the people in front forward.

The police fell back another step.

Kevin turned to the camera and swept the hair out of his face. "The authorities are urging people to remain calm."

A mother separated from the crowd and stumbled into the reporter. She held a young girl in her arms. The girl resembled Theresa at eight or nine. The girl's face gleamed with a sickly sweat. Her skin shone pale white with irregular, angry red welts. Yellow pus oozed from many of the sores. Her pupils were huge, the empty black nearly swallowing the surrounding brown. The whites burned red with veins like a roadmap.

The mother held a filthy white cloth to the girl's mouth. Dark stains showed it had been used several times. The woman clutched at the reporter's shoulder. Her fingers white with desperate tension. "Help my daughter! Please! She's sick."

The reporter froze. His mouth open and unmoving.

The girl's chest spasmed and a dark gout of blood exploded from her mouth. A fountain of gore splashed onto the reporter's face. The sticky liquid covered him, spilled out of his mouth. The girl continued coughing, sputtering red down her own shirt.

Her mother's eyes cratered open. Terror. She hugged the listless girl tightly. "It's okay, baby. It's okay. You're going to be fine."

The reporter clawed at his eyes, flinging away viscera that stuck to his fingers. He spat on the ground.

The woman grabbed at him again, apparently still convinced the poor guy could help her. He had a TV camera pointed at him, he must be able to save the world.

"Help my baby! Please!"

The reporter recoiled, trying to pull away. "Get away from me!"

He yanked her hand free like it was death incarnate. Maybe it was.

She reached for him again.

"Don't touch me," he shouted while stumbling backward.

She moved closer. "Please—"

He screamed and leveled her with a vicious shove that sent her sprawling backwards. She tripped and went down hard. Her arms wrapped tightly around her daughter, the woman had nothing to soften the blow as her head snapped back and slammed into the concrete curb.

Her body went limp as blood dampened her hair. It oozed onto the pavement under her head.

A middle-aged man parted from the crowd and knelt beside the woman. He scooped the girl into his lap and held her close, rocking her gently. The woman next to him tended to the injured mother.

"Oh my God! Oh my God!" the reporter shrieked as he continued digging gore out of his eyes.

The shot cut back to the anchor in the studio. A frozen look of horror stared into the camera. A dark shadow crept in from the side of the screen. A man with a headset stepped into the pool of light and nudged the anchor's shoulder. He laid a sheet of paper on her desk.

She blinked and slowly came to her senses. She read the paper silently and then turned to the camera, as if suddenly remembering millions watched on the other end.

"We've just received a couple of emergency alerts. The Federal Aviation Administration has closed the air space over Los Angeles. No flights will be allowed in or out of the city. No traffic of any kind will be allowed in the air space."

A thunder from the west grew louder and then the source appeared. A squadron of four F-22 Raptors screamed overhead and disappeared in the distance.

Everyone at the rooftop bar watched them go.

The news anchor shuffled her papers and continued. "The second alert is from the Mayor's office. It instructs citizens to remain indoors until city personnel get a handle on the situation. No specific information is given, but it appears some kind of outbreak has occurred. Medical facilities are overwhelmed and turning away people with the help of local law enforcement."

She glanced at the paper again and then to the camera. "Above all, Mayor Garcia urges every citizen of Los Angeles to remain calm."

A man at the bar turned away from the TV above his head and stumbled toward a trashcan in the corner. Before he made it, a fountain of vomit spilled out of his mouth, splashing the shoes of those nearby. Whether he was just a drunk who couldn't hold his liquor or something more serious, it didn't matter.

The thin crust of civility, the unspoken agreement society made to itself to make modern life possible, cracked and crumbled to dust.

Beneath the fragile crust, a vast subterranean insanity tore loose. The crowd of well-dressed beautiful people broke as one and rushed for the elevator. One thought thundered through the herd.

Escape.

Howling screams pierced the air as several of the weaker or less steady patrons were trampled underfoot.

Mason grabbed Iridia's arm and dashed for the same elevator, hoping to get in before the mob packed the narrow entrance and made it so nobody could get out. A man shouldered Iridia aside as he ran by. A couple of hipsters bumped Mason from the other side as he turned to her.

A dense group rushed for the elevator, sweeping Iridia forward in their frenzied wave. Her arm yanked free and she bobbed away.

In a flash, Mason had the Bonowi baton out and locked to full extension. With measured swings, he snapped the metal rod down on the shoulders of the people separating him from Iridia. Every swing sent another body crashing to the floor, howling in pain. The calculated strikes wouldn't break bones, but they were utterly debilitating.

The sea of people parted like Moses with the staff.

Mason made his way to Iridia and halted her forward motion.

The crowd packed closer together as everyone funneled toward the elevator. Elbows flew as people jockeyed for space, trying to push through others already stacked in front.

They weren't going to make it. He wasn't going to wade through that mess with Iridia. He turned back and fought to move away. He wielded the baton like a sword, whacking bodies that threatened to bowl them over. He parted the mass of rushing flesh and finally pushed free.

There had to be an emergency exit. Stairs that could get them to the parking garage. A single elevator that could hold five or six with more than a hundred people clamoring for a spot was not an acceptable option.

He pulled Iridia along as he scanned the rooftop. No signs that he could see made it obvious. They ran back to the upper level and turned the corner toward the bathrooms. Still nothing.

Surely this place didn't get permitted with no emergency escape.

He made it around to the bathrooms and was relieved to see a side door that led to the stairs. Not a single body crowded its entrance. Poor souls. If there really was some kind of outbreak, fighting through a mob of spitting, bleeding, drunken imbeciles wasn't a good way to avoid infection.

Mason threw open the door and pulled Iridia inside. He looked over the guardrails and down an empty, central column of air. Far below, he saw a few people winding down the steps in a rush.

Iridia pulled back and fought him to a stop. "Where are we going?"

"We'll worry about that later. Let's get down to the parking garage and get out of here first."

Mason looked her up and down. She was dressed for dinner with a director. Not for escaping a hotel filled with an increasingly dangerous mob. "Get rid of the shoes." She'd snap an ankle in those three-inch heels.

Her face screwed up in horror, like he'd suggested she abandon her only child. She reached down and slipped out of them. She looped them on a finger.

"I'm not leaving my Manolos," she said with a look that dared him to cross her.

"Fine. Let's go."

He took her hand and headed down the stairs as fast as she could follow.

36

November 2004
Fallujah, Iraq

MASON approached the next house to be cleared, his M16 in the low ready position. Third squad stacked up at the closed metal door in the concrete wall that fronted the property. A big padlock secured the door shut. Houses here weren't anything like back home in California. Here they were mini-fortresses surrounded by concrete walls six to eight feet high and a foot thick.

Mason waved to LCpl. Channing. "Channing, you're up."

In addition to his service rifle, Channing carried a Mossberg 500 twelve gauge shotgun. It could blast a crater in a body, and it also functioned well as a lock pick. Channing came to the front and aimed at the lock, less than a foot from the muzzle. He turned his face away and blasted the lock to bits.

Lucky had point and rushed through the open gate with his rifle up and ready to fire. It followed his eyes as he scanned the area.

"Going right." He turned right and disappeared into the courtyard.

Lopes pushed in with his M249 SAW sweeping the courtyard. The light machine gun could send lead downrange at eight hundred rounds per minute. It was a monster. And Lopes wielded it like a true artist. A deadly proficient one.

"Going left." He hooked left.

The rest of the team filed in, clearing their sectors and setting up their fields of fire.

Mason scanned the area. A two-story concrete house sat back fifty feet. He eyed two dark windows, but didn't see any movement. He scanned the roof. It looked like so many houses in Fallujah. A three to four foot high concrete wall surrounded a large, flat rooftop used as an outside patio. It was also a protected shooting position. Perfectly suited to rain down fire on anyone crossing the courtyard below.

Not a situation he wanted to end up in.

Third squad hugged the inside of the perimeter wall scanning for threats. None appeared. They hadn't encountered any resistance yet. Aside from the haji that ran across the street earlier in the day, they hadn't seen anyone. It was strange. Everyone knew it couldn't last, but it was hard to stay switched on every second of the endless day.

After clearing twenty or thirty houses with no contact, the brain got complacent. It expected the next room to be clear just as the last hundred had been. But that couldn't be true forever.

Mason wiped sweat out of his eyes. The searing overhead sun almost made the dark interior of the house appear inviting. Almost. He waved the breach team forward while the rest of the squad provided cover.

Channing examined the door and then slung the

Mossberg to his back. He rigged some C4 to the door and strung wires out as he stepped away, hugging close to the house's exterior wall.

"Fire in the hole," he shouted.

The wooden door exploded inward and the breach team swept into action. They disappeared into the darkness as the rest of the squad followed on. After clearing a large living room, they stacked up and proceeded down a hallway. Two men peeled off to clear the kitchen and Lucky took point. He moved down the dim hallway with his rifle at the ready.

They came to a closed door on the left. Channing kicked it in and Lucky went in and hooked left. Miro followed in to the right.

"Clear."

"Clear."

Mason rolled in behind them and noticed an attached room through an open doorway. He crossed the room and peeked around the corner. It was too dark to make out much. He reached up to his helmet and pulled down night vision goggles. The NVGs flared to life and a high contrast, green and black picture emerged. He leaned around the corner and took another look.

It was a small, bare area with a single item of interest. A large oak armoire on the far wall. Easily big enough to hold a man. Easily big enough to hold trouble.

He covered the closed doors and approached. With the rifle in one hand, he reached out and pulled the handle to open it. His Nomex glove glowed bright green. Images of a smoking barrel flashed through his mind. The brain anticipating death.

The door swung open and no hidden insurgent popped out ready to take them both to Allah. That was not to say the armoire was empty.

It wasn't.

Mason shook his head. They'd seen it too many times already. Though this was the biggest so far.

"Miro, take a look at this."

Miro pulled up behind him.

"Whoa! Nice find."

Inside was a stacked pyramid of RPGs. At least fifty. Next to them were twenty or so AK-47s. Along the floorboard sat a Russian RPK machine gun. Cans of 7.62 ammo waist-high. That much firepower could've done some serious damage. It was crazy for it to be abandoned.

But that wasn't the craziest thing.

The craziest thing was that they'd found weapons caches tons of times already. This was the biggest so far. Mason was shocked by the level of organization. The degree of preparation.

"Get Channing to blow it in place," he said.

"Copy that," Miro replied.

Gunfire erupted from the hallway. The sound was deafening. A Squad Automatic Weapon in action.

Mason ran back to the hall and found Lopes on point, his SAW probing the darkness further down the hall.

"I saw something, Sarge," Lopes said.

"Define something."

"Muj, I think."

Mason stared down the hall. Aside from the chewed up walls, the green and black picture showed nothing out of the ordinary.

As long as you didn't count hunting down killers in the dark corners of a strange desert city as out of the ordinary.

A bright green form flitted across the hall between two open doorways. The distinctive shape of an AK-47 at waist level.

Lopes opened up on the apparition. The muzzle flash lit up the corridor in blinding flares of brilliance.

Mason pinched his eyes shut to keep the NVGs from blinding him.

The SAW went quiet.

"Don't think I got him," Lopes said.

The first real contact they'd encountered.

Mason tapped Lopes' shoulder.

"Let's go ruin his day."

37

They crept forward. Their boots crunched over bits of concrete and slipped over spent shell casings. Mason glanced back. Miro and Lucky stepped in to cover the rear. Channing must've been prepping to blow the cache. The rest of third squad engaged with clearing other rooms in the house.

They stacked up on an open doorway to the left. The one the apparition disappeared into. Lopes prepped an M67 fragmentation grenade.

Mason took a quick peek into the room.

Lopes let the spoon fly off the grenade.

"Frag out!" he yelled and reared back to toss it in.

Mason edged a little further around to get a better view of what he was seeing.

The room contained three massive propane tanks. Each as big as a car. Five hundred gallons a piece. A frag going off would ignite the tanks and obliterate the house and everyone inside it. Probably level the half the block.

"Hold that frag!"

Too late.

Lopes' arm whipped forward and the baseball-sized ball of death flew into the room.

"No!" Mason screamed.

Mason dove into the room and followed the grenade as it bounced on the concrete floor and off the nearest tank. It ricocheted back and thudded into his boot. He snatched it off the ground.

A three to five second fuse.

How much had burned off already?

His legs wobbled. His brain screamed, knowing the thought would be its last. He couldn't toss it back into the hall where the rest of his men waited.

He saw a bathroom attached to the bedroom. Who knew how deep it was? All it would take was one shred of shrapnel to hit a tank and it would be over. He slung the grenade through the open doorway and heard a clang as it hit something.

BOOM.

A blinding light killed his night vision.

He couldn't hear a thing.

Was he dead?

A high-pitched keen rose in his ears. It felt like daggers driving into his eardrums. He stopped to consider. He could hear himself losing his hearing. That meant he was alive.

He looked up from the ground.

Lopes was above him, saying something.

Was this dying?

Slowly, a voice pierced the ringing.

"Sarge! Are you okay?"

Mason pushed his awareness to every corner of his body. Aside from a hundred small aches and pains, nothing felt fatal.

"Are you crazy? Why did you—"

"Lopes," Lucky said from behind. "Look at this."

Lopes turned and saw what Mason had seen. A death trap about to be set off.

"Whoa!"

Miro knelt in the corner with a flashlight tracing across the floor.

"Guys, these are wired. They're wired to blow!"

Lopes pulled Mason to his feet and steadied him.

Why didn't the insurgent fire rounds into the tanks? Was he still alive?

"Lucky, clear that bathroom!" Mason's voice croaked like a sick bullfrog.

The kid swung around and sliced the arc into the bathroom and disappeared inside.

"Clear."

He returned dusted in powdered concrete.

"No body?" Mason asked.

"Nope."

"Where did that muj go?"

"Over here!" Miro shouted.

Mason leaned on Lopes and they went around to the back side of a tank. A two foot hole was dug through the wall at the floor. A spider hole.

They'd seen them everywhere. The holes provided the muj a covert web of protected movement. Lead wires from the tanks ran into the hole and disappeared beyond.

Mason's spine froze. A glacial chill shoveling through his soul.

The insurgent had probably crawled into the hole, back to a protected position. A place where he could blow the tanks and have a decent chance to live and fight another day.

They all realized it at the same time.

Mason shoved Lopes at the door.

"Get everyone out! Get out now!"

Nobody moved.

Miro touched one of the huge cylinders.

"We're not going anywhere. If these blow, being outside the house ain't gonna help. I'll get Channing!"

Mason nodded. It was a good idea. Channing had the most explosives experience.

Mason knelt down to the hole and listened. It was quiet. And then a whisper floated down the tunnel.

"Allahu akbar. Allahu akbar. Allahu—"

The guy was praying to his god before he blew them all to pieces. Channing wasn't going to get there fast enough.

Mason had to do it. He yanked out the knife strapped to his chest and brought the blade to the two wires.

Should he cut the blue one? The white one? Both? He knew circuits could be booby-trapped.

Dammit.

He might end up doing the terrorist's job for him.

The whispered prayer floated down the tunnel.

"Allahu akbar. Allahu—"

The prayer would end and they would all die.

If he was going to die, it wasn't going to be waiting around for the enemy to kill him.

He grabbed a hank of wire, squeezed his eyes shut, and sliced through the wires.

"Sarge!"

Mason jerked so hard he nearly stabbed himself in the eye.

The propane tanks were still intact.

Channing ran up behind him.

"What the hell you doing, Sarge? You coulda killed us all!"

Vomit pushed up Mason's throat. His mouth filled with saliva. He coughed hard, fighting to keep down yesterday's MRE.

He wanted a frag in that hole, but couldn't risk it.

"Lopes, get your SAW in there and light it up!"

"Yes, Sergeant!"

Lopes maneuvered his gun into position and tore through a magazine. He slammed a fresh one home and burned through it as well. If the buried haji wasn't protected by a turn in the tunnel or a few walls, he had to be Swiss cheese by now. The guy was probably dead, but Mason couldn't take the chance. What if they left and the insurgent returned to finish the job?

"Lopes, keep your eyes on that hole," Mason said. "I'm gonna call this one in. Get an EOD team on it."

The radio squawked as he reached for it.

"Contact on the second floor! Contact on the second floor!"

Gunfire echoed through the ceiling above.

38

"Corpsman up! Corpsman up!" The universal cry for a Marine that needed immediate medical attention.

Somewhere upstairs, a Marine called for a medic. Mason ran out of the propane tank room and bumped into their squad medic as he made for the stairs further down the hall. Medics were a fearless breed. They'd kick the devil himself in the nuts to save one of their men.

Mason led him upstairs.

More gunfire shattered the air. Screaming voices accompanied it.

Mason pulled up his NVGs and rounded the corner at the top with his rifle at the ready. Light poured in from an open doorway to the roof outside. The afternoon sun nearly blinded him after being in the dark interior of the house.

A body lay on the floor in the opening of the doorway, also known as the fatal funnel of fire. The head was twisted back at a grotesque angle. Private Leo Lawrence. Half of his head was blown off. Pale gray brains spilled out onto the floor.

From the roof outside, AK-47 rounds thumped into

Lawrence's dead body. More shot through the doorway and peppered the opposite wall.

LCpl. Walder Kurtz struggled to pull the body out of the doorway. Kurtz was about half Lawrence's size but gritty as they came.

Their corpsman rushed over and helped pull the body out of the doorway and off to the side. He pulled out his kit and feverishly wrapped gauze and tape around Lawrence's wound.

It was no use. He was already dead. Still the medic worked, not ready to give up on his Marine.

"They opened up on us, Sarge!" Kurtz shouted. "Soon as we opened the door. Lawrence never had a chance."

Rage burned in Mason's gut. He'd lost a man. Lawrence would never go home. Thanksgiving was only weeks away, but he'd never share another holiday with family.

Kurtz looked chalk white. He watched as their corpsman gently tried to push brains back into a fractured skull. He muttered to himself.

"He was right there. Just opened the door. He was there."

Mason turned him around and smacked his helmet. "Kurtz! Listen up! We have to hit 'em. Hit 'em hard!"

The lost look in his eyes hardened into focus. He snarled. It was back. The killer. That's what Mason needed right now. They would honor Lawrence later. They would avenge him now.

A blood curdling scream tore out of Kurtz' mouth. He turned toward the door and emptied his M16 into the outside air. Return fire snapped by. Mason yanked him back before he stepped into the incoming barrage of bullets.

Mason dragged him back and shook him hard.

"Keep it locked down! We're gonna get 'em! But we have to do it smart!"

LCpl. Kurtz didn't reply.

"You understand me, Marine?"

He nodded.

A window shattered and Kurtz' head jerked to the side. His cheek exploded and blood splattered Mason's face. Kurtz collapsed and dragged Mason down with him. Kurtz held his face as blood squirted out around his hand.

"Corpsman up!" Mason shouted.

The medic looked over and saw another Marine down. One that maybe had a chance. He scrambled over and started treating Kurtz.

A hailstorm of enemy fire chewed through the open doorway.

Mason dug blood out of his eyes. Lucky, Lopes, and Miro appeared around the corner.

"Heavy contact, out on the roof," he said.

Miro nodded and stacked on the door with Lucky and Lopes following on.

"Prep your frags and hand 'em over!" Miro shouted.

Lucky handed him an M67 fragmentation grenade.

"Frag out!" Miro shouted and lobbed it out the door.

Lopes handed him another one.

He yelled again as he launched it through the door. Miro cycled through four more frags as explosions rocked the roof outside.

The sounds of incoming fire stopped somewhere in the barrage of exploding grenades.

Mason jumped up and got behind Lucky in the stack. Hate burned like fire in his veins. He wanted the people that hurt his men. He wanted their blood.

The stack rushed through the fatal funnel. Lucky peeled left so Mason went right. Thick clouds of swirling dust obscured portions of the roof. He scanned his sector, rifle at the ready. No threats.

"One dead over here!" Lopes shouted.

An M16 fired off several rounds. The sharp crack of the report echoed off the wall lining the roof.

"Another dead here!" Miro yelled.

The sound of moaning drifted out of the thick gray dust swirling in front of Mason. It sounded like a wounded man. He didn't love the idea of wading into the cloud, not being able to see more than two feet ahead. But he wasn't going to wait for the dust to settle and give the enemy time to recover and continue the fight.

He stepped forward a few paces and the fine fog swallowed him whole. The dazzling, afternoon sun filtered through the dust, making it a brilliant blinding white. He crept further into the choking cloud.

A dark form on the floor emerged. An amorphous gray blob with stable edges that set it apart from the whirling wind. The shape resolved itself as Mason got closer.

A severed, hairy arm. The fat hand still clutching a silent AK-47. Red splattered the ground nearby.

The moaning again floated through the fog.

Mason lunged through the white, no longer able to contain his bloodlust. A few paces further and his boot slipped out from under him. He fell to his knees and slapped a hand in a puddle of blood to right himself.

A jihadi lay in a twisted heap next to him. One arm conspicuously absent. The dying man lay on his side, his remaining arm reaching for an old MK2 pineapple grenade, just inches away. Blood gushed from his body in a hundred places. He turned to Mason and screamed impotent rage.

He rolled back and stretched for the grenade. His fingertips brushed the deadly metal.

Mason jumped over and kicked it away. He stood above the insurgent and felt nothing but grim satisfaction. The man screamed and blood and spittle sprayed from his mouth. He rolled to his back and shouted words drowned by the blood filling his mouth.

CRACK. CRACK. CRACK.

Smoke wafted from the muzzle of Mason's rifle. Three rounds pumped into the man's chest at point blank range.

The muj's body spasmed and he coughed up crimson fluid. His eyes flamed with enmity. He reached for Mason with his remaining arm, as if he might yet pull them both into oblivion.

CRACK. CRACK. CRACK.

Another three round burst ripped through the muj's chest.

Mason watched him, both disgusted and curious.

The ruined man refused to die. He spewed blood through punctured lungs. His heart geysered the life out of him. But he didn't go quiet.

"Why don't you die already!"

Mason set the M16's muzzle on the man's forehead and pulled the trigger until his magazine went dry.

"Jesus, Sarge!"

Lopes emerged out of the dust and looked at the dead man at Mason's feet.

"You messed him up, bro!"

The dead man's head was a fragmented pile of brains and bone. Like he'd shoved his head in a giant garbage disposal.

Mason noticed something sticking out of the corpse's side. A syringe. The needle still embedded in the stomach. He pulled it out and read the label on the clear tube.

Epinephrine.

Medical adrenaline.

The syringe was their first confirmation of what became commonplace as the battle continued. Muj fighters doped out of their minds on epinephrine, methamphetamines, heroine, and cocaine. The potent cocktail kept them alive and fighting far beyond what any normal body could absorb.

It made them a deadly dangerous foe.

39

The Last Day
Venice, California

THERESA pulled a stack of books out of her backpack and a paper fell on the floor. Holly picked it up and opened it without asking for permission. She didn't need to. Best friends didn't have to ask to get in your business. That was their job.

"Whoa," she said. "Five days detention. You're a bad girl now."

"You're the bad girl."

"Me?" Holly said with a fake wounded expression.

"Yeah, you. We're supposed to be at your house right now. My dad explicitly said that was the deal. But no. You insisted we sneak back to my house."

"That does make me look bad, doesn't it?"

Theresa nodded.

"But, in my defense, my parents would never let us watch *Death Before Life*! So we had to return here to watch it.

We'll head to my house afterwards and no one will be the wiser. Trust me, sister. It's all gonna be fine."

Theresa had heard that before.

Holly glanced at the detention slip. "Besides, you are officially the bad girl here."

"Shut up," Theresa said as she held her hand out for the note.

Holly teased it in the air.

"My mom won't want me hanging out with you when she finds out."

"Don't tell her! I'm serious!"

"Kidding. No way she'll hear it from me. Where else would I spend every day after school?"

"You could come to detention with me," Theresa said with a smirk.

"Sounds thrilling. Really. But no thanks. I heard you have to listen to motivational speeches the whole time."

"Seriously?"

"Yeah, like how to be a more responsible person and stuff like that."

"It's not like I'll even make it to detention. My parents are going to kill me first."

Theresa snatched the paper back and stared at it.

"I have to get it signed and returned on Monday."

Holly waved her off.

"That's no big deal. I'll forge a signature for you. Use my left hand so it can never be traced back to the source."

"Holly, you're a criminal mastermind. But it won't work. Apparently my flagging commitment requires a parent conference next week too."

Holly's eyes opened wide.

"You're screwed, girl."

"Tell me about it."

"Can't you say it wasn't your fault you were late today? I mean that accident is a legitimate excuse if I've ever heard one."

"I did!"

"That didn't get you out of it?"

"The problem was that the other six tardies didn't have such good excuses. I should've named names. Rolled over on you."

"Why, Miss Theresa West, are you blaming me?"

"*Blaming you* would imply there was some uncertainty about your being at fault."

Holly giggled.

Theresa stuffed the paper into a desk drawer. "I'll deal with it Monday morning. No reason to ruin the weekend."

"*You* are the bad influence on *me*, Theresa West!"

Despite the foreboding gloom of getting busted, Theresa laughed. Wasn't that what a best friend was for? To pull you up off the ground and make you laugh?

Holly could always make her laugh.

Theresa finished unloading her backpack. Some fruit she didn't get around to eating. Some stinky socks that had been in there for far longer than was remotely sanitary. Her house key on the LA Galaxy keychain. Her phone.

Holly flopped on her bed like it was her own. It kind of was.

"Anyway, tell me more about the encounter in the Principal's office."

Theresa dug through the remaining compartments of the backpack.

"It was just what you'd expect. All heavy disappointment on his part and fake repentance on mine."

"I'm talking about Elio. Oh, I guess you were, too."

Theresa giggled.

"Haha."

"Come on." Holly flicked her tongue in the air. "I want the hot, juicy bits."

"Gross, Holly!"

Holly threw her hands up like the world had gone crazy and she was the last sane person to understand it.

"What? It's biology. It's nature."

She circled her fingers and pumped her hand at her mouth while simultaneously poking her cheek out with her tongue.

"Yuck! Stop it!"

"What? Someone has to hold your hand through the baby steps."

"I know all about that stuff."

"You do? Since when? Where was I when all this happened?"

Theresa put her hands on her hips and shook her backside at her friend.

"You were probably working that night. I know those street corners get busy."

"You're so naughty," Holly said. "Seriously. What are you going to do when it's time to go there with Elio?"

"Gross, Holly! You're like a dog with a bone. A boner bone."

Holly bit her lower lip and rolled it out.

"I like big bones."

Theresa rolled her eyes. She knew Holly had a little more experience than she did, but she didn't love dwelling on it. It made her feel lacking.

"Look, don't worry about it. I'll show you how. What else are best friends for?"

Theresa could think of quite a few other things.

Holly pointed to her desk.

"Hand me that banana."

"You are not seriously going to do what I think you're going to do, are you?"

"I'm going to make sure you don't hurt him, or yourself. You can thank me later."

Holly held her hand out.

"I'm waiting."

Theresa could tell she wasn't going to give up on this one. And besides, Theresa was curious about how it worked. Holly had tried to glory in her few exploits a few times in the past, but Theresa had freaked out and changed the subject.

Something about Elio made her want to know more. It freaked her out too. But in a good way.

Theresa passed over the requested item of fruit.

Holly examined it with an expert eye. Or at least faked it really good.

"I'd say seven inches." She circled a thumb and pointer finger around it. "Bigger than you're likely to run into."

Theresa blushed. She wanted to look away, but couldn't.

"Like with fruit," Holly said, "you want to use a delicate touch. You're not playing tug of war with Max's favorite rope."

She stroked the length of the yellow fruit. She delicately turned down the peel.

"You won't have to worry much about getting the banana ripe. Smile at a teenage boy and their bananas are ready to blow."

She winked.

"If you know what I mean."

Theresa rolled her eyes, but couldn't help but giggle.

"Get a firm grip at the base, but don't choke it to death."

She held the base and brought the fleshy fruit to her lips. She kissed it.

"Disgusting, Holly!"

"What? Kiss it. Make friends."

"Right on the, there, on the tip?"

"To start, yes."

Holly licked the tip.

Theresa grimaced. Maybe this was a mistake. Give Holly an inch and she'd take a mouthful.

Holly licked the length of the firm fruit. She went up and down like she was cleaning the thing.

"I'm about to vomit, Holly."

"Girl, if this part makes you squirmy, you're in real trouble."

She brought the tip to her lips and lowered her mouth on it. A little fruit disappeared and then she pulled it out.

"A little at a time to start. To get you both used to it."

She kept that up and slowly worked her way down lower. In a minute, she had the whole banana disappearing into her mouth and then reappearing like some kind of farm fresh magic act.

Theresa still felt icked out, but fascinated, too.

"The whole thing?"

Holly nodded without stopping.

"Don't you choke?"

She pulled it out of her mouth.

"It takes practice." She held the banana out to Theresa. "Try it."

"You've been slobbering all over it. No way!"

"You're worried about *my* germs? Think about what we're talking about here. About what's going into your mouth."

Theresa pictured it for a second and her body trembled.

Partly from revulsion and partly from something else. Something tingly that launched a million butterflies in her stomach.

Her phone buzzed.

Saved by the bell.

Holly jumped up and grabbed it.

"Speaking of the gorgeous devil himself!"

She flipped the screen toward Theresa.

Elio had sent her a text message.

ELIO> Stay Safe! Insanity at your Whole Foods!

40

She clicked the provided link and a news broadcast segment filled the screen. A local news anchor that Theresa vaguely recognized set a paper down and looked into the camera.

"Violence erupts at the Whole Foods at Lincoln and Rose. During the lunch time rush, an unidentified white male wounded actor Ryan—"

A publicity pic from *Death Before Life* filled the corner of the screen.

"Tell me his face didn't get hurt!" Holly screamed. "He was so gorgeous."

"Shhhhh!"

"... LAPD officer was working at the time. Witnesses say he confronted the gunman and was attempting to peacefully resolve the confrontation when the unidentified man opened fire, seriously wounding the actor and killing the officer in a deadly storm of bullets."

"It's crazy," Holly said as she shook her head. "I masturbated to his abs two nights ago."

"No way."

"It's true."

"I mean, to his abs? That's kind of specific, isn't it?"

"Have you ever seen his stomach?"

"... say that a third person, described as a large Latino male, pulled a gun and tried to stop the rampage, but the killer escaped before police arrived at the scene."

The feed cut to a clip of a frazzled looking girl wearing a burgundy Whole Foods smock.

"It was a regular shift like any other, and then Ryan turned up in my line. He let me take a picture with him. He kissed my cheek! I'm never going to wash this cheek!"

She touched the apparently blessed cheek.

"Then everything went crazy. This insane white man pulled out a gun and shot Ryan. He shot the officer next and probably woulda killed me, too, but this vato guy pulled his own gun and ran him off."

She shook her head and burst into tears.

"It happened right in front of me. They're still scrubbing the blood off the floor. And the guy looked so normal. That was the crazy thing. Just some average Joe white guy. But isn't that who it always is? What's wrong with white folks these days?"

The feed cut back to the anchor as a drawing appeared in the upper corner of the screen.

"A forensic artist has sketched out what the suspect may look like. If you see anyone resembling this man, police warn you not to approach him as he is armed and dangerous. If you think you've seen this man, call 911 immediately."

The video paused as the final frame finished.

The suspect looked like nobody and anybody as those sketches often did. He wore an LA Galaxy cap. Dark glasses. Late twenties to early fifties.

Why did this maniac have to sully her favorite team?

The LA Galaxy shouldn't have been associated with this madman. Theresa handed the phone to Holly. That Whole Foods was less than two miles away. They went to it sometimes. Not frequently because her parents complained about how crazy expensive it was.

But still. Sometimes.

A murderer gunned people down in her neighborhood. He could be roaming the streets this very minute looking for new victims. She hoped LAPD found him and locked him up forever.

And to think that there wouldn't be a *Death Before Life 2* any time soon. Or that the officer woke up that morning having no idea that this was his last day on earth. It was scary how random death could be.

Wrong place at the wrong time.

Holly looked at the screen closer.

"That kind of looks like your dad."

Theresa took another look.

Yeah, it kind of did. Then again, her dad looked like a million middle-aged, white guys. Her dad would've taken care of that creep if he'd been there. She knew that for sure. He protected people. That was his job.

Holly grabbed the phone and started typing.

Theresa stood in disbelief. How could things like this happen? Happen so near to her life?

She fumbled over the questions when Holly handed her phone back.

"You're welcome."

"What?"

Holly flopped back on the bed and looked at the ceiling.

"Can you believe it? Doesn't seem real. Like it's a hoax or something. You think it'll end up like when a famous person fakes their own death just to get out of the spotlight for a while? I heard his supermodel girlfriend dumped him. Maybe he just doesn't want to face the press about it."

"I think it's real, Holly."

Holly twisted her mouth up, her eyes sad.

"I know. I just wish it weren't."

Theresa looked down at her phone and read the conversation.

THERESA> So crazy! So sad!

ELIO> I know right?! Might be a good idea to stay inside tonight.

THERESA> I am. Going to go to bed early... to think about you.

"Holly! I can't believe you did that! He's going to think I'm a total idiot!"

"He's into you, Theresa. Now you don't have to do all that awkward sixth grade note passing nonsense."

She drew in the air above her with an exaggerated, idiotic flair.

"Do you like me? If yes, check this box. If no, check this box."

"You just ruined my life!"

"You have so much to learn. Luckily, you have me to teach you."

"Am I supposed to thank you?"

"You're welcome."

"I didn't say thank you!"

"You didn't have to," Holly said with a smile.

41

The girls lay on their stomachs looking off the edge of the bed. Light from the TV splashed into the dark corners of the room. Theresa rolled a tattered bit of cloth between her fingers. Lambchops had been her number one stuffie for over ten years. Though his prominent position was more memory than reality now, she still reached for him sometimes. He stared up at her with his one remaining eye button.

She squeezed him tight and looked away from the screen.

"I hate this part."

"This is my favorite part!" Holly said. "You know this scene ends with him getting his shirt ripped off."

"That's not the part I'm talking about. What about the girl that gets it just before that? The one he was too late to save?"

"Yea, that's unlucky. She could've seen his luscious abs if she'd made it just a few more minutes."

"Fast forward to that."

"No! You can't ruin the build up."

Theresa didn't look up.

"Tell me when this part is over."

"Okay, it's over."

Theresa looked up. She shouldn't have.

A dark shadow crept down a dimly lit hall. The shadow's outline on the wall was not human. The shadow opened a door at the end of the hall. Through the crack, a teenage girl lay back on a bed with a laptop in her lap. Her fingers clacked on the keyboard. Her head bopped to the rhythm emanating from headphones.

She glanced up at the open door and her head stopped.

"Dad, I swear I'm doing homework. Close the door!"

The girl watched the door, waiting for an answer that didn't come.

A keening wail started softly in the background. Like crystal dragged across a chalkboard. A resonant, grating tone that stirred the hackles on your back, if you had any.

Theresa wanted to look away, but couldn't. She knew what was going to happen, she'd seen *Death Before Life* at least ten times. It was still scary, though.

The girl pushed her laptop to the side and yanked the headphones off her head.

"Dad, is that you?"

She rose from the bed, her body filled with an apprehension that guaranteed something bad was about to happen. She stepped toward the door.

"Dad?"

Her bedside light flickered and then went dark. The screen went dark.

Theresa held her breath and gritted her teeth. That girl needed to get out of there. Not walk right into it. She had a big front window there. She needed to jump out of that thing and run for her life! Theresa wanted to yell at her to not be an idiot.

A light flicked on and the girl's face was illuminated from below by her phone. She shined it in front of her as she took another step closer. She stopped a few feet from the door. Unsure.

"You'd better not be joking! I'm serious!"

Theresa covered her face with Lambchops. Unfortunately, the old stuffie was equal parts cloth and holes so she could still peek through.

The girl took another step closer. A growing fear crept into her face.

A huge body ran in front of the TV and landed on Theresa's bed.

Theresa screamed. The B movie slasher flick kind.

"Max! You gave me a heart attack!"

A long, wet tongue rolled out of his mouth and licked her face.

"Ewww! Yuck! You found some more of Mr. Piddles' poo. Disgusting."

Max turned to Holly, his tongue leading the turn. She rolled off the bed and jumped away.

"No way, Max! Keep that tongue to yourself."

Theresa wrestled Max to the bed, making sure to keep his mouth facing away. Max was better than Lambchops for snuggling when you were scared. If she was going to have to suffer through the scary parts, Max was going to have to do his part to make it bearable.

Holly sniffed the air. "Did you set a timer on the pizza?"

Theresa pulled away from Max's back and immediately smelled an acrid, burning odor.

"No!"

Theresa jumped off the bed and headed for the kitchen.

"I thought you set the timer!" she said as she went.

"Me? I thought you did."

Out in the hallway, the sharp scent was stronger. It had to be cheese charcoal by now.

Theresa ran into the kitchen and the fire alarm shrieked. Smoke curled along the ceiling. Max barreled into the kitchen, barking like crazy.

She turned the oven off and threw its door open. Black smoke billowed out and choked her. The roiling cloud stung her eyes. She squeezed her eyes shut and ducked out of the way. The alarm wailed.

Theresa grabbed a towel from the hook by the sink and reached into the oven for the crisp remains of dinner.

"Whoa!" Holly appeared in the doorway.

"Fan the smoke alarm!"

Holly grabbed another towel and fanned the alarm on the ceiling.

Theresa dropped the blackened disc into the sink as the scalding heat began to burn through the thin towel. She turned the faucet on and let the cool water run over her singed fingertips. The smoke was suffocating.

She threw open the window above the sink and flinched as the motion lights in the back yard switched on. She didn't see any movement. It was probably Mr. Piddles depositing another treat for Max.

Disgusting.

The fire alarm went silent as Holly succeeded in wafting the smoke into the living room.

Emergency over. Mostly.

Theresa got a spatula to scrape burned cheese off the oven bottom when her heart jumped into her throat.

A hideous screech came from the back yard and Mr. Piddles bolted across the yard.

What was up with him?

She was about to get to work on the mess in the oven when she froze. Her eyes locked on the backyard.

Long shadows swept over the grass.

Whispered voices moved with them.

42

A chill spidered up Theresa's back. It was probably the movie making her jumpy. It was just a breeze blowing the trees. She turned to Holly who was fanning the last gray wisps out of the kitchen.

"Did you hear something?"

"You mean like an ear-splitting siren? Yes."

"No, something from the backyard."

Holly gave her a look like she was crazy.

Theresa jumped as a scream echoed down the hallway.

Holly grinned. "Sounds like the girl just got finished off. Time for sexy abs!"

Theresa let out a slow exhale. Everything was fine. She shouldn't have let Holly talk her into watching that movie at night without her parents home. The alien things were too creepy. The actor had just died in real life, if it wasn't a fake.

It was all too creepy.

Max stopped circling Holly and froze looking at the glass back door. He tilted his head to the side. A shuffling sound came from the back yard. He tilted it to the other side. He launched at the back door, barking and growling, scratching at the glass with wild swipes.

BOOM.

The glass pane shattered inward and Max yelped as he spun backward and fell to the kitchen floor.

A remote part of Theresa's brain noticed that Holly grabbed a large knife out of the wooden block on the counter.

Theresa dropped next to Max, her hands gently running through fur that was normally a light tan, and was now a deep, wet red.

Max whined and looked up at her in confusion. He tried to stand and yelped as his back legs collapsed under him.

What was happening?

A big black boot kicked the remaining shards in and a huge tattooed man stepped inside. He was an enormous block of bulging muscles and dark ink.

"Get out of here!" Holly yelled.

She held the knife pointed at the stranger. Her stance awkward, yet tense and determined.

"Don't be stupid, blanca. Put the knife down."

She waved it at him.

"I'm warning you!"

Theresa could barely think, much less move. And there Holly was, ready to attack. Amazing.

The man snarled at Holly and pointed his mirrored gun at her chest.

"Drop it or die."

Holly didn't budge.

He wasn't bluffing. Theresa could see it.

"Holly! Do what he says!"

"Listen to your friend. I'm not here to hurt you. But I'd be fine with that, too."

He thumbed the hammer back and it clicked into place.

"Drop the knife, Holly!"

She frowned and narrowed her gaze at the dangerous man.

"Fine," she said as she laid the knife on the counter. "What do you want?"

"This your house?"

"It's my house," Theresa said. "My family's house."

The man took a picture from the bay window above the sink. The one with her mom and dad on the beach in Hawaii three years ago. He studied it and turned to her.

"Where's your dad?"

"He went to the store. He'll be back any minute."

"Good."

That wasn't the reaction she was hoping for. That was supposed to scare him into leaving.

"You should leave. My dad will hurt you."

"You think I'm afraid?"

"You should be."

The man glowered and took a step toward Theresa.

Even in pain and unable to rise, Max lifted his head and growled. His teeth snapped at the intruder.

BOOM.

Where a second before Max's head had been, now a pulped mess of tissue and gore remained. Her protector's body convulsed under her hand.

The stink of gunpowder burned her throat, like metal and acid. Her ears rang and the world seemed to sink away. Or maybe she floated back a few steps behind her eyes. Like the world existed at the other end of a tunnel where her senses still worked.

"You still think I should be afraid?"

Theresa wanted to cry. To scream. To run away and

never come back to this horrible scene. Maybe if she ran fast enough, it wouldn't be real. Maybe it would turn back time like Superman flying backwards around the planet. Maybe something would change.

Because the slick blood coating her fingers couldn't be all that was left of the best dog she'd ever known. The best friend that snuggled her every night. The best friend that made any nightmare dissolve and vanish.

How could life change so quickly? It was like the last six years of his life were a dream. All of her memories of their time together some cheap trick and now the blanket had been yanked back to reveal the emptiness of the illusion. He couldn't be gone. That didn't make sense.

The murderer dropped the family picture and the glass shattered when it hit the tile floor. He yanked Theresa up, practically pulling her arm out of its socket. A blinding pain shot through her shoulder and neck.

"We'll wait for him together. If either of you make trouble, you'll end up like that pinche perro."

"Jefe!" a voice sounded from the backyard.

Another man stepped through the shattered door. He was short and square with a face like the surface of the moon. Neck wider than his head. He had a phone in his hand and held it out for the much taller man.

The killer put it to his ear.

"Hola Mama, que pasa?"

His face turned dark. Angry. More than it already was. He tossed the phone back to the shorter man.

"Vamos. They're coming with us."

Before Theresa could react, she and Holly were being dragged out into the backyard. She fought like mad, dug her nails into the brute's arms. His hold on her didn't waver. She went for his face, trying to claw at his eyes.

A huge palm connected with her cheek and snapped her head to the side. Her spine popped with the torsion. Her face burned like she'd sat too close to a fire.

Fighting him wasn't helping. She went limp, trying to slow them down. That didn't do much either. The giant dragged her as easily as a sack of dirty laundry. Holly fared no better with the smaller man.

They went through the side gate and toward a red lowrider waiting in the street.

43

MASON pounded the steering wheel in frustration. Heading west on the ten freeway was a huge mistake. Everyone always talked about how it could be a parking lot during commute hours. That was the typical hyperbole that Los Angelenos used to joke about and to deal with the frustration of ever-worsening traffic conditions.

He tuned the police scanner mounted under the dash to LAPD Metro Dispatch. Maybe there would be some useful news about what was holding up traffic. A chatter of dispatch officers had responding units scrambling all over the metropolitan area.

A scanner was a useful tool in his line of work. Access to that information had literally saved a client's life two years ago. Tonight the stream was a nearly constant hum of voices. He'd never heard so much activity. The city had law enforcement on the ropes.

Nothing obvious surfaced about the predicament they faced.

Looking out at an endless stream of red brake lights, Mason shook his head. This wasn't the joking version of a parking lot. This was an actual one. He shot an irritated look at Iridia, as if she were the reason for all these people clogging up the pavement.

She wasn't. But she was the reason he had to deal with it.

He checked his watch. He should've never gone along with the meeting at the bar. It was a waste of time for both of them. Close protection was a delicate balancing act of being an employee while also being the boss when it mattered. Dealing with people like Iridia who thought the world was populated with personal servants made it a painful exercise.

Miro should've been here. He'd be ecstatic to rot in traffic with a supermodel.

Mason didn't have time for this. A mysterious sickness had the city teetering toward chaos. A dangerous gang leader was looking to harm him and his family. Yet, here he was babysitting this brat.

Sitting at a standstill on this six-lane freeway for the past five minutes had him about ready to shoot someone. Theoretically, at least. He knew better than anyone that you couldn't take back a bullet. Once it was out there in the world, it would continue on its path of destruction, changing lives and ending others without regard for second thoughts.

More and more people exited their vehicles, walking alongside when a few feet of space would open up in front. Horns honked and tempers flared. Motorcycles split lanes, weaving in and out of cars and people. At least Beth would be able to get home.

A few car lengths ahead, a knot of people formed. In the center of the group, two men stood face to face yelling and pointing wildly around.

Mason couldn't hear what they were saying over the

near continuous variable pitch siren of numerous car horns, but he didn't require words to see that the tension was escalating.

The man in a dark suit shoved the other guy backwards. He fell back into the crowd behind him and was immediately bounced back into the conflict. He threw a right cross and caught the business guy on the chin.

It was like a flare landed on a bucket of gasoline. Angry words turned to raging fists. The two in the center brawled and disappeared into the growing chaos of flying fists and crumpled bodies. The havoc grew as others joined, drawn to the fight like dogs ready for a brawl.

A sleek red sportbike zipped by Mason's side mirror and stopped a few feet short of the seething crowd. The rider honked several times, which did nothing to stop the fighting ahead. He cranked the throttle and the bike emitted an ear-splitting shriek.

Bad move.

The nearest edge of the mob stopped stomping on each other and turned as one to the new target. Several large men rushed the rider.

The rider was either insane or he panicked because the bike shot forward like an arrow. The lifted front tire knocked aside several people and plowed into the crowd, crushing those unlucky enough to be in the way.

The rider fell off the back and landed hard on the pavement. The enraged mob surrounded him like ants ganging up on a meal. He raised his arms, trying to fend off the avalanche of blows crashing down.

Mason had to get them out of there.

There would be no reasoning with the growing mayhem. The problem was Mason had no room to maneuver. He was less than a foot from the bumper of the Audi sedan in front.

He had to make room.

Mason threw it into Park and hopped out. He locked the hubs on the front wheels and jumped back in. He slammed the door shut and engaged the four-wheel drive.

He eased the Bronco's bumper up to the Audi's. It was more like bumper to trunk, but it would do. He pushed down the pedal and the throaty V8 growled. The Audi's sheetmetal trunk crumpled and then the car lurched forward as the Bronco broke the lighter car's traction. He shoved it forward until it smashed into the car ahead of it and they both ground to a halt.

The nearest edge of the crowd noticed and turned to Mason.

He backed up and immediately crashed into the car behind, which apparently thought the whole line had moved forward. He slammed it back a good ten feet.

A splinter of fighting people broke from the main group and ran at the Bronco. A big guy arrived at Mason's door and pounded on the window with his fist. He jiggled the handle, trying to open the locked door to get at Mason.

Ten or so people surrounded the Bronco. Fists pounding on the hood, the windshield, the doors.

Mason revved the engine and inched forward, threatening to flatten those blocking his way out.

The attackers refused to move.

Mason looked over as a baseball bat appeared in the hand of a man at Iridia's window. The glass exploded inward and Iridia screamed.

The man outside reached in and grabbed Iridia's hair, yanking her head to the side.

Mason whipped the Bonowi baton to full length and

jabbed her attacker's face. The man released his grip and fell back howling.

"Hold on," Mason said as he revved the engine again. One last warning to the guys kicking out his headlights.

Iridia grabbed the dash. "What are you doing?"

"Getting us out of here."

Mason cut the wheel to the right and smashed down the pedal. One of the guys beating on the hood went down and disappeared. The Bronco lurched into the few feet of open space between the four-foot high concrete barrier and his lane.

Mason bumped the front right tire into the barrier. It was tall, but his baby could do it. The people beating on his truck backed off, apparently not wanting to be the next in line to get up close with the undercarriage of the metal beast.

He pushed down the accelerator and the V8 engine growled. The Bronco bucked forward as the giant tires bit into the barrier. The forward momentum halted and the car fell back.

Mason let it roll back a little and then gunned it.

The engine roared and they slammed into the barrier. The right tire chewed up the side and the cab lifted, throwing Iridia to the left. She would've ended up in Mason's lap if not for the seatbelt.

The surrounding crowd dropped back and watched in awe. This wasn't in their playbook and they didn't know how to react.

He eased the wheel to the left a little and kept a steady foot on the gas. Too much and he'd drop the front right tire on the far side and land the axle right on top of the barrier. They'd be good and screwed if that happened.

The right rear tire hit and chewed up the side. The

whole vehicle tilted to the left with two tires on the pavement and two up on top of the barrier.

Iridia clung to the bar above the passenger door. "Are you insane?"

He straightened out the wheel and eased forward. He looked down to the left as his side mirror just missed the car that had been in front a moment ago. The old guy inside tugged his wife's shoulder, pointing at the Bronco, like it was hard to miss.

The attackers melted back through the surrounding vehicles, perhaps coming to their senses or perhaps looking for easier prey.

With inches of clearance on the left side and two tires riding the top of the barrier, the Bronco rolled forward.

They approached an off ramp that was nearly as clogged, but looked like he could edge through. Mason turned on his blinker.

He might as well be a courteous driver.

"You are insane!" Iridia said in a voice soaked with shock.

"Maybe."

44

Just as they arrived at the exit ramp, a shiny black Ferrari pulled right and cut them off. It didn't make it out of its own lane. It stopped diagonally in front, with its right front bumper inches from the barrier. Its engine growled like a trapped tiger. Round tail lights washed them in a red glow.

What was this idiot doing? He had no hope of squeezing through.

Mason honked the horn.

The Ferrari sounded right back, though the horn was weaker and almost musical.

Mason laid on the horn, about to blow his top. He shouted out the window, "Get out of the way!"

A hand emerged from the driver's window and communicated a single-fingered, distinctly rude gesture.

"Move it!" Mason shouted out the window.

The Ferrari responded with an ear-splitting howl of perfectly-tuned pistons.

Mason mashed the brake with his left foot and mashed the accelerator with his right. The beefy V8 roared as the Bronco inched forward.

Iridia grabbed his shoulder. "Don't do it!"

The Bronco's front bumper continued forward, until it hung above the side of the supercar.

The Ferrari driver jumped out of his car.

"What are you doing? Get back!"

"You cut me off! Get outta my way or I'll run over your Italian piece of crap!"

Iridia grabbed his arm.

"Don't do it, Mason! That's a three million dollar super car!"

Mason turned and detached her hand from his arm.

"Never touch the driver, and I don't care if it's a hundred million dollar sculpture of carbon fiber. He better move it. Now."

He turned back to the window just as the other driver ducked into his car. He came back out with an enormous forty-five pointed in the air. The gun bucked and nearly tore free in the man's weak grip as he fired a round.

"I said get away from my Enzo!"

Mason reached across Iridia's lap and yanked the recline lever. She fell back flat, out of harm's way. Better safe than sorry.

"Stay down," he said as he considered dropping this joker. He was certainly in the gray area of using justified lethal force. But this guy didn't have it in him to kill someone. Mason knew the type. Waving a gun around only worked if nobody called your bluff.

This guy was all bluff.

Besides, Mason had already been in one gunfight that day, and that was one too many already. He'd resolve this another way. A far more satisfactory way.

Mason gunned it and let off the brake. The Bronco's left front tire barely paused before climbing up over the quarter panel and onto the hood of the super car. The Bronco tilted up, like they were in a rocket about to blast into space.

The sound of crunching metal and shattering glass reminded them they were still on the ground. The front tire dropped to the street just as the back tire clawed up to continue the demolition. The Ferrari's engine choked, coughed, and sputtered to silence.

The Bronco pulled forward and the rear tire dropped to the ground with a thump. Mason held his hand out the window, returning the crude gesture he'd received.

The driver's impotent screams faded as they continued on, still canted up with two wheels on the barrier. They made the exit and pulled down the ramp. They passed wide-eyed people as they went.

"You just demolished a Ferrari Enzo, one of the most expensive cars in the world."

Mason grinned. "Not worth a zinc penny now."

They made it down the ramp and hit an intersection that wasn't completely clogged. Mason eased the wheel to the left and the Bronco bucked as the tires dropped to the street.

He patted the dash. "I wouldn't trade this baby for that Italian hunk of junk."

"It wasn't a hunk of junk."

"It is now."

Iridia didn't respond.

Mason mashed the accelerator to the floor and, tires squealing, headed north a couple of streets to get some distance from the insane freeway. He whipped a left on Pico Boulevard and headed west toward Santa Monica. To the local airport there. The surface street traffic was thick, but at least it was moving.

He had no idea how she was going to get out of LA with the airspace shut down. For all he knew, that rule didn't apply to the richest and most connected. Maybe she had a personal exemption waiting. The wealthiest often played by a different set of rules.

Even if she didn't have a flight waiting, he frankly didn't care. His job was to get her to the airport. One second after that, Iridia and all of her supermodel problems would be in the rear view mirror.

Mason almost smiled.

He didn't though because as the thought of dumping her crossed his mind, another part of his brain caught something coming through on the police scanner.

Iridia levered her seat back upright.

"Hello? Earth to bodyguard. Are you even listening to me?"

"Quiet!"

Mason turned up the volume.

All units, code ten. Adam three-six, code three.

Three-six, code three, go ahead.

Adam three-six, vehicle is a two-door, early model, tan Ford Bronco. Westbound on Pico at Normandie. Suspect is a white male, early forties, one-hundred-eighty pounds. Wanted for LAPD Officer's one-eight-seven. Presumed armed and dangerous. Break-

Go ahead.

Adam three-six, be advised ASD SWAT unit en route.

Copy. Three-six in pursuit.

A black and white in pursuit. Air Support Division SWAT en route.

And they thought he killed a cop.

And they were coming for him.

45

THERESA shifted in the backseat, an uncomfortable edge digging into her butt. Her phone, in the back pocket of her pajamas. She almost reached for it. She wanted more than anything to call her dad and get away from these killers.

The short, muscled guy with the pocked face drove. The huge man that killed Max sat between her and Holly in the back seat. If she pulled her phone out, he'd just rip it out of her hand and probably toss it out the window. She'd have to wait for the right opportunity.

They drove east on Rose, leaving the more gentrified neighborhoods closer to the ocean. They continued on down Fourth Street, heading past Indiana and into the rougher streets of Venice. Even with all the changes that had swept through the area, there were still a few blocks that none of the newcomers ventured through after dark.

They crossed Indiana and the homes immediately fell into disrepair. Like some invisible line held the future at bay. Behind them were remodeled houses occupied by the hipster avant-garde. In front of them stewed the dangerous soul of the old Venice.

The very character the hipsters clung to while at the same time wishing very much that bulldozers would level the place so new developments could be built. Ones that would raise their property values and make this neighborhood safe once and for all.

For now, this pocket of sporadic, violent defiance held. Small groups of sketchy looking men lingered on porches and street corners. Always in the shadows, just beyond the light.

The car stopped and the giant man dragged her and Holly out of the back seat.

Theresa's skin crawled at his touch. Thankfully, long sleeves and pant legs covered her bare skin. Holly wasn't so lucky. She wore some tiny, red shorts and a tight, black halter top that accented her ample chest. It didn't matter on a girls' night sleepover.

It mattered now.

Usually, Theresa was crazy jealous of her best friend's curves. It was like God took her portion and gave it to Holly. The girl could turn heads wearing a cardboard box.

She wasn't jealous of the attention now. Already, their captors had made big eyes. She had no idea what they had in mind, but Holly's curves on display weren't helping.

"Hey baby, where you goin?" a voice said from the shadows of a porch behind them. Four dark figures lounged on fold-up chairs. An old car sat in the yard with its front wheels on concrete blocks. A dilapidated chain-link fence surrounded the yard, as it did most yards in the area.

The lewd suggestion in the voice gave Theresa the shivers. Holly screamed when a pit bull slammed into the fence, its teeth bared, going crazy like it wanted to maul them. A hushed laugh floated over from a shadowed figure inside a darkened window covered by thick bars.

"Not quite like your neighbors, huh?"

The short brick of a guy holding Holly laughed as they dragged them across the street toward a two-story house that looked worse off than the other houses on the block.

Which was really saying something.

The street light on the corner didn't work. It was surprising how dark a neighborhood could get without the reassuring glow of nearby lights.

A rusted chain-link fence bordered that small lot too. The gate was open, the door detached and lying in the brown dirt that passed for a front yard. Thumping bass rolled out like thunder through a canyon. A group of three scary-looking guys chatted by the gate while another small group hung around the closed front door.

The house looked like it was built in the 60's and hadn't seen an ounce of upkeep since. Wood siding with traces of peeled paint. Half the windows covered with plywood. Two ragged couches up on the porch. Classic cars restored to perfection lined both sides of the street. Chrome wheels so big and polished you could check your lipgloss in them.

If you were on a date instead of being kidnapped.

"Cesar," one of the guys by the front gate said as he nodded to Theresa's captor. His low-riding pants seemed to defy gravity as they clearly had no butt to cling to. A thick gold chain sparkled on his bare, broad chest. A sling ran across his chest and over his shoulder.

"How's she doing?"

"Been out since a minute or two after I called."

Cesar nodded.

"Stay at your post."

The man with the huge gold chain rotated the sling around and a dangerous looking black rifle appeared in his hands.

"Seguro."

Cesar smiled. "Carnal."

The men by the gate parted like the sea before Moses. Cesar led their group inside the fence.

Theresa had the distinct impression they were entering a cage. One she didn't know how to escape.

Every eye followed Holly as she stumbled forward. She jiggled in the worst way possible for this crowd. Theresa wished more than anything Holly preferred sleeping in a bath robe.

Holly tapped on the guy's shoulder that pulled her along.

"Would you mind not throwing me in the dirt, please?"

He raised his eyebrows at her.

She continued, "What did you say your name was?"

"I didn't."

"It's just that I like to know the people kidnapping me and my best friend. You know, since we're getting to spend so much quality time together."

Theresa blanched. She knew Holly had to be just as terrified as she was. Especially after what happened to Max. But she didn't act it. She acted like they were coming over for dinner. Amazing.

"Evil."

"Pardon me?" Holly asked.

"They call me Evil."

Holly grimaced, her casual facade cracking a little.

"Nice name."

Evil leered at her chest. "It fits."

They marched up the steps and a group on the porch parted to make way. Evil kicked the door open and yelled something that got swallowed up by the audio assault from inside.

Cesar and Evil yanked them into another world.

The bass jabbed Theresa's eardrums. Every beat a vibration that set her jaw on edge. The rank stink of body odor wrinkled her nose. A stronger scent masked it. Something earthy and dank. She'd never smoked it, but she'd bet money it was pot.

Holly looked back and pursed her lips. The tilt of her mouth reflected the masked anxiety.

They took a right into a dim living room. The only light came from illumination not designed to brighten. The ends of cigarettes and rolled joints glowed hot orange as the holders sucked in deep breaths. Phone screens lit faces at odd angles. Many in that lit-from-below way that makes anyone look terrifying. Blinking stereo lights of different colors carved shapes out of other shadows.

A coffee table in the center of the room held an assortment of items, none of which was coffee. Empty and half-empty beer bottles littered the surface and the surrounding floor. A guy seated on the couch picked at a huge pile of clumped marijuana. The guy next to him chopped and sliced at a white ball the size of an olive. As he worked it with a credit card, powder crumbled off. Pills of different shapes and colors were scattered around like someone had spilled out the contents of a rainbow pharmacy.

Theresa's stomach churned. Her palms dampened. Her heart pounded under her ribs. The suffocating air tickled her throat and burned her eyes.

Her mind numbed, she almost didn't understand what was happening in the corner of the room.

A ragged leather chair, stuffing falling out of numerous tears, sat in the corner. Two people occupied it. That wasn't strange. It was easily large enough to accommodate two people.

Theresa squinted through the haze, not believing it at first.

They were screwing! Right there in the chair. Right in front of everyone. A girl with her top off and back to them rode on top of the guy sitting under her. Her skirt was pulled up around her waist. She bounced up and down, almost like she was following the bass beat. A loose tourniquet wrapped around her upper arm like an Egyptian fashion bracelet. The dull yellow rubber accented with black splotches. A hypodermic needle lay on the floor next to the chair. The man underneath grabbed the girl's hair and yanked down as he thrust up.

Theresa's legs went weak. Like her bones turned to jelly and were ready to collapse. She swallowed hard and looked away, trying her best not to scream like a mental patient. Only a couple other people in the room seemed to notice the activity in the corner.

Cesar led them through the living room and into a kitchen in the back. He threw open the fridge and pulled out two forties. Forty ounce bottles of Miller High Life. He cracked the tops off and handed one to each of them.

"Life ain't all bad, blancas. Drink up."

Theresa hesitated, wondering if a polite 'No thank you' would fly.

"Drink," he said in a voice so low it made the bass feel light.

Holly took a gulp from her bottle.

Theresa looked at hers. She brought the bottle to her lips and took a sip.

Disgusting.

Tasted like donkey pee. How anyone could seriously

enjoy this as a beverage was beyond her. She lowered the almost entirely full bottle.

Cesar lifted it back to her lips and leveled his eyes at her.

He didn't negotiate. Max's blood on the kitchen floor was the terrible proof.

Theresa took a few big drinks and sputtered as the foul taste bit her tongue and burned her throat. She coughed and some shot out her nose, doubling her over in a fit of coughing.

Cesar laughed hard and loud.

"Come on," he said as he regained his grip on Theresa's elbow. "Let's go upstairs."

Not good.

Theresa knew what happened upstairs, where the bedrooms were.

46

The grip on her elbow bordered on agony. Cesar's fingers dug into her flesh like a steel claw. Theresa had tried pulling against his grip a few times and only succeeded in tightening the vise-like hold. She and Holly half-walked and half-stumbled out of the kitchen. They passed a bathroom on the right and the stench emanating from it made her stomach heave. She peeked in as they passed, knowing she shouldn't but not able to stop herself.

A shirtless, chubby guy sat on the toilet taking a dump with the door wide open. Scratch that. There was no door. A huge vein in his forehead popped out as he strained. He noticed her and brought his fingers up to his mouth in a V. His tongue flicked out in a disgustingly suggestive motion.

She passed a number of people that stared at the two intruders with unveiled contempt. A girl with more black makeup than good sense stared as they approached.

Theresa tried to look away, but she couldn't. It was like taking your eyes off a rabid dog. You wanted to know where it was. You especially wanted to know where its jaws were.

As Theresa angled her body to slip by, the girl leveled a shoulder through her chest and pinned her against the wall.

"What are you lookin' at?" She spat the words into her face. A thin knife appeared in her right hand and she waved it inches in front of Theresa's cheek. "I'll cut you!"

Cesar watched for a second, evidently waiting to see if the girl would make good on her promise. After a moment, he chuckled and stepped between them. He leaned down and practically swallowed the girl's face with a rough kiss. She seemed to like it. He pulled her head back by the clump of her hair.

"Tranquilo, mija. She gonna get what she deserves."

Theresa's stomach clenched and vomit coughed up into her mouth. She snapped her mouth shut and swallowed it back down. Relief at being saved from the maniac knife girl mixed with that last part of what he said.

The part that didn't sound like it ended any better.

They turned a corner and came up to a guy the size of a basketball player. A dangerous basketball player. He flashed a hand signal and Cesar nodded as they ascended to the second level.

Theresa marched up like she was in a nightmare. Where you keep moving forward and you can't stop even when you know something terrible awaits. The dream pulls you forward, to the horrible ending that you know is as unavoidable as it is deadly.

Shag carpet worn bare in patches extended down the hall. The walls were a patchwork of holes and exposed wood beams. The single light in the center flickered, making it look exactly like a scene in a horror movie. A number of doors lined the hall. Some open and some closed. A guy stood by an open door at the end, facing them.

He looked like a soldier standing guard. Theresa

realized that she'd passed through a few already. The ones at the gate. The ones on the porch. The guy at the stairs.

They were being taken deeper into the cage. A scream bubbled up in her throat. She swallowed it down, knowing it would result in nothing more than provoking a response from their captors.

Cesar paused at a closed door on the left, halfway down the hall. He opened it and peeked in.

Theresa glimpsed an older lady in bed with a girl around her own age sitting next to her. The lady was asleep, or maybe dead. Her skin was ghostly pale with purple and brown bruises all over. The girl wore a white dust mask. She dabbed a damp cloth on the older woman's forehead.

Cesar said something she didn't catch and then shut the door.

Cesar pushed them ahead. She didn't want to know what was inside the far room. That was where this ended. That was where her options ran out.

The guard exchanged words with Cesar as they arrived. The whispered words mingled with the music filtering up from downstairs.

Theresa's belly cramped. She didn't want to die. She didn't want other things to happen either. Things that might be worse than death.

They stepped inside.

Two bare light bulbs hung by cords from the ceiling. The small room had none of the usual bedroom furniture. No bed. Thankfully, there was no bed. No nightstand. No homework desk. No dog bed. No dresser full of clothes. No comfortable chair.

She remembered the chair in the living room. Thankfully, there was no comfortable chair either. This wasn't a bedroom.

But that didn't make it better.

Theresa's breath caught in her chest. Her throat squeezed tighter than the fingers around her elbow. She couldn't breathe.

This was no bedroom. This was a war room.

There were guns. Many guns.

So many guns.

47

A couple of dark wooden chairs sat in the middle of the room. Two long tables lined the side and back walls. They were piled high with guns of every imaginable kind. There must have been a hundred or more altogether. Pistols. Tons of pistols. Small ones that could fit in a pocket. Several that looked like her dad's Glocks. Old style guns with barrels that spun. Quite a few bigger pistols, too. Though none as huge as the chromed one Cesar carried.

That wasn't it by half. Numerous shotguns. Several hunting rifles that looked like they belonged on some savannah in Africa. Fifteen or so black rifles that she didn't know the names of, but looked like the kind soldiers used.

Ammo of different types sat stacked in boxes along the wall. Individual rounds were all over the table tops. Long, thin rifle ones. Short, stubby pistol ones. Plastic shotgun shells.

Like confetti the day after a July 4th parade, drugs covered the tables as well. Syringes. Tourniquets. Rolling papers. Clumpy white balls wrapped in cellophane. Amber vials and clear ones. A trash bag with weed spilling out.

They had enough to open a pharmacy. A chain of pharmacies.

That would've been enough. Too much. But that wasn't all. At the far end of the table were two dark green, round metal balls. Like an apple with an oversized lighter top for the stem. A lever handle clung to the side. She'd never seen one in real life, but there was no question what they were.

Grenades.

Where did they get grenades? It wasn't like the local Wal-Mart carried them. You couldn't go to the farmer's market on Sunday and grab a few grenades with your groceries.

This wasn't Somalia.

There was enough gear here to start a war. Or finish one.

A tall, lanky guy wearing a black wife-beater stood at the end of the table, a shotgun in his hands. Thin, white scars criss-crossed his face and arms like latticework. He racked the slide and pointed it at the wall like he was about to blast a hole in it.

Maybe he was.

"Cuts," Cesar said. "How we doin'?"

"We gonna murder 'em, Jefe," he said.

Murder them?

Holly slumped against the wall next to the door. It almost startled Theresa that her best friend was still there because she'd never felt more alone, more powerless.

Murder them?

Theresa broke for the hall and bounced off the brick wall that was Evil's chest. He grinned. The smile distorted the holes in his face.

Cesar removed the giant gleaming pistol from his high-riding pants. He ejected the magazine and tossed it to Cuts.

"Two more rounds. +P hollow point."

Cuts nodded and starting sorting through the boxes of ammunition.

Two rounds. The two that ended Max's life.

Rage mixed with the terror in Theresa's belly. It boiled into a wicked cocktail that might explode in aggression or implode in surrender.

Cesar admired his chromed pistol. He wiped the side with a black bandana from his back pocket.

Holly swallowed hard and approached Cesar.

"What do you want with us?"

Cesar made no reply. He continued stroking his pistol like he hadn't heard her.

Holly took another insane step closer.

"We'd like to know what you intend to do with us. We have family that will be looking for us."

"I'm counting on it."

Cesar accepted the refilled magazine from Cuts and slammed it into the handle of his pistol. Metal scraped across metal as he chambered a round. He turned to Holly and grabbed her by the neck. She fought him and his grip tightened. He shook her violently until she gave up. Her arms fell to her sides.

He shoved a thick thumb under her chin and tilted her head back. His tongue extended like a snake's. He leaned over and slithered it over the tops of her breasts and up her neck.

He couldn't do this to Holly! He couldn't!

"Stop it! Why are you doing this?"

Theresa wanted to claw his eyes out and she was a hair's breadth away from trying.

Cesar pointed the pistol at her.

The hole in the end looked big enough to swallow her whole. It looked big enough to swallow everything she'd ever known. She couldn't look away. She didn't want to miss the last few seconds of her life.

"Like it?" he asked. He turned the huge gun in his hand. The chromed surface caught the light as it moved. "Desert Eagle Mark Nineteen, fifty caliber. Polished piece of beauty. Does massive damage. But you know that."

He waited for Theresa to respond.

She didn't. She couldn't. Fear froze her solid. She couldn't think. She couldn't move.

Cesar set the pistol on the table and picked up a rolled joint fat as a cigar. He picked up a Zippo and lit the tip. The paper caught and crackled. He drew in a deep breath and the tip glowed orange.

After an endless inhale, he stepped toward Theresa and blew out a hot, rank cloud directly in her face.

The acrid stink caught in her throat. She coughed and hacked. Tears welled up in her eyes. From the smoke or blind terror, she couldn't tell.

"You're at my house," Cesar said. He held the smoldering joint in front of Theresa. "Be a good guest."

Theresa stared at the offering, racking her thoughtless brain for a way to say no that he might accept.

"No thanks. I'm trying to quit."

Lame. It came out before she could stop it.

Cesar raised his brow at Evil and smiled.

"I wasn't asking."

He pushed the wrinkled paper between her lips and let his other hand rest on the silver pistol.

"Deep breaths. Show me you mean it."

Theresa sucked in and the fat tip glowed orange and crackled as hot smoke filled her lungs. She immediately doubled over, hacking and coughing.

The three gang members laughed.

"That was a skinny white girl hit," Cesar said as he turned to Holly. "Let me show you how a girl with curves does it." He wrapped a muscled arm around Holly and pulled her close.

Her wide eyes followed the crackling blunt. Cesar brought it to his lips. He drew in an enormous volume of air. His already large chest expanded half again. A half inch of paper burned away as he pulled on it.

Finally full, he passed it to Cuts and turned to Holly. He grabbed her jaw and squeezed until her mouth opened. He forced his mouth onto hers and exhaled.

She struggled to pull away but his iron grip held fast. His breath filled her lungs. Filled them until gray smoke billowed out her nostrils. Her eyes rolled up into her head. And still more smoke blew out her nose.

She collapsed in his arms and he finally pulled away. Her head lolled back. He yanked her top down, spilling her bare breasts out. He squeezed them roughly and bent down to suck on her nipples.

Theresa wanted to bite his face off. The room spun and her belly did a sickening flop.

He ran his thick tongue over her exposed breasts, up her neck, over her jaw, and shoved it between her unresponsive lips.

"Now that's a hit," Evil said with a laugh.

Holly didn't react. She was completely zoned.

Theresa wanted to scream, but her body seemed so far away. It all seemed so far away. Maybe it needed to be.

The distance might be the only way she'd survive.

48

November 2004
Fallujah, Iraq

MASON gulped down some water from his hydration pack. He looked at the fading daylight filtering through the black smoke that hung over the city. How much longer could they keep at it? They were all beyond exhausted.

They were the walking dead.

He scratched his face and wondered at how odd three days growth felt. Had it only been three days? It seemed impossible. It felt like a hundred years.

Third squad made its way up the street, heading back north. Reports came in that the muj had backfilled previously cleared neighborhoods to the north. So they had the aggravating mission of going back over liberated ground to ensure they wouldn't get surprised from behind.

Evidence of previous battles was everywhere. Houses and buildings flattened to heaps of rubble. Craters in the road where IEDs or bombs had hit. An old Toyota truck halfway down the street burned furiously, sending greasy smoke into the darkening sky.

Mason sniffed the air and grimaced.

The stench.

An unholy reek permeated everything. The air was a thick stew of raw sewage, rotting bodies, burning plastic, and other less obvious repulsive smells. It coated the insides of his mouth like syrup.

The men had begun to mirror their poisonous surroundings.

Most everyone had bouts of debilitating stomach cramps and explosive diarrhea. It was getting to the point where a Marine might find himself literally shitting and shooting at the same time. Oozing sores dotted any exposed area of skin. The smallest nick got infected in no time.

Personal hygiene was for the civilized. A peace time routine that the grueling pace of war made impossible.

Mason picked his way around a pile of rubble and heard a buzzing sound like a bee's nest playing a rock concert. The source came into view.

A hoard of black flies covered a dead body on the street. They were so thick no flesh was visible. Waves of motion swept through the mass.

A fly buzzed into his mouth. He gagged and coughed it out.

Disgusting.

The insects. How could there be so many insects in a desert city? Flies were everywhere. Like this one, hordes had taken over, feasting on the corpses. Once the city was secure, disposal teams would come in to clean up the carnage. But for now, the flies feasted and multiplied.

A wave of them shot into the air and Mason jumped back, smacking his hand at the air to fend them off. The body had been decomposing for a day or two. Half the stomach and ribcage was gone. The torso moved, sending another mass of flies darting for the air.

Mason leveled his rifle at the torso. There was no question it was not of the living. Right?

It jerked again.

"What the hell is that?" Lucky said.

Mason glanced over his shoulder and saw the kid wide-eyed with wonder.

A flap of skin wiggled and a viscera-covered creature crawled out of the torso. It looked up at them, bared its tiny teeth, and growled. Long hair was matted with human innards. Its fat little belly hung nearly to the ground.

Mason turned away, his stomach clenching and doing its best to push puke up his throat.

"Whoa, Sarge! Did you see that? A dog was in there. That was like Luke Skywalker in a Tauntaun! Cool!"

"You're a sick person, bro."

"Come here, Poochie Poochie," Lucky said.

"Leave that filthy mongrel alone. Let's finish this block and find someplace to go firm for the night. I'm beat."

"It's just a sweet little dog, Sarge."

"It just crawled out of a liquefying human torso!"

Lucky waved him off and stepped closer to the growling mutt. His boot landed on a patch of slimed pavement and slipped out from under him.

A single crack echoed through the air.

Lucky fell on his butt as a round snapped through the air where his head had just been.

They scrambled behind the pile of rubble as the continuous crack of automatic gunfire echoed down the street. The rest of the squad dropped behind the nearest available cover and returned fire. Mason checked Lucky over and found no wounds.

"Damn! That horseshoe up your butt amazes me, bro!"

Lucky laughed and shook his head.

"You see, Sarge? It was my being kind to that poor dog that did it."

"Maybe."

Mason glanced back at the rest of third squad.

"Anyone hit?"

All the men checked in okay.

The volume of fire and the distinctive report indicated at least one Russian RPK machine gun had them pinned down. A number of AK-47s added to the deadly fusillade.

Mason peeked over the pile of concrete and saw a dozen or so muj digging in behind a couple of burned out cars at an intersection about two hundred meters away. The strafing fire intensified as more of the enemy brought their weapons online.

An RPG sizzled through the air above Mason's head and exploded into a building no more than thirty meters away.

Another RPG whistled down the street and impacted the pile of rubble Mason was using for cover. Bits of shrapnel rained down and clattered off his helmet. A cloud of heavy dust swept by, leaving him coated in ghostly white.

Mason peeked over and started banging away with the M16. Two jihadis reloaded RPGs while others kept up a steady volley of small arms fire. Mason loaded a forty millimeter shell in the M203 grenade launcher attached to the underside of his rifle. After sighting the distance, he fired. The shell exploded in front of one of the torched cars.

A near miss.

He ducked as bullets pinged the concrete inches from his face.

This was about to go big time sideways. They were on the edge of losing fire superiority. They had to get in the fight or risk being overwhelmed.

"Lopes, go cyclic on those RPGs!"

Lopes nodded and started banging on the SAW.

"Miro, shower them with forty mike mikes!"

"Channing, get on the horn! We need fire support! Now!"

Mason popped up again and laid down suppressing fire. He emptied a magazine and then ducked into cover to refresh it. He looked around. All his men were in the fight. Their muzzles flashing in the deepening twilight. They were giving it their all, but they needed a better angle on the enemy.

A four-story building fifty meters ahead looked like the solution. They could get up a few stories then rain down hellfire on the muj. The problem was the approach. That fifty meters happened to be a patch of ground with no significant cover. Whoever sprinted for the entrance would probably get chewed to pieces.

Mason popped up and banged away. A skinny guy wearing a black bandana over his face collapsed as Mason found his mark.

Channing shouted from across the street, behind a smoking dumpster.

"Sarge, command has an Abrams en route."

An Abrams M1A1 tank. That beast could definitely swing the fight in their favor.

"ETA?"

"Less than five."

Mason got back into the fight. The air streaked with promised death. An RPG screamed in and exploded less than ten meters ahead. Mason ducked as shrapnel shot over the pile of rubble. Another RPG whistled in and hit the dumpster. The concussion knocked Channing on his ass. Miro dropped back to check on him.

Channing waved his arms wildly, screaming incoherently. Miro tried to calm him while calling for their medic.

"Corpsman up!"

He was there in no time, examining the blood pouring from Channing's face.

The Abrams wouldn't matter if they couldn't make it five more minutes.

A delivery van pulled out of a garage at the intersection. It was a patchwork of bare metal and rust. It turned down the street, and the enemy lines parted to let it pull through. The engine roared and the van launched forward.

"Concentrate fire on that van!" Mason shouted.

The jihadis were known for vehicle-borne IEDs. VBIEDs were essentially vehicles packed to the brim with explosives. Bigger ones could take out an entire city block.

The one barreling closer right now was about a hundred meters from being close enough to wipe out all of third squad.

49

Time seemed to slow as the van approached. As if its arrival was an event horizon beyond which there was no return. Mason popped up and fired a 40mm grenade. It exploded on the bumper but the vehicle kept coming. Lopes had the SAW zeroed and bits of glass and metal exploded off the target. But still, it charged forward.

Now fifty meters from being inside a guaranteed kill radius.

This was the end. At least it would be quick.

An instant of vaporized thought. An instant later scattered to the wind.

Mason raged at the inevitability of it. At the ruthless certainty that grasped for his men. For their futures.

An animal aggression reared inside him. A senseless rage that asserted its claim above all others.

He howled and ran to the center of the street, banging away with the rifle. Bullets zipped through his legs, pinged the ground around his feet, snapped by his head.

None of it mattered.

Only the rage.

He fired 40mm grenades in an almost continuous volley. A round hit the front right tire and it exploded. The van crunched to a stop.

Yes!

The engine roared and the van lurched forward. Sparks flew from the metal wheel mount as it dug a channel through the concrete.

The van kept coming.

Oblivion approached.

BOOM.

And then another explosion.

The ground thundered and flung Mason into the side of a building. He bounced to the ground and sucked at air that wouldn't enter his lungs. After slowly working breath back into his body, he propped up against the wall.

Less than a block away, a giant crater was all that remained of the incoming vehicle.

BOOM.

Mason jumped because the explosion came from behind them, to their sixes. Down the street, an Abrams tank rocked back as the concussion of its 120mm main gun sent another shell downrange.

The dozen or so insurgents at the intersection disappeared in a blink.

BOOM.

Another round fired to finish the job.

The hazy intersection flashed with the impact.

The sound of incoming fire went silent. Having a tank at your back made all the difference.

The tank chugged closer as Mason pulled himself up. He needed to check on his men. See how Channing was doing. See if anybody else got hit.

He stumbled as he got to his feet. His head spun with the

ringing in his ears. Like that squeal when someone gets too close to a microphone, magnified a hundred times.

It took them a good fifteen minutes to get everything squared away. Nobody got a direct hit, but there wasn't a patch of skin that didn't bleed from taking shrapnel. Only the clear ballistic goggles they all wore kept their eyes intact. Their medic went from soldier to soldier, taping and bandaging as needed. Channing needed it most. His whole head was wrapped in bandages with two little eye holes. It looked like a bad Halloween costume.

Mason thanked the Army 2-7 tankers before they got called away to another Marine unit needing assistance. He watched as the tank lumbered back down the street.

Lopes slapped his back. "Sure wish those Joes could stick around."

"You're telling me, bro. Make life a whole lot easier."

"Ahh, don't look so glum, Sarge. We're living the dream. Grunts in paradise."

Mason turned back to his men.

"Yeah, right. Where's my Pina Colada?"

"We don't serve sissy booze."

"Fine. Straight Jack will do."

Lopes pursed his lips and shook his head. "Man, wouldn't it?"

Mason laughed at the sudden change in tone. The wistful want of impossibility. He turned Lopes around and wrapped an arm over his shoulder.

"Don't get soft on me, Lance Corporal Lopez. I need badass, knuckle-dragging Marines."

"Well, this Neanderthal needs a rest."

Mason looked at the dark sky. The firefight had chewed up the last of the daylight. His men were wiped out and torn up. They needed to find a spot to hole up for the night. He scanned the area and saw a single story building that looked like it might have been a restaurant in better days.

He pointed.

"Lopes, let's go check that out. Might be a good spot to go firm for the night."

Lopes adjusted the SAW and nodded.

"Miro and Lucky, let's ride."

"Coming, Sarge!" Lucky yelled.

They cleared the place and found a basement level that made it perfectly suitable for a night's stay. There was even a pile of filthy rugs in the corner that they all passed around and used for blankets, despite the horrendous smell. Life in the infantry was like that. It stripped away all the artifice, until the smallest thing could mean so much.

Lucky swept the floor with a flat piece of wood. The floor was littered with discarded syringes and other medical paraphernalia. It must've been a muj hideout not too long ago.

Mason posted a couple of guys on the first floor and sent the rest of the squad below to get some deserved rack time. Within minutes, the sound of small arms fire started to pick up outside. Much of it centered on their position.

The insurgents had located them.

He got on the horn and called in for fire support. The last thing he wanted to do was to have to fight a protracted battle all night long. They were all close to the edge already.

The volume of fire outside picked up.

The Air Force responded a short time later. An AC-130 somewhere in the sky above unleashed on the insurgents outside. Its 30mm Bushmaster cannon buzzed death on the streets below. For his men, it was a guardian angel. For the enemy, it was a deadly demon.

The sounds of danger close fighting died down.

He did a final check on the men and then dropped to the dusty floor. Lopes tossed over a ratty rug. Mason accepted it with a nod. He was grateful to have it. A rug that in normal life he'd dispose of as toxic waste, he now wrapped tight over his body.

His eyelids drooped as he lay back on the floor. He was too exhausted to think. A couple hours would get him going again. The growing chill in the air guaranteed they'd all end up nuts to butts to keep from freezing to death. They'd already spent one night packed together like sardines with only their shared body heat holding back the bitter cold.

He watched flickering shadows cast by dim flashlights. Conversation went quiet as more of the squad drifted off.

What a long day.

The longest.

Day.

Someone kicked his boot.

"Sarge," a forced whisper hissed.

Mason came to the surface. Disoriented. Grumpy to so soon be back in the waking world.

His face itched. Like a feather tickled his cheek.

Another hissed word.

"Sarge."

It was Lopes, on his right.

Mason wanted to itch his face, but his arms were too heavy. Too beat to comply.

"Don't move, bro!"

The words louder now.

A flashlight blinded him and he saw the shadowed silhouette of long, articulated legs. Inches above his eyes.

"You got a camel spider on your face, dude!"

50

The Last Day
Venice, California

ELIO jumped off the South Lincoln blue bus at Venice Blvd. Towering palm trees lined the road west toward the beach. Cool marine air breezed in off the ocean less than a mile away. The salty tang sometimes strong enough to notice. A handful of stars peeked through a thick blanket of light pollution. Even on the clearest nights, you never saw more than a sprinkling of stars in Los Angeles.

He didn't mind.

Too many stars made your place in the universe too obvious. Like they were a thousand reminders that you were infinitely small and unimportant.

The usual dull orange that tinted the sky had a brighter color to it. Especially to the north, where the fires were going off. The hum of traffic faded as he got further away from Lincoln Boulevard. He cut north to avoid Abbot Kinney. It was a swanky street that always promised good cruising, but he wasn't in the mood for people watching tonight.

Venice had it all. He hoped to live here someday. If he could ever afford it.

But how could he ever? He barely made passing grades. No college would accept him. What were his prospects for a good career? None that were obvious. He'd be lucky to get a job washing dishes. There were always five guys in line ahead of him who wanted the same job. They had families to support and no school to interfere with their work hours.

The highway to the good life seemed to have all the entrance ramps shut down.

Which brought him back to the Venice 10. He knew banging wasn't a life that offered long-term security. He knew there were a hundred ways to die once you became a member. But his life wasn't panning out to be all that viable either.

As hard as his mom worked to give him options, it wasn't enough. She could barely keep them in a shared apartment in Inglewood. He didn't blame her. He just didn't look to her to solve his problems.

One thing above all others attracted Elio to Cesar and the life he promised.

No fear.

Those guys feared no one.

And for Elio, that was unimaginable. He lived in fear. Of disappointing his mom. Of not living up to the memory of his father. Of showing his feelings for Theresa. Of what might happen if he joined the gang. Of what might happen if he didn't.

Fear was his constant companion.

He pushed the jumble of thoughts in his mind aside as he arrived at the front gate of Cesar's house. The place was going off. He heard it from a block away. Crazy. The only reason nobody called the cops was because the whole street were either fellow members or lived in fear of retaliation.

If Elio had to choose, he wanted to be the one instilling the fear, not the one drowning in it.

Speaking of fear, he wondered how Cesar was going to react to what happened that morning. Elio had nothing to do with it, but that didn't guarantee anything. You could never tell with the shot caller. It might be nothing. Or he might be walking into the final minutes of his life.

The one thing he knew for sure was that Cesar could never find out that Elio knew Mason. He'd force Elio to give up his address. He'd go there to hurt Mason. Maybe to hurt Theresa.

Stupid Mason. Why did he have to stick his nose where it didn't belong? Did he have any idea of the tight spot Elio was now in because of him?

If Cesar thought Elio was holding out on him…

Elio shivered. He didn't want to think about how that would turn out. Best to claim ignorance and hope for the best.

"Yo Elio, pasale pasale," one of the guys at the front gate said. They all knew him. He knew some of them from kids, before they joined. But this was the first time he'd been to Cesar's house, the informal headquarters of the gang.

Elio nodded as he parted through three bodies that welcomed him in as their own. They knew he might be a fellow soldier soon and so extended him a little respect. Maybe word got around about him facing up to Evil. They either respected the move, or figured he was a dead man who deserved a last kindness.

Four dark figures loitered on the porch. Elio couldn't make out who was who until he got to the bottom step.

"You got a death wish, chavala?"

One of Cesar's soldiers bled out of the shadows and stepped into Elio's path. A long dagger glinted in a pocket of light.

"Nah man. Just showing up like Cesar wanted."

"Smart move. Maybe."

Elio dropped his gaze to show he didn't intend a challenge.

The soldier nodded toward the door.

"Jefe's gonna want to see you. Go ahead."

Elio nodded, trying to keep his legs from collapsing under him. One of the other guys pushed the door open and he headed inside.

The music buffeted his body with a physical force.

It was *loud*.

He wandered right and ended up in what appeared to be a living room. Not that it looked at all like one. Nothing his mother would recognize.

Elio had drunk more than his share of beer and even smoked enough weed to build a tolerance. But what he saw in the living room sent a stutter through his carefully orchestrated stride. The surface projection of confidence cracked.

He was glad Theresa couldn't see him here. This was so not her scene. Not that it was his either. But it was hundreds of miles from hers.

What would she think of him choosing to be around all this?

She'd see him for the lowlife thug the world had already decided he was. Maybe the world was right.

He glanced around. Obvious piles of weed, coke, smack, meth, and other stuff he couldn't identify buried the coffee table. There was enough to get everyone here locked up for life.

To get him locked up for life.

There was even a messed up couple in the corner going at it like doped-up bunnies. Elio shook his head and continued on, hoping to run into Cesar before Evil. He just had to show some face time. Let the shot caller see him hanging with the others. Assuming it went okay, he'd take off after that. His brain definitely wasn't prepared to soak up a full night of what was going on here.

He wondered if he ever wanted to call this normal.

He strolled into the kitchen and thought about raiding the fridge for a beer, but decided against it. His luck he'd be sipping a beer, one of Evil's beers.

Elio seriously wished he hadn't popped off that morning. Especially now, knowing he could run into Evil any second. It did feel good to lash out. Amazing to have gotten away with it. With nothing more than a bloodied nose and busted lip. But it might not be over. The scales not yet balanced.

Now, it seemed like a huge, stupid mistake. Standing up to the Venice 10 lieutenant was like a Chihuahua barking at a wolf. It was wasted noise. The outcome was never in question.

He left the kitchen and passed a bathroom on the right. A fat guy inside was passed out on the floor by the toilet. No shirt and his pants around his ankles. A girl sat on the toilet with her panties around her knees. Her black boots rested on his big belly like it was a foot stool. She raised an eyebrow at him and beckoned him in.

Elio didn't want to know more.

He kept going and saw some Goth Latina girl he didn't know stabbing gashes into the wall. He gave her a wide berth as he walked past. She muttered to herself as she slammed the thin blade home, again and again. "...gut that pretty pig..."

He nodded at a couple of guys he'd met before. He took a left, and bumped into a huge guy he'd seen once or twice. Like the gangster Shaq version.

"Sorry, man," Elio said as he edged to the side and made for the stairs. Maybe Cesar was up there. He'd check the backyard next if not.

The guy bumped him back and shook his head. A flat look in his eyes warned against any nonsense.

"Just looking for Cesar," Elio yelled to make sure he was heard over the music. "He said I should come by tonight."

"Wait here. Don't do something stupid," he said as he raised his shirt to reveal a semiautomatic pistol tucked into his pants.

Elio nodded. He had no intention of pushing this behemoth's buttons.

The guy lumbered up the stairs and disappeared. He reappeared a moment later and waved down to Elio. It felt like he was being ushered behind the velvet rope. Back to the secret party. The one all the regular folks never got to see.

This is what membership could be. Open doors, protected by his brothers. He skipped up the stairs and followed the hulking form down the dimly lit hall. He passed an open door on the right.

A half-dressed girl lay on a bare mattress on the floor. Her top was missing and she didn't seem to care. She scrambled around the room like she'd been bitten by a cobra and the antidote was hidden somewhere in the room. She caught his gaze and turned to face him. The tracks on her arms showed she'd been bitten by something, again and again.

"Don't look at me!" she screamed. Her voice raised another octave, to a shriek, "Don't look at me!"

His escort laughed, "Puta loca," never breaking stride.

Elio stayed on his heels, wondering if he should glance back to make sure the girl wasn't coming after him.

They arrived at the door and the giant literally ducked his head in the doorway.

"Kid's here."

He turned back to Elio and nodded toward the open door.

Elio flattened into the wall to get by.

He entered the room and nearly fell over.

His heart spasmed in his chest. Clenched so tight the pain shot through to his back. The music seemed to fade to silence. Twin bare bulbs hanging from the ceiling painted a surreal scene.

A nightmare.

51

Cesar sat in an old chair that looked like it could barely hold his muscled bulk. Theresa's best friend Holly sat on his lap. Her black tank top stretched under her boobs. Her nipples exposed and all. Cesar had an arm wrapped around her with his other hand snaked between her legs. Holly barely turned as Elio entered. She looked through him like he didn't exist.

Her eyes were glazed over and unfocused. Her head lolled from side to side. He doubted she had any idea what was going on. He hoped she didn't.

That was horrible enough. But the person standing by a table piled high with a huge collection of weapons made it infinitely worse.

Theresa!

What were they doing here? Why were they in their pajamas?

"Elio! Come in!" Cesar said with a grand wave. He took a huge hit on a nearly done roach and then turned Holly's head to his. His lips attached to hers and he blew his lungful of smoke into hers. She didn't pull away.

She was blitzed. In serious trouble.

Elio took a step in and watched Theresa. She leaned against the table, her eyes a little less dulled. She looked at him and recognition flared in her eyes. He shook his head and turned away, hoping she understood his meaning.

Cesar pulled back from Holly and squeezed her boobs. He finally turned to Elio.

"Glad you came."

Elio stood still as stone, at a total loss of what to say or do. As much as he wavered about entering this world, he wanted Theresa to have no part of it. She was better than this. She was too innocent. She had no idea what could happen. He had to get them out of here. But it wasn't like he could just tell Cesar to let them go.

That would gain him nothing more than a beating and the girls would still be no better off. Probably worse off. He did the only thing he could do. He played along.

"Hola, Cesar," he said, "you preparing for war?"

"Preparing to win one. You know what's going on out there?"

"Not really."

"The beginning of the end, ese. Chaos." He smiled like a shark. "Opportunity, for those willing to take it."

"Who is the enemy?"

Elio prayed his name didn't spring to mind.

Cesar ignored the question and leveled dead serious eyes at him.

"Did you know that hero from this morning?"

The threat in his voice was unmistakable.

"No, Cesar. No idea. Some wannabe Bruce Wayne."

Cesar watched him, studying him like a player at a high-stakes poker table. Because he was, betting his life instead of chips.

"I ran into him again. Found his house. Look what turned up there." He looked from Holly to Theresa.

Elio had to get them out of here. Before it was too late. It already felt like it was too late.

"A couple of dumb blancas? You should kick their asses out on the street. Send 'em back to the Third Street Promenade where they belong."

Cesar smiled.

Cuts stood by the table holding a shotgun.

"Let's smoke 'em, Jefe."

Cesar chuckled in appreciation. "You got one answer for every question." The words could've been an insult, except that Cesar said it with all the appreciation of a teacher addressing a star pupil.

"The problem is, I'm liking esta morena." He punctuated the preference by rubbing his hand over the silk cloth covering Holly's crotch. He licked his lips and grinned.

She didn't respond, like her body didn't work.

Elio couldn't let this happen. He had to do something quick. But what?

"And Evil here is liking the other one. He has a thing for flat-ass white girls."

Elio stumbled forward as a body shoved him hard from behind.

Oh no.

Elio turned to see a snarl of malignant glee directed at him. Cesar's right-hand lieutenant walked in. Evil pushed him aside and sidled up to Theresa. She shook out of a daze as his arm wrapped around her waist.

She looked at Elio and recognition sparked in her eyes. She glanced over at Holly and stared for a moment, as if she didn't believe what her eyes were telling her.

Evil squeezed Theresa. "You like me too, eh flaca?"

Elio tried to hide the horror in his heart. The terror in his mind.

As if that was possible in this crowd.

Fear and weakness attracted these wolves like bloody meat. They could smell it a mile away.

And right now, every pore on his body oozed panic.

If Evil figured out they were friends, nothing good would come of it for Theresa. If he found out Elio liked her, she'd suffer. Bad.

Evil turned to Cesar. "Jefe, tu madre esta despierta."

His mother was awake?

Cesar jumped up and shoved Holly to Cuts.

"Keep them here," he said as he left the room. Evil followed close behind.

Elio watched Cuts, wondering if he could grab a gun off the table and cap him without hitting the girls, then escape with the girls, somehow carrying Holly, all before anyone heard what happened and decided to stop them.

"Elio, vamos," Cesar said.

There went that plan.

He followed Cesar to an open door halfway down the hall. As soon as he entered, a foul stench assaulted his senses. So bad it made his eyes water. They filed in and shut the door.

Cesar dropped to his knees at the side of the bed. An older woman lay in the bed. Elio recognized Cesar's sister sitting in a chair next to the bed. She wore a white dust mask that had seen better days. Dark splotches of dried blood covered it. She dipped a rag into a bowl of iced water and then dabbed the woman's forehead.

The moisture evaporated the instant the cloth left her skin. Blistering red sores covered her exposed skin leaking creamy, yellow pus on the bedsheets. Streaks of red mixed with the lighter discharge.

With a tenderness Elio wouldn't have thought possible, Cesar twined his enormous hands around the woman's gnarled, wasted hand.

"Mama?" Cesar said in a whisper.

She turned her head toward him. Blood leaked from the slits of her closed eyes and down onto the pillow.

"Mijo?"

"Si, Mama. How do you feel?"

"I'll be with God soon."

The words cracked and rattled in her chest as they came out. A faint smile etched through the pain evident on her face.

"No."

"His hands now."

"How did this happen, Mama? You were fine yesterday."

"Only God knows, Mijo."

"Then I'll rip the answer from his bloody chest."

"Mijo!" Her thready voice transformed. "Never speak of the savior that way!"

She coughed and blood and spittle ejected from her lips and onto the bed sheets. She collapsed to her former weakened state.

"Tell me who did this, Mama."

"It's God's plan."

"Did they have you cleaning something dangerous? You shoulda quit years ago."

She patted his much larger hand.

"Cleaning kept food on our table."

The words brought more blood up. Her body heaved and collapsed onto the bed.

Cesar adjusted the pillow behind her head.

"You said you're working in labs now, right?"

"So shiny... glass and metal... so clean... Beautiful... except..."

She paused and took a labored breath. It rattled in her chest.

"Except what?"

"Got lost... stained floors... the walls... cages."

Her head lolled to the side and she opened her eyes to look at her son. The pupils were huge empty discs surrounded by red. The blood vessels in what should've been the white part were enormously swollen. One burst and blood streamed down her cheeks.

"Mama, what did you see?"

She whispered something. Her voice cracked and the faint words got lost in the muted background of music from downstairs.

Cesar leaned closer.

"What?"

Her body convulsed and went deathly still.

"Mama?"

Her fingers fluttered in his wide palm.

"Tell me."

She swallowed hard. The effort almost too much. Cesar turned his head and placed his ear by her mouth.

The faintest whisper escaped her lips and then she died.

Elio wondered at how her body somehow felt empty where a second before it felt occupied. As weak as she was, she was still there, animating it. Now, it felt like a vacated home. Shabby and dark without the light of the soul inside.

Cesar stood and kissed the top of her head. He tenderly laid her hands to rest on her chest. He reached across her body and squeezed his sister's hand.

"Take care of her, Julia."

His sister nodded and dropped her head. Tears streamed down her cheeks as she returned her heavy gaze to their mother.

Elio never expected this. That Cesar had a heart. That he was vulnerable. That he loved and could experience loss. The two pictures in his head wouldn't line up.

"I'm sorry, Jefe," Evil said. "Your mother was a saint."

"She was."

Cesar turned to face them. Whatever warmth or softness might have animated his eyes seconds ago was gone. Cold fury burned in them now.

"What'd she see, Jefe?" Evil asked.

"Sangre. Por todos lados."

Blood. Everywhere.

52

They filed out and returned to the war room. Evil awkwardly patted Cesar on the back. The shot caller batted his hand away.

"What do you think happened?" Evil said.

"Don't know, but I bet her boss does."

"We gonna pay him a visit?"

"Si. I'm gonna find out what happened. And then I'm gonna murder him."

"What can I do?"

"Round up some trigger pullers," he said to Evil. He then turned to Cuts. "Two rides." He pointed at Theresa and Holly. "Those two with me. Maybe we party after." He reached over, grabbed Holly's jaw and yanked her close. He leaned down and shoved his tongue into her mouth.

She didn't flinch. She barely remained standing. She was messed up.

Elio didn't want to think about what kind of party Cesar had in mind. He was sure Holly and Theresa wouldn't willingly do it. He was just as sure they wouldn't have a choice.

Cesar yanked her top up over her breasts and then Cuts pushed them out the door.

Elio picked up a heavy shotgun and wondered if it was loaded. He could turn it on Cesar and pull the trigger. He should do it. It might be loaded. But what if it wasn't?

Cesar would kill him. And then what would happen to the girls? To Theresa?

If only he could think of a way to save them. Like a traffic accident that you see just in time and swerve around at the very last second. But he couldn't. He wasn't the one driving.

Cesar took the shotgun out of his hands and loaded a shell into the tube.

SHUCK-SHUCK.

"Gotta load it if you want to do some damage."

Elio couldn't let them go alone. They'd have no chance if he got left behind.

"Let me go with you."

"You?" Cesar laughed. "You got it in you to kill somebody? It ain't like a video game."

"I want in. I'm ready."

Cesar narrowed his eyes, measuring the words. He clicked off the safety and turned the gun on Elio. The barrel came to rest on his chest.

Elio watched as Cesar's finger curled inside the trigger guard and rested on the trigger. Half an inch of a curled finger stood between him and his heart and lungs painting the bedroom wall. A cold sweat broke out all across his body. He shivered and bit down to stop his teeth from chattering.

The shot caller was going to murder him and then rape Theresa and Holly. So much for a brilliant rescue. Like so much of his life, Elio's final act would be a disappointment too.

"You know what you're saying?" Cesar asked. He pushed the barrel forward, pinning Elio to the wall.

Elio nodded, the signal subtle to avoid causing Cesar to accidentally pull the trigger.

"Okay. Blood in. Blood out. One way in. No way out."

Cesar let the weight of the barrel dig an impression into Elio's chest.

The gun clicked and his knees almost collapsed. He wondered what his heart looked like on the wall.

It was just the safety, he realized with a start.

The barrel pulled back. The hole at the end looked big enough to drive a car through. Cesar set the shotgun on the table.

"This one's too big for you."

He picked up another gun and slammed a long magazine into it. A flick of the wrist and a 9mm round fed into the chamber. He rotated it, looked it over with appreciation, and then handed it to Elio. "TEC 9. Thirty-two round magazine. Fully automatic. Sprays like a water hose."

Not like any water hose Elio had ever used.

"You gonna kill somebody tonight, ese."

Elio's knees went weak again. His legs buckled backward, locking out and keeping him up against the wall.

There was only one way to become a member of the Venice 10. Blood in. You had to kill somebody. Once you committed, there was no going back. If you failed or changed your mind, you were a dead man.

In trying to save Theresa and Holly, Elio had signed up to become a murderer.

53

THERESA noticed the dark tunnel strangling her world starting to open. The black edges around her vision shrank as the inner core of color expanded to closer encompass her normal vision. Sound still echoed in a disturbing way, like everything was on a time-delayed, fading loop. Her head spun and her stomach reeled.

She knew it was weed that Cesar had forced her to smoke. But there must have been something else in it. Her limbs felt like they were only half-connected to her body. She stumbled as Cuts shoved her forward.

"Guests of honor, tonight," he said as he marched her and Holly through the living room. His words seemed to play in her head, then play back and play back. Three or four times before fading away. Like echoes traveling through a canyon. Maybe it was the music dropping sledgehammer bass notes on her brain.

Everything was familiar in a distant and not totally significant way.

Everything but Elio. He was there. He'd come for her.

But then warned her away. She didn't know what to think of it.

They exited the house and walked down the concrete path. The guys she'd seen hanging out earlier in the front yard were nowhere to be seen.

Holly pitched forward and Theresa caught her before she planted face first.

"Are you okay?" she asked in a whisper.

Holly didn't respond.

She wrapped Holly's arm around her shoulder, partly to steady her and partly so she could whisper in her ear.

"Holly, are you okay?"

Holly turned her head as if hearing a sound she once knew, her eyes unfocused and jaw loose. Cesar had filled her lungs many times. The first time was more than enough to shut her down.

Theresa had choked on the puffs that Cesar forced her to take. Partly because it burned her throat and lungs. And partly because choking and coughing got it out faster.

Two four-door cars waited in the street. The one in front was sky blue. The one in back was the same red one in which she'd ridden earlier. Both were classics with shimmering paint and polished chrome. The frames inches off the pavement. Dark windows hid whoever was inside. The back door of the second car flew open and a cloud of smoke wafted out.

Cuts shoved them both toward it. As they neared the dark opening, Theresa leaned back, not wanting to go inside.

"Get in," Cuts said.

She grabbed the doorframe and braced herself to resist.

SCHWICK.

A knife appeared at her throat. The hard line of the blade bit into her skin.

"Don't make me tell you again."

She dropped her head and climbed in.

The same black leather bench seat. Empty beer cans on the floor. The driver looked at her in the rear view mirror. Holly fell in on top of her and Theresa scooted and pulled until she got them both up and seated. The door slammed shut.

Theresa glanced at the door on the opposite side. She had a vision of throwing it open and running away before anyone could catch her. That would still leave Holly in trouble. Holly could barely walk, much less run.

Theresa couldn't leave her.

Cesar had already violated her best friend. The disgusting pig wasn't going to do it again if Theresa could help it.

The only problem was, she didn't know if she could help it. She wasn't her dad. She had no weapons. No training in how to use them, even if she did. She'd never killed anyone. She'd never even fought anyone.

She needed her dad. Now more than ever. If anyone could save them, he could. But he had no idea she was taken, or where to go even if he knew. It was hopeless.

Or was it?

Wait. The app. The app on her phone!

The tracker, big-brother app that she'd fumed over. Activating it would send an alert to his phone showing her phone's location on a map.

Tracker 911, or something.

Hope sparked in her breast. Her dad might save them. That was his job.

She dug in her back pocket and pulled out the phone.

She thumbed it on and the screen flashed in the dark interior. Her fingers trembled as she raced to turn down the brightness. She peered up into the rear view mirror just as the guy in the driver's seat looked back. She smiled and he looked away with a snarl.

Evil, Cuts, and three other guys piled into the blue car in front.

Theresa looked back down and swiped through screens packed with apps. She was terrible at clearing out the old junk and enthusiastic about adding whatever new thing sparked her interest. She swiped all the way to the last screen and saw nothing that looked like Tracker 911.

Movement to her left caught her attention. Cesar and Elio walked through the open gate and toward the car.

She swiped through again. It had to be there.

Cesar opened the car door.

Then she remembered. It was in the Junk group. She found the group and tapped it to open the contents.

Cesar slid in next to Holly, shoving her and Theresa over as he entered.

There it was. Tracker 911. A little red cross with antennae waves coming off. Her finger shot toward it and smacked into Cesar's rough hand as he ripped the phone out of her grasp.

"Don't need this tonight," he said and passed it to the guy driving. The driver dropped it on the bench front seat.

Elio opened the passenger front door and slid in. The dark silhouette of a pistol-machine-gun-thing with a long magazine in his hand.

What was he going to do with that?

Elio slammed the door shut and caught Theresa's eye before looking away.

Cesar pounded on the back of the driver's seat.

"We going down the rabbit hole tonight! Vamos!"

The driver kicked up the music and speakers somewhere behind the seat shook Theresa's insides.

Holly's head lolled back on the seat. She stared at the ceiling like it was playing a silent movie.

Theresa wondered if this evening would turn out to be a horror flick.

54

The blue car in front pulled off with a screech. Theresa slid back into the seat as theirs did the same. Headlights came on as they rolled down the street.

Cesar pulled out a walkie-talkie and clicked it on.

"Hey, we're going to the Milagro Building downtown. Head up Lincoln and over on Pico. Stay on surface streets."

He leaned forward and smacked Elio's shoulder.

"Our boy Elio is gonna smoke somebody tonight."

The walkie-talkie screeched and then a blast of incoherent howls and yells responded.

"Pinche animales," Cesar said with something like love in his voice.

They continued on, leaving behind the seedier streets of Venice, and took a left, going north on Lincoln. They threaded through heavy traffic and entered Santa Monica as Theresa tried to think of something. Her brain moved thoughts like cars through waist deep mud.

What could she do?

She had to get her phone back. Her dad was their only

hope. He could save them. And he had to do it before Elio did something he could never take back.

But it wasn't like she could just reach over and grab it. How then?

The cars continued east and passed Santa Monica College on the right. Theresa figured her plans for going there for two years to help bring down the cost of a degree were meaningless now. Dreams for the distant future were meaningless when your life wouldn't extend much beyond the present.

They pulled up to a red light and stopped. Next to them, a police car eased to a stop. Two troopers looked over in their direction.

She doubted they could see much through the dark tinted windows.

The music in their car dropped to silence.

Would they hear if she yelled?

The urge to throw the door open and scream her head off contracted her muscles. Then something cold and hard touched her arm. She looked down.

Cesar's chromed pistol touched her arm.

"Want to live?"

She nodded, her eyes glued to the light reflecting off the side of the gun.

The stoplight turned green and the police car pulled off.

Her stomach rolled over and died.

That might have been their last chance. And she was too scared to take it.

The music kicked back up and they continued east, following the blue car. The night was lit by a blur of neon business signs. Between buildings, the towering, illuminated skyscrapers of downtown Los Angeles slipped into view.

An old Bronco approached in the opposite lane. The silhouette exactly like her dad's. Maybe he'd followed them. Maybe he was just waiting for the right moment.

It drew closer and the white paint and the stranger at the wheel shattered the dream. How could it've been him? He had no idea where she was. She had to change that.

But how?

An idea popped into her head. Stupid, but she didn't have any better ones trying to cut in line.

She leaned forward and spoke across Holly's immobile body. "Can I give Elio a lucky kiss? You know, put a little lead in his pistol?"

She bit her lip and tried to look sexy. It wasn't something she practiced so she had no idea how it came off. Probably ridiculous.

"Pop his cherry, blanca. He's gonna be a big boy tonight."

Theresa leaned over the front seat. She held his head forward and bit his jaw. He tasted salty and kind of good.

She bit his earlobe and licked the curve of his ear. She whispered, "Tracker 911 on my phone. Open it." She turned his head back toward hers and brought her lips to his. Her tongue slipped into his mouth. His teeth parted and she probed deeper.

Her heart raced and her stomach clenched. From fear or desire, she wasn't sure. She pulled back, praying the ruse worked. She fell back into the seat, licking his salt from her lips.

Did he hear her?

The music certainly covered her message. But did it drown it?

Elio glanced back at her. His eyes wide with wonder.

Cesar slapped his face forward. "Do it right tonight and maybe I'll share a piece of her."

Elio's back stiffened and his jaw twitched. "I'll do what has to be done." He looked back at Cesar. "How about a little more of that? I need to get my blood up, you know?"

Cesar grinned like a hyena. "Nothing like panocha to get you up for capping pendejos." He turned to Theresa. "Hop up there and give the kid a taste."

Theresa couldn't believe Elio would force her into this. She did it as a diversion. She didn't not like it, but she definitely didn't like being ordered around by this thug.

She must not have moved fast enough because Cesar grabbed her arm and yanked her forward. She pitched over the seat and got a slap on the butt as she went.

Her face landed in Elio's lap. She looked up and Elio's brown eyes were wide and white. She scrambled up and sat between him and the driver.

In the back seat, Cesar roared. "Blanca can't wait to get some!"

"Jerk," she muttered, only half-hoping the music muffled the comment.

Something jabbed in her hip and she was about to look down when Elio encircled her neck and pulled her forward. He kissed her ear.

"It's fingerprint protected."

She'd totally spaced the fact that her phone only opened to her thumb print, or the four digit code that she'd never shared with anyone but Holly and her parents. And her parents only because she had to.

Elio wasn't forcing himself on her. He was helping her pull off her plan!

He turned her to face him and his lips crushed into hers. Was it an act? His passion didn't feel fake. His other hand found hers. The smooth surface of her phone landed in her fingers. His tongue slipped into her mouth. He was full of surprises. She held it down at her side, sandwiched between their bodies.

"Get some, vato" Cesar shouted.

Electric tingles shot to her toes. The current made it hard to think. Harder than it already was. Her heart beat wild and fast. An intoxicating brew of fear and longing.

Still locking lips, she thumbed the phone on and the roof above her head caught the dim illumination. She tapped the tracker app. At least she hoped she did. She wasn't about to blow it by staring directly down at the phone.

She had to turn it off. They'd notice any second.

Elio twisted her head to the side and bit her neck. Chills swept down her spine and prickled the hairs on her arms. A warmth in her belly spread lower. Her breath came in ragged pants.

She somehow remembered the plan and peeked down to see that she'd launched YouTube instead. Taylor Swift was about to get her busted. A few swipes later and she activated Tracker 911.

The car swept through a section of West Los Angeles where the businesses were more spread out. The passing lights outside went dim and the illumination on the ceiling had to be obvious. She watched as the tracker map came up, pinpointing her position.

Please Dad. Please have your phone on.

She clicked the display off, knowing the app would continue broadcasting her position to the synced app on her dad's phone.

If he had it on. If he was checking it.

Elio pulled away and stared into her eyes. She nodded just enough to let him know she did it.

And then she realized something totally insane.

Despite the clear danger of the situation. Despite the likelihood that any number of terrible things were about to happen. Despite everything.

She wanted to kiss Elio again.

Maybe it was the fuzziness that made her brain feel like sun-soaked cotton. Maybe it was that she'd never been more certain about anything.

Whatever it was, she went with it.

She leaned forward into Elio's embrace and their lips pressed hard together.

55

MASON waited at a red light at Pico and Western. There had been no sign of police pursuit. Maybe he was wrong and they were going after someone else. There hadn't been an update since the original report. It was possible they'd shuffled over to a private channel.

He looked in the rear view mirror and up and down Western. No flashing lights.

A few more miles and they'd be at the Santa Monica airport. He could drop off Iridia to whatever fate would decide for her. Get back home to check on the girls and Max. He needed to call Beth. Something big was going down and he didn't like her being all the way over on the east side of the city. That was too much humanity between them.

If what the news showed was true, it was too many possible points of infection. Too many possible points of trouble.

He touched his phone to check in and started as it chirped at him. Not the ring of a call, but the chirp of an app notification. He pulled it from the change holder below the radio and flinched when he saw the illuminated screen.

Tracker 911 had an urgent message. He thumbed it on and the app showed an emergency alert from his daughter's phone. A map showed it heading east on Pico. Less than a mile west of his position.

Why was her phone not at home, where she should be? Was it stolen? Was it a glitch? He pulled up favorites. Only two slots were taken. His wife and his daughter. His mother needled him about that constantly.

He tapped his daughter's name and it went through to voicemail after the first ring, like she'd clicked it off. He left a quick message and then called again. Straight to voicemail.

Theresa knew not to play around with that app. He had stressed the importance of using it only in an emergency.

He had no idea why, but this was an emergency.

Maybe that was the definition of one. If it made sense, it wouldn't have happened in the first place.

Mason prayed it had nothing to do with the madness he'd seen on TV. Why would it? His chest ached. His fingers tingled numb. What was she doing?

If she was safe, he'd kill her. If she wasn't safe, he'd kill anyone that harmed her.

"What's going on?" Iridia asked.

The supermodel was still with him. He'd forgotten her completely. She could forget about getting to the airport. Professional responsibility fell a far cry short of parental responsibility. He had one mission now.

Get his daughter.

"My daughter. It's an emergency of some kind. I don't know, but it's serious."

He tapped on the brake and focused all of his mental power on changing the red light to green. It stayed red.

"Whatever," Mason said as he checked both ways and then floored it through the intersection, narrowly avoiding taking off the rear fender of a legally crossing car.

Red and blue lights flashed through the windshield as a black and white he hadn't seen coming north on Western flipped a left and blasted the siren. The cruiser pulled up on his bumper.

"Pull over," a loud speaker shouted.

He didn't have time for a stupid ticket. Or worse. What if they *were* looking for him?

Who knew what was going on with Theresa. Every fiber in his body wanted to floor it. The dispatcher didn't mention his name or license plate number. Mason knew they would have if they'd had it.

He had two choices. Pull over and hopefully get a quick ticket and continue on. Or two, initiate an OJ-style police chase. If he wasn't identified yet, that would blow it in no time.

He nearly punched a dent into the steering wheel as he turned on the blinker and pulled to the side of the road.

"What are you worried about?" Iridia said.

Mason snarled a response and didn't elaborate. He didn't have the time or inclination to fill in Ms. AllMeAlltheTime.

"Let me handle it," she said.

He shifted into Park but didn't turn off the Bronco. If they got wind he was wanted, he wasn't going to go quietly. He had no desire to break the law, but he didn't have a choice. Theresa was in danger. He had to get to her. Everything else was secondary.

He glanced at his phone. Her phone was heading in his direction, now just four blocks away. He looked down the street and didn't see anything obvious in the stream of traffic forcing their way through the congested lanes.

Tapping on the side window got his attention.

"Please roll down your window, sir."

An LAPD officer with a Maglite as big as a baton stood by the window. He looked young, barely out of the academy young. His head was level with the window, which made him on the tall side. At least six feet. He tapped the hard metal casing to the glass again.

"Down."

"Sure," Mason said and he complied.

"License and registration."

Mason leaned over to grab it from the glovebox.

Iridia stopped him.

She was weeping. Her face a puffy mess of tears and anguish.

Where did that come from?

"I'll get it, Uncle Mason," she said. She got his wallet and the registration paper and handed it over. The paper fluttered in her trembling hand. She collapsed forward, sobbing into her knees.

Uncle Mason? Did he have to be the old uncle?

The officer shined his light into the car, illuminating her face.

"Are you okay, ma'am?"

Iridia turned and wiped away the moisture on her cheeks. Mason would've sworn her favorite pet fish had died or something.

"Hey, are you that Sports Illustrated girl?"

Iridia nodded with a sad smile.

"Wow. The guys are never gonna believe this."

He coughed, as if remembering his position as enforcer of the law and not as lusty teenage stalker.

"Sir, are you aware you just ran through a red light?"

Mason was about to answer when Iridia let loose with another howl of anguish.

"Ma'am—"

She sniffed and turned to him. "Iridia. Call me Iridia."

His eyes widened like he couldn't believe it.

"Iridia, are you okay?"

Iridia shook her head and buried her face in her hands.

Mason decided to play along. He didn't know what else to do. He patted her back.

"There there, honey."

Iridia faced the officer again. She really was convincing.

"It's my mother. She's been in a bad accident. Uncle Mason was taking me to the hospital. If she dies…"

She let loose with another pained howl.

Mason almost forgot it was nonsense. He wondered what happened to her mother. That director made a huge mistake. She was good.

"I'm so sorry to hear that, Ma'… Iridia."

He handed the papers back to Mason.

"Listen, I understand wanting to get to her, but just slow it down. Getting into an accident yourself isn't going to make things better."

"Thank you so much, officer," Iridia said. "You're my hero today."

His face turned pink and he looked down. He patted the window sill. "Well, I'll let you off on this one. Just obey the traffic laws and we'll all get where we're going in one piece."

"Thank you, sir," Mason said. He tapped the brake, hardly able to keep his hand from the shifter. They needed to go.

Now.

The officer looked at Iridia again.

"I hope she's fine."

Iridia pursed her lips and nodded at him, doing her best not to break down again.

The officer walked back to his cruiser and shut off the lights.

Mason shifted into Drive and did his best not to squeal the tires as he pulled back into the lane.

"You're welcome."

Mason turned to Iridia wiping away the last bits of moisture from her cheeks. She was already normal again. Which meant irritating. But she did save him there.

"Thank you. And if I were a director, I'd hire you."

She grinned.

"You'd be an idiot not to!"

Mason checked the map on his phone. Theresa's tracker icon was right in front of his. Practically on top of each other. He scanned through the windshield.

And then he saw it.

The metallic red lowrider he'd seen cruising down his street earlier that day.

Of course. He should've trusted his instincts. Now Theresa was in trouble. And it was his fault. From start to finish.

The lowrider cruised past.

He stared at it but couldn't see anything through the dark tinted windows. He checked his phone again. Her icon passed his and headed away behind him.

He whipped a U-turn as soon as a car length opened up in the opposing direction.

The interior of the Bronco washed out white as a blinding light hit. Mason slammed on the brakes.

"Stop and exit the vehicle!" a loud speaker roared.

The light wavered away an instant.

A black LAPD Huey hovered above the next intersection, not fifty feet off the ground.

The red lowrider passed under the chopper and continued heading toward downtown.

"Stop and exit the vehicle!" the loud speaker thundered.

Black-clad SWAT guys fast-roped to the ground. The six man team spread out across the road, each taking cover behind a nearby vehicle. Their rifles all aimed at the Bronco.

Mason checked the rear view. Red and blue lights flashed from behind as two cruisers screeched sideways, blocking off both lanes. While looking in the mirror, he noticed a cloud of bright red dots swarming on his chest and face.

If he had any options, he couldn't think what they might be.

56

"Exit the vehicle and get on the ground! You have ten seconds to comply."

Mason remembered the police scanner and turned it up.

All teams, this will be a sniper initiated assault.

Team two, ready for go.

Team five, ready for go.

Team four, ready for go.

All teams, on my count. Wait for my count.

Mason shifted into Park. Was this really happening? He just wanted to get to his daughter. That was all. If they took him away in handcuffs, he'd never get to her in time.

"This is your final warning. Exit the vehicle now!"

Iridia grabbed his arm. "What do we do? I don't want to die! I don't want to die!"

Would they open fire? Surely it was a bluff. Where was due process? The right to life and liberty? But they thought he'd killed one of their own. They thought he was a murderer.

All teams, on my count. Three, two,—

Mason opened the door.

Hold fire!

Being hauled away in a body bag wasn't going to save Theresa.

He stepped out with his hands up and squinted hard when the blinding spotlight jabbed his eyes. He turned back and held a hand out for Iridia.

"Come on. Move slow and keep your hands visible."

She climbed across the seat and down out of the open door.

The loud speaker barked again.

"Both of you! Face down on the ground with your hands behind your head! Now!"

Mason lowered to his knees and helped Iridia do the same. This wasn't how he saw this job going. Putting a client in the middle of a SWAT takedown wasn't in the playbook. Or maybe it was, under the examples of the absolute worst things to do. This op had been a wreck from the start. That's what you got with no planning and a world famous client.

The Huey spun up and lifted higher into the air. Buffeting wind nearly pushed him over backward. He kept his hands up, not wanting to give anyone the slightest reason to pull a trigger.

Uniformed police officers rushed bystanders on both sides of the road away from the action.

Two SWAT guys broke cover. Running in a low crouch, they leapfrogged from car to car as they approached.

"Face down on the ground!" the loud speaker ordered again.

It felt like a Hollywood action movie, only he was the bad guy that everyone wanted to see get taken out. But for the knowledge that any sudden movement would result in his immediate death, he'd already have been sprinting down the road after his daughter.

A furious thumping approached from behind. Mason turned and saw the ominous silhouette of an AH-64 Apache gunship about a block north. It hovered with its M230 chain gun and missile bays aimed at them.

Wasn't this overkill? He wasn't an international terrorist. He wasn't even a bad guy, if anyone would take ten seconds to find out for themselves.

Team two, get back to cover!

The advancing SWAT soldiers retreated back to join the rest of their unit.

Mason watched as all their muzzles raised into the air and acquired a new target. The Apache.

The police scanner cut through the whirling winds.

Unauthorized Huey helicopter, I repeat, you are in restricted airspace.

This is LAPD SWAT! It's our airspace!

Unauthorized Huey helicopter, this airspace has been closed by presidential order. No local operations are approved. Ground your bird immediately.

We are about to apprehend a murder suspect! Back off!

Mason felt like a rabbit caught in a bear fight. This wasn't where you wanted to be if the claws started flying.

Unauthorized Huey helicopter, your mission has not been cleared by federal authorities. Ground your bird. We will shoot you down if necessary.

Back off! You can't order us down!

The Apache's chain gun let loose. Thirty millimeter rounds lanced through the air, less than twenty feet from the nose of the Huey. A warning shot.

Hold your fire! I've got six snipers zeroed on your fuel tank!

The Apache's chain gun roared again, this time shredding sheetmetal and glass.

Several SWAT guys went down. The howl of the chain

gun swallowed their screams. Cars didn't do much to stop the onslaught. One guy in black ran for the cover of a building. He fired bursts at the Apache as he went. He didn't make it. A volley from the gunship literally tore him in half. His upper body ripped loose and tumbled to a stop as his lower body ran another step before collapsing.

Iridia screamed. At least it looked like she did, but Mason couldn't hear anything above the whumping blades and the thundering cannon.

Several uniformed officers behind them opened up on the Apache with service pistols. Their bodies exploded. Vaporized by a torrent of fire. Their black and white cruisers crumpled and caved inward as rounds chewed them to pieces.

The scanner squawked.

Noooo! Noooo!

The Huey tilted up and clawed for altitude. It swung around as a gunner leaned out the side. He aimed at the Apache and went cyclic with an M4.

He barely got his finger on the trigger when a missile shrieked from the Apache. It lasered through the air not fifty feet above their heads and broadsided the Huey.

Mason grabbed Iridia and dove under the Bronco as an enormous fireball exploded in the sky. He curled around her as a blast of superheated air washed over them. Pieces of twisted metal fell to the ground like a tornado had touched down on a junk yard. Shrapnel exploded through glass store fronts. Store alarms went off, adding to the sonic tsunami.

Mason took a breath and choked on the acrid stink of burned oil, and worse. He lay still, curled around Iridia, a shell keeping her alive. He blinked to clear his head as much as his vision.

"You okay?"

The words croaked out, but she seemed to understand.

She nodded, eyes wide and unblinking.

Mason crawled out from under the Bronco, staying close to the side, wondering when a bullet would take off his head.

None did.

He looked around.

The cars in the middle of the street that the SWAT guys used for cover were hardly recognizable. They were twisted heaps of fragmented slag. Partly demolished by the chain gun. Partly melted by the Huey explosion.

Dozens of bystanders sprawled on the street. Some injured. Some worse. The lucky ones filled the street with their wailing voices. Mason turned back to the still-present whumping of the Apache a block away.

His shoe squished on something.

He didn't want to know.

The Apache's loudspeaker boomed.

"Citizens of Los Angeles. Return to your homes. Martial law is in effect. Curfew hours will soon be declared."

Mason had no intention of returning home. Not without his daughter. He reached under the Bronco and helped Iridia stand.

She leaned hard on him as she took in the scene.

He nodded toward the Apache.

"You're not getting out on a plane tonight. And I have to find my daughter."

"What about all these people?"

The gunship powered up and lifted higher into the air. It dipped its nose and disappeared over the roofs.

The screaming in the street grew louder. Or felt louder now that it no longer competed with the gunship's rotors.

A lot of people needed help here. Mason was no doctor.

And yet that didn't absolve him from trying. But what if Theresa got hurt because he delayed here? What if those precious seconds spent here ended up being the very same ones that meant life or death for her?

He'd never forgive himself. He wouldn't want to live with that hanging over his head. He knew baggage. He knew that aching weight more than anyone. And he knew with absolute certainty that losing his daughter would be the end of everything he cared about.

It was the fog of war. The uncertainty of knowing the right answer. The predicament of having no right answer. Only the one you went with and made work. He prayed he was making the right decision.

"My daughter needs me. I have to go."

57

November 2004
Fallujah, Iraq

MASON packed yet another oversized pinch of Copenhagen into his lower lip. The zing of nicotine couldn't arrive fast enough. He winced in pain. The bite wound below his right eye oozed creamy pus. The whole area was swollen, to the point where he couldn't see more than a slit through that eye.

Lopes slapped his shoulder.

"Like a little girl, bro!"

"Shut up," Mason replied.

The whole squad hadn't let it go for two days now. In their version of the event, he screamed like a little girl swatting the camel spider off his face. That wasn't how he remembered it.

He was fighting for his life! That monster had nearly chewed his head off!

He'd succeeded in batting it away, but not before the loathsome creature had gouged a chunk out of his cheek.

The whole squad chased the monstrous arachnid around the room for two minutes until Miro finally got a boot on it.

Big as your hand. Mandibles like a wood chipper. Eight long, jointed legs. Hairy. Repulsive.

Not venomous, though, so Mason figured he got away with minimal injury. And now two days later, the wound had half his face puffed up like a balloon. Touching anywhere near the area shot daggers into his brain. It had to be drained every few hours. The crud that spurted out was so revolting it was almost fascinating.

Lopes laughed. "I'm not saying I would've done it any different."

"I didn't scream."

"Sounded like a scream."

"I yelled. Roared. Howled. Bellowed. Manly stuff."

Not that he chose to get bit, but he was glad that it gave the men something to joke about. Some light humor while they moved through such a dark place.

So much of the last week had been filled with misery and heartache. He'd lost four Marines. Two killed in action, and two critically wounded that had been flown to Germany for further treatment. Down to nine men, they were a weaker unit for the losses.

However, they were also harder for it. More determined. More resolved. More certain than ever that every last terrorist would surrender or pay for what happened to their brothers.

The mental toughness juxtaposed with their physical condition. Every man had lost enough weight that their eyes looked sunk in and their cheekbones protruded in a grotesque way. They hadn't bathed in a week. Scrubbing moist towelettes over the filthiest regions was the best they could muster.

It wasn't enough, not by a long shot.

They'd devolved into base animals—comfortable, or at least resigned, with their caked filth. Their dreams had boiled down to three simple comforts. A good night's sleep, hot chow, and a hot shower. Things all the Rear Echelon Motherfuckers took for granted. REMFs lived comfortable lives behind the wire, inside the safety of the base. This gulf of experience created an invisible line that separated infantry from everyone else.

A grunt's life was sometimes torture, but Mason wouldn't have it any other way. He was here for his men. To see that the rest of his squad got back in one piece. There was no place in the world he'd rather be.

The nicotine buzz tickled his system, putting a little more gas in the tank.

They'd been reclearing backfilled neighborhoods for days. The enemy had an uncanny ability to melt away, only to reappear in neighborhoods that were supposed to be cleared. Going over old ground sucked big time.

Mason eyed the last house on the block. The surprise always seemed to wait until the last house. Like the muj knew that after a hundred empty rooms, it was impossible not to get sloppy. Impossible to keep your edge after so many dull hours.

This one-story house didn't feel right.

The hairs on the back of his neck prickled and stood on end. A tingle teased the edges of his awareness. He and a few of the other men were starting to develop a sense for when things were about to go sideways. Call it mind powers or maybe their brains picking out minute details that didn't register at a conscious level.

Whatever it was, it seemed to work.

This house had every alarm in his head going off. The

courtyard gate lay in the street. Probably dragged off by a humvee at some point. The place didn't appear occupied. Four large windows were boarded up. It was much larger than your average house. Maybe a minor member of Saddam's Baathist party.

The front door yawned open. A pitch black interior gave no further clues.

"Lopes, what do you think?"

"Gives me the creepers, Sarge."

"Me too."

"Wish we had a tank to flatten it."

"Yep."

They both stared at the ominous dwelling.

"Sarge?"

"What?"

"If something ever happened to me, you'd look after my boy, right?"

"Nothing's gonna happen to you."

"I know. I know. I'm just saying. If it did, you'd keep an eye on him, right?"

"First off, you'll be there for him. And second, you know I'd look out for him if it came to that."

Lopes stared into the infinite distance.

"A boy needs a father figure."

"Lopes, you're getting me all weepy."

"You promise you'd keep him safe, if I wasn't there?"

Mason could tell Lopes wasn't going to let it go so he turned and locked eyes with him.

"I promise you, bro. Now stop acting crazy."

"Thank you."

Mason rolled his eyes.

Lopes smacked his shoulder and Mason's face jolted with pain.

"Ow!"

"Pull your nuts out, Sarge."

"Very funny."

Mason waved to gather the squad at the courtyard wall. A violent shiver raced down his back. With the sun below the horizon, the temperature had begun to plummet. The sweat-soaked cammies leached away body heat.

"It's been a long day."

All the men nodded like they'd never heard a deeper, more profound truth.

"The longest," Lopes said.

"Longer than the longest," Miro said with a grin. "Lopes has been crying all day about not getting to shoot anything."

"I'll shoot you if you don't shut up," Lopes replied.

"It'd take every round in that box because your aim is awful."

"How about I aim it up your butt?"

"Why are you always talking about my butt?"

"Enough!" Mason shouted, though he couldn't help but laugh. "This is the last structure in this sector. Don't go to sleep on me. Stay switched on and let's do it by the numbers."

"Ooh Rah!" the squad barked in unison.

"Hydrate and check your NVGs."

The men gulped down water and then lowered their night vision goggles and looked around to verify operation.

"Good to go?"

"Ooh Rah!"

Mason motioned to move out.

Lucky took point and the rest of the squad got in the stack behind. They filtered into the courtyard, searching for targets in their fields of fire. Mason covered the two boarded windows to the right of the front door as they approached.

No bad guys popped out.

They stacked up to the right of the open front door.

"It's way dark in there, Sarge," Lucky whispered as he dropped his NVGs into place. The rest of the squad followed suit.

The inky night bloomed to life in green and black hues. The Marines filed through the front door, into the shadows.

Into the black unknown.

58

It was so dark inside, the NVGs weren't much better than unassisted vision. They cleared a large foyer. Cracked and pried out tiles marred an otherwise colorful mosaic floor. Mason didn't get what it depicted at first. Maybe that was because he was only seeing it out of one eye. He stepped back and it came into focus.

A portrait of Saddam Hussein in cammies wearing a black beret. His trademark bushy mustache faithfully reproduced in small tiles. He wore a toothy smile that promised salvation for all the suffering in the world. A smile could hide a monster.

"Hey, Sarge," Lopes said. "Look at those perfect chompers. I need to get on his dental plan."

"Lopes, I've never seen such sweet manlove," Miro said.

"Cut it out," Mason said with a growl.

The foyer had three closed doors, one to the left, front, and right. The middle one had the hairs on the back of his neck ramrod straight. What about it felt so wrong?

He pulled up his NVGs and flicked on a flashlight. The door in front was painted solid black. But that wasn't the most messed up part. A dark crimson hand print streaked into trails down the pale wall next to the door. Like a bloody hand fought to stay out of that hallway.

"That's messed up." Lucky said what everybody was thinking.

"Let's do that one last," Mason said.

Three doors. Three options. All or none could hold drugged up jihadis foaming at the mouth for American blood.

"Stack up on this one," Mason said, pointing to the door on the left. Waiting around wasn't going to make the choice easier. Besides, it was like a reverse lottery. The winner was the least lucky person in the world. You never knew when your number was up.

Lucky posted up next to the door and the rest of the squad got into position behind. Channing came around and tried the door knob. He'd only rejoined third squad that morning after receiving medical treatment for a face full of shrapnel. The doctors wanted to send him home. He refused. He wanted to be back with his brothers.

The strength of that loyalty was a bond they all shared. They'd fought through so much. Mason would rather he take a bullet than one of his men. He was sure each and every one of them felt the same way.

The door was locked.

Channing reared back and kicked it in. The frame splintered and the door swung open. Lucky moved in with the rest of the stack following. They swept in with a hard-earned, fluid grace. Not rushing. Slow was smooth, and smooth was fast. They worked like perfectly meshed gears. Each turning to support the one in front, while at the same time getting the same support from the man behind.

Mason entered and noticed a small table along the far

wall. A single candle burned in a bowl on the table. It illuminated a half-eaten plate of food. His goggles made the flame glow white tinged with green. An AK-47 leaned against the wall by the empty chair next to the table. An open doorway led to another room beyond.

Someone was here. They'd just missed him.

Mason waved Lucky forward. The kid jumped to his duty without a second thought. He shouldered up next to the open doorway.

"Allahu—"

The tallest muj Mason had ever seen appeared in the doorway. His lanky arm wielded a wicked-looking curved sword. He swung it at Lucky as he ran into the room. The blade struck the Private's chest body armor and stuck. The attacker didn't get a chance at another swing as every rifle in the room shattered the silence. Two feet from Lucky, his body jerked with every impact. The volume of fire slammed him backwards into the wall. Bullets ripped his flesh apart.

Blood spewed from his mouth, down his black garments. He slumped to the floor, leaving a brushed stroke of blood on the wall.

"Cease fire!" Mason shouted.

Their rifles went silent. The sharp stink of spent rounds filled the air. Wisps of smoke curled out of the ends of rifle barrels.

The insurgent raised a hand, reaching for them, his fingers curled into claws.

SHUCK-SHUCK.

Channing racked the Mossberg and stepped in front of the dying man. He didn't hesitate. He didn't call for last rites or forgiveness. He pointed the muzzle at the haji's head and fired. It was like a melon getting hit with a sledgehammer.

Like that old comedian used to do. People would laugh when the wet bits sprayed over them.

No one laughed. No one smiled.

They all stared at the body as the legs shuddered and went still. He'd never kill another Marine. That was enough.

Lucky turned and the sword stuck to his front rotated with him, the handle bouncing in the air. Miro grabbed it and yanked the blade free. He swung it through the air a few times.

"Nice balance."

He felt the edge with his gloved thumb.

"Razor sharp," he fingered a spot near the tip, "except for this bit that got stuck in your chest plate."

He swung it at Lopes.

"Get that thing away from me!"

"You scared of a little pigsticker?"

Lopes eyed the three-foot-long blade. "Texas pigs must be huge."

"Everything's bigger in the Lone Star state."

"Yeah, even the liars."

Miro poked it at Lopes. "You smell like a pig. Worse."

He turned before Lopes could respond and handed it to Lucky.

"A souvenir for your great grandkids."

Lucky held it in wonder. He touched the chink in the blade and then the tear in his vest.

"That was crazy, man! That could've been my neck."

He showed the weapon to Mason.

"What do you say, Sarge? Can I bring it along?"

Mason knew some REMF back at Camp Fallujah was sure to give them hell for carrying a giant sword around base. But whatever. The kid deserved to keep it.

"Sure. Leave it here for now. We'll come back for it after we get this place locked down."

Lucky stepped over the still corpse on the ground and laid it reverently on the table.

Lopes shook his head. "Don't you know stepping over a dead man is bad luck?"

59

The Last Day
Los Angeles, California

ELIO watched as they entered downtown Los Angeles. Skyscrapers rose like canyon walls, blocking out everything but the night sky above. He'd only visited a few times in his seventeen years. He didn't know if it was normal or not, but the lack of people driving or walking around didn't feel right.

One thing did feel right. Theresa's hand in his. Her delicate fingers. The soft curves of her palm. He didn't want it to end. And he didn't want to think about what he'd soon be forced to do.

He'd have to kill somebody.

Trouble was no stranger, but he'd never come close to killing anyone. He fingered the gun in his lap. Much like the gun, he would be Cesar's. But a gun had no sense of right and wrong. No ability to discern targets.

A gun didn't have to face Theresa after shooting someone.

What he was about to do was wrong. But what choice did he have? He'd opted in. Blood in. Somebody was going to die tonight. It was kill or be killed. And if he died, what would happen to Theresa?

Elio knew only one thing for certain. He'd do anything to save her. Even if that meant also losing her. She'd never give her heart to a cold-blooded killer.

And he wouldn't blame her.

Had the tracker app thing worked?

Maybe Mason would show up. As much as Elio didn't want her father meddling in his life, in his business, he had to admit that Mason would know what to do.

Theresa squeezed his hand. The gentle, warm pressure brought him back. He looked at their tightly interwoven fingers.

She was so beautiful. So everything he could ever want. Was her desire an act? It didn't feel fake. His longing seemed mirrored in her lips. If it was acting, she deserved one of those fancy awards Hollywood people were constantly giving each other.

The blue car ahead slowed down and turned left on Fifth. Their car followed. The one way street opened into five lanes and still Elio felt hemmed in.

A tall, brown brick building on the left stretched halfway down the block. A grid of hundreds of little windows dotted the plain exterior. Some held dim illumination. It stood out amongst all the surrounding glass and metal. It was what you'd expect to see in the Bronx. At least from what he'd seen on TV.

A family appeared out of a dark archway. A father and mother with two young children clinging to the woman's legs. What clothes they had were filthy rags. The man saw the cars and charged forward a few feet, beating his naked chest and waving his arms wildly.

The woman cowered down, wrapping her arms around the children. The man dropped to all fours and pounded the pavement with his hands. He screamed and hooted.

Elio noticed his eyes as they passed. The eyes were wild. Uncomprehending. Primal.

Small trees stood every hundred feet, each coming up through a hole cut in the sidewalk. Their faded green leaves almost an apology for trying to grow in such a place.

Cesar's walkie-talkie chirped and squealed.

"Coming up, Jefe."

"Good. We're looking for her crew boss, Frank. Met him once. Tall, skinny bald guy. Anybody tries to stop us, they're gonna die first."

"Understood."

Cesar smacked Elio in the back of the head.

"See that building up on the right? The white one with all the windows?"

Cylindrical glass pillars ringed the entrance. Lights in the lobby shined through enormous sheets of glass held in place by elaborate metal framework. The main cylindrical structure climbed higher than all the surrounding buildings. The top seemed to pierce the clouds above.

Three shiny, black SUVs were parked at the curb out front. The kind you usually see the President or rappers riding in.

"Yeah."

"That's the Milagro Corporation building. Tallest building in Los Angeles. Full of rich people that don't give a damn about you and me. We're going in, whether they like it or not."

Elio didn't respond.

"Cheer up, ese," Cesar said. "You're gonna become one of us tonight. It's gonna change everything."

That's exactly what Elio was afraid of.

The walkie-talkie chirped.

"We got movement out front."

Elio peered down the street as they rolled forward.

Four figures emerged from a revolving door and stopped by one of the pillars. All had broad shoulders and wore dark suits. Security guys, no doubt.

Their cars crept forward, now no more than a couple hundred feet away.

Another man exited the building and joined them. This one tall and lanky. His bald head reflected light. He joined the others.

"That's Frank!" Cesar screamed. "Elio, drop your window and get ready! The bald guy's mine. You're on the others. Got it?"

"Yeah."

Cesar thumbed the transmitter.

"Go! Go! Go! The bald pendejo is mine!"

Both cars launched forward, like wolves in the short sprint to finish prey.

Elio lowered the window and rested the TEC-9 on the windowsill. His fingers barely responded. His whole body was numb, like he was a body snatcher still getting used to the new controls. He tried to swallow and his throat gave up halfway.

He couldn't go through with it.

But he had to.

It was them. Or it was him. Or worse yet, Theresa.

60

As if by remote control, Elio's fingers encircled the pistol's grip and the barrel rose toward a future he wouldn't be able to take back.

His body pressed back into the seat as the engine roared.

All the security guys turned to see what was making so much noise. Their hands dug inside suit coats and pulled out dark shadows.

Elio watched as thin black barrels extended from the passenger windows of the blue car in front. Flashes of light exploded outward and the crack of gunfire filled the air.

The suits returned fire with pistols. One shoved Frank to the side behind a concrete planter. One of the suits dashed toward the street and ducked behind the nearest SUV at the curb. Flashing muzzles strobed the scene, like a death disco.

The car in front charged ahead.

"Blast 'em! Blast 'em!" Cesar yelled into his walkie-talkie.

The thunderous boom of his .50 caliber Desert Eagle deafened Elio's right ear. A keening whine accompanied a jolt of pain deep inside his head. He looked right to see a gleaming barrel extended from the back window, kicking out an enormous flower of flame each time a round fired.

Elio raised his pistol and pointed it at the suits.

Rounds peppered the car in front. Glass shattered onto the street. Their tires crunched as they sped over it.

The suits fell back, their semiautomatic pistols no match for the firepower leveled against them. The glass entrance behind them shattered and crumbled to the ground.

The tallest one jerked as a cloud of mist exploded from his chest. He jerked again and fell to the pavement.

Elio watched, paralyzed. He turned to see Theresa screaming. Her shriek just one more note amidst the roaring concussions of shots firing all around. He looked forward and the suit behind the SUV stepped into the road, blasting away at the lead car.

The driver's head snapped back and the car lurched right. It slammed into the suit, flung him back ten feet into the last SUV, and then slammed into both of them.

Metal crunched as the doomed guy's legs and waist disappeared in a metal meat grinder. Car horns blared as he screamed in agony.

His suffering was short-lived.

Cuts jumped out of the passenger side of the blue car and emptied a shotgun into him from point blank range. The trapped suit jolted back as slugs ripped through his chest. And then he collapsed forward onto the hood.

Evil spilled out the left back seat door and leaned low over the trunk, spraying his rifle at the two still standing. Another of Cesar's soldiers staggered out of the blue car and pitched forward. His body shuddered like an electrical current zapped it. He collapsed in the street, a puppet with the strings cut.

Elio's car skidded to a stop.

"What's happening?"

Elio glanced back and saw Holly looking around with a dazed look on her face. Cesar kicked the door open and wrapped a huge arm around her chest.

"Let go of me!" Holly shouted.

Theresa reached over the seat and grabbed Holly's hand. "No! Holly!"

Cesar yanked Holly free and pinned her to his chest. He ran straight at the spot where Frank had hidden, his pistol booming again and again.

One of the suits pulled Frank back and they disappeared into the ruined building entrance. The last guy stood his ground, the muzzle of his pistol jumping at Cesar's approach.

Holly's body jerked as a round hit her in the stomach. Another slammed into her chest. Another hit Cesar in the shoulder and Holly fell to the side. Cesar leapt at the suit. They landed hard and rolled to a stop. Cesar climbed on top and rained down punishing elbows. The blows crashed through the upraised hands trying to stop them.

Red covered Cesar's arms as he rained down blows, any one of which could've ended a man's life. The suit's face turned into a pulp of blood and lacerated tissue.

The poor guy's arms fell to the side and still Cesar didn't stop.

Elio wanted to turn away, but couldn't. Like watching a car wreck as it happened.

Evil approached, still aiming his rifle toward the entrance.

"Jefe, that one's dead."

Cesar stopped and lunged down. His teeth clamped on exposed neck. He jerked back, tearing the dead man's throat out.

Theresa screamed and her hand clutched tight on his knee.

Elio's stomach heaved and his mouth filled with spit.

Cesar turned and his face and frontside were covered in carnage. Like he'd chainsawed a cow. Torn flesh hung from his jaws. He spat it onto the ground.

Another burst of gunfire screamed into the night as Evil pin cushioned the body of one of the fallen suits. And then only the car horns and the gurgling cries of the injured remained.

Cuts staggered to the sidewalk, holding his right side. The shotgun he carried used as a cane now. "I took one!"

Cesar yanked the dead guy's ID tag from his chest and shoved it into his pocket. He then marched over and threw open Elio's door. "Get out!"

Elio didn't move. He could shoot him now. He could unleash a thirty-two round magazine at point blank range. Before this madman tore out his throat. Or Theresa's.

He could finish this.

Cesar's brow dropped like a hammer on the broad anvil of his glistening face. He brought his mirrored pistol to Elio's forehead. "Get out, now!"

Not waiting for a response, Cesar reached across him and yanked Theresa out of the car. He wrapped an arm around her and marched her forward in front of him.

More expendable body armor.

61

He had to do something. But he couldn't shoot Cesar now, not from behind. What if the bullets went through and into Theresa?

"Holly!" Theresa screamed. She reached toward her fallen friend as Cesar shuffled by.

Elio jumped out and scrambled to catch up.

Pushing Theresa in front, Cesar stepped through the mostly empty panes of glass in the entrance. Evil, Cuts, and another of Cesar's soldiers followed. Elio tried not to look at the suit with the torn out throat as he passed.

Pale brains oozed out onto the sidewalk.

He turned away, praying he'd forget and knowing he wouldn't.

He stepped over the bits of glass that remained stuck in the metal framework. His shoes crunched over safety glass reduced to rubble.

A thought came to him. He crouched down and picked up a shard sticking out of the metal framework, long and thick as a dagger, and carefully slid it into his back pocket.

If he didn't get a chance to shoot Cesar, maybe he could stab him.

He followed them into an enormous lobby. Beyond the wreckage of the glass, the floor was a large checker pattern of glossy beige and black stone. A long oval booth to the right of the entrance was empty.

Cesar walked around the booth and shuffled through papers on the table.

"Cleaning services are located on the eleventh floor."

"Elevators over here, Jefe," Cuts said pointing off to the left in the center of the lobby. "One's going up."

They all ran over. The red digital display above the closed doors stopped at the 55th floor. Cesar punched the call button and an elevator behind dinged and swished open.

They piled in and headed up.

Elio stood closest to the closed doors. He caught Theresa's eyes in the hazy metal reflection. Her eyes looked faded. Hollow. Empty of the life that normally animated them.

They reached the 55th floor and the upward movement slowed to a stop. The doors opened.

Cesar tapped Elio's shoulder.

"Take a look."

Elio crept forward and peeked to both sides. To the right stretched a long hall that looked like an infinitely nicer version of a typical hotel hallway. Instead of threadbare carpet, gray marble floors inlaid with brass designs. Instead of old 1980's light fixtures that threw hard light underneath and left the spaces between dark, modern recessed LEDs illuminated the ceiling with a warm, even glow. Both sides of the hall had closed office doors every twenty feet or so.

He stepped into the open space for a better look.

"Don't see anyone. Lot of rooms to hide in though."

The hall erupted with gunfire. At the far end, the suit that escaped earlier fired from inside an open doorway.

He ducked back into the elevator as rounds snapped by, some passing inches from his head.

Evil and Cuts leaned their guns around the corner and triggered off an answering barrage.

The air filled with the sounds of promised death. The loud crack of rifles emptying long magazines. The boom of shotgun shells delivering fatal slugs. The thunk of ammunition chewing into polished rock, lacquered wood, and textured drywall. The high-pitched whine as rounds zipped by.

Death reached for anyone unlucky enough to be caught. And Theresa was caught in the middle of it all.

Cesar dug something out from behind his back. He yanked a pin from it and a shim of metal popped away and clattered to the floor. He grinned at Elio and slung his arm around the corner, hurling a grenade down the hall.

Evil and Cuts retreated into the elevator as a massive bang destroyed whatever hearing Elio had left.

A cloud of particulate fog billowed past and curled into the elevator.

"Vamos," Cesar shouted.

They edged out of the elevator and into an impenetrable cloud of choking dust. Cesar waved Cuts forward.

His shotgun up and ready to fire, he disappeared into the obscured air. Evil and the other soldier disappeared next. Cesar followed with Theresa pinned to his chest.

She vanished into swirling eddies of particulate haze.

Elio took a deep breath and plunged in.

The shadowed forms of those ahead vanished and reappeared as Elio moved through varying densities of airborne debris. The hall stretched out into an endless choking cloud. They continued on for what seemed like forever.

The gray dust swirled as Cesar's darker form again disappeared. The world seemed far away, kept at a distance by the painful ringing in Elio's ears. Muffled echoes of his own coughing and hacking came through.

Panic grew in his chest. He couldn't see Theresa. He shoved his way forward and slammed into Cesar's broad back. The brute reacted with the speed of a mongoose. He whipped around, throwing an elbow out as he spun. It caught Elio on the temple and tossed him like a wet rag against the wall.

Theresa's face was sheet white.

A warm wetness trickled down Elio's cheek and jaw. He touched it and his fingers came away slippery and red.

Cesar waved his gun at Elio, motioning him to go ahead.

Elio stumbled forward while the hall tilted back and forth at odd angles.

Through the metal door at the end of the hall, stairs appeared out of the smoke. Evil, Cuts, and the other soldier waited at the bottom step for that floor. Cesar and Theresa came up behind.

Cesar shoved Elio and roared, "Go!"

The boom of a shotgun and the metal railing pinged as slugs filled the empty column of air in the middle and ricocheted around. Several floors above, the suit leaned out over the railing, raining down death.

The soldier screamed and spun to the wall as red blossomed on his white shirt. He slumped to the floor, leaving a crimson streak on the wall behind. Blood dribbled from his lips.

Cesar snarled and waved his gun up the stairs.

"Go!"

Evil took off up the stairs, his back hugging the outside wall as he went. Cuts followed with Elio behind. Cesar brought up the tail with Theresa stumbling forward in his grasp.

More slugs screamed down and caromed off the railings of the floors above.

Elio's feet pounded the steps as his brain searched for a solution. How could he save Theresa?

They made it up four floors, Evil and Cuts with their guns raised and sporadically blazing. The sharp stink of gunpowder burned Elio's eyes. The surrounding blasts created a deafening storm. And any second Theresa could get hit in the storm of lead.

Then the onslaught silenced. The suit above either got hit or retreated out of the stairwell.

Cesar's soldiers rounded the last bend and made it to the 60th floor. Spent shotgun shells and smaller pistol casings carpeted the concrete floor. Evil rounded the stairwell and ran halfway up to the next floor.

"Nothing up here, Jefe. They must be on that floor."

Evil rejoined the group on the landing to the 60th floor. He reached for the closed metal door partitioning the stairwell from the office space beyond.

"Wait," Cesar said. A barrel jabbed Elio in the back. "Get up front. Kill the one with the shotgun, or I'll kill you."

Theresa reached out and caught his sleeve.

"No!" she screamed. "Don't do it!"

If only that were an option.

He stepped out of the stairwell. More closed office doors lined the hall, about ten to a side. One of those rooms held the guy Cesar was after and the last suit. The silence hid which room it might be. They all appeared equally unwelcoming.

Gazing down the hall, Elio considered his situation. There were guns in front and guns behind. Both sides ready to punch holes in his body. He crept toward the first door on the right knowing only two things.

One, he would die.

And two, there was no escape.

62

MASON watched the tracker app as he and Iridia sped east on Pico. Theresa's phone hadn't moved in the last five minutes. He slowed the big Bronco as he turned left onto Fifth Street. A few blocks down was where her phone had stopped.

At the base of the Milagro Corporation Tower, one car blocked the middle of the road. The metallic red '64 Impala.

He'd driven like a madman to catch up, but now he approached slowly, reading the scene. He shut the lights off and parked halfway down the block.

"Iridia, don't get out. It's not safe."

She didn't answer. Those police officers that got mowed down. The destruction meted out by the Apache gunship. The brush with death. She was in deep shock. He'd be surprised if it were otherwise.

Anyway, he preferred the silence.

"Don't leave me!"

Of course, he wasn't lucky enough for her to stay quiet.

"I have to."

She stared at him, arms crossed and still looking supermodel beautiful. Anger worked for her.

"Listen, just stay put."

"Stop bossing me around! You aren't my manager!"

"No, your manager would have told you to screw that director to advance your career."

"Screw you!"

"I don't have time for this," he said as he got out of the Bronco. He so wanted to slam the door in her face. But stealth was more important than the satisfying pop of a bubbling outburst.

He eased the door shut and drew his Glock 19. He inched the slide back and verified the weapon was hot. In a low crouch, he moved forward keeping close to the buildings.

He swerved back into the street and approached the red Impala with his pistol at the ready, his finger extended along the slide, his head on a swivel scanning for threats. A sky blue lowrider had smashed into the last of three black, late model Cadillac Escalades. The kind close protection officers used for high-profile clients. The wrecked lowrider's horn droned continuously.

He scanned to the right and saw that the entire entrance area was a wreck of shattered glass and chewed up metal framing.

Several bodies lay on the pavement in front. None moved.

He side-stepped around the rear door, looking through the open window, slicing the pie as he went. The back seat was empty. He cut around the front seat and found it empty as well.

A quiet moaning surfaced below the much louder car horn. It was coming from over by the building. He moved around the back of the Impala and approached the source of the sound, a body partially hidden in shadows. The dark form lay on its side, curled up in the fetal position.

As he got closer, he realized with a shock that he recognized the clothes. And the victim.

Holly.

He holstered his weapon and knelt beside her. He touched her shoulder.

"No. Please."

"It's okay," he said. "It's me, Mason. I'm not going to hurt you."

"Help me."

The words croaked out wet and wheezing. Blood sprayed from her lips.

She held her chest with glistening, crimson hands.

She took a breath and Mason heard the sickening crackle of a sucking chest wound. Blood bubbled up out of her mouth.

Mason had seen similar wounds. Too many. And he'd never seen a soldier walk away from one like this.

The terror in her eyes morphed into confusion.

"Mr. West?"

"Yes, Holly."

He laid a hand on her shoulder. He didn't know what to say. She was dying, and he couldn't stop it.

"Am I hurt, Mr. West?"

He took her hand and kissed it. Warm blood coated his lips.

"You're going to be fine. Don't worry. Are you in pain?"

"Kind of. But not really."

Blood flecked from her lips.

"Good. That means you're going to make it."

It didn't mean anything of the sort. With a wound like that, her brain was overloaded and starting to shut down.

"Holly, listen to me. Where is Theresa?"

"I don't know. She was here. I'm not sure."

She glanced at the blood-soaked sheer fabric sticking to her chest.

"I got shot! I'm gonna die! I'm gonna die!"

He brushed the bangs out of her face and kissed her forehead. Her last moments should be peaceful. There was nothing more he could offer.

"You're not going to die. I've seen worse. Don't worry, you'll live."

Her face relaxed and her eyes fluttered. She opened them again and smiled.

"Is it scary, Mr. West?"

"What's that?"

"Dying. Because I'm scared."

"Just relax, honey. We'll get you to the hospital in no time. The ambulance is already on the way."

There was no ambulance. And a hospital was the last place he'd take an injured person right now anyway.

She turned her cheek into his hand.

"Thank you... thank you."

Her last words came out as an exhaled breath tinged with syllables.

With final words of appreciation on her lips, Holly died in his hands.

Her family would be crushed. Theresa would be devastated. How would he tell them? He kissed her forehead and left a bloody imprint.

Grief shadowed Mason's heart. But one emotion crested above all others vying for space in his soul.

Rage.

Rage at the taking of this girl's life. Rage for what might yet happen to Theresa.

He picked Holly up off the ground, cradling her in his arms. He wasn't going to leave her on the cold concrete as the warmth bled out of her. He carried her back to the Bronco. Iridia stared with wide eyes.

"Is she dead?"

He passed her door and walked around to the back of the Bronco.

"Tell me she's not dead!"

Mason flipped the hatch open and dropped the gate.

"Help me spread out this blanket. Now!"

Iridia jumped into the backseat and reached over to help out. With the old blue, emergency blanket spread out, Mason gently lowered Holly's lifeless body to rest. He pulled the edges over her as well as he could and then closed up the Bronco.

"Stay in the truck."

"What? Are you insane?" Iridia opened her door and Mason slammed it shut.

"Stay in the truck! Do you want to end up like her?"

The door stayed shut.

"Is she really dead? Tell me I'm not hanging out in a car with a dead body! Not after the night I've had! First, it was that scumbag director. I will not say his name. Ever again. Then—"

"Shut up, Iridia!" Mason shouted.

He needed to think for a minute. Theresa was likely in the Milagro Tower. In what condition, he didn't know. And the process of finding out might leave him in a bad way as well. Either or both of them might need medical attention, at a time when no medical attention was possible.

Except for Beth. She'd sewn him up a few times. And she had extensive care treating animals. She'd have to do.

He pulled his phone out of his pocket and called his wife.

"Mason? You won't believe—"

"Honey, sorry. It's an emergency. I need you home immediately with whatever medical supplies you can gather."

"What happened? Are you hurt?"

"Not yet."

"What do you mean? What's going on?"

"Some gang members have taken our daughter."

"What? Where's my baby?"

"I'm going to get her now."

"Don't let them hurt my baby! Mason—"

"Elizabeth. Listen to me. Bring whatever supplies you can gather and come home. You may need to treat gunshot wounds, lacerations. I don't know. But we can't go to hospitals right now. We need you."

"What are—"

"I love you so much, honey. I have to go."

"Don't let them hurt Theresa!"

"I won't."

He ended the call and looked at Iridia, waiting for another idiotic outburst.

"Go save your daughter."

You never knew how someone would react when it really counted. The toughest badass could break down crying like a baby. The most selfish supermodel could step up and show unexpected compassion.

Mason nodded and headed into danger.

63

Glock again at the low-ready, he bounded back down the street, head swiveling from street to building and back. He crouched past the red Impala and approached the blue lowrider in front. It was riddled with bullet holes. Like an entire fire team had let loose on it. The wailing horn grew louder as he drew near.

The hood was caved in from smashing into the parked Escalade. A man in a suit was squeezed between the two. He had the broad build and crew cut hair that screamed someone in Mason's business. His lower body a pulverized mess. He sprawled face down across the lowrider's hood. Blood pooled beneath him and dripped down the sides. The ragged exit wounds on his back told Mason that the car crash didn't finish him off. Shotgun slugs did.

After clearing the area, he turned toward the building. Several bodies lay still on the pavement. Their fallen weapons at their sides. One guy's head was pulped. His throat ripped out like a wolf had finished him off.

The muted stink of gunpowder lingered in the air. One

hint among plenty that a gun battle had gone down here in the very recent past.

He stepped around the mutilated body and cursed when his foot slipped on the gore. He fell to a knee and his hand squished into... something squishy. Looking away, he wiped the pale, spongy tissue onto the edge of a raised planter. The air reeked from bodies torn apart. He spat to get the filthy taste out of his mouth. It didn't work. The foul, metallic odor coated his tongue.

He noticed red footprints leading out of the blood. He took a closer look. Size sevens. Not a normal gait. Dragged along at times.

Could be Theresa.

The footprints led to the demolished entrance of the building. The exterior looked like it had taken several mortar rounds.

He crunched over a carpet of shattered glass and through the metal frame of a demolished window pane. He crept forward, sweeping left and right, knowing a threat could appear from anywhere. His daughter could be anywhere, too. And he didn't want to put a bullet in her if she popped out from behind a corner.

Mason followed the blood trail to a security booth and found it unoccupied. The papers on the desk thrown everywhere. He cast about and picked up the trail and followed it to the elevators. Three elevators on each side. He found a print in front of one and saw that the button had a red smear on it as well.

Still on their track. He wiped the button and smeared in a new pattern.

Not far behind either.

He punched it and waited to the side as the doors opened. A puff of light smoke billowed out. He sliced the pie and cleared the interior. Another smudge on the button for the 55th floor. He took a deep breath as it ascended into the heavens.

He prayed his daughter wasn't already an angel.

The doors slid open and he exited to find evidence of destruction everywhere. He moved down the hall, Glock covering the doorways as he passed. Through a metal door at the end and into a stairwell.

Evidence of a gunfight was everywhere. Spent shell casings on the floor. The concrete walls chipped and scored.

And then there was the body. A short gangbanger lay slumped over against the wall. A streak of blood on the wall showing his last fall to the ground. His mouth hung open, revealing a mouth full of gold.

A shot rang out. From somewhere above. A few floors if he guessed right. He rushed up the stairs. Most people didn't rush *toward* the sound of gunfire.

Mason wasn't most people.

64

BETH wrapped the tiny chimp in a thick, cushy towel. She tucked him into her messenger bag. He burrowed into the folds and settled. No doubt he needed rest. He'd had an exhausting start to life.

She grabbed another bag and stuffed it with electrolyte solution. He'd need it for a week or two while his body adjusted to formula. Next, she went to the medical supply cabinet and started grabbing things to treat various wounds. Hopefully not gunshot wounds. She had no experience with that type of injury, and didn't want to add to her resume working on her family.

Not that she hadn't worked on some ghastly wounds. She had.

The baboons in particular often ended up with gaping, deep lacerations when the males went after each other. The zoo did its best to separate the troublemakers and head off any scuffles, but a bloody battle could kick off for the most minor transgression. The males' aggressive attitudes were backed by canine teeth that matched any adult lion.

She doubted a puncture wound made by a tooth looked much like a puncture wound made by a bullet.

But even if the wound wasn't quite the same, she knew the treatment would be similar. She packed the bag full of heavy dressings, tape, blood-clotting packs, transfusion bags, IV ports, and other things that might come in handy.

Theresa was in danger.

The mother part of her mind butted into the doctor part.

She couldn't believe it. She didn't want to believe it. She didn't have enough information. A coil of worry squirmed in her belly. It twisted tight until she almost doubled over.

Mason would know what to do. If anyone did, he would.

Please God, keep her safe.

Beth hadn't been on a first name basis with the Almighty since leaving the strict regularity of her parents' home. But that didn't slow her down a bit. Once a Catholic, always a Catholic.

She saw her flashlight on the counter and grabbed it. The emergency power had kicked on a while ago, but you never knew. The returned power was a welcome change, but it came too late. Too late to save Jane.

When the lights came on, Diana left. Ostensibly to lead maintenance in the effort to figure out what happened and begin the repairs. She would likely succeed in only irritating the folks in Ralph's department. Especially since he wasn't there to buffer the interaction.

Diana had an almost superhuman ability to get under people's skin. To make subordinates feel inferior in fewer words than it'd normally take to establish that a conversation was taking place.

"You can't leave with zoo equipment or supplies," a voice said behind her.

Think of the devil and she appears. Like magic, only not fun. More of a curse.

Beth didn't pause. She continued filling the bag.

"What do you think you're doing?"

"I'm leaving, just as you requested."

"You're not leaving with those supplies."

Beth snapped the bag shut and grabbed her messenger bag and helmet. She was ready. Geared up for the ride home. She looked around the lab, pausing on the sheet covering the huge form that hours ago was Jane. The chimpanzee she'd raised from an infant.

Now it was an empty body. Devoid of the life she'd loved so much.

A stab of anguish pierced her chest.

She walked to the table and rested her hand on the sheet. The hard ridge of Jane's skull met her palm. Beth hated leaving her like this. It seemed so heartless. Such an undeserved end.

There simply wasn't time to do anything more.

Beth leaned down and touched her forehead to the spot on the sheet that covered Jane's forehead.

I'm so sorry. Your son will be safe with me. I promise.

She walked toward the door, toward Diana blocking it.

Would this be the last time she saw this place? After so many wonderful years. She didn't have any other dream jobs. She'd lived the only one that mattered.

Diana thumbed on the walkie-talkie. "Ralph, where are you? I told you to meet me in the operating room of the medical wing."

A voice answered, not from the walkie-talkie, but from the hallway behind her.

"Sorry, Mrs. Richston. Lot of things to deal with right

now and everyone else in Security took off after that newscast."

What newscast? Why would it make them abandon their jobs?

Beth realized she'd been sequestered in the medical wing most of the day.

"They'll all be looking for jobs tomorrow!" Diana said. "Ralph, Ms. West has medical supplies that belong to the zoo in her bag. She is attempting to steal them."

Ralph adjusted his pants, adjusting the slight paunch that hung out over his belt. He didn't move, caught between two people he didn't want to confront.

"Arrest her!"

"Is that true, Dr. West?"

Beth wasn't going to lie. She wouldn't give Diana the satisfaction of judging her.

"Yes. I'm taking them to help people who are hurt." She really hoped those people didn't turn out to be her husband or daughter.

Ralph's eyes went wide and he turned to Diana. His unspoken pleading fell upon deaf ears.

"I don't care if it's for the pope. Those supplies are mine and she can't have them!"

Beth stood quietly waiting for Ralph to choose a side. He wasn't a bad person and she didn't relish putting him in the middle.

A mewling cry escaped from inside her messenger bag.

The chimp squealed at exactly the wrong time.

65

Diana's eyes narrowed, like a hawk spotting prey.

"Where is the monkey?"

"Chimpanzees are apes."

Diana gave her a look like she was babbling in an alien language.

"In the incubation tank in my office."

"Liar. Ralph, you will arrest this woman for attempted theft of a priceless corporation asset."

The gall of this woman. Fury burned Beth's earlobes. She wanted to punch this ignoramus in the mouth.

"You didn't care about him one bit earlier."

"Ralph," Diana said. Her voice cracked like a whip.

He flinched and moved toward Beth.

She backed away. He wasn't in good shape, but he was big and there was probably a decent amount of muscle under that pudgy flab. If he was set on stopping her, she wasn't positive she could do anything about it. Not while also protecting a fragile, hours-old chimp in her messenger bag.

"Now, I don't want any trouble, Dr. West," he said as he

held his left hand up. His right hand reached down to his belt and grabbed a large can of pepper spray. "Please turn over the animal and we can avoid any problems."

"Stay away from me. I'm warning you."

That made him pause. He looked her over, clearly nervous that maybe she had a hidden weapon he hadn't seen. His eyes narrowed and he continued forward.

"Keep all the bandages and stuff," he said. "I'll take the heat. But you can't leave with an animal that belongs to the zoo."

"I'll give him back when you tell me what happened to the rest of the Bili chimps."

"What are you talking about?" Diana said. "They were transferred, as you already know."

"Then why can't I contact a single one of the zoos that supposedly received them?"

"That is none of my concern."

"They never went to any zoo, and you know it. So, where did they end up?"

Diana's fierce demeanor wavered.

"Don't try to hide your criminality with wild accusations. Give me the monkey!"

"If it wasn't for me, this chimp would be dead!"

"You recovered a corporate asset," Diana said. "Nothing more. And you destroyed another asset in the process."

"Jane might've made it if not for all your cost-cutting nonsense. Your relentless devotion to the bottom line has endangered the lives of animals and employees."

Diana's nostrils flared and her teeth clenched tight.

"Give it to me, Elizabeth."

Beth backed up, knowing she'd be cornered soon and probably on the ground hacking and coughing with that pepper spray in her eyes and mouth. She looked behind and saw no way out.

And then she found one.

The tranq rifle.

It was leaned up in the corner. On any normal day, that breach of safety protocol would have been enough to get someone chewed out.

But what did she care?

This wasn't a normal day, and she was already fired.

She lunged for the rifle and seated the buttstock in the hollow of her shoulder. The long black barrel pointed directly at Ralph's chest.

"There's enough Etorphine in this dart to kill a hundred humans. I'll shoot you if I have to."

She knew there was no dart in it. But they didn't. She was threatening a man's life. A man she knew well, and who had helped her that very morning.

What was she doing?

Ralph froze. A dark spot blossomed on his pant leg and a puddle of urine spilled onto the floor at his feet.

"You'll go to prison for this!" Diana shrieked.

Beth wheeled the muzzle over to rest on Diana.

She blanched, her skin pale and drawn.

"Get away from the door."

Diana's heels clacked on the floor as she skittered away.

"You'll never get out of here with my property!"

She was right. As soon as Beth left, Diana could easily call security and have her identity card deactivated. Then she'd have no way of getting out the employee exit. The main entrance and exit had mechanical locks and would've been locked up tight by now.

What was left?

She didn't feel confident about scaling a twenty foot gate

carrying medical supplies and an hours-old chimpanzee.

Who said she had to use her own card though?

"Take off your clothes, Diana!"

Diana's brows raised, confusion and surprise on her face vying for dominance. She glanced at Ralph, obviously uncomfortable.

"What?"

"You heard me! Don't make me ask again!"

Beth approached Diana with the rifle pointed at her chest.

"I should kill you now and be done with it."

Diana visibly faltered. Her eyes locked onto the tip of the barrel. She raised her hands with the palms out.

"Okay, okay."

Diana peeled out of her sleek business suit, while Ralph tried not to stare at the revealed bra and panties.

Beth gathered up the clothing and felt the hard edge of an identity card in Diana's pants pocket.

Bingo.

Diana covered herself as best she could.

"This is assault and battery! You'll rot in prison for this!"

Beth raised her left hand and extended the middle finger. She stepped into the hall and pointed the rifle at each of them in turn.

"I'm closing this door. I might leave. Or I might wait a while and put a dart in the chest of whoever opens this door."

She flashed a wicked smile and pulled the door shut.

That should keep them wondering for a few minutes.

A walkie-talkie chirped.

"Operations, this is Diana Richston. Dr. West has gone crazy and threatened to kill me and our head of security. Call 911! Deactivate her security card immediately!"

Beth tossed the rifle to the floor and fished Diana's card from her pants. She dumped the clothing and sprinted down the hall.

She had to make it to her bike before the police arrived.

If they caught her, she'd have to give up the chimp. Diana would probably let him die just to spite her.

She flew out the door of the medical wing and headed toward the main entrance. It was dark outside as only the emergency lights were illuminated. No patrons ambled down the normally busy paths.

A small group of zoo employees huddled on the path she wanted to take, the shortest one out. She dodged off to the left and took the longer looping path. She'd go a little further if she could avoid any more confrontations. Death threats weren't her thing.

She ran down a narrow path, past the flamingos and the petting zoo, and approached the employee exit, wondering if it would be blocked by a line of bodies.

It wasn't.

She was almost surprised. Something could go right today. Sucking wind as she arrived, she fumbled Diana's card from her pocket and swiped it. A red light beeped.

No.

She swiped it again, her hand shaking.

The red light beeped again.

No. No. No.

She looked at the card, ready to stomp it into crumpled plastic.

It was backwards. She'd swiped it with the metallic strip on the wrong side.

Seriously?

She was a terrible criminal. She was going to get caught for failing to do what any dimwit could easily do going through a grocery store line. Maybe the judge would consider that when she was sentenced.

She flipped the card and swiped it again.

A green light beeped and the electronic lock clunked open.

The modulated wail of a siren in the distance grabbed her attention. Out on the access road, two squad cars with lights blazing sped by headed for the parking lot entrance.

She shoved the gate open and sprinted toward employee parking, praying it was dark enough that they wouldn't see a lone figure running across the empty lots.

She arrived at her bike as the two squad cars pulled in, their headlights washing across her as they turned. Helmet on, key in the ignition, she cranked it and the old Vulcan rumbled to life. The vibration between her legs promised a quick escape.

She may have made a terrible criminal, but she was an excellent rider. She tucked the messenger bag in front, the supply bag behind, securing them both to her waist as the headlights found her again and this time didn't waver.

They'd seen her.

Red and blue lights splashed across the empty lots as the sirens grew louder.

Beth dropped the visor on her helmet, crouched low in the seat, and cranked back the throttle.

The Vulcan's 750 cc engine roared as the bike shot forward. The front tire kicked up before she shifted up and it settled back to the ground with a screech.

She cut to the side and blew by the squad cars as they fishtailed around to follow.

They didn't stand a chance.

Their sirens faded under the eager howl of her bike. She rocketed out of the parking lot and broke free into the night.

66

ELIO stood beside each office door in turn and tried to open it. They were halfway down the hall now and every door had been locked with no response forthcoming. Most everyone had gone home. If anyone remained, he didn't blame them for not being more inviting.

The sound of gunfire didn't make for a reassuring doorbell.

Maybe the suit and Frank would stay locked up and wait them out. That would be the best case scenario. He could show Cesar that he'd tried. That failure wasn't his fault.

Even within the agreeable confines of his own mind, Cesar accepting such an outcome didn't seem likely.

He crossed the hall and approached the next door on the right side. Maybe the tenth one or so he'd tried so far.

He stood to the side and tried the handle. Locked like the rest. He pounded on the door. No response like the rest. He took a step toward the door on the opposite side.

BOOM.

A shotgun fired inside the office. It tore a grapefruit-sized hole through the door and then another one on the opposite wall. Splinters exploded outward like shrapnel. Sharp bits of the door cut through his shirt and dug into his side. He fell back and pushed up against the wall. A cloud of smoke whooshed out and obscured the air.

SHUCK-SHUCK.

BOOM.

Another chunk of door vaporized, leaving the hallway filled with splinters and pulverized gypsum. Acrid smoke billowed out and burned his throat and eyes. Tears washed down his cheeks. He coughed and sputtered.

"Shoot him!" Cesar shouted from behind.

Elio raised the TEC-9 and held it at arm's length toward the door. Even being shot at, Elio couldn't bring himself to return fire.

"Matalo!" Cesar shouted.

What choice did Elio have?

He tilted the muzzle up and pulled the trigger.

The gun jerked as rounds ripped through the thick wood door, heading toward the ceiling inside. He hoped the bullets hit nothing but overhead lights and ductwork.

A voice inside the office yelled and doors slammed. They sounded faint and far away and Elio wondered if the ringing in his ears would ever go away.

A body shouldered him aside and Evil stepped in front of the door. He landed a hard kick on the mangled lock and the door swung inward. Cuts rushed through with his shotgun leading the way.

"Vamos! Vamos!" he said.

Evil moved in with his rifle raised and scanning for a target. Elio followed in behind and found himself in a front area with an unoccupied receptionist's desk facing the entrance. It was a long J-shaped, dark wood desk. Two empty chairs sat behind it. The fancy kind with the fine mesh backing and leather wrapped armrests. Thin computer screens silently waited to verify an appointment.

They didn't have one.

Off to the left was a minimalist, modern-looking couch with a few chairs surrounding a low glass coffee table.

Evil nodded at Cuts, pointing his muzzle down the wide corridor deeper in. The suit and Frank must've retreated into the office.

A voice rang out in the main hall.

"Don't move!"

Cesar and Theresa were the only ones still out there. But it wasn't either of their voices.

Had one of the suits survived and come up the stairs behind them? Were the police already here?

Elio turned to see what was going on.

Still in the hall, Cesar pivoted to face the threat and his brow screwed up in confusion.

"Daddy!" Theresa screamed, choking and coughing. "Daddy!"

Mason West was here?

The tracker app. It worked!

Cesar held Theresa pinned to his chest with the crook of his left arm around her neck. The chromed Desert Eagle came up and unleashed a volley of lead back toward the stairwell. "Coma plomo, cabron!"

Cesar dodged into the office, dragging Theresa with him. Evil aimed at the empty corridor further in and let loose. The muzzle flashed and did a brutal redecorating job on the interior space. Evil and Cuts ran past the desk, their guns kicking out rounds as they went.

Return fire exploded from an open doorway further down. A round snapped by Elio's head. So close it singed the skin on his ear. Evil and Cuts continued forward filling the space with deadly lead and choking smoke.

Cesar leaned his head out the door to look back toward the stairwell.

Shots fired and he ducked back in as the door frame by his head exploded with a double tap that just missed.

Elio froze.

Caught in a crossfire, between the suit and Frank fighting for their lives and Mason on the other side coming for Theresa. And then Cesar who probably didn't much care if they all died together in a ferocious blood bath. They wouldn't survive for long in this position.

What could he do?

He had to protect Theresa. That's what he had to do.

Cesar's back was to him, his attention on the empty doorway.

This was his best chance. Maybe his only chance.

So he took it.

He yanked a sleeve down and doubled it over his right hand and then pulled the dagger shard of glass from his back pocket. A chain-link glove would've been better. A few layers of cotton was pitiful protection. Maybe it would be enough to keep his fingers attached.

He lunged forward and jabbed the razor-edged glass into Cesar's back. His fingers slid forward along that same edge. The glass sliced through the cloth and parted his skin.

Cesar screamed and jerked forward. Theresa took advantage of his loosened grip and twirled in his grasp and threw a vicious knee to his groin.

He stumbled a couple of steps, and then whipped the butt of his pistol at her head.

She took it on the cheek and crashed to the marble floor.

Cesar turned in a circle, his left hand grasping at the shard lodged in the center of his back.

Elio dodged around him and dragged Theresa to her feet.

Cesar struggled to reach the embedded glass, but the width of his back and biceps made it an impossible task. He screamed with a ragged, guttural croak. "You're dead! Dead!"

The cacophony of gunfire coming from deeper inside the office ceased. Evil joined them.

"The security guy is dead. Cuts is looking for..."

He stuttered to a stop, looking around confused.

With Cesar blocking the open door, Elio dragged Theresa behind the desk. They swung around the corner just as Evil's rifle cracked to life and bullets chewed through the wood corner.

Elio pushed Theresa further into cover and then, with his right hand shredded, held the TEC-9 in his left hand and poked it around the corner. He triggered off a burst of fire. This time aiming waist-high and wanting nothing more than for those rounds to find flesh.

Furniture crashed and bodies tumbled to the floor. It went quiet. Maybe he killed them all.

Then the desk shuddered as bullets pounded into it. The whole thing shook and shivered but no rounds made it through. At least they had that.

The wood inches from his face exploded outward, peppering him with splinters. He fell back and landed hard on the harder floor.

"Get it out! Out!"

"You sure, Jefe?"

"Now!" Cesar said, and then screamed as somebody tore the glass dagger free.

"I'm gonna put a bullet through your teeth! And then

one through that puta's chest. I'm gonna rip your hearts out."

Elio had no doubt he'd do exactly that if given the chance. So he crawled forward and pushed his pistol around the corner and squeezed the trigger, determined not to give him the chance.

The hammer clicked and nothing happened.

He yanked the bolt back and saw the chamber was empty.

They were screwed now.

67

MASON jumped back away from the interior column of the stairwell when the report of a shotgun sounded. Then another.

They were close now. On the floor above. He held his Glock out and up, ready to squeeze rounds into any threat that entered his field of fire.

He continued up, slicing the view of the staircase above as he went.

An automatic burst of fire echoed down the hall and he froze at the landing to the 60th floor. Dust and smoke wafted into the stairwell.

This was it.

One of those events with consequences that rippled onward through time. The crests so high, sometimes, they could drown you.

The sharp cracks of rifle fire stabbed his eardrums.

Shouting voices and then a scream.

A scream he recognized.

Theresa's.

He rounded into the hall with his pistol ready and his

heart jumped into his throat. Cold fear clenched his gut. Not for himself, but for his daughter.

Theresa was held by some huge thug. Drifting smoke parted and Mason recognized Cesar.

He should've put him in the ground that morning. Forget the legal repercussions. Forget the dubious morality.

He'd put his daughter in danger. His motivations had been golden. Getting Elio out of a fix was holding to a promise that had few equals in his life. It was simply life. Sometimes your best call turned out bad.

Mason drew a bead on Cesar's head, preparing a kill shot.

Theresa jerked in Cesar's grasp and she pushed into his sight picture. He needed more separation to be sure.

"Don't move!" he yelled.

Theresa saw him.

"Daddy! Daddy!"

Cesar pivoted her toward him, using her as body armor. The lowlife.

He longed to release a barrage into Cesar's chest, but had no angle for it.

Cesar's pistol came up and kicked to life.

Mason ducked back into cover as lead thundered into the stairwell's far wall.

The firing stopped and he peeked out just as Cesar pulled his daughter into an office.

He scanned the approach and saw he'd have zero cover once he committed. It didn't matter. He set off in a low crouch, his front sight glued to the empty doorway.

"Go!" someone said and he stopped as a storm of gunfire erupted. All inside the office.

All in close proximity to Theresa.

Blind panic chewed at the edges of his brain. Echoes of past loss dulled his thinking.

He breathed hard and grounded his focus. Looking left and right as he passed closed doors. Ready to pivot in case any of them held a lethal surprise.

The walls wavered and existed in two places at once. Like a double exposure. Walls from a distant place and time. Thick walls made of clay and stone. White-washed walls dulled brown by layers of dust and debris.

A head that wasn't Theresa's appeared in the doorway. It pulled back as his pistol blasted two rounds in the empty space it had just occupied.

The head was familiar though. Hadn't he seen it...

When?

A memory that he daily fought to keep locked away broke free. A melancholy madness gripped him.

Cold sweat dripped down his forehead and ran into his eyes, blurring the world more than it already was.

A weight pressed into his chest. A tightness he dismissed as the heavy ceramic plate in the Interceptor body armor that had become almost like a second skin in Fallujah.

Mason blinked hard, trying to clear his mind.

Fallujah happened long ago. He'd buried those memories.

Buried them a thousand times.

But they always rose to haunt him.

68

November 2004
Fallujah, Iraq

MASON didn't have the patience to deal with a row right now. But he also had no desire to drop the hammer on his men either.

Miro smacked Lopes on the helmet. "Don't put that voodoo on Lucky!"

Lopes spit a glob of brown juice on Miro's boot. "I don't make the news. I just report it."

Miro examined his boot.

Mason waited for it. Now was not the time for these two to tangle.

Miro looked back up and grinned. "Sweet. I think your chaw spit washed some brains off my toe."

"You're welcome."

Now was not the time for their comedy routine either.

"Great," Mason said. "I'm happy you're bosom buddies again. Can we get on with our jobs now?"

"Yes, Sergeant West," Miro said in clipped tones. He

always used Mason's rank and name when he was worked up.

Good. Anger kept you on edge. Kept your senses awake.

"Clear that room," Mason said, pointing to the doorway that the muj had entered from.

The team cleared a sizable kitchen with no further surprises. They headed back to the foyer and stacked up on the door to the right. Door number two. Still avoiding door number three. The horror show door.

Nobody was in a hurry for that one.

Door number two was locked and a number of stiff kicks from Channing didn't faze it. So he blew it open with a couple shots with the twelve gauge. As soon as the door crashed open, they knew they'd hit a new record.

It was *the* arms cache of arms caches. This house must've been a muj headquarters. There was all the usual stuff, only way more of it: endless piles of ammo cans, AK-47s, RPKs, Dragunov sniper rifles, RPG rounds, drugs. Tubs full of drugs. But this one had a few things they hadn't seen before. A few things that chilled them to the bone.

Stacks of American military cammies. American Kevlar helmets. Body armor vests no different than the ones they wore. M16 and M4 rifles. Night vision goggles. Half the stuff there looked like gear straight from their own supply depot.

If the muj wanted to set up a deadly ambush posing as friendlies, they had everything they needed right here.

That would've set a new record for crazy. But that wasn't all.

The tables covered with gear also had something else they'd never seen before, not in all of the hundreds of houses they'd cleared.

Computers. Five networked laptops. Two metal filing cabinets.

"Jackpot," Mason muttered.

Lopes rubbed his finger together. "Vegas style."

Miro opened a filing cabinet and leafed through stacks of paper.

"Senior brass are gonna cream their pants."

"Channing, get on the horn. We need EOD and intel teams on this one."

"Roger that, Sergeant."

Mason waited to confirm explosive ordinance disposal and intel units were en route and then posted two men to guard the treasure trove. He pulled the remaining men back into the foyer.

He looked at door number three and chewed skin from his lip. The swollen half of his face burned. It was past due for another painful cleansing. His right eye was useless.

One good eye, viewing the world lit by headache-inducing night vision goggles. He wondered for half a second why he voluntarily signed up for this Bravo Sierra. He could be at home eating pizza and knocking back beers. Taking Theresa to an LA Galaxy game. Spending a weekend in bed with his wife. Swimming in the bracing waters of the Pacific Ocean.

He pushed the thoughts aside. They had no place here. The door in front of him was another barrier between him and that future. Overcome it and he'd be another step closer to home.

Mason squeezed his left eye shut. The right one already was. He had to pull it together. This door was just like all the others. A deadly game of Russian Roulette. The losers didn't get another chance. The winners faced another turn of the barrel.

Home.

Family. His wife and daughter.

So many Marines would never return. So many others would make it back in pieces.

Mason wondered if he was going crazy. His mind fought against his attempts to reel it in. To get it locked down.

"Sarge?"

Lopes was at his shoulder.

"You okay?"

Mason looked at his best friend. All he wanted in the world was for Lopes to make it home. For all of his men to make it through this. He studied each of their faces. They were spooked. He had to get himself together. They looked to him for strength. For guidance.

He buttoned down the whirlpool in his brain and locked it up tight.

"Fine," Mason said. "Stack up! Let's go!"

Lucky jumped to the front. The kid was all balls. Channing came around and turned the door knob. He pushed and it slowly swung open without a sound.

Mason's jaws clenched tight. The muscles ached from overuse. He was so sick of long, dark hallways.

69

This corridor was different from most. Usually a hallway was a passage leading to rooms on either side. A simple practicality of architecture that gave easy access to other areas. This one didn't follow that paradigm.

There was only one door. At the end. Ten meters away. The entire corridor was painted in creepy, flat black. The door at the end included. The walls were also painted with something much more horrifying. Handprints streaked the surfaces in crusted reds and browns. Other less recognizable smears added to the story of untold suffering.

Mason's danger sense raged like a five-alarm fire. It was a tunnel of terror. Silent testimony to the worst that mankind could dredge from their bestial natures.

They crept down the hall, senses attuned to anything that might be a threat. The only sound was their own breathing and the shuffle of their boots over a floor littered with discarded clothing and rags.

Lopes picked something up off the ground and studied it. A filthy t-shirt. Kid-sized. Brown stains splattered across the front. He flung it away.

They came to the end of the hallway and were surprised to find a blind corner to the right with a passage hardly wider than a man.

Lucky stopped on the near side at the corner.

Mason didn't like it. He wasn't going to send a Marine into that unknown. He was about to order them to prep it with a frag when the door at the end of the hall swung open.

The darkness flared with a blinding burst of automatic gunfire.

Bullets snapped down the corridor. One zipped by Mason's ear so close it seared the delicate skin. Tracer rounds streaked through the air like lethal lasers.

Channing shoved Lucky to the ground and rushed the unknown target, his rifle banging away. His body jerked as an enemy bullet found its mark.

Mason knew Channing couldn't last. It was a miracle he wasn't already cut to pieces. He rushed forward as Channing slumped to the ground, crossed the dark passage to the right, and barreled into the room with his rifle blazing. Something yanked his boot back and he crashed to the ground. Rounds zipped through the air two feet above his head.

He twisted around and saw a muj not twenty feet away, tucked in tight behind a concrete barrier. His crazed eyes illuminated by the muzzle flash of the roaring machine gun in his hands. Mason prepped a frag and tossed it over the barrier.

The blast vaporized the insurgent and nearly killed Mason as well. Shrapnel hits in his hands and face stung like a colony of fire ants had been dumped on them. His one good eye saw a blurred world that refused to come into focus.

Flickering orange hues lit the room. The frag had ignited

some of the debris on the floor. The flames quickly spread, pushed on by the desiccated rags.

Mason tried to stand and fell back to the floor. His right foot wouldn't work. The heel of his boot was soaked in red. Strangely, it didn't hurt yet.

He crawled over to Channing by the doorway. His demolitions expert lay there with a hand clutched over his chest. Mason peeked at the wound and grimaced. The shoulder and collarbone were a shattered ruin of bone and blood.

Lucky crawled toward them and another fusillade of fire erupted. This time from the dark recess now to Mason's left. Lucky fell back toward the rest of the squad and managed to avoid taking a hit.

Channing grabbed Mason's vest.

"I don't wanna die, Sarge," Channing said in a terrified voice. "Please."

A voice floated around the corner, out of the black depths of the narrow passage.

"Please, don't want die."

A thick Arabic accented voice mocked Channing's plea for life.

"Don't want die," it said again in a taunting tone, followed by a guttural laugh. "Alsh Shayatin al' amrikia."

Rage boiled in Mason's gut. A dark malignance burned through his brain. He'd rip the torturer's intestines out with his teeth. Cave in his skull and devour his brains while the light faded from his eyes.

"Please, Sarge," Channing said with a fading voice.

Channing needed immediate evac, but they were pinned down. Another cascade of fire blasted across the hall. So thick it was like a solid, wavering sheet of death.

There was no way they'd get through it.

The onslaught ignited more of the cloth and debris in the hallway. Lucky stamped on a burning pile and only managed to send glowing sparks into surrounding piles that also caught.

The gunfire stopped.

Mason pushed up his NVGs. The growing fire lit up the entire corridor.

The men across the impassable chasm turned sideways, clearing a path. Lopes was back by the entrance. Orange flames licked up the walls. Black smoke curled and thickened on the ceiling.

Lopes took off at a dead sprint toward them. Faster than he had any right to be, he sailed across the passage and gunfire exploded, just missing him. He scrambled to Mason's side.

"Get Channing outta here. Get everyone out. This place is gonna burn down on our heads."

"Sarge, your foot doesn't look so good," he replied.

"Don't worry about me. I'll make it."

Lopes didn't move.

"Get him out," Mason said. "I'll be right behind you."

Lopes nodded. He pulled Channing to his feet, carrying almost all of the injured soldier's weight.

"I'll cover you. Go when I fire."

Mason crawled to the edge of the doorway and pulled himself up. Flames licked up the walls. The debris on the floor crackled glowing yellow. An impenetrable layer of dark smoke obscured the ceiling.

"Don't stop. I'm on your six."

Mason poked his barrel around the corner. He nodded at Lopes and then hammered away into the narrow passage.

Lopes dove across the opening with Channing by his

side. Lucky caught them on the other side and helped carry their wounded brother down the hall.

Bits of flaming debris swirled in the smoke like fireflies in the night sky.

Mason blinked his eye and tried to pull the two versions of the hall into one. He put weight on his numb right foot and collapsed to the floor.

"Death comes for you, al' amriki. Allahu akbar."

Mason didn't care. He wanted only one thing. To kill the man behind the voice. He crawled toward the doorway.

A section of burning ceiling crashed to the ground, blasting a searing wave of heat at him.

He rolled back, shielding his face. Lying on his back, staring into hell. He breathed in and convulsed as the superheated smoke seared his lungs.

"Death is here, al' amriki."

Acid rage burned Mason's insides even more than the toxic air. Black hate boiled over in his brain. He would kill. He would take life before conceding his own.

"I am death! I am coming!"

Out of the blurred, swirling smoke and crackling flames, a dark form appeared.

The enemy.

Mason unleashed his rage. He emptied a magazine into the shadow that had come to claim him. Every bullet delivered his vicious intent. He screamed death as he gave it.

The form collapsed.

The body fell forward on top of him.

Mason rolled to the side and the body tumbled off. The head smacked the floor next to his own. The face of a dying man inches away.

"Remember your promise, Sarge."

Lopes blew a last breath across Mason's face and his eyes went dim.

70

The Last Day
Los Angeles, California

MASON doubled over, the decades old anguish a ragged knife tearing his bowels out. He pitched to the side and slammed into the wall.

He could never take back what happened. He'd die a thousand times over if just one would take Lopes' place.

A black void beckoned. Promised him a welcoming numb if only he'd let go. If only he'd take one step off the cliff.

The promise of oblivion rang false though. He'd drowned in it years ago. Almost given up his wife and daughter to it. The only things that mattered anymore.

He'd drowned himself in drink for those two dark years. He'd only reached for life after dying below the black waves. Died and then peered up through the warbling surface to see what he was choosing to leave behind.

A family that loved him.

A life that could mean something, if he'd give it more than a bottomless bottle of Jack Daniels. For his family, he chose more.

Dying was easy. Living could be so much harder.

Pushing the darkness aside, knowing it would never leave him, Mason rose to do what he'd been trained to do. In his last career and the current one. To end lives and to save them.

He stepped forward and a small, dark green metal ball clunked out of the open doorway and rolled toward him.

A frag.

Mason launched into the office door opposite him and crashed through as the world exploded.

A deafening blast twisted his guts and cranked up the piercing tone that muted everything else. A wave of pressure flung him to the floor.

Warm wetness leaked from his ears.

His vision blurred and his head ached.

A slender bald man wearing lime green glasses popped up behind a couch. He looked vaguely familiar. His clear blue eyes studied Mason with a calm intensity.

Whoever he was, he wasn't a threat.

"Get down!" Mason shouted.

The words rumbled in his chest, but they seemed far away. He checked his body and saw all his limbs attached and functioning. His suit was torn in a hundred places.

But he was lucky to be alive.

The man behind the couch nodded and ducked back down.

Mason found his pistol and crawled to the open door. The wall next to it was a ragged ruin of small holes, shredded beams, and dangling drywall. The hallway outside filled with smoke and swirling debris.

As the numbness faded and his mind reconnected with his body, he realized he didn't get quite as lucky as he thought. His back stung like a hornet's nest busted open inside his shirt.

He'd taken some shrapnel. He'd felt it before.

Mason forced himself up and held the doorframe as the ground settled beneath his feet. He thought of Theresa.

A hostage to that animal. A shield.

Something in his soul, something long restrained, tore free. A thirst that only made sense in the grim necessity of war.

The killer came forward.

It burned in him. An atomic fusion of vengeance and fury.

He screamed as the rage boiled over. His body vibrated from a massive adrenaline dump. He raised his pistol and charged into the hall, through the smoke and dust. His choking breaths a remote and trivial sensation.

Only the blood mattered. To make it spill. To make it flow.

A short figure with a pocked face jumped into view and the muzzle of his assault rifle unloaded a fusillade of fire in Mason's direction.

The whine and crack of bullets seared by, inches from his head.

Mason dropped to a knee as his trigger finger pulled again and again. His front sight locked onto the thug's chest. Seven rounds dug fatal channels through lungs and heart.

Mason raised the muzzle and sighted again as he squeezed off two more rounds.

Both impacted the target's head. The first round tore through his cheek and exploded in a pink mist behind. The second round pulped his left eye and blew out the back of his head. Gore splattered the wall behind and the guy dropped. The rifle went silent as it tumbled to the floor next to him.

Mason slammed a fresh magazine home and stowed the depleted one as he fast-walked forward and came upon the open doorway. He sliced the pie around the corner and came up face to muzzle with a shotgun barrel. A tall, lanky guy with more scars than minutes left on Earth squeezed the trigger.

A slug cut through Mason's jacket as he fell back and tripped over himself, landing on his knees. More shots pulverized the opposite wall behind him.

He lunged forward with his pistol angled up. The skinny guy looked down in shock, but it was too late. Shock wasn't an effective defense.

Mason unleashed five rounds less than two feet away. He walked them up the unlucky kid's torso until the last one caught him in the throat and blasted out the back of his head. Chunks of brain and bone plastered the ceiling. A geyser of blood spouted from a severed carotid artery.

The punctured body tumbled back and collapsed.

Mason rolled across the doorway as movement flashed inside and a pistol boomed. Pain shocked his calf as he rolled. Like a cattle prod touched the skin and jerked the muscle inside.

He pushed himself up on the far side of the doorway and stumbled a little as his left leg faltered. The cloth over his left calf glistened a shade darker. He tested it with a little weight.

A jolt of agony shot up his leg, but his weight held.

He set it aside for now.

"Let her go, Cesar!"

"I'll murder you all!"

Theresa screamed. The bleak terror in her voice nearly unhinged him. He fought to keep some measure of control. Simple madness wouldn't save her.

But killing would.

71

ELIO crouched behind the desk with Theresa behind him. Like that made her safe. He was out of ammo and out of options. He looked back to check on her.

Her eyes were watching his right hand. He tried to move the sliced fingers and agony jolted to his toes.

Theresa ripped at her tattered pajama bottoms and a long strip tore free. She held Elio's injured hand and wrapped the soft fabric around his fingers like a mitten. She secured the end, but didn't release his hand.

Their eyes met. A silent, eternal connection in a frenzied, ephemeral environment.

She brought his hand to her lips and gently kissed the bandage.

Elio gulped and wanted to say so much. Words he didn't know, yet felt. Things he couldn't speak, yet knew. But he had to save her first. That before anything else. He turned back and considered their situation.

Mason might be nearby, but he was too late.

Only Elio stood between Theresa and that rabid dog Cesar.

He needed a weapon. With his left hand, he yanked open a drawer and heard the jangle of metal. He couldn't stand up to see what was in it because his head would've popped up over the counter and been visible to the waiting room. He needed his head intact to save Theresa.

So he reached up into the open drawer and clawed at whatever he could get.

A razor edge sliced his fingertip.

"Ow!"

He yanked his hand back and pinched at the blood welling out. He reached up again, intent on grabbing whatever had sliced him. His hand closed around a handle and out came a plastic tape dispenser.

He cursed and slammed it on the marble floor.

He shoved his hand back into the drawer and felt a sharp point dig into his palm. He tried to pull out whatever got him. A letter opener hopefully. Even a pair of scissors. Anything that could protect Theresa.

Out came a wooden spoon.

A useless wooden spoon.

Were they allowed to eat at their desk? And if so, couldn't they have used a fork? A metal fork? Something he could stab with.

He was about to reach back up when the crack of shots rang out. Not knowing if they were aimed at him, he ducked lower and squeezed up against the cabinet.

"What are you doing?" asked Theresa. Her words cutting in and out as more gunfire erupted.

They both instinctively dropped as low as they could.

"I don't know!"

He looked at the spoon. Was he going to lull Cesar to sleep by tapping out a rhythm on his bloodied palm? Maybe break it apart and stab him with a splintered end? That could work.

He held the ends and tried to snap it like a chicken bone. It didn't bend. It didn't even creak. He lined up and slammed the middle down on his knee. The impact jolted through his body. He smashed the spoon again and again on the floor, and still it remained whole.

"What are you doing?" Theresa asked.

"Nothing that's working."

"Let me see it."

Theresa grabbed the spoon and placed it diagonally against the cabinet and the floor. She leaned over and kicked it dead center. It cracked in half, leaving one side with a sharp tapered point.

He grabbed it and turned just as Cesar barreled around the corner, his polished gun spitting lead and flame.

Elio launched himself up and spun as something punched him in the side. Like an angry donkey landed a kick. His momentum carried him forward even as his body jerked around.

He landed against Cesar's broad chest, and wrapped his arms around the shot caller's thick neck like they were a couple at a slow dance.

He slammed his head up and caught Cesar on the nose. The two fell back into the wall. Elio scrambled for a hold. Some purchase that might slow down his much stronger adversary.

Cesar spun around and slammed Elio off the wall like a rag doll. He brought the gleaming pistol up to his face and rammed the barrel against his skull.

Never mind the bullet, the muzzle ripped a gash into his forehead. The pressure so fierce it felt like his skull was going to implode.

Elio watched as time slowed and Cesar's finger curled around the trigger. The knuckles turned white as the finger curled in.

So this was how it would turn out. His violent end.

A sadness washed over him.

He would die. And that wasn't the worst of it.

The worst part was that he'd never know if Theresa made it.

"Don't do it, Cesar!"

Elio turned to see Mason with his pistol pointed in their direction. He'd come.

But he'd come too late.

72

MASON held a bead on Cesar's temple, and then the bridge of his nose as the man turned to face him. Everything inside him screamed to take the shot. The animal inside wanted blood. Wanted death. Wanted to kill and kill until no threat remained.

Elio.

What was he doing here?

A remote part of his brain registered the pressure of Cesar's finger on the trigger. Saw that a round through Cesar's skull might end up with another through Elio's.

Like father, like son.

Both dead at his hand.

The killer inside didn't care.

It pleaded. Begged. And then shrieked when his trigger remained unpulled.

It wanted blood.

But Mason was more than the soldier he'd been forced to become in Fallujah.

He was a husband.

A father.

A man dedicated to protecting lives.

He couldn't take the shot.

"Don't do it, Cesar," he said in a calm voice. Like you might speak to a vicious dog.

Mason released the grip on his pistol and let it pivot on his finger until the muzzle swung up to the ceiling.

Cesar watched him, perhaps surprised for an instant that another dog would roll over and expose its neck for the kill.

Mason bent over and laid the gun on the floor.

"Kick it away."

Mason did as instructed.

"You stupider than you look," Cesar said with a cold, mocking tone.

He swung the chromed Desert Eagle off of Elio's forehead and around at Mason.

Elio's left hand shot up and slammed into Cesar's face.

The brute roared and shoved Elio's head through drywall. Cesar spun, reaching for the short wooden spoon buried deep in his eye socket. He howled as his hand bumped the shallow cup, stirring the wound and spilling more blood down his cheek.

Cesar spun to Mason and unleashed a barrage of fire. The large, mirrored pistol bucked in his hand.

Mason dropped to a knee as a round ripped through his hair. More rounds sliced through the air inches above his head.

He yanked his right pant leg up and pulled out the subcompact Glock 26 from his ankle holster. In one fluid motion, his finger dropped inside the trigger guard and curled back as the sight picture lined up on Cesar's nose. Two rounds punctured his skull in quick succession.

The shot caller stood for a moment, a look of surprise frozen in his eyes.

Mason fired two more shots into his broad chest and the big man collapsed.

Still covering him, Mason approached. He stood above the body. The body of the man who'd put his daughter's life in danger. The body of the man who'd put Elio's life in danger.

Before he could stop himself, he unloaded the rest of the magazine into Cesar's chest.

The killer inside grinned. Vicious. Hungry.

Mason understood then that it would always be a part of him. And that he had to accept what he was. What he'd done. Perhaps he could even use it.

It might be a necessary partner in this new, chaotic world. So long as he kept it on a tight leash.

73

"Daddy," Theresa said as she rushed into his arms. He wrapped her in a hug he wished would last forever. A hug that would keep her safe from the world.

She buried her face in his chest and burst into tears.

"You're safe, honey. You're safe."

"Thank you, Mr. West," Elio said. A smile flickered across his face and then he collapsed back onto the wall and slumped to the floor.

Mason stepped over and spun around so he could inspect Elio while still keeping an eye on the fallen gang members.

There was a lot of blood. Too much.

Elio's face was waxy and pale. Several shades lighter than usual. His eyes fluttered and closed.

"Stay with me, Lopez!"

The relieved feeling in Mason's chest clamped back down, tighter than ever. Echoes across time lent their mass to the weight crushing down on him.

"Don't quit on me, Lopez!"

Mason peeled up Elio's shirt and found the wound. On

the side, at or just below the ribs. Maybe a lucky hit. Maybe a death sentence. He'd seen similar injuries go both ways. He felt around the backside and couldn't find an exit wound.

He ripped off the tattered remains of his suit jacket and packed it on the wound. The layers immediately saturated. He tore off his shirt and added that to the makeshift dressing.

"Theresa, I need you to be strong, honey. Elio needs help and we're the only ones who can give it."

"He saved my life, Dad."

"Hold this here." He took her hands and showed her how and where to keep pressure applied.

He found some duct tape in a drawer and wrapped Elio's torso, making sure the clothes stayed put. The kid needed immediate medical attention.

Mason had no choice but to hope his wife had made it home and could help. A call to 911 wouldn't work because where would the ambulance take them?

An ER visit was out of the question. From the chaos on TV, few were receiving medical attention. Besides, he had no intention of exposing any of them to the contagion going around. Those dense, desperate scenes were ideal transmission vectors. Sick people, uncontrolled physical contact in a tightly packed space. People would leave the ERs once they saw no help was forthcoming, or once violence broke out and drove them away.

In either case, newly infected people would walk away from the encounter. They would go on to infect others.

Mason needed to get them home. And minimize further contact with others. At least until they had Elio stabilized and then had a chance to gather more information.

He dipped an arm around Elio's good side and pulled him to his feet.

Elio responded with a mumbled grunt. His eyes opened and gazed on Mason with slow recognition.

"Let's get you out of here, Lopez."

Elio nodded.

"You're going to be fine. Just stay with me."

With Theresa helping to clear the way, Mason limped out of the office with Elio at his side. Elio's head hung forward, barely moving. He'd lost a lot of blood.

Not again. Please not again.

They got out to the hall and ran into the bald man that Mason had seen earlier. The lanky man adjusted his overtly fashionable glasses and smiled.

"I'd like to thank you."

"Who are you?" Mason asked.

"I'm Gabriel Cruz." He waved around to nowhere in particular. "This is my place."

The Gabriel Cruz. The richest man in the world. No wonder he looked familiar.

"Looks like you need some redecorating."

"True." Gabriel looked at Elio.

"He was one of the ones trying to kill me."

"He was just as much a victim as you."

Gabriel considered that.

"Well, as I said, I'd like to thank you."

"Wasn't here for you," Mason replied.

He nodded and pushed on as best they could. They walked down the hall and found the central elevators. By the time they reached the first floor, the thick wad of fabric stuffed under the duct tape was soaked through.

They descended to the lobby and exited the building.

The Bronco's door flew open as they approached. Iridia jumped out and stared with wide eyes.

"You did it!"

Theresa stumbled and caught herself. She gaped at Iridia. "Are you—"

"I'll explain later," Mason said. "Get in."

"Is this a normal day for you?" Iridia asked.

"Iridia, help Theresa climb into the backseat."

She held the seat forward and helped his daughter inside. She climbed in behind her and pulled the seat toward her to lay it as flat as possible.

Mason gently laid Elio in the reclined seat.

Iridia peeked forward and grimaced.

"Is he going to make it?"

Mason didn't want to conjecture. He didn't want Elio to hear conjecture. You assumed the best until reality forced you to accept something worse.

"He's banged up, but he'll be fine. Let's go."

He shut the passenger door and ran around the front. He climbed in and glanced back.

Iridia held Theresa's hand in hers. She picked debris out of his daughter's hair.

He cranked the throaty V8 to life and remembered to breathe.

"Holly! Daddy, wait!" Theresa yelled. "We have to get Holly. She's out there."

Mason studied the innumerable cuts on his hands. He didn't know how to tell her.

"We have to get her! She's hurt!"

Mason turned and his daughter froze when she saw his face.

"Holly didn't make it, honey."

"What? Where is she?"

Mason didn't know how to respond, so he defaulted to how his wife would've answered.

"She's in a better place now."

He wished he believed that as implicitly as Beth did. For her, that was simply the way of things. As natural a universal law as complementary angles always adding up to the right angle.

She had the right angle. He wanted to share it, but wanting wasn't believing.

"What do you mean?"

"She's gone, honey. Her body is in the back. But Holly is gone."

Theresa looked over the seat and sharply inhaled when she saw the covered body of her best friend. Of what used to be her best friend.

Iridia turned Theresa back around and cradled her in her arms. Theresa buried her face in Iridia's embrace. Her body shook with choked cries. Iridia stroked her hair, holding her tight while she unraveled.

"I'm so sorry."

Mason flicked on the lights. The devastation on the street ahead blurred into other, similar streets in his mind. In his past.

What was going on in Los Angeles? Why was it starting to resemble a war-ravaged city in a destitute, third world country?

Mason turned the Bronco around and accelerated away, determined not to let the past catch up to him.

Determined not to lose the son of the father he'd lost so long ago.

74

BETH wiped the sweat from her forehead, careful to use the sleeve of her shirt in order to keep her hands sterile. Somewhat sterile at least. Their bedroom wasn't the cleanest version of an operating room.

Mason sat in the overstuffed chair in front of her, his head leaning back against the headrest.

"How's Elio?"

Beth glanced over her shoulder at the stationary form lying on their bed. His feet rested on a pile of pillows. An avalanche of blankets covered him.

"Doing better."

The blue tinge to his lips and the pale skin of his face laid bare the lie. Mason didn't need the evidence. He could read the lines on her face as easily as lines in a book. They'd been together that long.

She'd managed to stop the bleeding and stabilize the wound, but Elio had lost a lot of blood. His heart had stopped and only an IV injection of epinephrine had brought him back. She'd already given him three pints of Mason's type O negative blood.

The Last Day

But he needed more.

Her husband was as healthy as they came, but losing two pints would knock anyone on their butt. Losing three started to put vital organs in danger. Losing more and he could end up in the same situation as Elio. And he'd already lost a good amount from the bullet wound in his calf, several bits of shrapnel in his back, and dozens of other minor cuts and scrapes.

Losing any more blood would be a huge risk.

"Take another pint."

She'd already taken two more than she felt comfortable with. Mason could barely move as it was. He was asking her to put his life in danger.

Her hands shook as she touched his cheek.

So cold.

"Mason, I can't. You're weak. There's no guarantee that one more will save him and it might kill you."

"Please, Beth. Take it."

"Why? I know you care for him, but think about Theresa and me. We don't want to lose you."

Tears welled in her eyes and streamed down her cheeks.

Mason tried to swallow and gave up. His voice came out raspy and quiet.

"I promised to protect his son."

"His son? You mean David?"

"Yes."

"Mason, I know you promised. And you've done your best. You didn't promise to die for him."

"To myself I did."

"Stop it! Why are you saying this?"

Mason looked at the ceiling and she wasn't sure if the conversation had ended.

"Talk to me. Please."

Mason looked back to her. His face a wan mask of grief. His lips pursed and trembling.

"I killed him."

"You didn't kill him. You said it was the gang leader that shot him."

"Not Elio. David."

"David? What about David?"

"I shot him. I killed him."

His eyes welled with moisture, but no tears escaped. He turned away.

She'd never heard this version of the story. David had died from enemy fire during a house breach. Mason had told it only once, long ago. But she remembered.

"No, you didn't."

He stared at the wall, and through it to a distant time and place.

"Beth, I did."

None of it made sense. What was he saying? He was probably too out of it to know.

"It was chaos. Explosions everywhere. An inferno. I was trapped. The op went sideways. Insurgents hit most of the squad. I went down. I thought it was the end. I thought I was dead. But then he came back for me. Only I didn't know it was him. I thought he was already down."

His eyes unfocused, or focused on the memory.

"He was just a dark figure in the doorway. I could barely see. My eyes were swollen shut. Flames burned everywhere. I was furious. So angry. I wanted to kill all those muj murderers."

Mason shut his eyes and shook his head.

"I thought he was an insurgent," he said, "and I reveled in killing him."

Beth grabbed the seat back to steady herself.

Suddenly, the two years following his return made sense. She'd known PTSD was a real thing. That Mason had lost squad mates. She'd known he took it hard.

But she never understood the depth of his suffering. Never understood the anguish that dragged him down.

She understood now.

"Why didn't you tell me?"

It would've helped her to help him. To support him. To give him space. To be more patient with his process. To understand.

"I couldn't. I didn't want it to be real. I half-convinced myself it wasn't."

"Does anyone else know?"

"I do now," a weak voice said.

Beth looked over her shoulder and saw Elio awake. His eyelids heavy and barely open.

"I'm sorry, Elio," Mason said. His chest convulsed as a ragged exhale escaped. "So sorry."

The room went quiet.

The faintest whisper broke the silence.

"Did your best..."

His words trailed off and he slipped back under.

Beth turned back to her husband. He looked crushed. Beaten. Such a contradiction to the man she woke up to every morning.

This morning that seemed like years ago. This morning when things made sense. This morning before the world went crazy.

What happened to normal, everyday life?

Was it always so delicate and we never noticed?

Did we ignore the fragility? Did we have to ignore it in order to keep going, day in and day out?

Mason caught her gaze. His jaw set, his eyes unblinking.

"Save him, Beth," he said as he rolled his arm over to expose the IV port taped to the crook of his elbow.

She wanted to collapse. Run away to avoid doing what he asked. Tears blurred her vision as she inserted the needle and watched as another vital pint oozed out of the man she loved. She watched his color leak away. Cold sweat trickled from his brow.

"I will, my love. I will."

She'd tell him anything to bring peace. To bring comfort where only black sorrow dwelt.

Mason managed a weak smile before his eyes rolled up in his head and he passed out.

75

THERESA lay on her parent's bed next to Elio. Sunlight speared through a crack in the curtain and blinded her. She looked away, at the clock on the side table.

It was morning.

Holly was gone. She'd watched from the front window as her mom and dad carried the covered body around to the backyard. Her best friend since third grade was gone.

Max was gone. Her two best friends in the world stolen from her. Grief stabbed at her heart. She pulled away from the sensation. Too overwhelmed to process it.

The later events of the night bubbled to the surface and she opened her eyes. And saw Elio watching her.

He smiled.

"Morning."

"Elio." She could barely speak his name. He'd nearly died a few times last night. She didn't know if he'd make it until morning. There was no way she could sleep. That was the last thing she remembered before waking up.

"You're alive."

She touched his lips, as if to test this waking reality. One she didn't yet trust not to be a dream. He kissed her fingertips.

"Couldn't leave right when things were getting interesting," he said with a strained wink.

"Are you hitting on me, Elio Lopez? Because if you are, I might remind you that we are in my parents' bed."

"I noticed that."

A slow smile spread across his face.

She didn't mean that!

If she could've seen him through an unbiased lens, she would've been forced to admit he looked terrible. But she looked at him with nothing but wonder. Nothing but love.

"You saved me," she said.

"No, you saved me."

Theresa edged closer and propped up on an elbow. She lowered her face to his. Her lips brushed his and a tingle of perfect connection passed between them.

"Ahem."

Theresa looked up. Her mom stood in the open doorway with her arms crossed.

"I'll need you to give my patient some breathing room. He's lucky to have pulled through."

Holding her close, Elio said, "You're right Mrs. West. I'm the luckiest guy in the world."

"Slow it down, Romeo. That's my daughter you're swooning over."

"I know."

Her mother's eyebrows shot up.

"I saved you last night. Don't make me kill you this morning."

"Mom!"

Her mother grinned, a sadness tinging her good spirits. "Only kidding. Mostly. Theresa, can you help me with a bottle? I've been up every hour and a half all night. I'm wrecked."

Only then did Theresa notice the blanket in her mother's crossed arms.

Her mom looked down and smiled. Tender and protective. She tilted the swaddled bundle down to reveal a tiny chimpanzee.

"Sure."

Beth walked over and deposited the wrapped bundle in Theresa's lap. "I'll get the bottle."

She headed back to the kitchen.

Elio peeked over and creased his brow.

"Maybe I'm still out of it, but isn't that a monkey?"

"No. It's a chimpanzee. Isn't he the cutest thing ever?"

He really was. Eyes closed and mouth puckered. Delicate little fingers pushing at the air. It squirmed when the air ended up not being filled with warm milk. It squealed and turned its head.

Elio's gaze returned to Theresa.

"He's the second cutest."

Theresa's cheeks burned. Her ears felt warm.

"You are an unrepentant flirt, Elio Lopez."

He looked up at the ceiling and smiled.

"What?"

"I like the way you say my name."

Her mom returned with a bottle of warm electrolytes. Theresa knew it wasn't milk yet from her experience with Jane's first few months.

Her heart broke again knowing Jane was gone. And the loss swirled with the wonder of holding her baby. Like a grand cycle of life playing out in her hands.

In her heart.

She didn't understand the depths of it. She didn't know

it could go this deep. The full depth and meaning was a hint and a promise.

She didn't have to understand right this minute.

It felt significant. Like a moment you never forget. One that changed everything.

That was enough for now.

76

MASON pushed himself up on the living room couch and rubbed his eyes. He felt like Rip Van Winkle after only an hour of sleep. The events of the night had not yet receded beyond the comforting distance of a good night's sleep.

Scratching the gunk out of his eyes was exhausting.

"Good morning, honey."

Beth walked in from the kitchen with a tall glass of orange juice in her hand. She gave it to him accompanied by a kiss on the forehead.

"Get back under that blanket. You're still too cold."

"Yes, doctor."

He threw the blanket over his legs and then took a sip. The citrus tang hurt his mouth. He took another drink and then gulped it down.

"Thirsty, huh?"

Orange juice dribbled down his chin.

"A little."

"I'll get more."

"How's Elio?"

Beth paused and turned back. "He's doing better. The soft tissue damage will heal. No vital organs were affected. But he got pretty torn up. Infection is the big question mark. I've got him pumped full of what antibiotics I had, but it's too soon to tell."

"He'll make it. He's tough. Just like his father."

"I wish I had your confidence."

Mason remembered carrying Holly's lifeless body to the backyard, and down into the storm shelter where the cool air would slow the tissue decay. He would take the corpse to her parents as soon as he had the strength. The thought of initiating their nightmare turned his stomach.

An endless well of grief awaited them.

No other future would come to pass. And yet, not knowing what happened provided a limbo of uncertainty. Like the cat in the quantum experiment that is both alive and dead at the same time.

He knew he was partly to blame for her death. He hadn't pulled the trigger. He knew exactly what that felt like. This was different. It was a burden. A guilt. But he'd carried greater for years.

And for his family, he would shoulder a new one and carry on despite the weight.

"Mason," Beth said, "about what you told me last night. You—"

"Let's hold on that, if you don't mind. I'm glad you know the truth. But I'm not ready to revisit it right now."

Beth looked at the floor, chewed her lip, and then nodded.

"I'll get the juice."

Mason realized again for the millionth time, he was so lucky to have her.

She'd gone into the kitchen, so he raised his voice for her to hear.

"Where's Iridia?"

Another voice answered.

"Here."

She appeared in the hallway to the bedrooms. She wore his old UCLA sweatshirt. Bright yellow lettering on dark blue cloth. It hung low for a top, but rode high for a dress. Her long, thin legs drew attention to themselves. She probably planned it that way.

How did a swimsuit issue model end up in his home? How did she end up in his sweatshirt? Beth was going to be grumpy, no doubt.

Mason gave her a smile he didn't totally feel. His body hurt and he wasn't sure how his wife was going to react to their interaction. Mostly, he wished Iridia wasn't his responsibility. What was he supposed to do with her now? He was too beat to deal with it.

So, he faked a smile and acted like a regular human being.

"Good morning," he said.

"It's too early to tell."

Maybe she wasn't all bad. He felt the same exact way.

Beth returned to the living room with another glass of orange juice.

Mason salivated so hard his jaws ached.

Iridia waved her away.

"Just put it on the table. I'm still waking up."

Beth did a double take and then chuckled.

"It's not for you. There's more in the fridge if you want some."

Iridia looked confused. Like the idea of getting her own juice in the morning was incomprehensible.

"You know, you might be more comfortable with some shorts on," Beth said with a raised brow.

Iridia pinched at the cloth.

"This is fine. A bit rough. But okay."

Mason accepted the offered glass and took a big swig. The sugary juice acted like a battery charger. He literally felt the energy seeping into his limbs.

He leaned back against the couch and looked out the window.

The old Woodie classic was in the neighbor's driveway. Otis must have gotten home after they did last night. Mason remembered the scene at the Reagan Medical Center and that Otis went to see his wife there yesterday. Hopefully, they got out before the chaos broke loose.

And then another memory pinged for attention and he grimaced.

Beth's slow morning demeanor kicked into doctor mode. "What is it? Pain?"

"No. I didn't get a chance to check on Mr. Piddles last night."

Beth looked out the window and saw the car in the driveway.

"They're back now. I'm sure he's fine."

Mason started to get up.

"I should go. You know how they are with that demanding devil."

Beth stepped in front of him and gently pushed him back down to the couch.

"You're not going anywhere, Mr. West." She turned to Iridia.

"Iridia, can you please be a dear, and go next door to make sure Mr. Piddles didn't die from starvation or meet some other improbable end?"

"Really?"

Iridia looked scandalized at the thought of doing anything more than leaning against the wall.

"I'll pour you a glass of orange juice, and I'll consider making you some toast and jam."

Iridia nodded. She understood the give and take.

"Deal."

"Put some pants on first."

Iridia tugged at the sweatshirt and it lifted for an instant, revealing black lace panties.

"What's wrong with this?"

"You'll give old Mr. Crayford a heart attack. That's what's wrong with it."

Beth left for a moment and returned with a gray pair of old sweatpants. She dropped them into Iridia's arms.

Iridia yanked up the sweatshirt and wiggled into them. Right there in the living room. Like it was her own private changing room.

Mason looked away and caught Beth watching him as he did. Her arms crossed and lips pressed tight together.

"We have a bathroom, Iridia. Feel free to use it for changing or whatever."

Iridia adjusted and primped the ratty old clothes like it was a fashion shoot.

"No need."

Beth exhaled, in a pointedly exasperated way that nobody could miss.

Iridia did. She combed fingers through her hair and then put it up in a bun with a red hair band.

"Go Trojans. That's UCLA, right?"

Beth groaned and shook her head. "No, the Trojans are USC."

Iridia rolled her eyes like the correction was so minor as to not merit a mention in the first place.

"It's all sports stuff."

Mason stifled a laugh.

Beth turned on her heel and marched to the kitchen.

"Go check on the cat. I'll get your juice."

77

One small bite of bread with butter tasted delicious, so rich Mason could barely swallow it. He washed it down with more OJ. Liquid wasn't a problem. He set the glistening triangle of toasted wheat back on the saucer.

"Where's Theresa?"

"She's sleeping in our bed with Elio."

The hackles on Mason's back prickled up. His jaw clenched and teeth ground together. The next bite of toast forgotten.

Elio was a good kid. And Mason was overjoyed that he'd made it through the night. But that sure didn't mean he got to sleep in the same bed as his daughter!

As weak as he was, his brain urged him to stomp in there and toss the injured boy out on his ear.

Beth giggled.

"You are such a dad."

Mason hardly heard.

"Relax. He's in no shape to do anything that might set off your dad alarms."

"No more sleeping together."

"What are you worried about? What could they be doing in there? All alone. No adult to monitor their blossoming desires."

Mason knew she was playing him, and he still got more worked up. But he knew how to play games, too.

"Iridia seemed to really like my sweatshirt. Fit her well, too, don't you think?"

Beth's game face cracked and she scowled.

"Don't you even start that!"

They both giggled and she snuggled up under his arm. Their lips touched and her needed warmth spread through him. She was the most amazing woman he'd ever known.

Even if she could be a little jealous for no reason.

The enjoyment of their intimate moment shattered with a scream coming from outside. Mason thought it was Iridia, but he couldn't be sure. He was certain it came from next door.

"Help me up."

Beth paused while the doctor and the wife inside her battled to make the call. She helped him up and wrapped a blanket around his shoulders. He was grateful she understood when a protective doctor needed to compromise with a protective husband, father, and neighbor.

Biting through the sharp, stabbing pain in his left calf, Mason got to his feet. With a little help from his doctor, he made his way down the front steps, remembering to skip the second one even in his diminished state.

Especially now, when a slip would assuredly send him on a collision path with the pavement.

They walked next door and found the door open. As they entered, Iridia nearly bowled them over on her way out. Her face washed white with panic. Words stammered and stumbled out of her mouth, over and on top of each other like an avalanche.

"I came, the door, walked in, was open." She waved toward Otis and Mabel's bedroom. "Just walked in."

Of course she would just walk in. The world was an open door for her.

"I can't, alive, he's there."

Mason held her shoulders, trying to calm and bring her back to the ground.

She went silent and looked at each of them with eyes wide as dinner plates.

"The blood."

A warbling scream burbled up in her throat.

"The blood."

It was clear she would offer no more.

"Stay here."

He walked toward the bedrooms in the back, Beth following along in his wake. As he drew near, the sweet stink of putrid flesh assaulted his senses. He knew the smell. He'd fought through a devastated city choked with it.

Death.

He gagged and covered his nose and mouth with the blanket.

"Mason," Beth said in a whisper at his ear. Her hand pulled on his shoulder.

He stepped into the open doorway and wished he hadn't.

Mabel Crayford lay sprawled on the bed, posed indecorously with her legs sprawled wide. There was no shame. That and every other human emotion no longer remained. Dark blood soaked the bed sheets and congealed puddles covered the floor. Crusted over open sores covered her gray skin. Like the skin simply split apart and spilled bile onto the bed. Her lips were drawn up tight above her teeth, showing too much gum. The torment of her suffering frozen on her face.

Otis sat next to her, his back to the door. He wore what once might have been a white t-shirt. It was mostly black with dried blood. It stuck to his torso in damp patches from sores seeping pus underneath. More weeping wounds oozed from his exposed skin.

The stench poisoned the air. Mason tasted it, swallowed it. Breathed it into his lungs.

His stomach heaved and he fought to keep vomit down. He swallowed hard.

"Otis." He waited. "Otis."

Otis didn't respond. He dipped a filthy rag into a bowl of dark liquid. He then dabbed at Mabel's eyes. Or what was once her eyes. Her sockets were crusted black.

She had not died easily.

Otis whispered incoherent words.

Mason started to take a step into the room and Beth dropped an arm in front of him. She shook her head and mouthed the word *No*.

This was the sickness. The contagion. The thing affecting those people on TV.

At the very hospital where Mabel was receiving treatment.

Mason took a step back and the wood floor creaked.

Otis turned. Bright red blood trickled out of his nose, over his lips, and dripped from his chin to the sheets. Huge red veins in his eyes crowded out the whites. The center a black pit.

Dark streams leaked from his eyes, painting his cheeks variations of red, brown, and black.

He barely looked human.

78

The old man blinked and wiped at his eyes. The pressure burst fragile veins and fresh blood seeped down his cheeks.

"Is someone there?"

He couldn't see. A small blessing.

"Otis, it's Mason."

Are you okay?

The words almost came out, but he cut them off knowing how absurd the question was. This man was as far from okay as was physically possible.

"What happened?"

The old man reached for his wife's hand, patting the blanket until he found it.

"How is Mabel? She went quiet some time ago. She needs rest. Some time to get better."

Mabel wasn't going to get better. She was gone.

"I won't leave her now. Not after fifty years together. Where she goes, I go."

Mason wondered if he knew what he was saying. Because it looked like he was dead right about that.

"Otis, what happened?"

The cloth dropped from his hand and he licked his lips, licking a break in the line of red dripping from his nostrils. The line continued and spilled over his lips in its continuing descent.

"I went to pick up Mabel this morning and the hospital was a mess. Doctors and nurses running around like chickens with their heads cut off."

He coughed and blood spewed out onto the filthy sheets. The new addition only visible by the wet sheen it caked on the older, dried areas.

"They'd moved her and nobody knew where she was. What kind of yahoo operation does that?"

He shook his head.

"It took forever to get someone to help me. To find her."

He covered his mouth and coughed. A wet, crackling hack. Blood oozed between his fingers.

"Such a disgrace. The way she was. Unforgivable."

He turned back to his wife and ran his fingers along her body until they found her face.

He continued speaking, his words wet and mushy.

"I brought her home. So we could be together."

He doubled over, hacking and spitting chunks of fibrous slime onto the sheets. A fresh wave of putridity filled the room. His arms went limp, one on each side of his wife. One final hug before going to join her on the other side.

Beth pulled Mason back.

He didn't budge. It didn't compute. Or maybe it computed too easily. He'd seen gore as bad as this in another place, another time. Mangled bodies left to rot in the streets. Bodies turned inside out like a pair of pants.

Having endured it before didn't make it easier now.

This was closer to home.

Right next door to home.

Beth dragged him back down the hall.

"We can't be here. We have to leave, Mason."

They found Iridia at the entrance and pulled her outside. Mason closed the door, thinking that he'd never walk through it again welcomed by the delicate, rich scent of homemade rhubarb muffins. He'd never sit with Otis on a lazy Sunday afternoon and hear about how much the world had changed. Hear about the cases he'd won in his long career.

Otis either had a perfect record or he never chose to discuss the times he lost.

The Crayfords had survived wars, depressions, and more. And they'd done it together. Side by side through the best and the worst. As horrific as their end was, Mason was glad that they at least faced it together.

He wondered what future he and Beth might have to endure.

79

His chest ached. A suffocating sadness bore down like he was breathing against double the usual gravity.

Beth crossed over to the Crayfords' flower bed and plucked the tallest Gerbera daisy of the bunch. Its petals shone like sunlight. She carried it back and gently set it by the front door.

A single flower at the peak of its ephemeral vigor.

The most pitiable meowing echoed through the closed door.

Beth cracked it open and Mr. Piddles slunk out, his head low. He howled and sniffed at Beth's outstretched hand.

"What are you doing, Beth?"

Mason had a pretty clear idea. He just didn't know if it was a good one.

Beth picked up the rotund cat and crossed back to their driveway. She stopped.

"Hold up here."

She turned to their house. "Theresa! Theresa, come outside!"

Theresa stumbled out a moment later in her second

favorite pajamas. Beth had thrown out the ones she wore last night. This set was long sleeves top and bottom too, thankfully. Mason had never realized how much of a blessing long sleeved pajamas could be. Never realized it until his daughter woke up in bed next to a boy two years her elder.

"Get the mop bucket and a few rags from the pantry closet. The bleach and a heavy duty, black trash bag from under the kitchen sink. And four towels from my bathroom."

Theresa stood there, her brows knitted together in confusion.

"What are you doing with Mr. Piddles?"

"Now, Theresa!"

"Okay. Okay."

She reappeared a few moments later with the requested items.

Beth pointed at a spot ten feet away on the driveway. "Put them there. Don't come closer!"

"Okay. What's going on, Mom?"

"Just do it, honey. I'll explain later."

Theresa did as she was asked.

"Get back now."

Theresa backed up to the bottom step of the porch.

"Go inside, Theresa."

"Why?"

"Theresa!"

She turned and sprinted inside without another word.

Beth turned to Mason and Iridia.

"We need to dispose of our clothes and wipe down completely with a bleach solution."

"What?" Iridia asked.

Beth started stripping down.

"Get naked. Isn't that what supermodels do?"

"Often, yes," Iridia responded without a tinge of sarcasm.

What a strange world she lived in.

Then again, the normal world wasn't all that normal lately.

Beth set Mr. Piddles on the ground. He sat back on his haunches and watched. The occasional sorrowful meow testament to his grief.

Mason took the blanket off his shoulders and stretched aching, exhausted muscles. Sharp pain radiated from his calf and numerous places on his back.

They all peeled out of their respective clothes, right down to their birthday suits. Mason and Beth stood awkwardly, not knowing where to put their hands. Wondering if they should or should not be covering this or that part. Their eyes darted here and there, trying to find a comfortable place to linger and being drawn to places they didn't consider appropriate.

Iridia looked as natural as ever. She stood with her hip cocked to the side and her hand resting on it. She was a vision. Utterly confident without a stitch of clothing on. She studied both of their naked bodies without a hint of discomfort.

"You two keep fit for being so old."

Beth's nostrils flared. "Thanks. I think."

She turned and piled their clothes in the trash bag and then knotted it closed. She knelt down by the bucket and measured out capfuls of bleach.

"One part bleach to eight parts water will kill anything known. Get the hose, Iridia."

Iridia brought it over and Beth filled the bucket. The biting antiseptic scent filled the air.

"We need to scrub every part of our bodies with this solution. Thoroughly. And leave it on for a few minutes."

"You want me to put *that* on *my* body?" She said it like the bucket contained hydrochloric acid. It wasn't quite that strong. "That will murder my skin!"

Beth grabbed a rag and swished it around in the water. Mason couldn't help but admire the curve of her backside as she knelt there.

Beth stood up and held a dripping rag out to Iridia. "There are very likely microbes on your skin right now that will murder you. Murder you like they did those poor souls next door."

Iridia gulped and her deer legs quivered. She accepted the rag.

"You have moisturizer, right?"

She started wiping down her chest and neck.

"Ugh, it stinks."

"That means it's working."

Mason accepted a soaking rag and started scrubbing his shoulders down. Water slid down his back. He winced as the solution washed over fresh wounds.

Beth joined in the cleansing ritual.

"What are you guys doing?"

Theresa on the porch. Her eyes wide and jaw dropped open.

Mason looked at himself, at Beth, at Iridia. They shouted ludicrously. They looked like a high school car wash gone old and illicit.

"Your mother told you to get inside!"

Theresa squeaked and flew back through the door.

They all finished wiping themselves down. All the parts they could reach.

Mason looked over as Iridia strained to wipe the center

of her back. The rag got close but never quite hit right in the middle.

"Let me help," he said without thinking.

He grabbed the rag and scrubbed her back and only when he finished did he feel Beth's gaze burning holes in his back.

He turned and her face was red. Her eyes practically smoking.

"Just being helpful."

And it was true. It wasn't until he'd swiped her back a few times that his eyes unconsciously dropped lower. Even then, he didn't let them linger.

"You're a saint," she said. "Mind getting my back?"

"My pleasure," he said with a wink.

Gallows humor. He'd been here before. When the ugliness of the world pushed you to the edge, humor was the thing that kept your toes attached to dirt.

Mason scrubbed his wife's back, making certain he spent twice as long so there would be no question later.

He finished and, for a brief moment of black comedy, wondered if he should ask Iridia to scrub his. One look at Beth told him she wouldn't understand a soldier's humor.

Her lack of understanding pleased him. Normal people shouldn't have to endure so much misery and suffering.

The thought stopped him cold. He shivered despite the warming morning sun.

What if the normal world no longer existed?

80

The Jefferson Hotel
Washington, D.C.

DR. ANTON RESHENKO touched the ancient silver Dirham in his left pocket. Genghis Khan himself may have once held it in his hand. He rubbed the inscription, marveling at how the coin connected their souls through the ages. A popped blister on the pad of his thumb made it a painful meditation.

He didn't stop. Pain was an obstacle to be overcome, like anything else.

He paced back and forth across the immaculately shined parquet floors in the living area of the Thomas Jefferson suite. The Washington Monument proudly reflected the warm afternoon sun through the open doors to the veranda. There had been many such uncharacteristically warm winter days of late.

An elaborate chandelier hung from the ceiling in the center of the room. Tiny electric candles, one of the few concessions to a modern sensibility, cast warm light through hundreds of sparkling crystals.

They'd tried to dump him in a deluxe suite and only acquiesced to reason after he'd threatened to leave.

The analog clock on the wall indicated his meeting with Senator Rawlings should've started three minutes ago. His teeth squeaked as he ground his jaws together.

He squeezed the coin tight and felt a stab of pain in his thumb. He drew it out and watched as a tiny rivulet of blood welled up and traced down into his palm. He clenched his hand into a fist.

Blood would flow.

One didn't change the course of history with endless talk and diluted consensus.

But he never thought that blood would flow so close to his heart. His daughter. Was she a necessary sacrifice upon the altar of his destiny? Had Genghis Khan done the same?

Perhaps. Then again, Khan had many children. If he lost one, he had many more to garner his attention. Anton just had one. As stubborn and misguided as she was, she was still his flesh and blood. The only reminder left in the world of her angelic mother. His dear Katerina. Taken too soon. Stolen, was more accurate. Murdered, still more.

If only his daughter had listened, none of this would've happened. She'd be safe with him, not trapped at ground zero of what would soon be the biggest transformation humanity had ever seen.

Bigger even than the conquests of Khan.

He could've told her that the future she dreamed of would no longer have meaning. Modeling, acting, being famous. Those were empty ideas nearing their expiration.

But he didn't. And so she disobeyed and went without

telling him. He was too soft on her, because she was the remaining soft part of him.

Iridia.

His fatal flaw.

He wouldn't let her die, because he couldn't.

And that meant getting her out.

Only, he didn't have access to the manpower or equipment necessary to effect such an operation. Hence the meeting.

A knock at the door.

"Yes?"

It opened and his bodyguard, Mr. Pike, appeared.

"Senator Rawlings is here."

"Get out of my way!"

The gray-haired Chairman of the Senate Armed Services Committee pushed by the much larger, much younger man. His bodyguard raised a brow, an unspoken question if he should toss the intruder out on his ear.

Anton would have very much liked to do exactly that. He shook his head.

"Good to see you, Charles."

The door closed as Mr. Pike resumed his station outside.

"Don't glad hand me, Anton," the senator said. "I'm the career politician here. You don't operate on my level."

That was true. Though not in the way the senator intended.

"Why didn't you just come to my office on the hill?"

"I don't come like a dog when called."

"Don't get cute with me!"

The old man unbuttoned his suit coat and loosened his tie.

"Have anything to drink?"

Anton waved him toward the small bar in the corner.

"By all means, let me get it myself."

The senator stalked over to the bar and dug out a glass and a bottle of Jefferson's 17 Year Old Presidential Select whiskey.

"At least you have the good stuff."

He measured out two fingers and raised the amber glass with an air of appreciation. After a stiff gulp, he turned to Anton.

"Could you please explain to me what the hell is happening in Los Angeles?"

"Selective depopulation."

"People are dying!"

"Isn't that what I said?"

The senator adjusted his glasses, as if doing so would change what he saw.

"The Darwin Protocol was intended to be a selective sterilization. That's what you guaranteed. We are the United States government! We don't murder people for no reason."

"Don't you? Anyway, I did what needed to be done."

"And I stuck my neck out for you. You offered an acceptable solution. A solution that would safeguard the future of this great nation without also destroying the values upon which it was built."

"Every empire must one day crumble."

"Stick your platitudes up your ass!"

Anton strode over and slapped the older man across the face. The senator's head snapped to the side and his spectacles tumbled to the wood floor.

"Don't speak to me as you do your high-priced whores."

The senator held his cheek, stunned to silence.

"I have asked you here not to talk, but to listen."

Anton waited to see if the older man would interrupt. Wisely, he did not.

"There has been an unforeseen complication."

"You don't have to tell me that."

Anton glared and considered dealing out another punishing reprimand. The senator cowered.

"My daughter, Iridia, is in Los Angeles."

The senator's bushy brows lifted.

"Now, isn't that a peach pit of irony?"

"You will get me the resources required to retrieve her."

"And why would I do that?"

"Because I have the cure."

THE END OF BOOK 1

Turn the page for a preview of *The Final Collapse*, book 2 in the *Edge of Survival* series. Preview only available for ebook format.

WANT BOOKS FOR FREE?

Join the Readers Group to get a free copy of The Last Day, Sole Prey, and Saint John. One novel, one novella and one short story, all for free. You'll also receive exclusive discounts on new releases, other freebies, and lots more.

Go to WWW.WILLIAMODAY.COM to find out more.

OTHER WORKS

Extinction Crisis series
SOLE CONNECTION, a Short Story
SOLE PREY, a Prequel Novella
SOLE SURVIVOR, Book 1
SOLE CHAOS, Book 2
THE TANK MAN, a Short Story
THE PLUNGE, a Short Story

Edge of Survival series
THE LAST DAY, Book 1
THE FINAL COLLAPSE, Book 2
THE FRAGILE HOPE, Book 3
THE DESPERATE FIGHT, Book 4

The Best Adventures series
THE SLITHERING GOLIATH
THE BEEPOCALYPSE
THE PHARAOH'S CURSE

Short Stories
THE GENDER LOTTERY
SAINT JOHN
SHE'S GONE

QUESTIONS OR COMMENTS?

Have any questions or comments? I'd love to hear from you! Seriously. Voices coming from outside my head are such a relief.

Give me a shout at william@williamoday.com.

All the best,
Will

THE GOAL

I have a simple storytelling goal that can be wildly difficult to achieve. I want to entertain you with little black marks arranged on a white background. Read the marks and join me on a grand adventure. If all goes well, you'll slip under the spell and so walk alongside heroes and villains. You'll feel what they feel. You'll understand the world as they do.

My writing and your reading is a kind of mechanical telepathy. I translate my thoughts and emotions through characters and conflict in a written story. If the transmission works, your heart will pound, your heart will break, and you will care. At the very least, hopefully you'll escape your world and live in mine for a little while.

I hope to see you there!
Will

MY LIFE THUS FAR

I grew up in the red dirt of the Midwest, the center of the states. I later meandered out to the West Coast and have remained off-center ever since. Living in Los Angeles, I achieved my Career 1.0 dream by working on big-budget movies for over a decade. If you've seen a Will Smith or Tom Cruise blockbuster action movie, you've likely seen my work.

The work was challenging and fulfilling... until I got tired of telling other people's stories. I longed to tell my own. So, now I'm pursuing my Career 2.0 dream—a dream I've had since youth—to write stories that pull a reader in and make the everyday world fade away.

I've since moved to a more rural setting north of San Francisco with my lovely wife, vibrant children, and a dog that has discovered the secret to infinite energy. His name is Trip and he fits the name in four unique ways.

WILLIAMODAY.COM

Made in the USA
Middletown, DE
15 June 2020